Hitler
and
Mars Bars

Dianne Ascroft

Note for Librarians: A cataloguing record for this book is available from Library and Archives
Canada at www.collectionscanada.ca/amicus/index-e.html

Cover design by Alan Taylor

ISBN: 978-1-4251-4591-0

*We at Trafford believe that it is the responsibility of us all, as both individuals and corporations,
to make choices that are environmentally and socially sound. You, in turn, are supporting this
responsible conduct each time you purchase a Trafford book, or make use of our publishing
services. To find out how you are helping, please visit www.trafford.com/responsiblepublishing.
html*

*Our mission is to efficiently provide the world's finest, most comprehensive book publishing
service, enabling every author to experience success. To find out how to publish your book, your
way, and have it available worldwide, visit us online at www.trafford.com/10510*

 **Trafford** PUBLISHING™ www.trafford.com

North America & international
toll-free: 1 888 232 4444 (USA & Canada)
phone: 250 383 6864 ♦ fax: 250 383 6804 ♦ email: info@trafford.com

The United Kingdom & Europe
phone: +44 (0)1865 722 113 ♦ local rate: 0845 230 9601
facsimile: +44 (0)1865 722 868 ♦ email: info.uk@trafford.com

10 9 8 7 6 5 4 3

In memory of my mother,
Marjorie Dineen (Stone) Smith
1936 - 2007

ACKNOWLEDGEMENTS

I WOULD LIKE to thank the Irish Red Cross; Thomas Weiss, City Archivist, Stadtarchiv Hattingen, Germany; and Liam Kennedy, Professor of Irish Economic History, Queen's University, Belfast for answering my questions and providing needed information for my background research. I must stress, though, that they are not responsible for my interpretation of the information or any liberties I have taken with it.

German language translation was undertaken by Sue Ginda and I would like to thank her. I greatly appreciate her help.

PREFACE

OPERATION SHAMROCK was an Irish Red Cross project, in co-operation with the German Save The Children Society, which helped hundreds of children recover from the deprivation in post-war Germany. After the Second World War conditions in Germany were appalling and many people were near starvation. Ireland was one of the first countries to send donations of money and goods to the damaged country. The Irish people expressed particular concern for the children of the nation and as a result the German Save The Children Society was formed in October 1945. Its stated aim was to bring German children to Ireland to save them from starvation. Similar organisations were also founded in England, Sweden, Switzerland, Denmark and South Africa.

In March 1946 the Irish Red Cross, on behalf of both organisations, applied to the Allied Control Council to bring one hundred German children to Ireland; the request was approved on 31st May. On 27th July, 1946 the first eighty-eight children arrived. By April 1947 over four hundred children, aged between three and fifteen, were in Ireland. Most of them came from the devastated Ruhr area which had been heavily bombed by the Allies during the war.

On arrival the children were taken to the Red Cross centre at Glencree, Co. Wicklow where they were cared for by nurses and Red Cross workers. Malnutrition and other health problems were treated and when their health improved sufficiently they were placed with foster families. Each child was fostered by a family of the same faith as himself. The children received good care and nourishing food; most formed strong bonds with their foster families.

At the end of the planned duration of the three year project, between April and September 1949, most of the children were returned to their families in Germany. They returned home healthy and happy though many missed their foster families. Approximately fifty children remained in Ireland permanently.

This story is loosely based on these historic events. I have re-searched Operation Shamrock and spoken to many people who had first hand experience of this worthwhile endeavour. While their recollections have fuelled my imagination and I am grate-ful to them, the events and characters in this story are purely fictional.

1

THE GINGERBREAD HOUSE
Bredenscheid, near Hattingen, Germany
March 1945

"WAKE UP, Erich," his mother said softly.

Leaning over him, she gently shook his shoulder.

Shrugging away from her touch, he turned over in the narrow metal bed. She shook a bit harder and he opened his eyes, squinting at her silhouette in the moonlight.

"*Mutti*! You're here!" Erich sat up and threw his arms around her neck.

"Yes. Get up, quickly now."

"I knew you'd come!" he cried.

"Shh...don't wake the other children," she hushed him as she pulled back his thin, woollen blanket.

Shivering in the cold air, he jumped out of bed and scurried the few steps to the fireplace. The embers from the fire, set before bedtime, still glowed and occasionally crackled in the open grate. The waning fire radiated a modest heat and Erich savoured its warmth. The moon was low in the early evening sky, but its light streamed through the partly drawn curtains.

Erich's mother pulled his white cotton nightshirt over his head and he hunched forward, shivering as cold draughts eddied around him. She quickly threaded his arms into his shirt. Erich squirmed against the prickly fabric which scratched at his back.

"It's itchy! I don't want to wear it!"

"You don't have anything else so you must. Hurry now!" she

9

urged him.

She pulled up his short brown trousers and leaned over to lace his boots. She pushed his arms into his ragged woollen coat, then pulled it firmly around him, noticing how baggy it was.

"You are so thin!" she exclaimed. "You must eat!"

"They don't give us much. And it's rotten! It makes me sick. And I'm so tired," he complained.

The food shortage was severe as the war drew to an end. Everyone struggled to get enough to eat. Malnutrition and the poor quality of available food frequently made the children ill. To conserve energy they went to bed after their evening meal.

She frowned, looking at him. The waist of his trousers was loose and his bony knees seemed large on his thin legs.

Putting her arm around his shoulder, she ushered him out of the dormitory and down the stairs. At the foot of the stairs Erich stopped. "*Mutti* has come for me, T-T-Tante Gretchen!" he called excitedly to the staff member standing in the downstairs hall. Nodding to the woman as they passed, his mother said, "I will return him by breakfast. Good night."

As they stepped out of the door the darkness enveloped them; no street lights lit their way. Their eyes adjusted to it as they walked briskly down the country lane. Erich held tightly to his mother's hand. He pressed against her, almost tripping her in his eagerness to be close to her on this rare visit.

The steady movement lulled Erich. The wheels clicking rhythmically were a muted lullaby. He dozed, his head rocking on his soft, flesh pillow. The carriage, rolling steadily forward, suddenly came to a halt, brakes squealing as it lurched and stood still. His head jerked forward on his mother's knee. Throwing his arm across her legs, he clung tightly. Her thin arms steadied him.

"Where are we?" He tried to sit up but his mother gently pushed him back onto her lap.

"We're still in the yard. Go back to sleep."

"I want to stay here. D-D-Don't take me back. We c-c-can live here."

"Go to sleep. We're staying here tonight," she reassured him smiling, her lips a gentle crescent in her pale face. She crooned a lullaby, her hand resting on his shoulder. "Sleep little one sleep, outside are the sheep, the black and the white." He knew the song and, in his mind, he saw the black and white sheep chasing the naughty child. I will be good so they will not bite me, he thought sleepily.

"We'll live here forever. I'll d-d-drive the t-t-train."

"You'll be a good train driver. I'll be so proud of you. Now go to sleep, *mein kleine*." She murmured the words of endearment as she stroked his hair.

Outside in the blackness other trains shunted back and forth in the yard. They were imposing shadows, brakes hissing and screeching. She peeked behind the blind, into the darkness, watching the silhouettes move, pensively stroking his head. Turning on his back and pulling his knees up, Erich searched her face. Pale and thin, it was framed by light-brown hair, pulled back into a bun. Her pale blue eyes were dark-ringed above her smiling mouth.

She felt much older than her twenty-six years. Several years of enforced work for the Fatherland in Poland had given her too much experience. Erich was born in November 1940 in Wroclaw, while she was working there. In October 1941, while she was on leave in her home town, Essen, her second son, Hans, was born.

"Go to sleep, *mein liebling*." She smiled down at him and he closed his eyes.

"Can I drive the t-t-train tomorrow?"

"We'll see," she murmured.

Heavy footsteps tramped along the platform, sometimes passing the window. Beyond the blind the only other sounds were just the normal ones of a railway yard.

The industrialised Ruhr Valley had experienced heavy bombing since 1943. Essen and the surrounding area was one of the prime targets and had sustained severe damage. But no flashes of light or explosions disturbed them tonight. The air raid sirens were silent.

The light in the carriage shone through Erich's closed eyelids. He turned over, the velvet seat dragging at his bulky coat. The smell of smoke embedded in the velvet mingled with his mother's warmth. He clutched her skirt, anxious lest she disappear as he slept. As he drifted into sleep he sighed, his hand relaxing, imagining himself driving the big engine. I'll drive it tomorrow, he thought as sleep overtook him.

A streak of amber light, flecked with red, shone in as Erich's mother pulled the blind back slightly. It shone palely onto the seat across the aisle. The blind rustled as she let it slip back against the glass and Erich opened his eyes. His mother shifted slightly, straightening her legs and stretching. Yawning, she looked down at him. Gurgling noises resonated in his empty stomach.

"I'm hungry."

"You'll get breakfast when we go back."

"The porridge is just water," he moaned, thinking of it.

"They give you what they can."

"I-I-I don't want to go back. I w-w-want to stay here with you. I'm g-g-going to drive the train!" he pleaded.

"You know you have to go back. I have to go to work. Who would look after you?" she asked.

"I'm a big boy."

"Four isn't big enough yet. Someone must look after you. And you must look after Hans for me."

Erich didn't want to look after Hans. He wanted it to be just his mother and him. He didn't want to share her with anyone. But he didn't want her to be annoyed so he didn't say this. He frowned, sitting on the edge of the frayed seat, his legs dangling.

"You are so like your father. He would be proud of you," his mother continued. She ran her hands through his blond hair, pulling the wavy mass into order. "I know you will be very good for me when I'm working," she wheedled.

Erich still said nothing. He slid off the seat, ducking under the blind to put his nose against the cold glass. She pulled the blind up and peered over his shoulder.

Though the sun had barely risen there was already lots of activity in the yard. Men in overalls walked along the tracks, shouting at drivers leaning out of cab windows. An old man pushed a large broom along the platform and a woman, a bucket beside her, swirled a mop across the entrance to the men's toilet. Steam rose as the water sloshed across the floor.

"We have to go now. I should be at work." Erich's mother took his hand and pulled him reluctantly down the narrow aisle of the carriage. At the doorway, gripping the metal frame, he stretched his short leg towards the step below, barely able to reach it. Holding his other hand, she steadied him as he wobbled down the steep steps. Still holding his hand firmly, she led him along the platform past the woman mopping the floor.

"Good morning, Fraulein Schmidt."

"Good morning, Frau Schnell. Are you not working today?"

"Yes, but first I must take Erich back to the Home."

"You should hurry. You do not want Herr Kramer to notice you are late."

Glancing around quickly for any sign of the station master, she led Erich toward the door. As they emerged from the station the small boy stopped and stared. Bells clanged loudly and a metal rail slowly lowered. The long, thin arm, covered in glistening crystals of ice, moved seemingly on its own. How did it move like that? Were there strings pulling it? Erich wondered. Fascinated, he inched closer to have a better look. It was even better than the trains which rolled through the station, he thought, awestruck.

"Erich, don't go too close to the barrier. A train is coming. You must stay back."

His mother gripped his hand more firmly and pulled him

13

away. A train, wagons loaded with coal, rumbled through the station. Disappointed, he peered over his shoulder as he was led away, watching the lights flash and the barrier slowly rise.

Leaving the road not far from the station, they took a shortcut through the fields. Delicate white snowdrops, their flowers gently tilting forward, peeped up amid scattered patches of snow. The sun was climbing and its muted warmth crept over them. Birds twittered, darting in and out of the hedges.

"There used to be lots of cows in these fields," his mother said.

"Where are they?"

"The war has caused lots of bad things. Meat is very scarce," she said, not answering his question directly.

"I don't like the meat they give us. It makes me sick."

"You must eat whatever you're given. Food is very hard to get."

"But it's horrible!"

"I know but there's nothing else. You must eat it so you will grow up to be a big, strong man like your father was. He was very handsome in his uniform," she said, half to herself.

"When will I see him?"

"Not today," she said, thinking of the man who died before his second son was born.

The small boy tugged at his mother's hand, pulling her to a stop.

"W-W-When can I-I-I go home with you? I-I-I d-d-don't want to live there."

She bent down and looked into his steady blue eyes. He focussed his unwavering attention on her face. She swallowed, trying to make her voice sound steady.

"One day you will come to live with me. But right now I have to work to earn money for us. So, for now, you have to stay at the Home." She smoothed his unruly blond hair. "You are lucky. You have lots of children to play with there," she said, trying to cheer him.

14

Cupping his small hand in hers, she straightened up and walked on. He trotted along beside her.

"We're almost there and your breakfast will be waiting."

As she spoke, the tall, peaked roof of the building came into view. Its brown slates were visible through a dusting of snow. Several tiny windows popped out of the slates like flaps lifted on an advent calendar. The roof ended abruptly at the second storey windows. Beneath, white walls were tied with brown ribbon-like stripes, criss-crossing horizontally and vertically as if wrapping a large gift. Their orderly pattern only deviated at each corner where they appeared to have stumbled and dangled drunkenly. Surrounded by leafless trees and hedges, the building resembled a large gingerbread house dropped into the barren, winter forest.

"Isn't it pretty?" his mother asked, gazing at the postcard view.

"I don't think so," Erich sulked.

"It's just like a gingerbread house," she replied.

"What's that?" he asked.

"Like a big, sweet biscuit," she replied. She remembered that he had never seen or tasted gingerbread. Such treats were scarce during wartime. "Did you know the Goldschmidthaus was a farmer's cottage many years ago? Then a very rich man, Theodore Goldschmidt, bought it and made a holiday home for his factory workers to come to visit."

"Will they come to stay with us this summer?" Erich asked.

"No, Herr Goldschmidt has loaned the building to Essen's government so children who have no parents or whose parents are working will have a place to live and someone to care for them."

Erich's frown deepened as he looked at it. He wished Herr Goldschmidt hadn't been so kind.

"Good morning, Frau Schnell and Erich." A large, middle-aged

woman greeted them as they entered the hallway.

"Tantchen Trude, I'm g-g-going to d-d-drive the train!" the boy exclaimed, fidgeting as his mother undid his coat.

"Are you? Well, go and get your breakfast first." Smiling, the matron nodded towards the dining room.

On tiptoe he reached up and threw his arms around his mother. She hugged him tightly.

"Don't leave," Erich sniffed, tears welling in his eyes. "When are you coming back?"

"I'll see you soon. Be good." His mother's eyes were also moist. She hugged him again, then pushed him firmly towards the dining room. "Don't be late for breakfast."

"Bye bye, *Mutti*." Erich's eyes never left her. He made no effort to move.

"How's Hans?" she asked, turning towards Tantchen Trude.

Erich frowned at the mention of his brother. Reluctantly, after another gentle shove from his mother, he left them and entered the dining room.

"He's fine," Tantchen Trude replied.

"I wish I had time to see him today, but I'm late already. It's such a relief to know they are safe here. The bombing is so heavy in the towns. So many buildings are destroyed and the railroad is a constant target. Anywhere near the railway line even in our village is dangerous. I would never stop worrying if they were with me."

"Don't worry about them. We'll care for them well."

"I come as often as I can. When Hans is a bit bigger I will be able to take him out with Erich. But he is too small to walk as far as the station yet. I know it is risky to take them there but I have nowhere else."

"In these times how can we know anywhere is safe? Come when you can. They love to see you."

The heavy wooden chair scraped the tile floor, echoing in the

large, bare space as Erich pulled it away from the table. He hauled himself onto the seat, shivering in the cold room. On either side of him Karl and Eva ate silently, without enthusiasm. A bowl containing a small quantity of runny broth was set in front of him. Congealed lumps of porridge clung to the rim; it didn't look enough to fill him. As he poked the spoon gingerly through the broth an odd lump surfaced. He filled his spoon and blew on it, scattering some of the mixture across the table. Watery broth slid down his throat; there was very little porridge in it. His stomach felt warmer but still empty after he finished it. Looking along the table he could see nothing else to eat. Experience had taught him it was pointless asking for more.

Tante Gretchen stood near the kitchen door. Seeing most of the bowls were empty, she called for attention. "Bring your bowls to the basin then go back to your dormitories."

Sliding from his chair, Erich lifted his empty bowl. Even the congealed lumps on the rim were gone. He trooped silently to the kitchen door behind a tall girl, yellow braids hanging over her protruding shoulder blades. Placing his bowl in the bucket, he smiled at Tante Gretchen. She smiled back and ruffled his hair.

As he turned away the smell of freshly baked bread wafted from the kitchen making his unsatisfied stomach rumble. He could not ignore the tantalising smell. Quickly checking that the staff were occupied, Erich slipped through the kitchen door.

A shiny, warm world greeted him. He marvelled at the large pots, tendrils of steam still rising from them, on the gleaming range. A row of utensils hung high above his head. They would clang like bells if I hit them, he thought. He reached up, attempting to set them swinging, but they were too far above his head. Jumping up he flailed his arm, hitting only air. A white coated woman pouring boiling water into the sink spotted him.

"Boy, what are you doing? You are not permitted here!" She set the pot down and walked toward him. He stood silently staring at her, apprehensive but too hungry to flee from the smell of

the baking bread.

"He won't do any harm." Another white coated figure appeared from behind the long central table. Cook looked down and beckoned him with a flour covered finger. He sidled towards her, reassured by her kind voice. She scrutinised his square, serious face gazing up at her.

"What are you doing in here?"

"It's warm and smells good. I'm hungry."

Cook opened the oven, pulled out a tray of freshly baked bread and set it on the table. The hot sweet smell wafted over them. She watched Erich eyeing the bread and licking his lips. Cook reached down a long, black-handled knife and sliced straight narrow lines through the cooling bread. She handed a piece to Erich. He ate it quickly, stuffing it into his mouth.

"Why are you giving him that? There's little enough to go around without giving him extra!" the cross dishwasher admonished.

"One piece of bread will make little difference." Turning to Erich she said, "Now run along before Tantchen Trude finds you here." Cook ushered him out of the kitchen.

Slightly less hungry than before he returned to his dormitory.

The sun shone patchily melting the snow until it looked like a moth-eaten christening blanket. Its brightness gave an illusion of warmth. Despite their constant hunger and tiredness, the children, walking in a column, laughed and jostled each other, glad to be outside. Erich grabbed Eva's hair. She shook her head, pulling it free.

"Stop that!" she cried. Erich laughed, reaching for her hair again. She darted out of his reach, giggling.

Entering the woods near the Goldschmidthaus they left the sun behind though its beams occasionally danced through the waving branches to light small patches of ground. Erich threw his head back, trying to see the tops of the trees. They are so tall,

he thought.

"I can see the top of that tree," Erich said to Eva.

"No, you can't!"

"I can!"

Erich spotted two pairs of steel cables running between the trees, suspended from silver, pyramid-like pylons. As he watched wagons were pulled along steadily by the cables, like a horizontal ski lift. It would be so much fun to ride in a wagon, high above the ground and see everything below, he thought.

"Tante Gretchen, how do the wagons stay up in the sky? Where do they go?" Erich asked his favourite staff member.

"The wagons hang from cables which are like a road in the sky. They carry the wagons from the coal mine near Bredenscheid where we live to Hattingen."

"And sometimes coal falls out and we can have it," Erich said.

"That coal isn't for us. It's very dangerous to take anything that falls from the wagons. The soldiers would be very cross if they knew. You must never mention it if you see anyone lift any coal," Tante Gretchen warned him. Erich nodded seriously.

A cuckoo, like its famous mechanised replica, gave its familiar "cuckoo, cuckoo" cry.

"Where is it?" Eva asked, looking around. Erich turned his attention from the wagons to the bird's cry. He scanned the trees for the bird.

"Maybe over there," he replied, pointing to a treetop. Both children stared upwards. The bird's cry was repeated, echoing through the woods, but there was no sign of it. The elusive bird preferred to welcome spring covertly.

Tante Gretchen began to sing in a clear, thin voice. "Cuckoo, cuckoo calls from the forest." The children joined in, shouting back to her, "Let us sing, dance and jump." She motioned for them to join her for the last line, "Spring, spring comes soon."

The path emerged from the shade of the trees into a clearing. From well-established habit Tante Gretchen and her co-worker,

Tante Helga, crossed the clearing and sat on a fallen log. They could see the children easily from this vantage point. Erich joined several older boys poking through bushes at the edge of the clearing, looking for insects, mice or frogs. Ever hungry, they sought anything edible. But nothing moved in the undergrowth on this early spring day and the boys eventually abandoned their search.

Bernhardt, an earnest boy, with furrowed brows and a strong voice, organised a game of hide and seek. *"Eins, zwei, drei…."* he counted, eyes closed, with his back to the clearing.

Erich disappeared behind a large bush. His small stature made it unnecessary to crouch down to hide himself from view. When Bernhardt reached twenty he opened his eyes and whirled around. Glancing to either side he strode towards Karl, who was hiding behind a tree. But before he reached his target, branches cracked and an engine roared, getting nearer. The children peered out from hiding places around the clearing.

An army lorry, its swastika visible between the branches, rumbled along the path. The women stood up hurriedly, calling the children to them. They drew them into a tight group as the lorry approached.

"Hello, meine Damen." A soldier, steel helmet set low, framing his eyebrows, stepped out of the vehicle and addressed the women cordially. As he came towards them, the children craned their necks to peer around him at the lorry. Some of the taller boys peeked into the cab, hoping to spot any food scraps it might contain. Even standing on tiptoe Erich was still too short to see anything.

A second soldier sat in the passenger seat, neck protruding thickly from his stiff black uniform collar. His steel blue eyes regarded them indulgently.

"Do you have any bread?" a thin, blonde girl asked hopefully. She stood on tiptoe, leaning towards the cab.

"Come and find out for yourself," he replied. He got out and lifted her into the cab. Several boys peered in after her. The girl in the cab found an empty egg shell and popped it into her mouth. The soldier drew her attention to a piece of bread lying on the dashboard. But before she could move two boys also spotted it and reached for it, tugging it between them. The girl whimpered, watching them helplessly.

"Children, come here," Tante Gretchen called before any more squabbles over scraps erupted. They reluctantly moved away from the lorry and clustered around her. The soldiers watched them, assessing the group.

"Children, attention!" the driver commanded. The children shuffled and straightened up, arms held rigidly at their sides as the older ones had learned to do in school. "Who is our great leader?" he asked.

"*Der Furhrer,*" Bernhardt replied.

"*Der Furhrer* would be pleased with you," the soldier said approvingly. Stretching his arm in a salute, the soldier shouted, "*Heil Hitler, heil das Reich.*" Erich flinched, jarred by the noise. The soldier waited expectantly for the children to repeat his words. After a slight pause, the words tumbled out in a discordant tangle of voices, each independent of the others. Looking at Erich standing silently, the soldier singled him out.

"*Heil Hitler,*" he said to Erich. Erich shrunk towards Tante Gretchen, unsure what was expected of him and frightened by the soldier's imposing manner. The soldier bent down, waiting for the boy's response. Erich backed away, then turned and ran behind the bush where he had been hiding a few minutes earlier. The soldier frowned as he straightened up.

"Come back here," he commanded, clicking his black-booted heels together as he spoke. There was no answer from behind the bush.

Unused to his orders being unheeded, the soldier said, "This behaviour is inexcusable. Come back at once!" Erich still did not appear. The grey figure, black boots crunching on the ground, moved towards the bush.

"Come here, Erich," Tante Gretchen called gently.

Erich slowly emerged from behind the bush. Head down, he edged towards her. Tante Gretchen took his hand and pulled him to her.

"This boy must learn respect and obedience."

"He meant no disrespect. He is only four. He does not understand," she said, trying to appease the soldier. He stared at Erich for a long moment. Abruptly he walked to the cab and climbed in. Without another word, he revved the engine and they drove away.

"Come, children, it will soon be dinnertime," Tante Gretchen said. She herded them along the forest path towards the Goldschmidthaus. Erich clung tightly to her hand.

Erich swallowed the last bite of his sandwich. He hated the taste of the acrid, nearly rotting meat. Its stringy, tough fibres stuck between his teeth. His stomach heaved as he swallowed and he struggled to keep the food down. Even if it were palatable, a quarter of a sandwich was not enough to fill his empty stomach. His stomach still rumbled, the muscles clenched in anticipation of food that was not coming; the contents of his stomach churned. He knew he would be very hungry before morning. Erich tugged at Tante Gretchen's sleeve as she passed.

"Can I have more bread?"

"No, Erich, *mein kleiner.* That's all for tonight. You will be in bed soon and will forget about your hunger when you sleep." She smiled kindly at him, knowing how hungry the children were.

Erich picked the last crumbs of bread from the plate as Tante Gretchen called for attention.

"Bedtime, children. Go to your dormitories, get undressed and into your beds," she instructed.

Erich slid off his seat and into the queue that snaked around the room. He passed the wash basin and set his plate in it. Lethargic and weary from lack of food, he dragged himself up the stairs with the other children. The long line divided at the top, boys

and girls going to their separate dormitories. The toddlers were already asleep in their room.

Erich's stomach still churned as he undressed; he felt ill. He hoped he would not be sick; he hated that feeling. But he could not help it if he were, he thought miserably.

He sank onto his bed as Tante Gretchen entered the room. She opened the Bible, which lay on the mantelpiece, and read the story of Noah and the Ark. When she finished he knelt beside his bed and Tante Gretchen led the boys in their nightly prayers.

"God bless *Mutti* and let me see her soon," Erich finished.

When they were all tucked in bed Tante Gretchen closed the door and left them to their dreams. A few sighs, coughs and restless shifting in beds were the only sounds at first. Erich closed his eyes, trying not to think about his stomach.

Karl sat up in the next bed, whispering, "Erich!" Erich opened his eyes. "It's still light outside. It's too early to sleep." They heard women's voices in the garden, chatting. Karl threw his covers back and put his bare feet onto the wooden floorboards.

"I want to see who's there. I'm going outside," he announced.

"You can't go downstairs. They'll see you!" Erich said.

"I'm not going downstairs." At eight Karl had learned a few tricks. He crept down the middle of the room. Wolfgang and Franz slid out of their beds near the balcony door to join him. They cautiously pulled back the bolt on the door and it swung open. Pushing the door open wide, they stepped onto the balcony. Erich, despite his tiredness and sore stomach, could not resist. He slid from his bed and padded down the aisle.

The four boys tiptoed to the railing, their bare feet just visible under their white nightshirts, hunger, tiredness and illness forgotten briefly in the excitement of the adventure. Karl peered over the railing. The women's voices wafted up with their cigarette smoke, but the boys couldn't see them. Wolfgang went to the balcony door to keep watch.

Erich forgot the conversation below. He jammed his face against the rungs of the railing and stared into the distance. If he could see through the trees he would be able to see where *Mutti* was working, he thought eagerly. He squinted in that direction but he could see nothing. Maybe she would come tomorrow. He hoped he would see her again soon.

Footsteps tramping along the path towards the front door made the boys jump. Erich tried to squeeze his head between the bars for a better look. He could see shiny black boots and belt contrasted with a pale uniform. Karl, leaning over the railing, also saw them. The soldier glanced around him but did not look up. Erich thought of the soldier who had yelled at him earlier; he backed away from the railing. The other boys followed and they crept as quietly as they could into the dormitory, then raced, floorboards groaning, for their beds. Erich dived into bed and pulled the bedclothes up under his chin. His stomach churned and he was suddenly shivering, his bare feet tingling from the cold balcony. Maybe the angry soldier has come to punish me, he worried.

Other boys, still in their beds, whispered, asking what happened but, shaking their heads, they shushed them. Coughs were stifled and breath held. Erich lay very still, listening. The soldier he had met earlier in the woods had been very angry with him. Maybe he's looking for me, Erich thought. Maybe he'll punish me. Erich closed his eyes very tightly, feigning sleep.

A loud knock on the front door echoed up the stairs. Soft footsteps clicked across the tiles and the door creaked open. The soldiers' commanding voices drowned out the women's soft tones.

"We have come to inspect your premises."

"But the children are all in bed."

"We cannot wait. We have orders."

"The children are weak from hunger. Let them sleep. Please do not wake them."

"Step aside. We must make our report tonight."

The heavy footsteps echoed through the hallway; the lighter ones tripped behind. The footsteps continued through the dining room and kitchen as they made their inspection. Next they mounted the stairs. A cough in the boys' dorm was hastily stifled. The dormitory door opened, light flickering in. Eyes remained firmly closed and bodies lay rigid. No one dared to give any sign he was awake. The soldier glanced around quickly, sizing up how many soldiers the room could accommodate.

"Close that door." He indicated the balcony door, lying open after the boys' dash back to their beds. Tante Gretchen hurried to comply.

"It is small but might be satisfactory for a short period," he said to his comrade. He turned away without a backward glance. "If we require the premises we will inform you," he threw over his shoulder to the woman following him.

The door closed abruptly. The odd giggle or cough was hushed until the footsteps retreated and there were no further sounds from the hallway. Erich turned on his side, pulling his knees up to ease the pain in his belly. Closing his eyes, he wished his mother were here. She would take him away and they would live together. He hoped she would come before the angry soldier returned.

The bodies were piled one on top of the other on the hill, arms and legs flung in every direction. Jackets flapped open in the wind, blood dripped from ripped shirts. Dirt and blood covered their faces. An arm hung partially severed from its body. Erich crept closer to look at them, horrified and fascinated. There was such a huge pile. He grimaced at the sight confronting him, too frightened to make a sound.

Erich tossed restlessly until shuffling and banging in the large dormitory penetrated the images racing through his mind. The horrible scene faded as he opened his eyes. Boys pushed and shoved, scrambling under beds in search of their boots. The sky was lit with a red glow. Erich stared out of the balcony door. Sharp bangs punctuated the night. Each small explosion was answered by a larger one and flames leapt into the air. It was closer than he had ever seen before. Erich craned his neck upwards watching white sparkles popping and floating towards the ground. The sparkles marked the bombs' course as they fell.

"Are the bombs falling on our garden?" Erich asked Karl.

"No, it's not that close. Tante Gretchen says the oil tanks at the plant in Hattingen are on fire. Don't they make a great bang!" Erich nodded wide-eyed as he watched the display outside.

Staff rushed to and fro, urging the boys to hurry as they herded them towards the door.

Tante Gretchen said, "Erich, get up. We must go to the shelter." She pulled his bedclothes back.

He sat up and pulled on his boots. Tante Gretchen threw his coat over his shoulders and bundled him towards the door. The dying embers of the fire, glowing in the dark room, warmed him briefly as he passed. The boys jostled each other to be first out of the door. Pushed into the melee, Erich grabbed the doorframe to brace himself against a taller boy's shove. Ducking down, he pushed through the doorway and stepped into the hall. A muffled pounding rose from the wooden stairs as the children descended.

Small, even for four years old, Erich could not see through the throng. His nose brushed the torn pullover of the boy in front of him as he was pushed forward by the others. On the ground floor Tante Helga stood at an open door, ushering them down the stairs into the musty smelling cellar.

Several years of heavy bombing in the Essen area made these night-time forays a familiar occurrence. The staff counted heads as the children settled wearily into whatever space they could find. Erich laid his head on the lap of an older girl, Hilde, wedged between her and his friend, Karl. Hilde leaned her head on the shoulder of the girl next to her, her hand resting on Erich's hip.

"Maybe they'll bomb us tonight. It might just be rubble when we go out in the morning!" Karl exclaimed.

"Don't say such things! Where would we live?" Hilde scolded.

"No talking," Tante Helga said firmly. "You must sleep now."

Silence descended and only the occasional cough disturbed the regular breathing of the roomful of dozing children. Explosions were heard in the distance as the night wore on. But nothing landed near the Home. The bombs fell in the more heavily populated areas.

Dawn broke sending a sliver of light creeping under the door at the top of the stairs. Erich woke and sat up.

"Is the house still there?" Karl whispered.

"You snore so loud, Karl, that you would never hear it if we were bombed! But I think it is still there," Bernhardt answered the younger, dark-haired boy.

"Maybe everything is gone except our house!" Karl cried.

"Even the forest?" Erich asked.

"Every tree," Karl asserted. Erich frowned; he liked to go to the forest.

Exaggerated claims and assertions dominated the children's whispered conversation. After what seemed an unbearable wait, Tantchen Trude led them upstairs. Erich and the other children darted around the house and out into the grounds looking for damage, grey metal fragments or bodies that may have fallen from the sky. But everything was as it had been the night before. Despite the carnage in nearby Hattingen it was another ordinary morning. With a sigh Erich trooped upstairs to his dormitory with the other children to wash and dress. He wondered if his mother would come today. Maybe she wouldn't have to work if the railway station had been hit. Excited by this thought, he hurried to get ready.

❦

April 1946

Erich stared at the brown, hardboiled egg in front of him. Biting his lip and frowning with concentration, he dipped his paintbrush into a blob of paint and moved it towards the Easter egg, a few blue drops splashing onto the surface of the wooden table. The children around him were also absorbed in the task. He finished the last couple of strokes of his design and put down the paintbrush. Holding the hardboiled egg up, he admired the bright colours spattered over it.

"Look at my egg!" he shouted to Tante Gretchen as she walked past.

"It's lovely, Erich!" she said, squeezing his shoulder.

"I'll s-s-show *Mutti* w-w-when she comes," he said.

Tante Gretchen said nothing, merely smiled sadly. No one had seen his mother in more than a year. During that time, Allied troops had occupied Essen and the war had ended, bringing changes though not obvious ones. Soldiers still patrolled the area but they wore a different uniform and spoke a strange language. The ravaged country was trying to recover but there were terrible hardships and food was still scarce.

Erich turned to look at the creations of other children seated at the table. Each egg had its own individual design in brilliant colours. Eva held up her red and yellow egg proudly.

"When can we eat them?" Erich asked.

"Tomorrow morning - after the egg race. But now it's time for bed." Tante Gretchen clapped her hands, instructing the children to go upstairs. Reluctantly they put their eggs in the basket set in the middle of the table and left the room. Erich willed his mother to come for Easter Sunday tomorrow. He had so much he wanted to tell her. She hadn't been to see him for a long time but she must come tomorrow. He closed his eyes and wished.

Next morning, as soon as it was light, the children were out of bed. Tante Gretchen brought in the basket of eggs and each boy grabbed his. Clutching his egg, Erich ran into the hallway. He

lined up with several other children to roll his egg down the long
stairs. When Tante Gretchen shouted "Go!" Erich shoved his egg
and watched it bounce down the stairs. It arrived at the bottom
intact and he cheered. He didn't care if he won the race; he just
wanted his egg to survive its journey.

He raced to pick it up, broke it in half and bit into the centre,
enjoying the yolk's rich taste. It was a welcome change from watery porridge. He ate every morsel, then admired its colourful
shell. He would keep it to show *Mutti* when she came.

As the day wore on Erich waited for his mother to appear,
carefully guarding the fragile eggshell. He stared out of the window, wondering when she would arrive and growing more agitated, unable to sit still.

"When w-w-will *Mutti* c-c-come, Tante Gretchen?" he asked.

"I don't know, *mein kleiner*," she replied, drawing him away
from the window. "Let me see your beautiful egg again," she
said, hoping to distract him. She had lost track of how often he
had asked the question and she didn't know what she could truth-
fully tell him.

Why doesn't Mutti come? Erich wondered. When she still
had not arrived by bedtime, he admitted to himself she was not
coming. Sad and defeated he undressed. She had promised to
come back for him. Why didn't she? Have I done something to
make her angry? I try to be good and I'm nice to Hans whenever
I see him, Erich thought. He didn't know what else he could do
to please her. He agonised over what he might have done to upset
her until he fell into an exhausted sleep.

August 1946

The August sun, hot and glaring, high in the afternoon sky, beat
down with no breeze to counter it. Thin, wispy clouds floated
across the still, blue expanse. Sweat trickled from Erich's tem-
ple, dripping off his jaw, and his curls lay damp and flat on his

forehead. He coughed as dust caught in his throat. Walking was tiring in the heat.

Tante Gretchen looked back and counted five heads of differing heights; they were all there. The small group of children moved slowly, heads down, arms swinging listlessly. Erich usually enjoyed coming with the staff to the village when they had errands to do, but today the walk was an exertion and he could hardly push himself forward. The food shortage was even worse since the war had ended and he, like the other children, struggled constantly, weak from lack of food. The heat took the remaining strength he had.

"We will be there soon," Tante Gretchen said as the village came into sight.

"It's such a long walk," Erich groaned as he trudged along.

"You must be very tired with the heat. You don't usually mind the walk, Erich. I know it must seem a long walk into Bredenscheid today. But we've only come from just outside the village. On a cooler day we could almost walk to Hattingen and Essen is only a few miles further," Tante Gretchen replied.

Though the Ruhr Valley, in which they were situated, was the industrial centre of Germany, Bredenscheid was a quiet, rural hamlet. Nevertheless, because of its proximity to the larger, industrial towns and cities, it had also suffered the ravages of war.

One of the most visible marks left on the village by the war was the railway station's mangled shell. Bits of roof dangled motionless, only disturbed when a breeze blew. Heaps of rubble lay scattered on the platform, visible through holes in the wall. It stood silent and deserted. The children took little notice of it as they passed. It had stood thus for many months. Only Erich hung back to take another look. His mother worked there. Where is she? How will I find her? he wondered. He looked through a hole in the wall for some sign of activity. Nothing moved within. Where had all the people gone?

"Where is my mother? She works here. I-I-I want t-t-to see her." Erich tugged at Tante Gretchen's hand.

"I know she did, Erich. But I don't know where she is now. Many people are missing. It may take a long time to find them." Tante Gretchen did not tell him that many of the people missing were dead.

"Are you tired? We're stopping to rest there," she distracted him, pointing at a tavern ahead.

Stopping outside the tavern, the children clustered around Tante Gretchen. Her colleague, Tante Helga, went inside. Bernhardt disappeared around to the back door. Through the open door Erich saw Tante Helga standing at the battered wooden counter. Her blonde braids contrasted with the dark wood surrounding her. She spoke to the man behind the bar and he reached down two tall, thick tankards from the shelf behind him. Setting one under a tap, he tilted the glass and pulled the handle. Golden liquid flowed into the glass, a slight froth rising in it. Erich watched the liquid flow. It gleamed, a beautiful gold with white swirls snaking through it. Water came from a bucket carried from the well and milk sat in a jug on the dining room table. But this beautiful liquid flowed from the shiny tap when the man pulled the long tapered handle. Erich stood mesmerised by it.

When he had finished pouring, Tante Helga carried the tankards to a table outside the door. Tante Gretchen sat opposite her. Erich stood beside Tante Gretchen, leaning against her shoulder. Bernhardt returned carrying a bucket filled with water and a tin cup. The children eagerly passed the cup around and gulped the cool water. Then they sprawled on the grass.

"What's that?" Erich asked. He licked the water from his lips as he eyed the golden liquid.

"Taste it." Tante Gretchen held the heavy tankard to Erich's lips. He was still thirsty and took a large mouthful, swallowing quickly. The cold liquid slid down his throat, making him shiver. He pursed his lips and grimaced, screwing up his nose at the bitter aftertaste. He tried to spit but the liquid was already gone.

"I don't like that!" he complained.

"When you are older you will like it. Do you want some

31

more?" Tante Gretchen held the glass towards him but Erich pulled away.

"No! It's horrible!"

Tante Gretchen and Tante Helga sipped their beer. Wasps buzzed around, landing on the women's glasses and crawling inside. The women nonchalantly swatted them away. The wasps were not easily deterred and hovered out of reach, returning and landing again and again. The beer and the heat made Erich light-headed and he sat down on the bench, leaning his head against Tante Gretchen and closing his eyes.

Heavy American army lorries rumbled past, raising a cloud of dust. The driver of the first one waved and the children watched hopefully. The occupying troops were friendly and sometimes had treats for them. But they passed by without stopping today.

The women finished their drinks and stood up. Erich yawned. His head buzzed and he felt too heavy to move. He stood up slowly. The staff herded the children together. Sluggishly they trailed after the women onto the main street. Erich paid little attention when they stopped outside several shops. He waited with the other children until the women emerged, uninterested in what they had bought. He was glad when they turned and re-traced their steps. Erich paused as they passed the railway station to look once more for *Mutti*. Maybe I could ask someone if they have seen her, he thought. But, seeing no one there, he trudged on.

As he entered the long neglected garden behind the Home, tired and hot from the walk, a movement caught Erich's attention. A large orange and black speckled butterfly hovered close to him. White spots blinked on its fluttering wings. It was almost within reach but, as he stretched towards it, the butterfly flew off, alighting a couple of feet away on a small bush. It hung sideways, its wings flapping to balance. Erich crept towards it, hands outstretched; again it fluttered off. He followed its zigzag path, meandering through the garden, away from Tante Gretchen and the other children, his eyes fixed on the butterfly. Suddenly it soared upwards, wings beating rapidly. It flew above Erich's head and flitted away above the tall grass. Erich threw his head back, watching the vivid colours disappear into the blue sky. Then looking around he saw only tall, thick grass. He had wandered into the middle of the garden in pursuit of the butterfly and now he could not see which direction he had come from. He had trampled the grass all around him during his butterfly hunt. A fly buzzed at his ear and he slapped it irritably. Where is the house? How will I get back to it? he wondered, growing worried. He didn't know which way to go. His stomach rumbled, ever hungry. It would soon be dinner time and he was lost. Tears welled in his eyes and his lips quivered. No one would ever find him.

Even standing on tiptoe he could not see above the grass. It swayed and brushed against his face, making him scratch. He pushed it away angrily. Frustrated he jumped in the air. He caught a brief glimpse of colours and shapes in the distance. Jumping again he tried to get a better view. There were only tree trunks and various odd shapes. Turning in the opposite direction, he jumped again. The brown and white patterned house was briefly visible. Relieved, he rushed towards it, tramping down grass and weeds as he went. Stopping briefly, he jumped again to check he was heading in the right direction. The building was nearer. He could see Karl and Eva peering into the garden.

Charging forward he flattened the stalks of grass in front of him, creating a path, like a drawbridge lowering. He emerged beside the daisy littered path leading to the back door. A few feet away Tante Gretchen and the other children were standing together, staring into the garden.

"There you are, Erich! We were looking for you!" Tante Gretchen said with relief.

Erich ran to her and hugged her tightly. "I got lost in the grass. I couldn't see you," he sobbed. "I missed you so much!"

"It's alright. We've found you now. Let's go in for dinner."

Tante Gretchen smiled at him then she wiped his wet face and led him inside. Erich was cheered at the thought of food. Even a small bite would ease the gnawing hunger and make it bearable for a while. As he entered the hallway he heard engines roaring, getting closer. Curiosity overrode his hunger and he stopped to peer out of the window.

2

LORRIES, TRAINS AND BOATS

UNABLE TO see the front gate from the downstairs window, Erich ran upstairs to look out. Green lorries with large red crosses on their curved roofs and sides trundled up the driveway. One stopped directly under the balcony.

Doors slammed as Red Cross workers got out of the cabs. The staff greeted them warmly and led them inside. A few workers remained outside, lounging against lorries. They chatted sporadically, their lit cigarettes dangling from their lips or their jaws, stuffed with chewing gum, moving rhythmically during the silences.

Erich leaned over the railing to stare at the large red cross, like a bulls-eye on the lorry directly below. He wanted a closer look. Climbing onto the railing, he balanced precariously before jumping onto the vehicle. The driver felt the vibration, looked up and smiled at the small boy standing on the roof. Hesitantly, Erich smiled back then turned and dashed the length of the lorry and back again. Captivated by the bold red cross he ran to the centre of its brilliant colour then around its edges, tracing its outline.

Absorbed in his game, he didn't hear the driver approach him. The friendly man held out his arms. He looks like a soldier but he's not scary, Erich thought, watching the uniformed man. He leaned forward and let the man swing him down in a semi-circle as if waltzing in the air, and set him behind the steering wheel.

Children ran in and out, between the lorries, shouting with excitement as they whizzed around. Some of the bigger children climbed into the lorries. Their feet echoed on the grooved metal floors as they explored. Eva leaned out of a cab window, laughing. The Red Cross workers stood watching the excited children, amused by their antics.

Sitting high up in the cab, Erich pulled himself up as tall as he could, grasping the steering wheel. He peeped over its rim. Revving his imaginary engine, he hauled at the wheel, hands clenched, attempting to turn it. He tapped the horn, jumping as it beeped loudly, then fearfully looked around. But, seeing no disapproval, he did it again, laughing.

After a few minutes the driver peered into the cab. Smiling he held out his arms, motioning Erich forward. Reluctantly, the boy slid across the seat, allowing himself to be lifted out. But his disappointment at leaving his game was soon forgotten when he spotted Karl peering into the back of the next lorry. He ran over to him and stood on tiptoe to see what he was looking at. Several large boxes were stacked in it.

"Let's get in and look inside them!" Karl exclaimed. Erich nodded enthusiastically.

"Children, dinner!" Tante Gretchen called from the front door.

Erich and Karl groaned, loath to abandon their exploration, but they knew they must. They filed into the dining room with the other children. Erich sat in his usual seat, glancing frequently out of the window to be sure the lorries were still there. Maybe we can go out again after we've eaten, he thought.

A bowl of steaming soup was set before him. A few pieces of limp cabbage floated in the clear liquid as he swirled his spoon around. They had soup most evenings and he hated it. Dipping his fragment of bread into the soup he ate the soggy morsel. He quickly finished the bread and he spooned up the rest of his soup. It wasn't much but inadequate portions were all he remembered; food shortages had existed for most of his life.

After dinner, as usual, the children were sent straight to bed. Disappointed, Erich trudged up the stairs. He wanted to play in the lorry again. Once he was in bed he found it hard to sleep knowing the lorries were parked outside. The low murmur of the Red Cross workers' voices chatting with the Children's Home staff carried up the stairs. Maybe the man would let him drive the lorry tomorrow, Erich thought excitedly. He couldn't wait to tell *Mutti* about the lorries. He had so much to tell her. Thinking of his mother, Erich's high spirits plummeted. When would he see her again? She said she would come back for him. Tears slid silently down his cheeks. He wished she would come soon. He tried to imagine her face as he settled to sleep, hoping this would make his wish come true.

The next morning Erich was puzzled. The staff were behaving strangely. After breakfast they rushed around, ignoring the children's questions. Even Tante Gretchen had no time to talk when Erich tugged at her sleeve. Each child's meagre possessions was packed into bags and boxes - whatever was available - and stood labelled beside each bed.

Erich asked Karl, sitting in the hallway, "What's happening?"

"I don't know. I think we're going somewhere."

"Where?"

"I don't know."

Erich wandered down the hall. Leaning his chin on the windowsill, he peered down at the lorries parked in the driveway. Nothing moved outside except the white heads of daisies fluttering in the slight breeze. A cloud drifted past, hiding the sun and shedding a few drops of rain. But it quickly moved on and the sun re-appeared, drying the ground.

The children milled around from one room to another, watching and waiting, unsure why. Time dragged slowly. Erich wanted to play in the lorry again but Tante Gretchen said they must stay inside. Eventually one of the lorry drivers walked past Erich, ruffling his hair as he headed to the front door. Several other workers followed him. The watching children raced after them out of the door. The youngsters headed straight to the vehicles and began climbing on them. As soon as the lorries were unlocked the children begged to be lifted into the cabs. They darted from one vehicle to another, shouting excitedly. Erich ran to the lorry he had sat in the night before. No one was near it. He eyed the cab but it was too high for him to climb into without help. He stood beside it, considering what to do.

Amid the pandemonium the staff began carrying bags and boxes to the lorries and setting them inside. It did not take long to store the children's meagre possessions away. Before Erich could find an ally to lift him up, Tantchen Trude called the children back inside.

"Stand along the wall, children," she instructed them.

Staff walked along the row of children, pinning pieces of beige cardboard with large numbers printed on them onto dresses and shirts. Erich looked down at his number. He traced the six with his finger.

"Children, you're going on a journey to a place called Ireland. It's very far away and we don't want to lose anyone, so don't take your number off," Tantchen Trude instructed them.

"Where's Ireland?" Erich whispered to Karl.

"It's a long way from here," Karl answered, not wanting to admit he didn't know.

Tantchen Trude led the children outside and the staff took them in twos and threes to the waiting lorries. Erich held tightly to Tante Gretchen's hand when it was his turn. He tried to climb into the lorry unaided, pushing away attempts to help him but he was too small to haul himself up. A Red Cross worker, impressed by his plucky spirit, grinned as she lifted him up and set him on his feet in the middle of the lorry. He sat down on the narrow bench beside Eva. When the benches on both sides were full the woman raised the tailgate and closed it. Erich leaned forward to keep Tante Gretchen in view. The children were inside the vehicles and their belongings were stowed. Red Cross workers climbed in beside them; Tante Gretchen made no move to join them. Erich watched anxiously.

"G-G-Get in!" he said to Tante Gretchen.

"No, Erich, I can't," she said, shaking her head.

"Aren't you c-c-coming?" Erich asked, alarmed. Again Tante Gretchen shook her head.

"You be a good boy in Ireland," she said, tears glimmering.

The grounds were empty, but shouts and snatches of conversation echoed from inside the lorries. Erich silently watched Tante Gretchen, still hoping she would get in. He couldn't believe she wasn't coming with him.

The engines started and one by one the lorries rolled down the path to the gate. Tantchen Trude and her staff waved as they left. Erich waved back vigorously to Tantchen Trude and Tante Gretchen, tears springing to his eyes as they disappeared from view. Several children around him whimpered, faces crumpling.

He didn't want to leave Tante Gretchen. No one else, except *Mutti*, really cared about him. He wanted to stay with her until *Mutti* came back for him.

To distract them, a kind, young worker sang, "Cuckoo, cuckoo calls from the forest". Comforted by the familiar melody, the children joined in one by one. Erich remembered Tante Gretchen singing this song with them as they walked in the forest. Fresh tears slid down his face.

The familiar woods and village slipped by but Erich barely noticed. They continued into unfamiliar territory; the passing flat countryside was like a large screen moving picture. After the first hour or so the children quieted, lulled by the steady rocking motion of the vehicles; some dozed on the benches. Erich's eyelids began to droop and he also dozed. The sun, high in the sky when they left, gradually slipped lower and the light faded.

Suddenly the first lorry stopped, backed up and turned into a long, winding driveway almost hidden by overgrown shrubs. The other lorries followed and they stopped outside a large, silent house. Erich awoke, weary and hungry. We would have had our dinner at the Home by now, he thought. The children shuffled out of the trucks and into the house. The workers distributed sandwiches to them and, despite his weariness, Erich ate ravenously. Afterwards he lay down on the floor where he was sitting, wrapped himself in the blanket he'd been given and, wanting to forget everything, succumbed to his tiredness and depression. Muttering, "God bless, *Mutti* and Tante Gretchen," he dropped off to sleep.

The next morning they were woken early. Erich noticed Hans across the room as he sat waiting for breakfast. They rarely saw each other in the Home. I promised *Mutti* I would look after Hans, he remembered. When bread and hot drinks were distributed Erich grabbed two pieces of bread and walked over to where Hans was sitting on the floor. He handed a piece of bread to Hans; Erich ate his standing. When breakfast was finished everything was quickly loaded back into the lorries. Erich led Hans to the lorry he had travelled in the day before then returned to his. The children were counted as they boarded, then they set off again.

After what seemed a long time to Erich, the lorries left the road and drove up a narrow lane to a large, imposing stone building. A few holes and broken slates pockmarked the roof but the train station's structure was solid.

The lorries stopped in a row at the station's entrance, occupying all the parking spaces. The Red Cross workers opened the tailgates and the children spilled out. Erich was set on the ground and, after a quick glance around, joined the throng flowing towards the entrance. Through the wire fence he saw belching engines standing at both platforms. He hurried, following Karl and several other boys, wanting a closer look at the engines. Inside the station a man with a Red Cross pin on his lapel directed them to the nearest train. Erich hesitated for a second, scanning the crowd to spot Hans, but he was too short to see anything and quickly abandoned his quest. He raced after Karl and the other boys, along the platform, ignoring orders not to run. Despite be-

ing the smallest, Erich caught up and kept up with them. They
sped past identical grimy, black carriages until they were at the
one behind the engine.

Puffing, Erich hauled himself up the steep steps and entered
the carriage. He dodged wrestling boys as he walked down the
narrow aisle between metal bunk beds. The boys jumped on the
lower bunks, bouncing up and down on the thin mattresses. Karl
picked up a pillow and swung it at Erich. He ducked and lunged
at Karl. There were shouts and groans as the boys fought over
the bunks.

"This is my bed!" a boy in a grey coat shouted, jumping on
the mattress.

"No, it's mine!" Karl replied, trying to shove him off.

Erich climbed up the metal frame of a bed in the corner.
Holding the top post, he hauled himself up and rolled onto the
bunk.

"T-T-This is mine!" he shouted.

He stood on the bunk, bouncing in the centre of the mattress.
The floor was dizzyingly far away. Not liking the sensation he
flopped down and stretched out on the itchy woollen blanket,
leaning over the edge to watch two boys tussling below.

Eventually all the bunks were claimed and the boys sat or lay
on top of them. Shouts, pounding feet and ringing metal were
heard in nearby carriages. A crash followed by a girl's high
pitched cry came from the next carriage.

Erich looked out of the window. Men and women in blue
Red Cross uniforms rushed up and down the platform, setting
boxes and bags into carriages. Men in khaki uniforms wandered
around the platform or lounged against the wall, flicking cigarette ashes onto the ground. They waved at children peering out
of the windows.

A tall, sandy-haired man came and leaned against their carriage, his shoulder resting against the window frame. Erich
stared at him, unblinking. The man smiled, pushing his peaked
cap back on his head, then slowly closed and opened his right

eye. Unfamiliar with the gesture, Erich copied him. The soldier laughed as Erich returned his wink. Erich winked again, grinning back at the man.

"The train will depart in one minute," a railway employee shouted as he walked up and down the platform, slamming doors. The soldier straightened up and stood back from the train.

The carriages shuddered and brakes creaked. With a jerk the train lurched forward and slowly rolled out of the station. The boys pressed their faces against the windows, watching the platform slowly fade from view. Erich saw the man raise his hand to wave as they pulled away. Once clear of the station their speed increased and the countryside flashed by, green dotted with the odd house or heap of rubble. Abandoned carriages lay at intervals beside the tracks.

Two Red Cross workers came into the carriage, counting the boys and checking their identification tags.

"We'll bring you something to eat soon," one of the women said, smiling at them. The boys cheered and shouted.

Erich climbed down from his bunk and perched on the lower one. Bending over, he peered underneath. Shiny specks dotted the floor. Erich leaned forward for a better look. Curious, Karl also peered under the bed and spotted the small shapes glittering. With excited shouts, both boys scrambled under the bed, reaching for them. Being smaller was to his advantage and Erich slid furthest under the bed. He swiped his arm across the floor, knocking Karl's hand away. When he pulled his hand out, he found he was holding a broken string with several beads on it, some loose beads lay in his palm. Karl faced him, clutching the remaining beads. Erich grasped the broken necklace and loose beads tightly. Accustomed to want and hardship, hoarding whatever they could get was second nature to the children irregardless of whether they needed it.

"Let me see them."

Ignoring Karl's demand, Erich pushed the necklace onto the upper bunk in front of him and climbed up.

He sat upright on the bunk, examining the necklace. Setting the loose beads between his spread legs, he lifted them, one at a time, threading them carefully back onto the string.

"Erich, let me see! Give me some," Karl pleaded, peering onto Erich's bunk.

"No! They're m-m-mine. I g-g-got them first!" Erich eyed the other boy suspiciously, threading another bead onto the string. With a scowl, Karl lay down on his bunk, flicking the round beads across his mattress. Erich continued threading, frowning as his hand jerked with the motion of the train.

Erich held up the glass necklace; he had most of the beads back on the string. In the light they glinted, some clear, others a deep, burnished red. He lay with his arm extended, watching them swing with the train's motion. They were the most beautiful things he had ever seen. He would give them to *Mutti* when she came to get him.

That night, when he climbed under the blanket to sleep, the necklace was safely tucked in his coat pocket. The coat lay on top of the blanket and Erich clutched it tightly. He wouldn't take any chances with his treasure. It was for *Mutti*.

The next morning when Erich woke the carriage was silent except for low snoring in one of the bottom bunks. Erich propped himself on his elbow, watching the countryside roll by. Mattress springs creaking below made him look down.

"W-W-Where are we?" Erich asked Karl.

"I don't know," Karl answered, peering up from the lower bunk opposite.

"Are we in Ireland yet?" Erich asked.

"I don't think so. But we'll get there soon!" Karl asserted, uncertain whether this was true.

The other boys began to stir and soon they were all out of bed. Two of them clouted each other with their pillows as the others jumped on the bottom bunks. Erich liked bouncing on the lower ones. The ground was much closer; he didn't feel dizzy.

"Boys, that's enough! Sit on your beds for your breakfast." A middle-aged Red Cross woman came into the carriage handing them bread and cheese. Erich ate quickly, glad not to have lumpy porridge.

After breakfast Eva, her hair in plaits, peered through the door from the next carriage, pressing her small button nose against the glass. Erich opened the door and waved her in.

"What are you doing?" he asked.

"Not much," Eva answered.

"Have you seen Hans on the train?"

"Yes, the youngest children are in the carriage after ours. If you walk through our carriage you can get to them." Erich nodded, satisfied to know where his younger brother was.

"Do you want to see my beads?"

"Yes."

Erich pulled them out of his coat pocket and held them up. They glimmered as they twirled in his hand. Eva stared at them, enchanted.

"They're beautiful!" she cried.

"They're for *Mutti*, but I'll give you one." Erich reached into his pocket, pulled out a loose one and handed it to her. She stared at the rich coloured bead in her hand.

"Thank you."

Erich and Eva admired the beads, chattering happily.

They were still engrossed in their treasures when the Red Cross worker returned.

"I have been looking everywhere for you, Eva. You know you must stay in your carriage. Come with me," she scolded as she took the girl's hand. Eva smiled over her shoulder at Erich as she was led out of the carriage.

Erich climbed onto his bunk and watched the countryside roll monotonously by. Sometimes he saw men working in the fields or a woman walking along the road, a basket hung over her arm. There were many burnt out buildings and piles of rubble and stones. The war had caused destruction everywhere. Erich paid little heed to these signs of carnage; it looked very much like where he came from.

Bored, he climbed down and searched under the bed for any other treasures they might have missed. Finding nothing, he wandered restlessly around the small space in the carriage. He would like to go to see Hans but he knew he wasn't allowed to leave the carriage.

The train suddenly slowed, then inched forward steadily. Erich pressed his face against the window to look at the engine in front of them but something else caught his attention. He stared wide-eyed. The land had disappeared on both sides; there was only water. He pressed his face flat against the glass, looking through its grimy surface. Looking down the side of the train he could not see the ground, only water. Frantically he climbed onto the bunk opposite and looked down. Again there was only water. He leaned his head against the glass, pulling his knees up to his chin. He screwed his eyes shut, then opened them again. There was still only water. We'll sink! Erich thought, panic-stricken.

"The t-t-train is on w-w-w-ater! We'll d-d-drown!" Erich shouted.

Bernhardt looked out of the window and laughed. "We're on a bridge," he said.

The other boys, following Bernhardt's example, barely glanced out of the window at the narrow railway bridge. Erich said nothing more. He stared out, waiting to feel the train sinking. The blue-grey expanse seemed to stretch forever. He clutched his beads tightly in his pocket, so he wouldn't lose them when they sank. Then, without warning, land appeared just ahead of them. Suddenly they were surrounded by green and the train was gaining speed. Erich lay back, sighing.

He closed his eyes, beginning to doze, but in his mind the water surrounded him. He jumped and peered out of the window to reassure himself they on land. Seeing it was still there, he dozed again until the train slowed once more. Looking out of the window this time, he saw water ahead but no bridge.

Fearfully he asked Bernhardt, "How will we get over this

water?"

"We're going on a boat," he replied.

"Why can't we stay on land?" Erich asked.

"Because Ireland is across the sea," he replied.

Unhappily, he watched the water get closer.

Erich hurried across the gangway, trying not to look at the water below. Reaching the security of the deck, he plodded down the steps, peering through the gaps in the latticed metal to the lower deck. The steps rang with the clatter of feet as a steady chain of children wound down them and into the cabin below. Erich lifted his feet over the high rim of the watertight doorway and stepped into a large room.

The room was filled with children; a few adults in uniforms moved amongst them. They sat or stood in every available space. A girl raced past Erich to grasp her friend standing beside the doorway. The two girls giggled, linking arms and walking away. Erich wandered aimlessly until he spotted Karl standing on a seat, looking through a small, blue-rimmed porthole. Erich climbed onto an empty seat next to Karl and stretched towards the porthole. He could just see out. Thick ropes held the ship against the concrete dock, stretching taut as the ship bobbed against them. The dock was nearly empty now. Erich frowned. He didn't like all this water around him. He wanted to get back onto the dock, but the gangway had been removed. There was no way out now. Feeling trapped, he turned around and slid down the seat. Karl slid down and sat on the seat beside him, look-ing around the room. At the other end of the room a Red Cross worker was handing out sandwiches.

"Let's get something to eat!" Karl cried.

From habit, unsure if he were hungry, Erich got up and fol-lowed Karl into the queue. The worker handed Erich a sand-wich with a greyish-white filling. Walking back to his seat he inspected it dubiously then bit into it. He chewed slowly, forcing it down; it had a strong fishy taste. Erich didn't like it but he persevered. He was used to unpalatable food and knew there would be no alternative. Karl ate his, seemingly unaware of the rotten taste.

Several loud, deep blasts sounded, echoing around the room. Erich jumped. The floor vibrated as the engine shuddered to life. Erich's feet didn't touch the floor but the vibration travelled up through his seat and shook his whole body. Through the porthole the boys saw buildings retreating from them. A black and white ship glided past. A breeze, pungent with the smell of salt and dead fish, blew through the open porthole.

As the ship gathered speed it rocked up and down over oncoming waves, a bit deeper with each wave. Sometimes it shuddered as a wave hit it sideways and it rolled but it quickly righted itself and dipped forward again. Karl whooped, enjoying the motion. Erich's stomach churned with the confusing movement. The rocking made him dizzy. He dropped the last of his sandwich onto the floor.

"Put your head between your knees if you feel ill," a kindly woman in a white uniform said, gently pushing his shoulders downwards.

Erich bent forward and closed his eyes. The motion seemed to be inside his head. He could feel each dip throb in his temples while his stomach churned. He wished the motion would stop. His stomach heaved and he felt the greasy bile of the sandwich in his throat. He swallowed, hating the bitter taste in his mouth. Tears welled in his eyes. I want it to stop! he thought. As the ship plunged into another wave, his stomach lurched and the bitter taste spewed out. He leaned outwards so only a few drops landed on his shoes. The smell of the grey mush at his feet made him feel worse.

"Get a mop and bucket," the kindly woman said to a co-worker. "I think you need some fresh air," she said to Erich. Taking him by the hand she led him out of the room and onto the rocking deck. Erich stumbled, putting his hand on the wall to steady himself. The breeze ruffled his hair and cooled him. The woman led him to the rail and he leaned on it until his head cleared. She stood beside him silently.

"Feel a bit better?" she asked after a little while. Erich nodded, unsure if he did but wanting to agree with the nice woman. She led him back inside to his seat, saying, "You're looking a bit better now. I'll come back to check on you in a while."

Erich slouched in the seat and dozed, flinching at the shouts and laughter of children playing around him. Footsteps raced past him. He knew he should try to find Hans but he had no energy to look. The engine hummed loudly. Erich's stomach rolled and he squeezed his eyes tightly shut. He wanted to get off the boat. Why did he have to be on it? Why hadn't *Mutti* come to get him so he didn't have to go to Ireland? As they got further from port the water calmed and the boat bounced less. Its monotonous motion lulled him and, despite his unhappy thoughts and his queasy stomach, he lay down and drifted off to sleep.

It was dark when he woke. Several boys' voices, including Karl's, were raised, fighting over seats. He glanced over with no enthusiasm. After a sharp word from a Red Cross worker they settled down and stopped squabbling. Erich went back to sleep.

The next time he woke light shone through the round portholes. Karl climbed onto a seat to look out. He called to Erich, telling him what he could see but Erich couldn't concentrate on what he was saying. There were shouts and shuffling noises as children around them woke. Erich tried to raise his head but put it down again. He felt terrible. He was dizzy and unable to raise his head, and hunger gnawed at his churning stomach. The kindly worker sent the children around him to join the queue for their breakfast. They trooped across the room, laughing and shoving. Eva stopped beside Erich.

"Come and get breakfast," she said, watching him with a concerned expression. Erich shook his head. He sat up slowly, resting his shoulder against a thick, grey pillar.

"Have you seen Hans since we got on the ship?" Erich asked.

"Not since we left the train," she replied.

"You should try to eat something," the worker said to Erich. She sent Eva to join the queue for breakfast.

The kind worker brought a bowl of porridge to Erich. He looked at the hot mass. Its creamy smell made his stomach lurch and he pushed her hand away.

"Try some," she urged but he shook his head. She set it down near him and moved on to another seasick child. He reached into his pocket, grasped the bead necklace and pulled it out. Seeing its shiny beads didn't make him feel any better. He put it back in his pocket and put his head down between his legs, closing his eyes.

Time passed very slowly. Children around him were eating and talking; he didn't know why they didn't feel ill. He couldn't keep his head up. He wished for the thousandth time that the motion would stop. But the ship kept rolling steadily forwards. He hated this boat. Erich leaned his head against the pillar. If only *Mutti* had come to get him. If he could even see her, everything would be alright. When I get off the boat I will find her and then I will give her the necklace I have for her, he decided. I should check on Hans, he thought listlessly. *Mutti* would expect him to do so. But he felt too ill to get up. I'll do it later, he decided.

Dun Laoghaire, Ireland
September 1946

The motion had finally stopped. Erich dragged himself up on the seat to stand beside Karl and peer out of the small porthole at the huge grey dock rising above them. Where are we? Erich wondered, feeling better now that the rocking motion was not warring with his stomach.

"Is it Ireland?" Erich asked Karl.

"I guess so," he replied.

"Off the seats, boys! Queue up here, children." A woman attempted to herd them into an orderly group, but the children pushed and shoved as they rushed to the door, eager for it to open. Erich trailed listlessly behind them, letting Karl run on ahead of him. Several other slightly greyish children also hung back, reluctant to join the jostling mass. The engine was silent and the floor had stopped vibrating. After what seemed a long wait, they were allowed to file out of the door. A strong breeze ruffled Erich's hair. Grasping the metal handrail and copying the boy in front of him, he stamped his feet as he climbed to hear the steps ring.

Stepping off the boat, he found himself at the foot of a flight of concrete stairs. A solid wall of the same material stretched upwards well above his head on one side while the other was open. Climbing upwards Erich huddled in against the wall, trying not to look at the drop beside him to the water lapping, and sometimes crashing below.

At the top he looked around. Another large ship was docked along the pier, its crew flitting around it like bees around a hive. The wide, bare concrete was crammed with milling children and the adults, who were trying to herd them into order. Women in white uniforms, a red cross emblazoned on their chests, and men and women in blue uniforms, Red Cross pins on their lapels, moved to and fro, gathering the children together and leading them along the pier. Erich shuffled along with the crowd, dragging his feet. He was tired and his head ached from the lack of food.

Where are we going? Where is Karl? he wondered, anxiously. He couldn't see him in the mass of children. Where is Hans? I never looked for him. *Mutti* will be annoyed if I lose him, he worried.

The grey concrete stretched out like a road. A sharp wind blew, splattering rain against him. Erich ducked his head, grasping the beads in his pocket tightly, and plodded on.

At the end of the pier they entered a large concrete building. Erich looked around, wondering where to go. All around him were long tables filled with food. Bread heaped with butter lay on trays beside glasses of milk. Orange and yellow balls lay in piles. What are they? Erich wondered vaguely, not really caring.

After escaping the motion of the boat, Erich was hungry. He crept over to the nearest table. Standing to one side he reached up, surreptitiously, and grabbed a piece of bread, quickly stuffing it into his mouth. A woman, in a white uniform, behind the table said something to him, smiling. He didn't understand what she was saying and darted away, not noticing the plate she held out to him. Another woman bent down and spoke to him. He didn't understand her either. What is wrong with them? Why are they speaking like that? he thought.

The children chattered to each other, pointing out the wonders on the tables. Erich watched a woman hand a small, pocked sphere to Eva. She bit into it, skin and all, the juice squirting across her face as the woman watched her in amazement. The woman pulled the orange away from Eva, whose face crumpled. Peeling it she broke off a section and handed it back to the girl. Eva popped it into her mouth and sucked, her eyes widening and her cheeks tightening at the bitter taste. She grimaced, then laughed, quickly taking another piece. The citrus smell made Erich's stomach rumble.

"It's good!" she said, noticing Erich watching her.

Around him adults were talking, but he didn't understand them. What are they saying? He glanced around, watching people hurry to and fro. Everyone was moving and the din never stopped. Too tired to bother, he sat down. Voices enveloped him but they didn't make any sense. Here and there he picked out a German conversation between other children and was reassured by the familiar sound. He couldn't think clearly and just wanted to sleep. A woman in a white uniform, the red cross blurring as she knelt in front of him, spoke to him. He stared at her blankly. She spoke again. This time, as she spoke she grasped his hand, pulling him to his feet. Too tired to protest, he let her lead him out of the building. He wondered vaguely whether he should look for Hans. He hoped that someone would look after him. But he was too tired to go back and search that huge building. He hoped that Hans wouldn't tell *Mutti* he'd left him.

The rain splattered him as she led him to a bus brimming with children. He flopped down in the nearest empty seat and rested his head on the one in front. He didn't care where they were going. He just wanted to sleep.

❦

Glencree, County Wicklow, Ireland

Erich balanced on the thin plank. Stepping forward he slipped, almost toppling off. He tensed, pulling himself upright. He looked fearfully into the deep, black water below before taking another cautious step. His foot found the plank; he sighed as he put his weight down. He was almost there. Hopping on his left foot he overbalanced, tumbling sideways and shrieking as he fell.

He jerked awake, expecting to feel the icy water. He looked down into the murky water, but saw a wooden floor. Gasping, he darted glances in all directions. He found he was in a large dormitory. There were about fifty beds stretching along both sides of the room. He looked at the boy in the next bed, who regarded him curiously.

"Where are we?" he asked.

"We're in Glencree," the boy replied.

"Where's that?"

"Ireland. Just as my father told me, it's a long way from my home. I wish it wasn't so far away."

"*Mutti* will come to get me," Erich replied confidently.

He got out of bed and padded over to look out of the window. Grey, granite walls met him. He was on an upper floor of a tall, drab building. He frowned at the grey walls opposite. They were so cold.

"I don't like this place," Erich said.

"It's not so bad. You get lots to eat, not like at home," the other boy replied.

"Most food make me sick."

"This food is better than at home. Some of their food is strange but you get used to it. There's always enough to eat too."

"Why does everyone speak so funny?"

"The staff speak English. Most don't speak much German but there's a few who can."

"Do we have to stay here forever?"

"I don't think so. Most of the children go to live with families after a while. One day we'll go back to Germany and I'll see my father."

Erich thought about this information. He wanted to go back to Germany as soon as possible so he could see *Mutti* again.

The Red Cross Home in Glencree cared for refugee children from Germany and France until they were strong enough to be sent to foster placements. They arrived thin and malnourished, after the deprivation they had endured. Nurses oversaw their care, paying close attention to their diets. Most children were unable to tolerate a normal diet and rich foods made them ill. Their milk was thinned with water and they were fed very bland food. Luxuries like butter, oranges and bananas were all new to them and had to be introduced gradually. The children stayed up to three years in Ireland before they returned to their parents.

The Home was a Victorian type building, very imposing and sombre. Its intimidating grey exterior contrasted with the rolling, green hills of the Wicklow Mountains which surrounded it. Many of the children came from cities flattened by bombing and had never seen such a fairytale place before. This was not the barren, war-scarred land they had come from, but a lush, vibrant one.

Erich turned from the window, shivering as he went back to his bed. The hot summer was in full blaze when he left the Goldschmidthaus, but there was a cold breeze here. His coat lay across the end of the bed. He suddenly remembered his beads and dived into his pocket. With a sigh of relief he felt the uneven jewels. They were safe. No one had taken them while he'd slept. He started to dress.

As Erich pulled on his short trousers a very young volunteer entered the dormitory. She glanced uncertainly around the room. When she spoke to them the boys looked at her blankly. She doesn't make any sense either, Erich thought. After a moment's hesitation, the woman waved her arm towards herself, walking to the door as she did so. Regarding her curiously, the boys followed her. Erich spotted Karl amongst them and ran to catch up with him. She led them down the hall, then through the last door on the right, turning to check that they were still behind her.

Erich glanced around as he entered the large room. In the centre there were several tables, some already occupied by children. Erich followed Karl to an empty table nearest the window and raced to grab the end seat. Hans was at the next table; Erich smiled across at him. He was glad to see Hans. Now he knew his brother was safe. He could tell *Mutti* he was watching him just as he'd promised. She would be so proud of him when she came to get him.

The smells of fresh bread and porridge cooking wafted through the room, making him aware that he was very hungry.

A bowl of porridge, with milk running down the creamy mound, was set before him. He spooned into the thick, heavy mass, eagerly. After a few mouthfuls his stomach bulged uncomfortably. He took another spoonful and gagged, unable to eat any more. This porridge was much thicker than he was used to and years of near starvation had shrunk his stomach. He pushed the bowl away. A staff member came by and set it in front of him again, smiling encouragingly. When he pushed it away once more she said something to him. Erich looked at her uncomprehendingly, then shook his head and stared at the floor.

"What did she say? Is she cross?" Erich whispered to Karl.

"I don't know but I don't think so. It sounded very strange," he replied.

The Red Cross nurses and the volunteers were strict, but caring and worked tirelessly. Several interpreters tried to bridge the language barrier. But there weren't enough interpreters and the children were often unable to understand their carers.

Erich left the table and wandered over to the window. Outside was quiet and deserted. What is this place? Erich wondered. Is it a Home, like the Goldschmidthaus? Will I live here now? How will *Mutti* find me here? Except for the other children, no one understood what he said so there was no one he could ask. Questions filled his mind but no one could answer them. He sat down beside the window and stared out.

Time passed slowly for Erich as there was little to do. Sometimes he played with Karl and the other children but often he stared out of the window, hoping to see *Mutti* coming for him.

As he looked out of the window one morning a tall man, wearing a white clerical collar, walked out of the main entrance. A petite woman in a dark raincoat walked beside him holding a small, dark-haired boy's hand. The child looked familiar; it was Hans. Erich usually only saw him at meal times as the toddlers were in a separate dormitory.

Where are they taking him? Erich wondered. Worried, he ran to the front door in time to see the man speaking to a nurse at the bottom of the steps. Smiling they shook hands. Then he led Hans and the petite woman towards a black car parked in the driveway. When he opened the door the woman ushered Hans inside.

"Hans!" Erich shouted, racing down the stairs. Pleading silently Hans turned his large, brown eyes to Erich, startled and unsure like a deer's caught in headlights. The woman, smiling reassuringly, gripped his hand and guided him into the back seat. She got into the front passenger seat beside the minister. Hans turned around to stare at Erich.

"Erich!" the nurse called, holding out her hand to him. Racing past her, he ignored it. The minister started the engine and the car rolled forward before Erich could reach it. He lunged and grabbed the bumper, falling as he clung to it. He held on as the car moved off, half dragging him.

"Erich!" the nurse shouted, running after him.

Hearing the commotion behind him, the minister stopped and got out. Together they prised Erich off the bumper and the nurse, gripping him tightly and speaking sharply, pulled him inside. Twisting he shouted, "Hans!" over his shoulder at the disappearing car.

Hans is gone. How will I find him? Erich thought desperately. What will I tell *Mutti* when she asks where Hans is?

He was supposed to look after him. *Mutti* said so. Now Hans and *Mutti* were gone. He hadn't seen *Mutti* for such a long time. He had no idea where she was either. Everyone had left him. Erich felt very alone.

The nurse was still talking. She seemed to be scolding. Erich stared at the ground, tears rolling down his cheeks.

The nurse sat him down on a chair, then disappeared. Reappearing a few minutes later with white gauze she dabbed at the cuts on his knees, putting a clear liquid on them which stung. Erich cried as the liquid bit into his skin. The nurse said something to him. He frowned, trying to understand her.

"*Ich verstehe sie nicht!*" he shouted, frustration making him angry. The nurse looked at him and shook her head.

"We need more translators," she said to another worker nearby. "I don't know why he was so upset about that boy going to a foster family."

After she finished cleaning his knees, she patted his shoulder, then went to check on some children playing across the room. Erich slouched over the back of the chair, staring disconsolately. He wondered where Hans was going. He couldn't even ask anyone. Tears rolled down his cheeks again.

Karl and Erich leaned forward, ready to race each other across the room, but a tap on his shoulder made Erich pause. A worker beckoned towards her. She looked at both of them and repeated the gesture.

"What does she want?" Erich asked Karl.

"I don't know," he replied.

Puzzled, the boys followed her from the dining room and down the long hall. Turning into an unfamiliar room, she motioned for them to join several other boys and girls already there. Erich smiled when he spotted Eva among them. Around the walls several couples stood watching them. They pointed and whispered to each other as they circled the children, studying them. One woman reached over and brushed a girl's long brown hair back from her face. She inspected the pinched, strained face carefully. A man put his hand on Karl's shoulder and squeezed it, peering intently at the boy. A couple pointed to Eva and spoke to the worker standing beside Erich. The woman put her hand on the elfin girl's shoulder and guided her towards the door.

"Where are you going?" Erich asked Eva, alarmed.

"I don't know," she replied.

"Don't g-g-go with t-t-them," he said. Erich tried to follow her, but the worker blocked his way. Eva walked slowly, looking back frequently.

Hans went away with strange people and now these people were taking Eva. Where do they take them? Erich wondered.

The adults milled around the children who instinctively huddled together like herded sheep. They were centre stage, unsure why and trying to avoid the spotlight. The children avoided the strangers' gazes, shyly aware they were being scrutinised. The staff took no part in matching children and foster parents. They left the couples to make their own choices.

Erich eyed the adults, unsure what they wanted. A man, with small, piggish eyes and the smell of stale tobacco on him, stopped in front of Erich. He grasped the boy's chin and regarded his face carefully. His wife spoke to him softly and he let go. He moved on, stopping in front of a taller, blond boy. With a grunt he nodded towards the boy. His wife smiled at the boy and motioned for him to follow her. A small woman with a hawk-like face peered over her glasses at Erich. He backed away from her outstretched hand. As she advanced, Erich backed further away. Shaking her head, she moved on.

A stout woman, smelling of bacon fat and grease, approached him. The smell made Erich feel ill and he backed quickly away. He darted between two women chatting near the door and tore down the hallway. He ran into an open toilet door, locked it and leaned against it, shaking. What are these people doing? he thought anxiously. He didn't like them touching him and poking at him. He wanted them to go away. They had taken Hans and now Eva. What if they took Karl too? he worried. He would have no one then. Tears welled in his eyes.

Distantly, he heard hard soles clicking on the linoleum. The footsteps got louder until they stopped outside the door. The nurse knocked loudly and spoke to him, but he didn't answer. He didn't know what she was saying, but he thought she was probably angry. He stood very still, hoping she would forget about him.

Finally, getting no response, she walked away. The hallway was very quiet. No one passed the door.

After what seemed like a long time, he heard sounds at the end of the hall. Footsteps left the room, heading towards the front entrance. Men's and women's voices echoed in the hall mingled with a few clatters and giggles. Then the sounds stopped.

When it had been silent for a few minutes, Erich unlocked the door. He peeped around it, but saw no one. Cautiously he stepped out and walked nervously down the corridor.

As he approached the dining room the nurse popped her head out of the doorway. She spotted him and strode quickly to him. He blinked rapidly, watching her.

"*I-I-Ich…*" he began, inhaling sharply, but knew she wouldn't understand what he wanted to say. She gripped his hand firmly and led him to a corner at the end of the corridor, speaking sharply to him. He had no idea what she was saying. She left him facing the wall, with his hands behind his back. Erich cowered and hunched his shoulders. It was obvious that she was annoyed he had run off. He didn't even know what he had run from. He had just wanted the people to stop looking at him and touching him. Tears welled in his eyes again and he sniffed loudly.

"*Mutti...*" he cried, wondering again why she didn't come for him.

Erich looked at the clump on his plate. It was mushy and a thin trickle of greenish liquid ran from it, settling on the plate's white rim. A pungent smell rose from the pulpy mass. Erich pushed his plate away, empty except for the green mass. He liked potatoes and bacon and had devoured them. But this was awful. He couldn't eat it. He had never seen so much food before but some things were very strange.

A volunteer passing by looked at the pile of mushy peas, untouched on his plate. She pointed at them, speaking to him. Looking away, he pretended not to hear her. She spoke louder but he stared fixedly out of the window, blinking rapidly. Again she pointed at the plate, and he flinched, avoiding her gaze. He worried that she would make him eat the terrible mess. He pushed the plate away roughly and it slid off the end of the table. The mushy peas flew off the plate en masse, like jelly. Shaking her head wearily, she grasped his arm, led him out of the room and left him standing, in the corner, at the end of the corridor.

When her footsteps had retreated, he leaned over to look out of the window. The breeze blew in, chilling him. Branches swayed and dipped and leaves scattered across the well-manicured grounds. Some of the leaves falling were yellowed and crumpled. A gust of rain swept across the lawn, driven by the sharp wind. Autumn was well established.

I must have been here a long time, Erich thought. How much longer will it be until *Mutti* comes for me?

Several cars surrounded by a group of people were parked at the entrance. A woman ran her hand through her short hair, flipping her fringe away from her eyes. A thin, serious man stood with his head inclined towards her. A small girl clung to his hand, swinging from it. A potbellied man, trailed by a shrinking, hesitant woman stood next to them. Erich hoped they weren't here to poke at him. He hated going to that room where people looked at him. Karl said these people came to choose children to take home. But he didn't want to go with any of the people who had looked at him. I want to go home with *Mutti*, he thought miserably.

Footsteps approaching made Erich pull away from the window. He stared into the corner. The woman would be annoyed if Erich wasn't where she left him. The footsteps stopped behind him and she said something to him. Taking his hand, she led him down the hall. His heart sank as they neared that room again. He slowed his pace but she pushed him forward. There were only other children in the room but he knew that wouldn't last. Karl stood at the window and Erich went to join him. Staring out, he saw that the people were gone from the entrance. He heard shuffling behind him and knew they must be entering the room. He looked at them briefly, then turned back to the window.

One of the staff came over to them. Taking Erich's hand, she led the boys to the middle of the room. The potbellied man walked past Erich and he held his breath. He hated the smell that wafted from him. The little girl looked over, twirling on her father's hand, and smiled. Half-heartedly Erich smiled back. She giggled and ducked her head. Her father followed her gaze, then walked towards Erich. He tensed as they approached, waiting for them to touch him. The thin man knelt, smiling at Erich.

"Hello," he said.

"Hello," Erich replied cautiously, keeping a safe distance.

The girl giggled again and her mother shushed her. The woman bent down to look Erich in the eye.

"Hello," she said warmly. Turning to her husband she spoke

quietly and he nodded. They turned to Erich and smiled. They hadn't touched him and he started to relax. The girl peered around her father's legs but quickly retreated again, giggling.

The couple spoke to one of the staff standing nearby and moved towards the door. As they did so, the woman turned to Erich. Her smile was so warm, he reached out and clasped her outstretched hand. They walked to the door. Erich turned back to Karl and waved, sadly. He didn't want to leave his friend but it seemed that he would have to go with someone and these people seemed nicer than the others who had poked and prodded him. Where will Karl go? Where am I going? he wondered. He couldn't ask anyone so he just followed them.

3

SHE'S MY MAMMY!
Bray, Ireland
Autumn 1946

ERICH STRETCHED up to gaze out of the window at the wild, hilly countryside which gave way to narrow roads, lined with large houses huddled together. Palm trees swayed in the breeze behind well manicured hedges. An elderly couple sauntered along the footpath. The car turned onto a wide, straight avenue. Gazing between the front seats, Erich caught sight of the sea, a thin blue line just visible on the horizon.

Where are we going? Erich wondered. Back to the boat? His chest tightened at the thought. He didn't want to get on a boat again. Where did Hans and Eva go when they left that place? he wondered.

The short-haired woman in the front seat turned and spoke to Erich and the small girl beside him. He looked at her blankly. Her husband said something to her and she nodded. The girl chattered without pausing in the guileless way of a young child, sometimes staring at him. Erich felt uneasy, wondering what they were saying.

The car slowed and turned into a driveway. The woman got out, opened the back door and the little girl, who was sitting beside it, slipped out quickly. Hesitantly, Erich followed her.

His shoes crunched on the gravel driveway as he walked towards the pebble-dashed, grey bungalow. Set well back from the wide road, an open archway almost hid its recessed, white front door. Red slates swept down the roof, nearly meeting the archway. Bay windows protruded on either side of the entrance.

A dark-haired boy, taller than Erich and perhaps a year older, peered out through the square panes of the left bay window. Beside him, a white-haired woman stood with her hand resting on his shoulder. She spoke to him and he nodded then his gaze returned to Erich.

The short-haired woman walked up the path, motioning to Erich to follow her. At the door he stood with her and the little girl in the alcove, waiting as the man locked the car and strode up to them. He unlocked the door and they stepped into a narrow hall.

"Hello!" the man called out as the little girl disappeared into a room beside the door. She quickly reappeared, followed by the boy and the white-haired woman. Both children were talking at once. Erich listened, uncomprehending.

Another voice drew his attention. As she undid Erich's coat and slipped it off, the short-haired woman spoke. She glanced at the boy to prompt him and he turned to face Erich.

"Hello," he said. At least this was a word that Erich understood.

"Hello," he answered cautiously. The girl giggled, pressing against her father's leg.

Drawing Erich's attention, the woman pointed at her son. "Paul," she said. Then she pointed at the little girl, now hanging onto her father's hand. "Margaret."

The white-haired woman leaned towards him, smiling, and the younger woman said, "Granny Quinn." Next she pointed to the man, saying, "Uncle Richard." Lastly she pointed at herself, saying, "Auntie Alice."

Erich nodded and pointed towards himself, saying shyly, "Erich."

Uncle Richard led them from the cool hall into the sitting room. An open fire, opposite the bay window, gave the room a pleasant heat. A breeze blowing against the window rattled some of the panes set in the wooden frame. Erich went to the window, looking out as far as he could in either direction. A few stray leaves drifted across the neatly kept lawn. Trees obscured his view of the nearby properties but he caught glimpses of brick and red slates. Red-roofed buildings, set back on large lawns, peeped through the gaps.

Granny Quinn settled in a high-backed chair beside the hearth stretching her legs towards the heat. Instructed by their father, Paul and Margaret sat on the sofa. Margaret bounced on her seat, competing with her brother for his attention. Reaching inside his jacket pocket, their father pulled out a small brown paper bag. Margaret tugged at his sleeve, bouncing harder.

"Erich!" The man motioned for Erich to join them. He held up the bag and pointed to it, then pointed to the sofa. Erich cautiously came over and sat beside Margaret, who was still chattering and bouncing.

Margaret squealed and shoved her hand towards her father as he opened the bag and rummaged in it but he shook his head. He pulled out three small, brightly coloured objects from the bag and handed the first to Erich. Then he gave one each to Paul and Margaret. The wrappers crackled as Paul and Margaret unwrapped theirs and popped them into their mouths, sucking and slurping. Turning to look at Erich, Margaret's eyes suddenly widened. She said something to her father, tugging at his sleeve and pointing at the boy. Erich was sucking the sweet, wrapper and all. He tried to bite it and grimaced as his teeth met the wrapper. Uncle Richard made a spitting motion to him. Erich tried once more to bite into the wrapper then, disappointed, he spat out the sweet. Reaching into the bag, Uncle Richard pulled out another which he unwrapped and handed to him. Cautiously Erich put it into his mouth and rolled it around on his tongue, tasting its tart flavour. It was different from the soft, pliable sweets Tante Trude had occasionally given them; it was hard and juicy. He bit into it, breaking it into small fragments, which he devoured eagerly.

Margaret went to the tall bookshelf in the corner and standing on tiptoe pulled down a large, thick book. She half carried, half dragged the heavy blue volume to the sofa and sat down, hauling it onto her knee. Opening the thick cardboard cover, she flicked through the pages holding it so Erich could see it too. Colourful illustrations adorned most pages. A wolf in a night-dress peered out from the bed at a girl in a red cape on one page and a large goose, a white starched cap on her head, stood surrounded by chicks on another. Erich stared at the pictures, fascinated. They did not have many books at the Goldschmidthaus. This was the most beautiful one he'd ever seen. He watched eagerly as she turned the pages of the nursery rhyme book. As he leaned forward to look more closely at its wonderful illustrations, his bead necklace dropped from his pocket. Margaret stopped turning the pages and bent to retrieve the necklace. Erich dived after it, scooping it up and quickly stuffing it back inside his pocket. Margaret spoke to him but Erich moved away, clutching his necklace tightly.

Uncle Richard and Aunt Alice silently watched the children for a few minutes, then slipped out of the room.

"We can't even imagine what he's been through," Uncle Richard said, standing in the kitchen.

"No, it must've been terrible for him. The matron at Glencree said they were told that he and his brother, Hans, have no living relatives that they know of. Their mother has been missing since before the end of the war and is presumed dead. They have no one. Young children like that on their own - it's just unimaginable! The food shortages were dreadful in Germany last winter. We'll probably never know all he went through," she replied, replacing the lid on the potato pot.

"Well, he won't have to be afraid now. God willing, we'll care for him the best we can. With your cooking, sure, we'll have him fit in no time!"

"That necklace must have been his mother's. Poor lad, it's all he has of hers."

"Indeed. How terrible to lose your whole family and every possession."

"The first problem now is that he doesn't speak any English."

"He'll soon pick it up. For now we'll just have to play charades! When he starts school he will learn it in no time." Uncle Richard smiled at his wife.

The butter and jam dripped over the edge of his soda bread. Erich ate every crumb. I've never seen so much food! he thought ecstatically. Full after supper, he felt sleepy. The sun was low in the autumn sky; it was almost dark. Auntie Alice lifted dishes from the table and whisked them to the sink. Trying to imitate her, Margaret lifted a couple plates, balancing them unsteadily with both hands. Auntie Alice made several trips, clearing the table quickly. Granny Quinn washed the dishes and set them on the drain board.

Erich watched them. Slim and dark-haired, Auntie Alice was a bit like *Mutti*. She didn't wear her hair in a bun as *Mutti* did, but she smiled the same and fussed over him. He wondered again where *Mutti* was. Would she find him here?

Auntie Alice, with Margaret behind her, came back to the table. Pulling Erich's chair away from the table, she motioned for him to follow her, saying to all of them, "Bedtime." The children followed her out of the kitchen and down the hall.

Margaret disappeared into her room and the boys continued to the end of the hallway. The room had two beds in it, one directly opposite the door and the other against the far wall. Paul flopped down on the bed furthest from the door; Erich took the nearest one. Auntie Alice undid the buttons on Erich's shirt, helping him undress. He pulled the necklace from his pocket and slid it under his pillow, watching Auntie Alice warily. Smiling reassuringly, she spoke to him. Although he didn't know what she was saying, Erich thought he could trust her. His necklace would be safe. She wouldn't take it from him. He relaxed and pulled his hand out from under the pillow.

Once they were in their nightshirts Paul knelt, bowing his head and Erich did the same. Auntie Alice led them in their prayers. Erich said the prayers he had been taught at the Goldschmidthaus ending with "God bless *Mutti*, Tante Gretchen, Karl, Eva and Hans and let me see them again soon."

When they were finished and under their blankets Auntie Alice kissed each of them good night. She is so like *Mutti*, Erich thought, I like her. He reached up and hugged her tightly. She smiled and hugged him, pleased at his trust.

After she left, closing the door behind her, Erich lay on his back looking up at the ceiling. The room was dark but a skylight above his bed gave him a view of the stars. He couldn't see Paul but heard his breathing. He slid his hand under the pillow to re-assure himself the necklace was still there.

"Your mother is very nice," Erich said in German, sitting up in the bed. Paul said something which Erich did not understand.

"She makes such lovely food!" Erich thought of the chicken and potatoes they had for dinner earlier. "I could eat and eat!" He paused briefly. "Goldschmidthaus was very different. I had cabbage soup every day."

Again Paul said something Erich didn't understand. He wondered why Paul couldn't speak properly. No one here seemed to be able to do so. He wondered when he would meet someone he could talk to again.

He tried once more, "Where are we?"

Paul sat up on his elbow and looked at Erich, "Shh...."

Erich lay back in the bed and looked through the glass above him. It wasn't much use talking to him if Paul couldn't under-stand what he said. But Auntie Alice was so nice and the food was wonderful. He liked it here. Still he wished he could talk to them.

Paul's breathing was very slow and even. He was almost asleep. Suddenly Erich felt very alone in the dark. He didn't know where

Karl or Eva were. All his friends from the Goldschmidthaus had vanished. And where had those people taken Hans? He was supposed to watch his brother but he couldn't stop them taking him. Tears welled in his eyes and he sniffed loudly. He liked Auntie Alice but he really was alone. Erich sniffed again and hummed part of a hymn he had learned at the Goldschmidthaus. He remembered lying in his bed at the Home singing with Tante Gretchen and the other boys before they went to sleep. She always sang his favourite hymns. Thinking of Tante Gretchen, more tears ran down his face.

"Jesus, tender Shepherd, hear me. Bless thy little lamb tonight. Through the darkness be thou near me. Keep me safe till morning light," he sang softly as Tante Gretchen had taught him. She always smiled as she pulled the blanket around his shoulders when she tucked him in. Singing the hymn, for a few minutes he felt as if he was back at the Home with his friends.

Across the room there was a sharp "Shh!". Erich hummed lower and closed his eyes, tears still trickling down his face. Gradually his breathing became slow and steady. The room was quiet as both boys slept. Erich sang to lull himself to sleep many times over the next few weeks.

December 1946

Erich and Paul sat at the table, dressed in their best short trousers, white shirts and blazers. Margaret, in a matted red cardigan, leaned on the corner of the table.

Auntie Alice, carrying breakfast bowls to Granny Quinn at the sink, said, "Come on, lads. You've to hurry!" She motioned to Erich to stand up, as she spoke. Turning on the kitchen tap, she cupped her hand under it. Granny Quinn moved out of her path.

The water tap fascinated Erich. He remembered the golden liquid that flowed from the tap in the tavern in Germany. It was pretty but tasted horrible. He knew that beer came from taps. It never ceased to amaze him to see water coming out of this one. Why isn't it beer? he wondered.

Erich shoved Paul so he could stand closer to Auntie Alice. Paul leaned against him, trying to squeeze him aside until Auntie Alice noticed and fixed him with a stare. He stopped, glaring at Erich. Auntie Alice sprinkled water on each boy's head. Picking up the comb on the windowsill, she quickly combed Erich's hair. His curly locks straightened then bounced back as the comb slid through them. Unable to tame them, she patted them down and took a final look. Then she turned to Paul and ran the comb easily through his straight hair.

"Off you go now! Straight to school and no messing or you'll be late!" she said. Erich didn't understand everything but caught a few key words. The final sweep of her arm told him what he needed to know. The boys picked up their exercise books and hurried out of the front door.

The wooden sign, "Rosemount", on the black iron gate, rocked as Paul swung the gate open. Standing on the footpath they leaned forward to see up and down the long, wide road. Nearly identical, squat, red-roofed bungalows behind concrete walls lined the opposite side of the street. To the right the sea sat flat and grey-blue, just visible on the horizon.

Bray, south of Dublin on Ireland's east coast, had been a thriving seaside resort in the Victorian era. Its heyday was past but there was still evidence of its grand history. A large white and black building, Bray Head Hotel, sat at the end of the promenade a little apart from the other hotels and B&Bs as a reminder of its elegant past. The long, straight promenade with its wide, sandy beach, once thronged with holiday makers, was still a popular destination for family day trips. The narrow streets near the promenade harboured once grand houses, hidden amongst palm trees and shrubs.

No traffic was in sight as they crossed the road and headed along a side street. Sprawling villas, once majestic, lined both sides, typical of an old seaside town. Behind their walls and ornate iron gates lacy fascia boards framed doorways and palm trees dotted lawns and gardens, lending an air of gentility to them. Half-moon fanlights over the doors let light stream into formal hallways. Each property spread out lazily, not crammed for space.

A steady breeze flicked Erich's unruly hair as he walked. In autumn the breeze was refreshing but this winter morning it bit into his ears and nose. Without seeing or hearing it, the salty smell wafting on the breeze made the sea's presence felt. Beside him tall, black iron rails rose. Behind the rails lay a small, immaculate park inhabited only by the ghosts of Victorian nannies pushing prams and courting couples with parasols and top hats. Its locked gates kept it pristine and quiet.

Following the park's high iron railings around the corner brought the boys opposite the French School. The three storey, red brick building was founded in 1864 and one of its original purposes was to promote language learning. Erich looked up at the tall, rectangular windows. The peaked arches over each window sported white lines, like eyelashes, fanning around them. They stood out gaily, like a clown's eyes. Matching towers propped up each end of the building. The door sat squarely in the centre of the building at the top of a short flight of steps.

Erich hurried across the street, up the steps and through the door. Grasping the solid wooden banister and sliding his hand along the smooth wood, he climbed the stairs. The banister swept in a wide arch upwards; Erich leaned over it to see the large foyer below. Paul dallied in the centre of it with some of his classmates. Girls and a smattering of young boys were heading to their classrooms. The French School accepted boys for the first two years of their education, then they transferred to all boys' schools.

Erich took his seat at the back of the classroom. His teacher wiped the blackboard with a wet cloth as a few stragglers shuffled into their seats. The children fidgeted and whispered; books thumped on desks. The teacher, a young blonde woman with steady blue eyes, turned to face the class. Standing beside her desk, she silently and steadily regarded them. Gradually they became aware of her gaze. The room quieted; the children sat up straight and still.

"Good morning, children," she said.

"Good morning, Mrs Murphy," the class replied.

"Now take out your copy books and write down the sums I will put on the board," Mrs Murphy said.

Only the floorboards creaked under Mrs Murphy's shoes as the children jotted down the sums and began to work on them. Reading and spelling followed arithmetic. Erich listened carefully, trying to make sense of what he heard. Many words were becoming familiar so he understood part of the lessons. When the last word written on the blackboard had been spelled correctly Mrs Murphy leaned back in her chair and smiled.

"Now, children, since it's our last school day before the Christmas holidays we'll sing some carols."

In a high pitched but melodic voice she led them singing, "Silent night, Holy night. All is calm, all is bright."

The children's high, thin voices joined hers. Erich, recognising the tune, sang, "*Stille nacht, ….*". He remembered standing with Tante Gretchen and the other children singing the same carol last Christmas. *Mutti* sometimes sang it to lull him to sleep. His chest felt tight as he thought of *Mutti* and Tante Gretchen.

As they finished the carol there was a peaceful hush. In the silence he heard *Mutti's* soft voice, humming. She would find him soon. He was sure of it.

Margaret ran back and forth, in and out of the sitting room. Her father shooed her out repeatedly but she continued to get under his feet.

"Margaret, don't be so bold. If you don't behave, Father Christmas won't stop here tonight," her father said, looking at her sternly. Margaret retreated a few steps to the doorway and watched him.

Erich peered into the sitting room, wondering why there was such activity. Auntie Alice had been busily cleaning all day and Uncle Richard had just carried a pine tree into the room. What would he do with the tree? Maybe he might burn it on the fire. It would make a lovely big fire, Erich thought. At school yesterday all the children were talking about Father Christmas bringing gifts tonight. When he lived at the Goldschmidthaus Father Christmas had brought a few sweets for him but he didn't remember any other gifts. Christmas had been much like any other day. Why is everyone so excited? Erich wondered.

Margaret finally retreated from the doorway and came to stand beside Erich in the hall, carrying her favourite doll. Looking earnestly at the doll, she said, "You must be very good!"

Erich watched her wagging her finger at the doll. "You'll go straight to bed if you're bold," she admonished.

Uncle Richard appeared at the sitting room door, holding a paper bag. He held it up saying, "You may each have a sweet if you are very good."

The wrappers rustled as he dropped the sweets into their outstretched hands. Erich unwrapped his, saying *"Danke."*

"Daddy, can we see the tree?" Margaret pleaded.

"When I'm finished. Go and help Mammy in the kitchen," Uncle Richard replied.

Margaret reluctantly headed to the kitchen. Erich followed her. Auntie Alice was peeling apples, dropping them onto a pastry shell flopped inside a thick, grey baking tin. Paul was sitting on a chair at the table, watching her. Erich squeezed in between Paul and Auntie Alice. After a warning glance from his mother, Paul reluctantly shifted his chair to make room for Erich. Margaret leaned on the opposite side of the table. Auntie Alice handed them each a slice of apple. They watched as she deftly kneaded and rolled a ball of dough. She flipped it in the air then laid the dough on the table, lightly sprinkling it with flour, and ran the rolling pin over it. She gingerly lifted it, setting it on top of the apples piled high in the tin.

"Will Father Christmas come tonight, Mammy? I tried very hard to be good," Margaret asked.

"We'll have to wait and see," Auntie Alice replied, setting the pie in the oven.

She dropped the rolling pin into the sink. Dishes rattled in the soapy water as she washed them.

From the sitting room Uncle Richard called, "Does anyone want to see the tree?" Margaret rushed down the hall. Paul slipped around the table and ran after her. Erich looked up at Auntie Alice.

"I stay here," he said seriously, glad to have her to himself.

She smiled. "Go and see what Uncle Richard has to show you." She gave him a push towards the door and reluctantly he left her. Margaret's squeals echoed down the hall. He wondered what was so exciting. Entering the sitting room, he was astounded to see it adorned with paper streamers criss-crossing the room. The tree sat in front of the bay window. Tinsel was draped over its branches and baubles dangled below them. The fire and the lights on the tree provided the only light in the room, creating a flickering glow in the semi-darkness. The silver, red and gold baubles glinted as the tree lights caught them.

Erich stood speechless, eyes wide, captivated by the soft flickering lights. Margaret jumped up and down beside him.

"Daddy, can I put the angel on top?" she shouted.

Uncle Richard handed her the white angel, its silver halo stuck to its black head, and lifted her up. She leaned over and pushed it onto the top branch. He set her down and they stood together, admiring the tree.

"Isn't it lovely!" Auntie Alice exclaimed as she entered the room.

"That's a grand tree," Granny Quinn agreed from her place beside the fire.

"Father Christmas not come?" Erich asked, thinking of the

Christmas Eve festivities at the Goldschmidthaus. Even though he only had sweets to give them Father Christmas always visited them on Christmas Eve.

"Father Christmas will come while you're sleeping tonight," Uncle Richard answered.

"He go my house first," Erich said, thinking he must be late because he would visit the Goldschmidthaus first. Uncle Richard gave him a puzzled look.

"Daddy, can we have more sweeties?" Margaret asked.

"Just one and then it's time for bed. Or Father Christmas won't come."

Uncle Richard picked up the paper bag from behind a sprig of holly on the mantelpiece and handed each child another gaily wrapped sweet. Erich tore the wrapper off without taking his eyes from the tree. The children sucked the sweets silently, still gazing at the twinkling tree.

When they were finished Auntie Alice said, ushering them towards the door, "Come, children. Time for bed." Erich's eyes never left the tree.

Erich and Paul sat up in their beds as the grey light streamed in the skylight and window.

"I hope Father Christmas brought me a lorry!" Paul said.

"He come?" Erich asked.

A door creaked, then footsteps padded along the hall carpet. Margaret shrieked with glee. Erich and Paul rushed into the hallway. A trail of silver flakes ran along the red wool carpet from their bedroom to the sitting room.

"What that?" Erich asked, pointing at the glittering carpet.

"It's angel dust. It leads us to the gifts," Paul replied.

The flakes scattered under their bare feet as they ran to the sitting room. Margaret was seated cross-legged on the floor in front of the tree. Gifts, wrapped in bright patterns and plain colours with handmade tags, were piled under the tree almost touching the lower branches. Paul leaned over to read the nearest tags.

"That's mine!" he exclaimed, after inspecting one.

Erich bent to look under the tree, surprised to see so many parcels sitting there. He looked behind the sofa and then pulled the curtains back to look behind them. Uncle Richard and Auntie Alice came in, dressing gowns wrapped around them and tied securely to keep out the chilly early morning air.

"What are you looking for, Erich? All the gifts are under the tree," Auntie Alice said, noticing him prowling around the room.

"Angels," Erich replied.

Auntie Alice looked at Erich, puzzled. Erich looked up at the top of the tree and then around the back of it. Paul stopped trying to read the tags and glanced at Erich.

"He's looking for the angels who left the angel dust," he said.

Auntie Alice smiled.

"Oh, I don't think you'll find them there. You're not meant to see them. Now, children, go and get dressed while Daddy lights the fire. Then you may each open one gift before church." As the children trailed out Uncle Richard set to work lighting the fire.

There was a crackling fire in the grate when the family assembled again. Dressed and seated on the sofa, each of the children held a small, colourful parcel. Erich opened his and found a pair of thick blue mittens Granny Quinn had knitted for him. Margaret held up a pair of red ones; Paul also had blue ones.

"What do you say to Granny, children?" Auntie Alice asked.

"*Danke*," Erich said, looking over at the old woman sitting beside the fire.

"Thank you," the other children echoed.

"You're welcome, my dears," Granny Quinn replied.

"Can't you say thank you?" Paul asked, nudging Erich.

"*Danke*, I say," Erich replied.

"It's thank you," Paul insisted.

"Whisht, Paul, enough of that. Now get your coats or we'll be late for church," Auntie Alice said. She helped them put on their coats and button them.

A constant breeze nipped them as they walked along the main street to the far end of town. Ahead Erich saw the square fortress-like steeple of St Paul's Church. The austere, grey church was set high on a hill above the Dargle River. Three peaks adorned with crosses faced them as they climbed the steps; the steeple stood at the far end.

They passed the small graveyard and filed into the church, the click of their shoes on the tiles breaking its silence. Uncle Richard slid into the pew, followed by Auntie Alice holding Margaret by the hand. Erich squeezed past Paul to sit beside them.

Erich sang each hymn lustily not caring whether he knew all the words but squirmed in his seat during the minister's sermon. He couldn't wait to get back to the house and open the parcels under the tree. What's in them? he wondered. There are so many! They never had presents like that at the Goldschmidthaus. To Erich's relief the service finally ended and they headed home.

The smell of the goose cooking and the sound of Granny Quinn rattling pots in the kitchen greeted them as they entered the house. Auntie Alice went to help her in the kitchen.

"Can we open the gifts now?" Margaret pleaded a few minutes later.

"We must wait for Mammy and Granny Quinn," Uncle Richard replied. As he spoke, the rattling stopped and the women appeared, still wearing their aprons. Wiping her hands on hers, Auntie Alice sat down on the sofa. Granny Quinn took her usual seat beside the fire. Erich sidled over and squeezed in beside Auntie Alice.

There were shouts and squeals as Uncle Richard reached under the tree for the first gift. He handed a parcel to each of them. Erich found a black, shiny miniature train locomotive inside his parcel. It's wonderful! he thought, holding it up to examine it from every angle. Paul received a similar one. Margaret unwrapped a new doll. Brown, curly hair framed the doll's porcelain face and the most beautiful blue eyes stared back at her.

When she laid the doll down the eyes closed. Standing her up again they popped open. Margaret hugged the doll then cradled her in the crook of her arm. Fascinated, she watched as the doll's eyes closed again.

"Lads, do you want to try your new locomotives on the track?" Uncle Richard asked, walking over to the corner where the Hornby train set was laid out. The track wound around in an oval with a miniature station against the wall. Paul put his engine on the track and Erich rushed to set his in front of Paul's. Paul then put his in front of Erich's.

"M-M-Mine first!" Erich said.

"No, mine is!"

"N-N-N-o!" Erich tried to push past Paul to lift his locomotive.

"That's enough, boys! If you can't behave no one will play with it," Uncle Richard warned. "Do you know that I've had train sets ever since I was your age, Erich? I've always loved them. We get the track out most weekends and every holiday all year round."

Erich made no reply. The boys glared at each other as Uncle Richard set the trains in motion but the trains' movement quickly drew their eyes to the track. Forgetting their argument, they watched, fascinated, as the miniature engines chugged around in a figure of eight.

They were lost in the movement of the tiny locomotives when Auntie Alice called, "Dinner's ready." Reluctantly the boys left the train set.

Erich had never seen such a feast before. Without food shortages to contend with portions were generous in Ireland compared to what he had had in Germany, but this was exceptional. The goose sprawled in the centre of the table, surrounded by bowls of potatoes, carrots, turnips, peas, cranberry sauce and gravy. There was barely room on the table for their plates. Uncle Richard carved the goose as Auntie Alice dished out the vegetables, pouring gravy over everything. Erich hungrily surveyed the mound on his plate. Despite the size of the portion, he cleared every scrap. He felt his belly bulge.

After dinner the whole family sprawled in front of the fire, too full to move. As they dozed, the light outside began to fade; the Christmas trees lights shone more brightly. Eventually Uncle Richard roused himself and brought a large box into the room saying, "Who'll help me build a crane?"

"Me! Me!" Paul and Erich chorused. They crowded around Uncle Richard as he unpacked the steel Meccano pieces. He set out a square base on the floor then piled the pieces on top of it, interlocking them with miniature nuts and bolts. Uncle Richard and the boys built it up until they had a square structure with a thin arm hanging in front of it. The crane's arm stood level with Erich's head. Both boys surveyed it with pride.

Margaret sat on the floor in front of the fire rocking her new doll. Erich wandered across the room and peered over her shoulder at the doll.

"Shh...She's asleep," Margaret whispered.

"Make eyes open," Erich said.

"She's asleep," Margaret insisted.

"Open eyes," Erich repeated, staring at the doll.

"Oh, alright," Margaret said. She raised the doll and the eyes slowly opened. Then she laid the doll down again and the eyes swung smoothly closed. Erich watched with interest. Paul also came to look at the doll.

"How do they work?" he asked. He tried to grab the doll but Margaret pulled it away from him.

"Let's see it," Paul insisted. He leaned over her but Margaret twisted away, hugging the doll tightly.

"Let her alone, boys," Uncle Richard said. "It's nearly time for bed. Go and get ready."

A few minutes later the boys were in bed, prayers completed. Auntie Alice kissed them and closed the door. After all the excitement of the day Erich was wide awake.

"My train best," he said to Paul.

"No, mine's faster!" Paul replied.

"No!"

"Boys, be quiet and go to sleep. If you don't, the bogeyman will come," Uncle Richard called from the sitting room.

The boys quietened and soon Erich heard Paul's light snoring.

"What we do in morning?" he asked but got no reply. He shifted in his bed, unable to settle, chatting to himself and humming tunes of familiar hymns. He didn't feel so alone when he sang.

"I have pie tomorrow," he said. There was no response so he continued to mutter to himself. The bedroom door opened and Uncle Richard poked his head in.

"Shh...Or no pie tomorrow," he said. Erich closed his eyes promptly, thinking happily of his gifts and the Christmas dinner. He finally drifted off to sleep.

"Sure, he's such a chatterbox since he started to get a grasp of English. But I think he'll be quiet now," Uncle Richard said to Auntie Alice when he returned to the sitting room.

The Christmas holidays sped on. The boys woke early on Saturday morning. It was an unusually cold winter. From the bedroom window they could see Bray Head's imposing form covered in a white blanket of snow rising behind their garden. The boys stared at it in awe. Erich remembered that Uncle Richard had promised to take them sledding if there was enough snow. He raced down the hall to the adults' bedroom followed closely by Paul and flung the door open.

"It's snowed! It's snowed!" the boys shouted.

"I see that," Uncle Richard said, as he headed down the hallway to the bathroom.

"We do sledding!" Erich shouted.

The boys jumped on the bed, on either side of Auntie Alice, shouting in her ears. She tried to hush them.

"Go away! I sit here!" Erich ordered Paul.

"No! She's my Mammy!" Paul shouted.

"Go!"

"No!"

"Now stop that, boys!" Auntie Alice exclaimed.

Erich, glaring at Paul, pushed him away from her. Paul shoved him back. Erich shoved again, landing on top of Auntie Alice. The boys wrestled and vied for her attention while she tried vainly to pull them apart. Hearing the noise, Uncle Richard came into the room.

Grabbing them each by an arm, he said sharply, "Stop that or neither of you will go sledding today!" They stopped and silently glared at each other.

"Now go and get dressed." Uncle Richard gave them a stern look.

After breakfast they donned their new scarves, hats and mittens; Auntie Alice buttoned their coats tightly. Uncle Richard got the sled from the garden shed and they climbed Bray Head, Margaret trailing slightly behind up the steep hill. It was cold but the boys danced around with excitement, barely noticing their red noses and cheeks. Uncle Richard took Margaret on the sled with him on the first run. The sled, metal gleaming, raced down the hill, stopping only feet from their back garden. The boys each took a turn afterwards. They shrieked as the sled gathered speed down the hill. After each run there was the long trudge up the hill but they didn't mind. They raced up to slide down again. They were wet and exhausted after many tumbles in the snow as they made their way home for lunch.

Their outdoor clothes were soaked and they were tired after their energetic morning, so they stayed inside after lunch. As soon as Auntie Alice cleared the table they crawled under it, pulling the table cloth down until it nearly touched the floor.

"We hide here," Erich said.

"We have to watch for the enemy," Paul said. "You stand guard."

"We shoot them," Erich stated gravely. He kept guard, peering out to spot any threat to their hideout. Margaret sat beside them, her new doll cradled in her arms.

With nothing else to interest him in their hideout, Paul regarded it curiously. "How do her eyes open? Let me see it."

Margaret pulled the doll away from him but he was quicker than her and grabbed it. He held it up, looking at the eyes. Turning it around he scrutinised the back of the head but could not see what made them work. Erich helped Paul to examine the doll thoroughly. They looked under its dress but found nothing to explain it there. Then Paul tried to pull its head off. Margaret cried, trying to grab the doll from him.

"Give her back! Don't hurt her!"

Paul held the doll out of Margaret's reach. He tried once more to pull the head off but it didn't budge so he slammed it against the floor. After several blows the head smashed and the pieces scattered around them.

"Mammy! Mammy!" Margaret cried.

The doll's curly hair hung limply over the gap at the back of the head. Pushing the hair aside, Erich and Paul stared intently at the mechanism inside, repeatedly tilting the doll horizontal and vertical to watch it work.

Hearing Margaret's hysterical cries, Auntie Alice hurried into the room to find the girl, red eyed and sniffing, sitting amid the broken pieces scattered across the carpet.

"That's very bold!" Auntie Alice said to the two boys. "Go to your room at once!" She hugged Margaret and then began picking up the broken pieces. Erich watched Auntie Alice anxiously over his shoulder as he followed Paul from the room. He didn't like her to shout at him. He wanted her to like him. He didn't break the doll. He hoped she knew that. He scowled at Paul's back. It's his fault Auntie Alice is mad at me, he thought crossly.

"I'm sure Daddy can glue it together again for you, pet," Auntie Alice said, as she hugged the weeping girl.

"Glue what?" Uncle Richard asked as he entered the room.

"Margaret's doll," Auntie Alice replied. "The boys have broken it."

"Don't worry, pet. I'll have her mended in no time," Uncle Richard said giving the girl a quick hug. "But first I must punish the boys for being so bold."

Uncle Richard went to the boys' bedroom and opened the door. Erich lay on his bed dejectedly while Paul stood staring out of the window at the snow.

"You know that breaking Margaret's doll was very bold, don't you, boys?" Uncle Richard asked. Paul nodded meekly but Erich opened his mouth to speak, anxious for Uncle Richard to know he didn't break it.

"You will both stay in your room for the rest of the day and you will not have any tea tonight," Uncle Richard said, not giving Erich a chance to speak. Erich groaned, frustrated that he was sharing the blame for Paul's actions.

"Enough of that, Erich. You must accept your punishment. I won't allow you to behave like that," Uncle Richard said with finality. Erich didn't reply.

Easter 1947

The school term flew and soon it was the Easter holidays. After breakfast on Saturday morning Erich went into the bedroom; Paul was sitting on his bed.

"Let's play camping," Paul said. He dragged his blanket off the bed and pulled their chairs into the middle of the room. Erich helped him drape the blanket over the chairs and soon they had a makeshift tent. They crawled in and sat looking out.

"Margaret, come in!" Erich called when she peeked in the door. Margaret crawled under the blanket and sat beside him.

"I have sweeties. You can have one," she said, handing it to him.

Auntie Alice came into the room and stared.

"Boys! I'm only after making that bed and you've torn it apart.

We'll never get to the Beattys if you keep messing about!"

The children crawled out of their tent looking sheepish.

"Now help me put this back where it belongs," Auntie Alice said, as she lifted the blanket. "And no more messing." The children helped her re-make the bed.

By the time they were finished Uncle Richard was waiting for them in the car. They drove along the coast road to the Drumms' old friends in the next town.

A carpet of vibrant yellow daffodils lined the path to the Beattys' front door. The ground was covered with them and the air was filled with their scent. Erich stared at the bright and cheerful plants. I must pick some for *Mutti*, he decided.

As he grasped the stem of one, Uncle Richard said, "Don't pick the flowers, Erich. They're not yours."

Irked, Erich let go of the flower. It would have made a lovely gift for *Mutti*. He wanted to keep it for her. He wished she would come for him like she had said she would. He knew she would like it here if only she would come. Wondering when he would see her again he felt suddenly deflated. Head down, he followed the other children to the front door.

They went through to the back garden and the children were soon running about on the lawn while the adults sat in garden chairs drinking tea and gazing at the sea. Erich liked to visit the Beattys. They had a big lawn and were even closer to the sea than the Drumms. As long as he didn't have to venture onto it Erich liked to watch the water.

He stopped running, his attention drawn by the metal arched hoops dotted around the lawn. What are they for? he wondered.

"Do you want to play croquet, Erich?" Auntie Alice asked, seeing him eyeing the hoops.

"What croquet?"

"Paul'll show you."

"I want to play too," Margaret said as Paul went to get the mallets.

Paul showed Erich how to hit the ball through the hoop. Erich had a try but the ball swivelled away, rolling to a stop a couple of feet away.

"My turn!" Margaret shouted. She grabbed the mallet and swung it high behind her, preparing to hit the ball. Paul let out a yelp as the mallet hit him.

"Ouch! Margaret!"

"Ohhh!" Margaret shrieked.

Margaret and Erich watched horrified as blood spurted from a cut on Paul's forehead. Hearing the commotion, Auntie Alice hurried over, gasping when she saw the blood. Taking a hankie from her pocket, she pressed it against the cut. While she was trying to stop the bleeding Uncle Richard appeared. He surveyed the situation and turned to Erich.

"That's enough of this fighting, boys! And you can't just hit people, Erich! That's very bold!"

"Erich has such a temper at times. But we can't have this," Uncle Richard said to Mr Beatty, hovering nearby while his wife went to get some water and a cloth.

Margaret started to sniffle.

"It's only a small cut, Margaret. There's no need to cry," Uncle Richard said.

"But I'm very bold. I didn't mean to hit him." Margaret continued to sniffle.

Uncle Richard looked at her. "Well, that's another matter if it was an accident," he said. He said quietly to Mr Beatty, "The boys fight so often I thought that's what must have happened. We've been having some problems with Erich. He's very jealous of Paul."

Mrs Beatty reappeared with a wet cloth. When the cut was cleaned up it was much smaller than it had first appeared. Mrs Beatty brought Paul a lemonade and he sat beside Auntie Alice. Erich hovered on her other side. It wasn't fair that Uncle Richard got angry at me when I didn't do anything. Paul always causes me trouble, he thought angrily.

Red Roses Cottage, Near Glendalough, Wicklow Mountains
Summer 1947

Auntie Alice bent over and pulled out another handful of weeds. They grew so fast and she was only here weekends and a couple of weeks each summer. But the roses were blooming well this year she noticed. The cottage, a corrugated iron structure, painted green with a wooden interior, was very simple but comfortable. It was named for the lovely red roses Auntie Alice cultivated.

"The roses are grand this year, my dear," Uncle Richard said.

"There are quite a few blooming. Much better than last year," she agreed.

The children raced around them.

"L-l-l-ook how far I can jump, Auntie Alice!" Erich shouted excitedly, hopping up and down. He ran and jumped but landed on one foot and fell forward.

"I can jump further than you!" Paul shouted, as he also leapt across the lawn.

"Very good, both of you!" Auntie Alice replied.

"I can jump higher!" Paul shouted.

"N-n-n-o! I-I-I-I can!" Erich replied.

Both of them leapt into the air, stretching their hands above their heads. Paul, several inches taller than Erich, had the advantage but Erich refused to give up. After a few minutes they stood puffing, chests heaving.

"Now, maybe you'll be able to sit quietly in the motor, boys," Uncle Richard said.

"Where are we going, Daddy?" Paul asked.

"To Glendalough for a picnic," he replied.

Glendalough's long, steep valley rose on either side of them as they sat beside the smaller of the two lakes. The popular tourist attraction was a favourite place with the Drumm family for picnics when they were staying at Red Roses Cottage.

Auntie Alice opened the picnic basket and set out the potato salad, green salad, cheddar cheese and ham slices. She swatted away a wasp, that was hovering over the potato salad.

"Children, come and eat," she called to the three children playing nearby. Erich raced over to sit beside Auntie Alice, elbowing Paul away. When they were seated on the grass she handed them plates, then spread butter on the soda bread and handed each of them a slice. They helped themselves to the rest of the food, set out on the blanket, and ate hungrily.

"The water's very dark today," Auntie Alice remarked looking at the deep, murky lake.

"There's rain coming but not for a while. We should be able to have a walk before it comes on," Uncle Richard replied, looking at the grey clouds floating overhead. There were still large blue gaps between them.

When they finished eating Auntie Alice began to pack the food away. Uncle Richard, glancing at the sky, said, "I think we'd better not delay." He stood up and led the children to the path along the shore.

Erich looked over his shoulder. "C-C-Come, Auntie Alice?" he asked.

"No, I'll clear up and put the dishes away while you're gone," she replied.

Disappointment etched on his face, Erich followed the others. He turned to look at Auntie Alice every few steps. They walked around the edge of the Lower Lake to the graveyard. Grey, imposing stone buildings, the remains of a monastic site, were dotted around. The children went into the graveyard and wandered amongst the headstones, some weathered beyond reading. Celtic crosses adorned the tops of many of them. Paul looked at a very weather-beaten headstone.

"Daddy, why aren't there any words on this?" he asked.

"Because it's been there a very long time and the wind and rain have worn them away. It's been here for hundreds of years," Uncle Richard replied.

Erich stood looking up at the tall, thin tower nearby. The round tower, with its conical top, was a solid stone edifice. Only a couple of slits were visible on the sides of the thick stone walls.

"We climb tower?" Erich asked.

"I could climb it faster than you!" Paul said.

"N-N-No! I could!" Erich replied.

"Could not!"

"Now boys, that's enough. We can't go inside it anyways," Uncle Richard replied.

The boys glared at each other but knew better than to say any more. Disliking the tension, Margaret reached into her pocket, pulling out a couple of sweets. She handed the first one to Erich saying, "I saved this. You can have it." Erich popped the sweet into his mouth, pleased that Margaret had given him the first one.

Uncle Richard looked up at the sky. The grey clouds were getting thicker with fewer blue patches between them and the breeze was getting stronger. A few drops of rain fell.

"I think we'll head back now. It won't be long before the rain gets heavy," Uncle Richard said.

They hurried to where Auntie Alice was waiting.

"We saw big rock! I-I-I could climb to top!" Erich shouted as he ran to her.

"Could you now. Isn't that grand," she replied.

"It wasn't a rock it was a tower and I'd be faster than him!" Paul shouted.

"Let's get in the car before we get drenched," Uncle Richard said, ignoring their competitive boasting. Pushing and shoving to be first, the boys got in the car. The adults exchanged a weary look.

Bray

Autumn 1947

Erich's nose dripped. He wiped it with his sleeve as he looked listlessly out of the window. At midday the dark, rainy sky cast a gloomy shadow over the sitting room. But he didn't really mind because his cold allowed him to spend the day home from school with Auntie Alice and Margaret. Rustlings and soft thuds came from the dining room as Auntie Alice dusted. Margaret sprawled on the floor in front of the fire, her nursery rhyme book open in front of her. She looked at a large goose wearing a white lacy bonnet.

"You don't know who that is," Margaret said, pointing to the goose on the page.

"*Mutter* Goose," Erich replied, glancing over from the window.

"It's not "*Mutter*"! You can't talk properly!" Margaret said.

"Is *Mutter* Goose!" Erich insisted.

"You talk funny!"

"I-I-I talk g-g-good," Erich said, annoyance making him stutter more than usual.

"You talk funny! You talk funny!"

"S-S-Stop!" Erich shouted, tensing his jaw and glaring at her, as Margaret chanted the words.

Margaret closed the book, stood up and skipped to the dining room, chanting as she went, "Erich talks funny! Erich talks funny!"

"S-s-s-top it!" Erich shouted, running after her. Aware that he sounded different to other children as he struggled to learn English, he was very sensitive about any teasing.

At the dining room doorway Margaret turned and stuck out her tongue, then ran to hide behind her mother, still chanting. Erich, fists clenched, followed close behind.

"Margaret, stop that. It's very bold," Aunt Alice said, not looking up.

Erich stopped at the doorway. An idea struck him and on

impulse, he turned and scurried down the hall to the kitchen. Reaching into the drawer he pulled out a knife then raced back to the dining room with it grasped in his hand. Margaret stayed behind her mother, poking her head out to stick her tongue out again, still humming her chant.

"Margaret!" Auntie Alice admonished.

"I-I-I n-n-not like that!" Erich cried, glaring at Margaret.

"Margaret, did you not hear me? Stop teasing Erich," Auntie Alice ordered, continuing her dusting.

Margaret's chanting died away as Erich waved the knife. Auntie Alice glanced up, duster held in mid-air above the picture frame she was dusting, to see Erich standing with the knife clenched in his fist.

"Erich, what are you doing?" Auntie Alice said with a slight tremor, seeing the knife. Margaret clung to her mother.

"Erich, put down the knife," Auntie Alice said, her voice shaking noticeably as Erich inched closer, knife outstretched. Margaret looked up at her mother. Hearing the tremor in her mother's voice, she whimpered, tears rolling down her cheeks.

"N-n-no!" Erich replied, shoulders hunched and eyes blinking rapidly.

"Erich, I said put down the knife," Auntie Alice repeated, her voice still shaking. Erich watched them silently. Auntie Alice and Margaret stared back at him for what seemed like an hour. No one moved. Finally, under Auntie Alice's steady gaze, Erich set the knife on the table. He dropped his gaze to the floor, shoulders slumped.

"Erich, that was very bold. You can't attack people when they make you angry. You'll go to your room until Uncle Richard comes home from work. He'll decide your punishment." Auntie Alice spoke briskly, with only a hint of a tremor in her voice. "You were very bold too, Margaret. You may also go to your room."

Erich continued to stare at the floor. He didn't want to hurt Auntie Alice or Margaret; he liked them, especially Auntie Alice.

He just didn't like to be teased. He didn't want Auntie Alice to be mad at him. He hadn't thought about the consequences before he grabbed the knife. Now he knew he was in trouble. Dejectedly, he went to his room.

Uncle Richard came through the front door, whistling. He popped his head into the sitting room. Paul and Margaret, her punishment finished, sat in front of the fire; Granny Quinn, awake after her afternoon nap, was in her usual place beside it. Auntie Alice came along the hall towards him.

"Where's Erich?" he asked her.

"Come to the kitchen. I need to speak to you," she murmured.

In the kitchen she told him what had happened during afternoon. He frowned and rubbed his forehead.

"At least you're both alright. It could have been more serious. I will have to think of a suitable punishment. We can't allow that behaviour," Uncle Richard said, shaking his head.

"I don't know what we're to do. I don't know if we can manage him. We never expected anything like this when we offered to foster a child. I know he's been through some terrible experiences but we can't endanger our children," Auntie Alice said.

"You're right. I was thinking the same thing myself. He's so jealous of Paul and wants your undivided attention. They do be fighting constantly. Sure, children have their spats but now we can't be certain anyone is safe if he gets angry. I know he's lost his family and has no one but he's getting to be more than we can manage," Uncle Richard said soberly.

Auntie Alice nodded.

"I'll ring the Red Cross office and see what can be done. I'll also ask at church to see if anyone knows someone who would foster him. Meanwhile I had better speak to Erich," Uncle Richard said.

"I don't want him to go," she said.

"Neither do I but we have to think of the whole family," he replied. He put his arm around her shoulder, smiling sadly.

4

CHRISTMAS IN CAVAN
County Cavan, Ireland
December 1947

THE LIGHT was fading as they arrived at the farmhouse. Dejectedly Erich followed Aunt Rose up the long, dirt track from the lane. The boundary wall's dark form guided them in the semi-darkness. Rose Elliott, tall and big boned, carried herself with almost military bearing. Her long, fawn coloured coat swished as she strode purposefully to the farmhouse she had grown up in.

Erich trudged behind her, hand in his trouser pocket, clutching the necklace. He'd almost given it to Auntie Alice before he left, but decided to keep it for *Mutti*. If he couldn't stay with Auntie Alice he would have to find his mother he had decided. He didn't want to live with strangers.

He saw the outlines of an assortment of farm buildings and a two storey farmhouse across the field. The earthy smell of turf burning floated towards them from smoke streaming out of one of the two chimneys in the middle of the peaked roof. When they reached the end of the field they stepped through a gap in the boundary wall into the farmyard. Large, grey slabs protruded from the ground, in the dirt haggard. This was very different from the bungalow he had left this morning, set back from the neat road in a manicured garden. He wished he was back with Auntie Alice.

Two dogs came to meet them. Patch, a wizened black and

white sheepdog, approached, head lowered and alert. Gipsy, a boisterous brown spaniel, bounded over sniffing around them. Erich eyed the dogs warily; dogs he had met in Germany were half starved and vicious. Patch returned his stare as Gipsy leapt at Erich. He stepped back startled and the dog craned forward, licking his hand vigorously. Tentatively Erich patted the dog's head. The dog licked harder.

"He'll not hurt ye. Yon's too daft to do ye any harm," said a tall man, seeing the fear in Erich's eyes. His broad chest strained against his jumper and tweed jacket, as he leaned over to pat and reassure the wary sheepdog. His eyes crinkled good humouredly as he regarded the boy gradually relaxing with the spaniel. The man's calm, friendly manner eased Erich's distrust.

"Hello, Davy," Aunt Rose greeted the man. They stood roughly the same height and shared the same distinctive elongated face and forthright gaze.

Davy Elliott, Rose's brother, had inherited Derrykeane, the family farm. Smiling, he watched the small boy patting the spaniel.

"You must be Erich. I'm Uncle Davy. You're very welcome." He led them in the back door, through a partially completed extension. Brick walls rose on both sides of the doorway, standing unsupported, without a roof to join them. The grey stone slabs, from the haggard, extended inside to form the floor of the large, unpainted kitchen.

Uncle Davy's wife, a thin woman, hunched and wiry, stood with her back to them at the open fire.

"Hello, Elsie!" Aunt Rose called, her voice slightly raised. The woman turned from the fire and smiled, returning the greeting. She hurried over, smiling kindly at the boy.

"This is Aunt Elsie," Aunt Rose said to Erich.

"Hello," he said.

She regarded him with a piercing stare; her declining hearing made it necessary to observe everything carefully.

"You're very welcome, Erich. Ye must be foundered after that long journey. Come sit down and we'll get a cup of tea," she said slowly and distinctly, enunciating every word carefully. She put her arm around his shoulders and led him to a seat by the fire, squeezing his shoulder before letting go.

Aunt Elsie busied herself preparing a meal for them. She slid the kettle onto the metal oven top set in the chimney breast and set bread on the table. Aunt Rose hung up her long coat and began setting cups and plates on the table. Her regular visits to her childhood home ensured she did not feel like a stranger. Erich let his coat slide onto the chair as the fire warmed him.

"Are ye busy at Jacobs these days?" Aunt Elsie asked, as the women worked.

"This is always a busy season for us," Aunt Rose replied. "Everyone wants our biscuits for Christmas and in the accounts office the work never stops until we shut on Christmas Eve. I was lucky to get this Saturday off to bring Erich here."

"How's Olive?" Aunt Elsie asked.

"She's grand. It's fortunate the Drumms mentioned to Olive they were looking for a place for Erich. She asked me if I could keep him but I couldn't manage it on my own. But I knew you had plenty of room with the girls away at school. This is a great place for a boy," Aunt Rose said.

Aunt Elsie nodded in agreement. "We'll love to have him. It's quiet with the girls away."

By the time the kettle boiled, Erich was shyly studying the table laden with soda bread, ham slices, cheese, butter and jam. He was hungry after the journey and came to the table quickly when he was called. Besides, unfamiliar with the routine at this new house, he did not know when he would be offered food again and didn't want to miss it. The food shortages in Germany had left him anxious about getting enough to eat.

In the easy atmosphere of the house he soon lost his shyness. After grace was said, he tucked into the food in front of him, listening silently to the adults' conversation. When he finished he felt full and drowsy.

"You'd best go to bed," Uncle Davy said, noticing Erich's eyelids begin to droop. He lifted the paraffin lamp from the wall.

"Goodnight, Erich," Aunt Rose and Aunt Elsie said in unison. Aunt Elsie reached over and kissed him on the forehead.

With the lamp held aloft they climbed the stairs to the first bedroom beside the staircase. Several grey woollen blankets were piled on the metal framed double bed set against the far wall. On top of the blankets were a new shirt, a pair of short trousers and a shiny, blue Dinky toy. Erich rushed to the bed excitedly, forgetting his tiredness. He lifted the lorry and danced around the bed.

"*Danke!*" Erich shouted.

"We can't take all the credit. It's from the Red Cross as well as us," Uncle Davy replied, laughing. When Erich's excitement finally subsided he undressed. Kneeling on the bare boards beside the bed, he said his prayers, ending with "God bless *Mutti*, Hans, Aunt Rose, Aunt Elsie, Uncle Davy and God bless Gipsy and Patch."

And help me find *Mutti*, he prayed silently as he climbed into the bed. Uncle Davy pulled the covers up and said goodnight, then he was alone in the dark. He reached out and grabbed his trousers which were lying on the floor beside the bed. He pulled out the necklace, thrust it under his pillow and set his Dinky toy beside it. He lay there, one hand under the pillow clutching his treasures, unable to see anything in the black room. A clicking noise crossed the bare floorboards accompanied by a steady panting. He tensed as the bed springs bounced and a wet tongue licked his face. Pulling his hand out from under the pillow, he hugged Gipsy delightedly, rubbing his head against the dog's silky body. Maybe I will like it here, he thought as he snuggled against the dog. With a contented sigh he closed his eyes and drifted off to sleep.

Erich looked down from the plank, into the menacing water. He

*couldn't see anything but water. He would never get out if he fell
in! He breathed rapidly, fear seizing his muscles. He couldn't
escape. The waves lapped against the plank. Losing his balance, he wobbled and toppled towards the icy water, screaming
as he fell.*

Erich awoke from the familiar nightmare, gripping the blanket
and shaking. Uncle Davy was sitting on the edge of his bed.

"You're fine, lad. Twas just a bad dream," he said,
reassuringly.

"The water..." Erich began, groggily.

"There's no water. It's alright. Go back to sleep."

Uncle Davy rubbed his back and murmured soothingly as he
relaxed again. Erich felt better knowing he was there. He felt safe
and he trusted this man to keep the bad dreams away.

"You protect me. Like my daddy," Erich said, despite having
no memory of his father. "You're my Daddy Davy."

Daddy Davy pulled the blanket around Erich and sat with him
until he slipped into a sound sleep.

After breakfast the next morning Erich followed Daddy Davy out
of the back door. Gipsy bounded after them across the haggard;
Patch followed at a safe distance. Two well-fed, white geese waddled around the yard. Erich watched them curiously. Spotting
the newcomer, they rushed at him, necks outstretched, honking.
Erich jumped back as the first one nipped him.

"Daddy Davy!" Erich shouted, backing away.

"If you run, they'll chase you. Show them you're not afeered o'
them, lad," Daddy Davy advised him.

Erich straightened up and hesitantly faced them. The goose
advanced, beak open, towards him. He walked towards the bird
and it stopped, watching him. Keeping his eyes fixed on them,
Erich walked past. He made a triumphant noise as he entered
the byre.

Daddy Davy sat down on a small stool beside a brown and

white cow. He squeezed her teat gently and a thin stream of milk shot into the bucket in front of him. A black cat sat nearby, eyeing the milk. Daddy Davy aimed the stream at her and she opened her mouth, expertly catching it. Erich went to stand beside Daddy Davy, reaching out tentatively to touch the soft side of the placid cow. He liked the smooth feel of her coat. He reached up and stroked her wet, velvety nose. Her mouth moved slowly and rhythmically as she calmly watched him. Barely interrupting her chewing, she snorted and tossed her head. Erich jumped back, alarmed. Daddy Davy looked up, half smiling.

"She'll not harm you, lad," he said.

When the cow quieted Erich moved closer and continued stroking her. He had never been so close to such a large animal before.

When the bucket was partially filled, Daddy Davy reached down a cup from the wall, dipped it in the bucket and handed it to Erich. He took a sip of the rich milk. He had never tasted such warm, lovely milk. He quickly drained the cup.

When Daddy Davy finished milking the cows they went into the stable next to the byre. A quiet, brown pony stood in the nearest stall, flicking one ear absently, and a narrow faced donkey looked at them arrogantly, head held high, from the next one. Daddy Davy brought hay in and set it in the animals' troughs. Chomping loudly, they plunged their heads into the hay.

Erich approached the donkey's stall. The animal turned, ears pulled back, nostrils flared in his white muzzle. Daddy Davy glanced over.

"Don't go too close to yon fella. He's a mean-tempered beast."

Erich stopped, watching the donkey. The beast's black eyes returned his gaze, unwaveringly.

"Come ye here and see this boyo," Daddy Davy said, patting the pony's neck.

Erich entered the pony's stall, staying back against the wall. The pony shifted his hind legs, snorting. Erich jumped away.

"He'll not hurt you. Come you here."

Erich advanced cautiously. The pony continued to chew, standing calmly. Erich reached up to stroke his neck. The pony turned his head towards the boy, thrusting his nose down, nuzzling against him as the boy reached up and stroked him.

"What his name?" Erich asked, stroking the animal's nose.

"Paddy," Daddy Davy replied.

Looking at the donkey, Erich asked, "What his name?"

"He's Paddy as well. I didn't know what else to call him."

Erich laughed.

"S-s-so many a-a-animals here," Erich said, excitedly. The donkey shied to the far side of his stall as Erich raised his voice.

"You can help me tend them," Daddy Davy said.

Erich jumped up and down. The pony lifted his head and snorted then went back to munching on the hay in front of him.

"I-I-I h-h-help you!" he stuttered, excitedly. He had never seen so many animals in one place before except when Uncle Richard and Auntie Alice had taken him to the zoo. He frowned, remembering Auntie Alice. He wished she was here. But even missing her couldn't dampen his pleasure in the animals. He loved them. Gipsy bounced around him, excited by Erich's enthusiasm. He leaned down and hugged the dog tightly.

Erich helped Daddy Davy carry the holly branches in. They set them on the kitchen table.

"Thank you, Erich," Aunt Elsie said, giving him a quick hug. She lifted a few sprigs and fastened them behind the pictures hung on the walls. The deep green holly, with red berries dotted through it, gave the bare plaster walls some colour. Paper chains were already fastened in the corners of the kitchen ceiling, criss-crossing in the middle of the room, giving the drab room a festive air.

"I have a surprise for you after tea, Erich," Daddy Davy said.

"W-W-What it is?" Erich shouted.

"You have to wait and see or it wouldn't be a surprise," Daddy Davy replied laughing. "Come and have your tea."

Erich ate his meal hurriedly, then fidgeted impatiently until Daddy Davy pushed his plate away. He jumped up, barely able to contain his excitement, when Daddy Davy said, "Go and get your coat. We're going to the Christmas party at the school."

Erich raced to get his coat from the peg in the hall, feet clanging on the stone floor. He jumped up, grasped a sleeve and hauled it down, nearly pulling the rest of the coats down with it. With coats tightly fastened, they set out on the three mile walk to Rathnane School.

Laughter and music rang out as they approached the single room school. Erich followed Daddy Davy inside. Children milled around the room chattering excitedly. A large Christmas tree stood in one corner, handmade paper decorations dangling from it. Its candles gave a soft light. Erich let out an excited squeal when he spotted it.

Daddy Davy guided Erich across the room to a big boned, handsome woman, her wavy, brown hair brushed untidily to one side. Several children clustered around her, shyly waiting for her attention. Her seemingly aloof, wide-set eyes turned from them and regarded Erich for a moment, then she smiled.

"This is Mrs Baird, Erich. She'll be your teacher after the holidays," Daddy Davy said.

"Ye're very welcome, Erich," Mrs Baird said, her broad, serious face regarding him kindly, "Perhaps you'll give us a wee song or maybe a poem tonight."

Blushing, Erich nodded mutely. Mrs Baird smiled, satisfied, then strode to the harmonium and called for silence. Daddy Davy led Erich to seats near the front of the room as she placed her hands on the keyboard, pumping the pedals. She began "Joy to the World" to the reedy accompaniment of the harmonium; the children joined in. When the carol ended Erich listened as children went to the front of the room, singly or in groups, to sing or recite a poem. Struggling to understand the poem a small boy was reciting, his mind wandered and his eyes strayed to the Christmas tree's lights dancing in the dim room. He watched them entranced.

"Now we have a wee boy who's come such a long journey from Germany to live wi' us. He'll be joining us at school after the holidays. Children, make Erich welcome," Mrs Baird said.

Everyone clapped. Erich looked up startled as Mrs Baird motioned him to come forward. Nervously he walked to the front of the room.

"Would ye like to sing a song?" Mrs Baird asked.

Erich shook his head, bashfully staring at his toes.

"Will ye say a poem then?" Mrs Baird asked.

Erich nodded and began one he had learned from Margaret's nursery rhyme book, "Mary had a little lamb. Its fleece vas vite as snows. Everyvere Mary vent, lamb vas sure to goes."

When he finished he walked quickly back to his seat, blushing as everyone applauded loudly. He glanced furtively around the room, embarrassed but warmed by the applause. They didn't seem to be laughing at the way he talked. Daddy Davy smiled at him and he felt pleased with himself. It didn't matter that his face flamed.

As Erich recovered from his embarrassment, there was a knock at the door. The children roared, "Come in!" A chubby man in a red suit and white beard entered the room. All around Erich the children were cheering. The man sat down on a hard-backed chair beside the Christmas tree. Small, brightly coloured packages were piled underneath it. Erich wondered what was in them. There won't be one for me, Erich thought. Father Christmas doesn't know I'm living here now. The man pulled out one of the parcels.

"Doris, where are ye?" he asked. A small girl, blue eyes peering out from under blonde eyebrows, stood up. She walked forward pushing behind her ears wisps of her blond hair, that had escaped from her ponytail. Shyly she regarded the red-suited man, smiling and giggling as he gave her the parcel.

Father Christmas called out one name after another. Erich watched them go forward to receive gifts. When his name was called Erich, surprised, went forward. Embarrassed and excited, he brought the parcel back to his seat, tearing the wrapping off as soon as he sat down. He lifted a multi-coloured paper coil from the wrapping and examined it. He put the open end in his mouth and blew. The coil unfurled, making a hooting noise. Erich jumped, then looked around to see if anyone would chastise him. Seeing no disapproval, he tried it again, laughing at the noise it made. It was marvellous!

"Look, Daddy Davy!" he cried, blowing it again.

When they left at the end of the evening Erich stuffed the hooter in his pocket, beside his necklace, clutching it tightly. They had only walked a short distance when he took it out and blew it again; watching the paper coil fly out in front of him noisily.

They walked through the dark village; the post office and few shops in it had been shut for hours. As they turned towards home at the edge of the village, a bright moon lit the dark road. The hedges were encroaching shadows, squeezing the dirt road. Erich took no notice of the odd rustle in them. He walked happily in the chilly night beside Daddy Davy chattering about his gift and occasionally blowing it. The three miles back passed quickly.

A gust of cold air blew into the kitchen the next evening as Daddy Davy, followed by two teenage girls, walked through the door. Erich, sitting across the table from Aunt Elsie, eyed them shyly. The girls took off their coats, laughing and chattering. The taller, sandy-haired one noticed Erich sitting there.

"Hello. You must be Erich," Nell said. Her blonde sister, Rose, almost a head shorter, also greeted him, smiling.

"Hello," Erich said quietly. He looked uncertainly at Daddy Davy.

"Remember I told you that our daughters were coming home

for the holidays? This is Nell and Rose," Daddy Davy said pointing to each of the girls in turn.

The girls nodded again and continued to talk, raising their voices slightly, telling their mother all the news from Sligo Grammar School. Aunt Elsie nodded and smiled as they talked, glad to have them home from boarding school. Occasionally she would stop and peer at them to better follow their steady stream of chatter.

Aunt Elsie reached for a loaf of freshly baked bread on the dresser, drawing Erich's eyes to the Christmas cake beside it. He remembered when Aunt Elsie had made it. She had put the ingredients for the Christmas cake into a blue, thick-rimmed porcelain bowl, sprinkling sultanas, raisins and currants in last. Then she opened a bottle of Guinness and poured in a small measure. Erich had watched fascinated as she stirred the dark mixture vigorously. When it was well mixed she had poured it into a battered baking tin and set it in the oven in the chimney breast. It had smelled so rich when she took it out of the oven later.

"Can we eat cake tonight?" Erich asked her.

"Indeed no. It's for Christmas," she replied.

The girls questioned Erich about himself and received muffled, monosyllabic answers. He felt uneasy with the noisy, boisterous girls. Saying as little as possible, he watched them until bedtime. They were friendly and interested in him but had disrupted the calm order and routine of the house. He wasn't sure if he liked it.

Erich swallowed his last mouthful of potatoes. Nell, who Erich noticed since she arrived a couple days ago was always moving, was already collecting the plates to wash. Reaching for his plate, she leaned over his shoulder and stopped. She leaned closer to him, sniffing.

"You smell!" she exclaimed.

"I not!" Erich replied.

Rose came over and sniffed at him. "You do indeed," she said.

"When did you last have a bath?" Nell asked.

Erich lowered his head and didn't answer. He didn't like baths especially in winter. "I not smell," Erich reiterated. But the girls, accustomed to the town, noticed the farm smells lingering on him. Nell looked at the back of his neck.

"Look at the dirt!" she exclaimed. "You need a bath!"

"No!" Erich shouted.

"A bath is a good idea," Aunt Elsie said. "You'll feel grand afterwards." She smiled at him encouragingly. Even her coaxing did nothing to warm Erich to the idea.

Nell went to fetch the tin bath and set a large pot of water over the fire to heat. Erich watched her preparations mutinously. When the water was hot Nell set the bath in front of the blazing fire and poured the hot water into it. After adding some cold water, she tested the temperature.

"Come you here," she ordered Erich.

"N-N-No!" he shouted.

He sat stubbornly glaring at her as she walked towards him. Catching his arm, she tried to drag him but he pulled away. Rose grabbed his other arm and the two of them dragged him, feet scuffing the stone floor trying to get a foothold, over to the tin tub. His clothes flew in all directions as he squirmed and shouted. Still trying to pull free, they pushed him into the tub. Water sloshed over all three of them.

"Mind, don't hurt him, girls," Aunt Elsie said.

Nell poured water over his head, lathering him with soap. He shouted and squirmed as they scrubbed him. When they were finished, Nell briskly dried him and wrapped him in a large towel. As soon as she loosened her grip he hurried to a chair by the fire, pulling the towel tightly around himself.

"Isn't he grand now - squeaky clean," Nell said.

The girls looked at the scowling Erich, proudly surveying their work.

When Erich was dry and dressed he sidled over to the kitchen window. Heavy rain lashed against the pane, thwarting his desire to play outside. He sat down on the bench under the window, staring out. Aunt Elsie noticed his glum face.

"Sure it's no day to be going out but I'm sure it will blow over soon," she said.

Nell busied herself helping her mother while Rose huddled by the fire, reading a book. The rest of the afternoon passed slowly.

After tea was finished and the dishes washed, the children joined Daddy Davy by the fire. He calmly smoked his pipe, looking out at the rain which still hadn't abated. The children were restless after being cooped up all day. Nell looked at Erich, eyeing him up and down.

"Have ye got a pot belly?" she asked him.

"No," he replied.

"I think ye do! Stand up," she ordered him.

Nell lifted his jumper and stared at his waist. Erich had arrived in Ireland thin and malnourished, after enduring the severe food shortages in Germany, but months of wholesome food had transformed him so that now a slightly round tummy was visible.

"We needn't have fattened a goose this year. You'd do grand," Nell said jokingly. "You're fat as a snail! But we'll soon sort that."

Erich eyed her suspiciously. Since the girls arrived they had taken charge. He knew he didn't stand a chance when they had an idea or made a decision. He was discovering what it was like to be the youngest in a family. While he liked their company, he sometimes wished that things would go back to what they were in the few days before the girls arrived.

Nell and Rose went to the piano in the corner. Curious, Erich trailed behind. The girls whispered between themselves briefly then fixed their gaze on Erich. I know that look, he thought resignedly. Nell began playing a bold march on the out of tune piano, shouting instructions as she played.

"March in time to the music!" she ordered him. "Arms up, arms down! Feet higher! Don't stand still!"

Erich tried to co-ordinate his arms and legs to keep up with her barked instructions. She speeded up until he got his arms and legs tangled up and almost tripped himself. He stood puffing as Nell continued to thump out tunes.

"You do exercises!" Erich demanded, still puffing.

"Who would play the piano then?" she replied. Erich shrugged. I don't care as long as I get a rest, he thought.

The back door opened and Aunt Rose stepped in, rain dripping from her fawn coat. The exercises were forgotten as the children clustered around her, shouting greetings.

"You got here then. I didn't think you were coming when it got so late," Aunt Elsie said.

"I didn't get out of work until late and the bus was slow. I walked from the Cross," Aunt Rose replied.

"Gracious, that's no day for walking! I'd have asked Davy to fetch you from the bus if I'd known you'd be on it. You'll be wanting a drop o' tea," Aunt Elsie exclaimed, hurrying to set the kettle over the fire to boil.

Aunt Rose hung her coat on a peg in the hall and then rummaged in her carrier bag, lying where she'd dropped it beside the table, until she produced a tin of Jacobs biscuits. Employees got boxes of broken biscuits free and every Christmas Aunt Rose brought a big box. The children squealed with delight when they saw it. Erich was glad of the diversion. The exercises were forgotten and he couldn't wait to taste the biscuits.

Christmas Day dawned. Erich awoke, peering around eagerly in the grey morning light until he spotted a dark mound at the foot of the bed. He sat up to see it better. A bag containing a new white shirt, a grey jumper and a pair of brown short trousers lay against the metal frame. He crawled to the foot of the bed and rifled through the bag, exclaiming excitedly when he found a new

Dinky toy hidden in it.

Erich ran the toy lorry up and down over the folds of his rumpled wool blanket pretending he was crossing a steep mountain range. He was happily engrossed in his adventure when Aunt Elsie came in.

"Look what Father Christmas brought me!" he exclaimed.

"You're a very lucky boy. Wasn't he very good to you!" Aunt Elsie replied, not mentioning that the Red Cross and the Elliotts were responsible for the gifts he had received. Smiling, she watched him gleefully steering the lorry across the bedclothes.

"Time to get dressed, Erich. We don't want to be late for church," she said after a few minutes. After a last rush across the bedclothes, Erich put the Dinky toy under his pillow beside the necklace and his other Dinky toy. He picked up his clothes lying beside the bed and dressed quickly.

When everyone was ready to leave, Daddy Davy brought Paddy, the pony, to the door. A soft dusting of snow on the ground had replaced yesterday's rain, muffling the clip-clop of the animal's hooves. Erich danced with excitement as he stepped onto the white carpet. Cupping his hand, he stooped to scoop up some snow and began rolling it into a ball, eyeing Rose. Daddy Davy saw him and shook his head.

"No messing before church," Daddy Davy warned. "It'll still be here when we get home," he added, grinning.

Disappointed, Erich dropped the partially formed snowball. He stuck his tongue out at Rose, mouthing, "I get you!" She smirked at him as Aunt Elsie climbed into the trap.

"Anyone fancy a lift wi' us?" Daddy Davy asked. Rose quickly climbed in beside Aunt Elsie, giving Erich a taunting wave as the trap moved off. Nell and Erich walked with Aunt Rose, following the vehicle.

Situated at the top of a hill, Christ Church, Kilmullagh was three miles from Derrykeane. The trap rolled silently over the white ground as the pony leaned into his harness, pulling determinedly. Sometimes his hooves slid and he snorted anxiously, stumbling on the slippery snow. As the trap skidded, Daddy Davy kept the pony's reins tight, clucking reassuringly. Erich laughed watching them career about, oblivious to Aunt Elsie's nervous glances and her sigh of relief when they arrived safely at the church.

The building was decorated festively and the congregation, in the holiday spirit, sang the carols heartily. Standing between Nell and Rose Erich didn't have to be reminded to behave himself, he was too engrossed in the singing.

As they filed out after the service parishioners wished each other a Happy Christmas. Several men clapped Erich on the shoulder and asked him what Father Christmas had brought him. Erich grinned, standing taller. Everyone had been so friendly to him since he arrived; he felt welcome here.

The downhill journey home was easier. Aunt Elsie gasped as the pony sometimes slipped on the snowy roads, but he nimbly stayed on his feet and they arrived home without mishap. Erich ran behind the trap, sliding in its tracks.

The heat from the fire and the smell of dinner cooking hit them as they entered the kitchen. Erich took a deep breath of fatty goose cooking which wafted from the oven.

"That smells good," Daddy Davy said.

"Well, we'd best get some water boiling. It wouldn't be dinner without the praties," Aunt Elsie replied.

The women took off their coats and set about preparing the meal. Aunt Elsie swung the crook with a large pot hanging from it off the fire to put the potatoes into it to boil. An assortment of smaller pots sat on the top of the chimney breast oven simmering. Erich watched them, his mouth watering.

"It won't be ready any faster if you watch it," Aunt Elsie said, patting Erich's shoulder as she passed.

"Come you here and help me, Erich," Daddy Davy said, grasping one end of the table. Erich helped Daddy Davy pull the table away from the wall and set it in the middle of the room. The women bustled around setting the table and checking the pots cooking on top of the oven. Daddy Davy lifted the goose from the oven and set it on a platter at the head of the table. When everything was cooked and they were all seated around the table he said grace.

"Thank you, Lord, for the food we are about to eat and for the family we are blessed with. Thank you also for Erich, the newest addition to our family. Amen."

Erich grinned from ear to ear at the mention of his name. Daddy Davy began carving the goose, passing the plates to each member of the family. They helped themselves to potatoes and vegetables heaped in bowls on the table. Erich ate until he thought he would burst.

"Where did you put it?" Nell asked. "We won't be able to tell you from the goose!"

"He'll have to do lots of exercises now!" Rose said gleefully.

Erich didn't mind their teasing. He'd had so much lovely food! And Daddy Davy was glad he was here. One day he would find *Mutti* and she could come to live here too. Everything would be perfect then. He smiled contentedly.

When dinner was finished and cleared away everyone slumped in front of the fire, dozing. The turf's strong smell drifted over them. The girls, also full from their dinners, finally left Erich in peace. Tired and satisfied, he dozed. In a very short time the family's warmth had drawn Erich in and he didn't feel like a stranger. He hadn't thought he would like it here when he arrived but now he couldn't imagine living anywhere else.

On the first morning after the Christmas holidays, in the creeping, greyish light, Daddy Davy hitched gentle, placid Paddy to the trap. With Erich sitting high on the seat beside him, they drove, wheels crunching on the frosty roads, to Rathnane School. Erich looked over the thick, leafless hedges at the white-tipped grass, brittle and bent, in the fields around them. The cart bounced on the potholed road and their breath made ghostly patterns in the

January air. Erich stuffed his hands into the pockets of his knee-length, double-lapelled woollen coat to keep warm.

Erich wondered about his new school. What are the other children like? he thought. Living furthest from the school, he hadn't met any of them yet except briefly at the Christmas party. A frown crossed his square, serious face as he thought about it. Everyone seemed very nice at the party but at his last school they noticed the way he spoke. He hated people mentioning it. He didn't want to be singled out. I don't want them to tease me, he thought, panic starting to grip him. He blinked rapidly, drawing his breath in sharply.

"Alright, lad?" Daddy Davy asked, hearing him. He nodded. Then, shrugging his shoulders, he pushed his hands deeper into his pockets. He wished he could just stay at home with Daddy Davy and Auntie Elsie. The house was quiet again now the girls were back at school.

They sped along the frosty roads and the two storey, white-washed building soon came into view. Erich hadn't seen it clearly in the dark on the night of the Christmas party. Now he saw that the school was set back from the road in a field with a row of tall trees standing guard behind it. A narrow stream gurgled in front and a small, rounded hill rose behind it.

As Daddy Davy pulled the reins and Paddy halted outside the door, Mrs Baird came out to meet them. Her piercing, wide-set eyes scrutinised Erich, dressed in his new white shirt and short brown trousers, but her full mouth smiled warmly. Her capable appearance, broad shoulders encased in a plain brown woollen dress, and her straightforward manner exuded authority.

"I'm after telling the children about ye, Erich. Come in and join us."

Mrs Baird spoke forcefully but smiled kindly at Erich and some of his anxiety disappeared amidst the warm tone of her greeting.

"He'll be grand with us, Mr Elliott," she said, nodding dismissal to Daddy Davy.

She ushered Erich inside, barely giving him time to say good-bye, through a small cloakroom littered with coats and boots. Inside the single room class thirty faces watched him silently from rows of battered, wooden desks. Afraid to make eye contact, Erich scanned the walls covered with children's drawings and essays, then fixed his gaze on the floor. Mrs Baird directed Erich to a seat near the front. A black stove in the corner provided the only heat for the large room.

Mrs Baird taught all the children at the small country school from their first day until they left at fourteen. There were children of all ages and sizes; the smallest, including Erich, were seated at the front of the room. Girls, in woollen dresses and skirts, some covered with ragged cardigans and jumpers, sat amidst boys in worn cardigans or jackets over their short trousers. Most items of clothing had had more than one owner. Bare, bony knees protruded beneath skirts and short trousers. All but the poorest children wore socks, mostly drooping around their ankles, in their laced shoes or Wellington boots.

Children seated around him glanced furtively at Erich as Mrs Baird began the lessons. Erich blushed, trying to avoid their gaze. The morning passed in a blur of discomfort and anxiety. At dinner hour Erich ate the sandwich Aunt Elsie had made for him at his desk, stealing glances at the other children. They regarded him shyly, unsure how to approach him. They had known each other from birth; they rarely had newcomers to the area.

As he finished eating Erich looked up to see a fair-haired boy, bolder than the rest, standing over him. George was somewhat taller than him and a couple years older. He laid his hand flat on the scratched surface of the desk.

"Hit me. Go on," he said.

Erich looked at him uncomfortably but, with an intent stare, George nodded towards his hand, spread-eagled on the desk.

"Ye can hit me as hard as ye like," he said, with bravado.

Anxious to be accepted and not wanting to refuse a challenge, Erich clenched his fist, raised it high above the desk and slammed it down towards the outstretched hand. Just before he connected with it George pulled his hand away laughing. The desk shook as Erich hit it with full force. He lifted his stinging hand and looked at George, dismayed. Some older children watching scowled and muttered.

"What a cruel trick on the poor, wee lad," a girl said, disapprovingly.

"Twas only a bit o' fun. I didn't mean any harm," George replied.

"Take no heed o' him, he's an eejit," the girl said to Erich.

Some other children standing nearby nodded in agreement. A dark-haired boy with a cheeky grin came over to Erich.

"Never mind that carry on. He tries that trick on everyone," Bobby Crawford, a great nephew of Aunt Elsie, said with a slight trace of an English accent. "When me Mum and I first came here after the war he did the same to me." Erich was glad to find he wasn't the only one who had been singled out because he was new and different.

As George moved away, Bobby rolled his eyes. Erich grinned, glad to have an ally.

"C'mon, let's go outside."

Erich followed Bobby gratefully.

Spring 1948

Erich sat, huddled over, beside the fire as Daddy Davy's sisters, Aunt Rose and Aunt Sarah, visiting for a few days, bustled around him. Aunt Elsie came into the kitchen. Spotting Erich she said, "Did ye have your breakfast, lad?"

Erich kept his head lowered, not answering her. She came over to him, bending to see his face. Tears ran silently down his cheeks.

"He's crying, Aunt Elsie," Aunt Sarah's daughter, Helen, said, regarding him sympathetically. About the same age, they had taken an immediate liking to each other when they met.

"Whatever's the matter wi' the child?" Aunt Elsie asked.

"He's fretting because you'll be away," Aunt Sarah answered.

"Who said he couldn't play?" she asked, her voice rising. "Why did you tell him that?" She looked around the room fiercely. Her declining hearing sometimes made it difficult for her to understand what was said.

"No one said that, Elsie. He doesn't want ye to go," Aunt Sarah replied, her voice raised.

Aunt Elsie looked at her and then back at Erich. He kept his head down. In the few months since he arrived he had become very fond of Auntie Elsie and Daddy Davy. *Mutti* hadn't come back when she went away. He didn't want Aunt Elsie to do the same but he couldn't explain it to her.

"You will come back soon?" he asked her worriedly, putting strong emphasis on 'will'.

"I'm only going to visit my sister, lad. I'll be back in a few days," she said, putting her arm around his shoulders. He hoped this was so.

Peering into his face she smiled. "Don't ye fret now. Come and get your breakfast so."

Erich, wiping his eyes on his sleeve, went to the table and sat down.

"Maybe I shouldn't go," Aunt Elsie said to Aunt Sarah.

"Nonsense. It's all arranged. Sure, didn't we come to see to him and Davy. He'll be fine wi' us," Aunt Sarah answered.

Heading home from school the next day, Erich walked through the village, turning right at the post office. He walked slowly. He wasn't in a hurry to get home. The house seemed empty without Aunt Elsie. She was always glad to see him and listened as he told her what he had done at school each day. Even Helen's company didn't fill the void. He craved Aunt Elsie's motherly care. He didn't know Aunt Sarah and Aunt Rose very well. They were different from Aunt Elsie, often busy and chatting to each other. Erich would be glad when she got back. Four days was a long time.

A few sweets would make him feel better he decided. He would share them with Helen. Half a mile outside the village was Miller's family grocery, seed and hardware shop. Erich stopped and went into its dark interior. He surveyed the small drawers that lined the walls, each one carefully labelled. Farm families didn't make frequent trips to town so the shop stocked a bit of everything; the necessary staples as well as a few treats were all there. The drawers contained everything from tea leaves to screwdrivers to sewing needles. Tinned goods sat on shelves and bacon slices in a barrel beside the counter. Sweets filled the jars on the counter. They also sold meal for sheep and cattle. Daniel Miller and his wife knew where to find everything in the overflowing room.

He could barely see over the high counter but Erich eyed the jars, filled with a wonderful assortment of sweets. He chose a farthing's worth of hard-boiled sweets, then carefully counted out his pocket money and handed it to Mrs Miller as she weighed the sweets. Eye level with the cash drawer beneath the counter, he watched as she opened it. Inside, laying half buried amongst the other coins, a shiny half crown gleamed. Its brilliance caught Erich's attention. He stared at it, unaware of her outstretched hand. Never having many possessions Erich was drawn to the beautiful coin. Mrs Miller, in her mild manner, brought him back to reality.

"Here's your change, Erich," she said.

In a daze Erich put out his hand and took the change. With his other hand he scooped up the sweets from the scale. As he dropped them into his pocket Mrs Baird entered the shop.

"Good day to ye, Mrs Miller," she called loudly as she strode in.

Several of her children as well as a couple of others they had picked up along the way home were sitting in her trap outside the door. The pony stood patiently.

"Sure it's not a bad day but there's little heat in it. God willing, we'll get a good summer, " Mrs Miller answered. Small and thin, the cold plagued her and she always struggled to keep warm. "Those were fine eggs ye left in this morning," she added.

"Thank ye. The hens are laying well this weather," Mrs Baird replied.

"I've your messages ready for you so," Mrs Miller said.

"That's very kind. I'll put them in my basket."

Erich stood listening to their conversation and thinking of the shiny coin he'd seen. He'd seen few coins in his short life and none that glinted like that one did. He could give it to Aunt Elsie when she got home. She'd like it and be so pleased with me, he thought. As Mrs Baird held out her basket for her purchases, Erich quietly pulled open the cash drawer, reached in and picked up the shiny coin. Putting it in his pocket, he left unnoticed as the women continued to chat.

Once out of sight of the shop Erich pulled the coin out of his pocket, his sweets forgotten. He held it up, watching as the light danced on it. He put it back in his pocket but drew it out again and again to admire it. It will be a wonderful present, he thought excitedly. He barely noticed anything else on his walk home.

Aunt Sarah and Aunt Rose, busy in the kitchen, called out greetings to him when he opened the back door. They bustled around him as he sat down by the fire. Helen sat huddled by it, her nose running with a heavy cold. She smiled as he sat down, dabbing her nose with a handkerchief. The delicious smell of potatoes boiling in the pot over the fire reminded him how hungry he was. The women worked, pulling the crane out from the hearth to stir the contents of the pot and then swinging it back onto the flame again. They continued chatting, taking little notice of him. Erich sat scuffing his shoes on the large, grey stone slabs of the kitchen floor, then reached into his pocket. Drawing out the coin he turned it over in his hand and examined it again. Helen leaned over to look at the shiny coin.

"Where did ye get that?" Aunt Sarah asked, catching sight of it.

"I f-f-found it," he said, not meeting her eyes. "It's f-f-for Aunt Elsie."

"What do ye have there?" Aunt Rose enquired, looking over Aunt Sarah's shoulder. Taller than her sister, she could easily see the coin in his hand.

"Half a crown!" she exclaimed. "That's a right bit o' money. Where'd ye find it?"

Erich continued to stare silently at the floor, still holding the coin for them to see.

"Now then, tell me where ye got it," Aunt Rose insisted. "Did ye find it on the road or is it from the Post Office or maybe Miller's shop?"

Erich sighed, turning the coin over in his hand. "M-M-Millar's shop. They have lots. They w-w-won't miss it."

"That's not the point. It's stealing. Ye'll take it back straight away," Aunt Rose said.

"Sure, the tea's nearly ready. He'll take it back after he has a bite to eat," Aunt Sarah said, setting plates on the table. Helen nodded in agreement with her mother, knowing better than to voice her opinion. She was always on Erich's side.

"No, he'll take it now. I'll not give him a morsel until he returns it and apologises to Mrs Miller."

"He's had a long walk already. He'll have his tea and then take it straight back. He's only wee and meant well," Aunt Sarah said, smiling at Erich. Helen nodded vigorously, smiling encouragement to Erich.

"He has to learn right from wrong. He can't steal even if he meant to give it to Elsie as a gift. He'll take it back now," Aunt Rose insisted, looking sternly at Erich. Under her unwavering gaze he shuffled, head down, towards the door.

She led him grimly back to the shop and marched him through the front door. Mr and Mrs Miller stood behind the counter.

"This wee lad has something to tell ye," she said, looking at

Erich.

Head down, shoulders slumped, Erich took the coin from his pocket. He held it out to them, still admiring its shiny gleam. Mr Miller, tall and thin, towered over Erich, regarding him with a serious expression.

"Well, what have ye got there?" he asked.

"Tell Mr Miller what ye're after doing," Aunt Rose prompted him.

Looking down at the floor, he said in a muffled voice, "I t-t-took it from your drawer. It s-s-so shiny. I want g-g-give it to Aunt Elsie. I s-s-sorry."

Mr Miller put the half crown back in the drawer.

"Ye can't take things not belonging to ye. Good lad for owning up to what ye did."

To Aunt Rose he said, "They must learn when they're young."

"Indeed. He's had no tea yet so that should help him remember the lesson."

Ravenous and tired, Erich trailed behind Aunt Rose back to Derrykeane.

Erich jumped up and down, aiming for the yellow flowers. His aim was improving quickly and he could land on the plant he targeted on most tries. He was pleased with his skill. The flower bed beside the front door was filled with spring daffodils. He jumped as high as he could landing hard on the flowers. He was quickly making a flat area in the middle of the bed. The trampled flowers lay around him. He was so engrossed in his game that he did not hear Daddy Davy open the door.

"Stop that at once!" he shouted, glaring at Erich.

Erich looked around, startled.

"That's very bold. You're ruining them. God created them and you've no regard for that." He looked sternly at the boy. Erich guiltily eyed the damage around him. He hadn't realised he had destroyed so many flowers.

"God doesn't want you to squash and trample the flowers. They aren't toys for you," Daddy Davy said.

"I s-s-sorry," Erich said, meekly. "I d-d-don't do it again."

"Good boy. Now then, I was looking for you. I've some news," he said softly.

Erich looked at him expectantly. "What?" he asked.

"Your brother, Hans, is coming to live with us."

Erich looked at him stunned, considering this statement.

"I don't have b-b-brother," he said flatly.

"Yes, you do. The pair of you were in the same orphanage in Germany and you came to Ireland together. He's been staying with Reverend Anderson and his family in Virginia, a few miles from here. I know you haven't seen him in a right while but don't you remember him?" Daddy Davy asked.

Erich tried to ignore the image of the small boy in the back seat driving away from him. That boy was gone now. It couldn't be Hans who was coming here. It must be some other boy, he rationalised. Erich frowned. Hans went away; he wasn't coming back. Erich knew it. Karl and Eva didn't come back. No one ever came back. Besides, he liked being alone with Daddy Davy and Auntie Elsie. He didn't want another boy coming to share them.

"No, I don't have brother," he stubbornly insisted.

"Your brother will be here soon," Daddy Davy said.

Erich looked at him but said nothing. Everyone kept talking about his brother but Erich refused to think about the boy who was coming to live with them. His brother went away a long time ago. He couldn't be coming back now.

Looking out of the window he didn't see anyone coming. He went upstairs and flopped on the bed. Shoving his hand under the pillow he felt around to check the necklace was still there. He found his Dinky toys beside it and pulled them out. Making a roaring sound he crawled across the bare floorboards, racing them in front of him. Today I'm crossing the desert, he decided.

Engrossed in the imaginary hum of the lorries' engines he didn't hear the car at first. It stopped outside. Erich looked up when he heard a car door shut. He dropped his Dinky toys on the bed and slowly came down the stairs, stopping on the landing. Daddy Davy's voice mingled with another man's as the door opened and a thin, dark-haired boy followed Daddy Davy and Reverend Anderson through the front door. The boy, shrinking into his coat, eyes narrowed and fearful, looked up the stairs. Erich glowered at him. He did not want to meet this boy. He didn't look like the toddler Erich remembered. He couldn't be Hans. Erich knew he wasn't his brother. The boy, hands in his pockets, timidly approached Erich.

"Erich, this is your brother, Hans," Daddy Davy said.

"Hello," Hans said, almost in a whisper. He stood slightly taller than Erich despite being a year younger.

"Hello," Erich replied, curtly. He wished the boy would leave.

"Hello, Reverend Anderson. You're very welcome, Hans," Aunt Elsie called from the kitchen. "Come in, I've the kettle on."

Erich brushed past the boy and went in first. Silently, head bowed, Hans followed. His hurt eyes followed Erich's retreating back hopefully. Daddy Davy raised his eyebrows at Reverend Anderson.

"They haven't seen each other in more than a year. It will take some adjustment. I think a bit of time may be all that's needed," the minister said.

"Indeed, I hope you're right," Daddy Davy replied.

As the boys entered the haggard, a few days later, Gipsy raced to meet them, jumping around and barking excitedly. Erich patted and hugged Gipsy, giving Hans a warning glance when he reached to pat the dog. They set their school books on the wall.

"Let's play game. Hit me," Erich said.

Hans frowned at him, perplexed. "Why?" he asked.

Erich repeated the order. "I want Gipsy protect me," he said.

Hans looked uncomfortable but, hoping to please Erich, he raised his hand and stepped forward. As he did the dog growled, low in his throat. Gipsy crouched and the sound grew menacing. Hans lunged towards Erich and the dog sprung at him but before the dog could sink his teeth in, Erich grabbed him and pulled him off. Gipsy barked loudly, straining towards Hans, who drew back fearfully.

"Good dog," Erich repeated over and over, happily hugging the silky spaniel. He could barely contain himself. The dog followed him everywhere and usually slept beside him on the bed. And now Gipsy had protected him. No one could replace him in the dog's affection. Gipsy is truly mine, he thought, satisfied. The display this afternoon reassured him of the dog's loyalty. Gipsy licked Erich's face, tail thumping on the ground. Erich, lavishing praise on the dog, was oblivious to Hans's forlorn look.

Erich stared up at the grey, almost black, spire with its bayonet-like stone spikes, just visible at the top of the hill. He loved the sight of it towering on the hill in the misty morning. The church at Kilmullagh stood plain and solid on the hill. Despite the mist settling on their coats and gradually seeping in, the walk to church on an April morning was easier than on a December one. Though at Christmas Hans wasn't here, Erich thought wistfully, half wishing he could return to that time. Erich didn't let this thought trouble him for too long. Daddy Davy told them last night that this was a special service today. He wondered what would happen. Maybe it would be like Christmas with holly in the windows and everyone happy.

"I don't know how we could check the German records. That's if they still exist after the bombing in that area. We'll never know if they were baptised when they were wee," Daddy Davy said to Aunt Elsie.

"Indeed, you're right. We'd not want to chance leaving it," she replied, concern wrinkling her forehead.

Daddy Davy led them inside to their regular pew, standing aside to let his wife and the boys in first. Ignoring Hans, Erich hung back to sit beside Daddy Davy. Happy to be sitting in this prime position, Erich sang heartily and squeezed his eyes tight shut for the prayers. Trying so hard to please Daddy Davy with his piety, he didn't concentrate on the service and was surprised to hear Reverend Downey call his name from the pulpit. Then he also heard Hans's name called. Puzzled, he looked at Daddy Davy, who had stepped out of the pew and motioned for them to follow. Daddy Davy and Aunt Elsie led the boys up the aisle to the baptismal font. Willy and John Graham, Aunt Elsie's nephews, came from the back pew to join them. Erich giggled as Willy gave the boys a wink. Whatever is happening will be fun with Willy here, Erich thought. Then he saw Daddy Davy's warning glance and quickly suppressed his laughter.

Erich listened, uncomprehending, as the minister read the words of the ritual of baptism. The adults stood behind the boys listening solemnly. As the minister finished he dipped his hand in the water and made the sign of the cross on each boy's forehead. Hans closed his eyes as the minister reached towards him; Erich regarded Reverend Downey steadily. As the water dripped down his forehead Erich shook his head like a spaniel emerging from a lake. Willy grinned but Erich's answering laugh was choked by Daddy Davy's nudge. The boys returned to their seats, still puzzled.

After the service many of the parishioners came and spoke to them, smiling and clapping their shoulders. Erich did not understand what the fuss was about but he enjoyed being the centre of attention.

"You have new names now," Daddy Davy said to the boys on the walk home.

"What mine?" Erich asked before Hans could say anything.

"Your name is Erich Elliott Schnell. You're named after my family. And Hans is Hans Kerr Schnell. He's named after Aunt

Elsie's family," Daddy Davy replied. Hans smiled shyly.

Erich repeated the name quietly to himself, listening to the sound of it. He liked having Daddy Davy's name. Hans didn't have it. Now he knew Daddy Davy loved him best. It didn't matter that Hans was here; he must be Daddy Davy's favourite. Reassured, he smiled at Daddy Davy.

Daddy Davy shook Paddy's reins. As he set off along the lane, Erich and Hans ran after him and jumped on the back of the milk cart. It was easier than walking the three miles to school. Erich sat, legs swinging over the back end, watching the road they had just travelled snake away from them into the distance. Hans sat behind him, his back against a milk can. They stopped at Mr Maguire's farm next door and the two men swung his milk cans onto the cart. The men took turns taking the milk cans to the Ballylea Co-op creamery depot.

Bobby Crawford caught up with them while the men were loading the milk cans. Hans hopped off to walk with him. Although timid, Hans was easy going and people liked his quiet manner. He and Bobby had quickly formed a friendship. Though Bobby was Erich's first friend and ally when he started school, he felt on the outside when the three boys were together.

In the preceding weeks Erich had got used to Hans living with them. Though they argued frequently he now had someone to play with. But he still wasn't completely sure he liked the change. He had to share Auntie Elsie and Daddy Davy's attention and his friend preferred Hans's company to his. I was here first, he thought, disgruntled. How could Hans come and change everything?

Hans and Bobby were quickly left behind on the road and his mood improved as he put them out of his mind. The road was bumpy and the cans rattled but Erich didn't mind. It was just Daddy Davy and him for a while. Pleased to find himself in this coveted position, he shouted to other children heading in the same direction as himself as the cart passed them.

When they arrived at the creamery men who were waiting their turns to unload their milk cans called greetings to Daddy Davy. Half a mile outside Ballylea village, the creamery was a central meeting place for the local farmers. Men from the surrounding farms brought their milk to the Co-op and chatted as they took their turns to pull up to the open doors, at the wooden platform, to unload. Erich jumped off the cart. Standing close to the blue, wooden structure, he dallied, listening to Daddy Davy talking with the other men as he set about unloading the milk cans. Hans and Bobby walked past but he didn't notice. Setting a milk can on the platform, Daddy Davy turned around and spotted him standing there.

"Are you still here? Away wi' you or you'll be late for school, lad," he said.

Reluctantly Erich headed off, arriving at the school as Mrs Baird finished ringing the hand bell. He filed into the classroom with the stragglers and took his seat. Hans and Bobby were already seated. They continued talking unaware of his arrival; Erich pretended not to notice them.

Mrs Baird stood beside her desk, surveying the room and waiting for silence.

"Good Morning, children," she said.

"Good Morning, Mrs Baird," they chorused.

She picked up a bag of Cerebos salt laying on her desk and pointed to the trademark ink drawing of a small boy, crouched behind a chicken, trying to sprinkle salt on the tail of the uncooperative bird.

"*Cen t-ainm ata air?*" she asked in Irish, balancing it on one hand so the class could see the picture on it and pointing to the chicken trying to flee.

"*An eireog,*" replied the class in chorus.

"*Litriu eireog,*" Mrs Baird commanded, pointing at a thin girl in a tattered beige cardigan sitting near Erich.

"*E-I-R-E-O-G. Eireog,*" she spelled in the lilting, singsong tone the children adopted when reciting their lessons aloud.

"*Go maith*," she said, approvingly.

Erich imagined the boy running after the chicken like he did when he tried to put the chickens and geese into their coop at night. Sometimes the geese bit him; he had to be very quick to avoid their beaks.

Erich paid close attention to his teacher. He had found lessons very confusing when he first arrived in Ireland. But, with his determination and enthusiasm, he was making good progress. His English was improving steadily and he was beginning to grasp the Irish language lessons as well. He liked school and eagerly tackled every exercise. Absorbed in his tasks the day passed quickly.

Before Mrs Baird dismissed them that afternoon, she turned to the class, "Who'll help me clean the blackboard today?" she asked.

The children shuffled in their seats, eager to get outside. But Erich didn't mind helping with the chore; he craved praise. His hand shot in the air. As the rest of the children filed out of the room, Erich got a wet rag to wipe the board. Unable to reach the top of the board, even standing on tiptoe, he pulled a chair over and stood on it. He swished the rag across the board and jumped down from the chair. Dragging the chair along he repeated the process across the width of the blackboard.

When he was finished he hopefully approached Mrs Baird's desk. Her head was bent over the papers she was marking but she looked up as he stopped beside her.

"That's a grand job," she said, looking at the shining blackboard. "Thank you, Erich."

Erich beamed at her praise and took the apple she handed him. He bit into it as he stepped out of the door and he was still crunching it as he reached Jemmy Murray's carpentry shop at the edge of the village. The door was open and Erich peered inside.

"Hi ya," Jemmy called, glimpsing Erich outside the door. He

held a piece of wood firmly with his left hand as he plunged a saw through it. The pleasant smell of fresh sawn wood rose from the plank. Erich liked the smell but would not venture into the sawdust strewn building. The whine of the saw frightened him. It conjured images from the nightmares he frequently had. He wasn't sure exactly what it reminded him of. Maybe it was guns firing or bombs exploding but he knew it was a sound he didn't like. He tensed, listening to it. As the whine reached a crescendo he gave a quick wave, backed away from the door and headed up the road.

On the opposite side of the road, a few yards further along, was the post office. Situated in the centre of the village, it functioned as a post office and family grocers. Mrs Henderson and her daughter, Emma, were behind the counter as Erich walked in. Since Erich's transgression at Millar's shop had been discovered he avoided calling there. Now he rarely missed calling into the post office on his way home from school and often bought sweets when he had pocket money. He eyed the familiar array of sweets on the counter top.

Dark-haired, small and stout, Emma bustled around behind the counter serving customers. She greeted Erich cheerily. "Hello, Erich. Fine day, isn't it?"

"Hello," Erich replied, nodding in answer to the question. He liked Emma as she always made time for him. She didn't treat him as a pesky child to be shooed away. He carefully studied the sweets before choosing two liquorice sticks.

When most of the customers had concluded their business and left the shop, Emma motioned to Erich. She led him through to the parlour. She loved to sing and seated herself on the piano bench, pulling Erich up beside her.

"Will ye sing me a song?" she asked.

Erich sang "Jesus loves me this I know," in a high, steady voice. He knew it was one of her favourites.

"What a grand boy ye are! Twas lovely!" she said when he finished, handing him a hard-boiled sweet. Erich popped it into his mouth, leaning back against her shoulder. Erich loved Emma's soft, encouraging voice, motherly way and the sweets she doled out. Sitting with her reminded him of the nights he spent in the train carriage with *Mutti*. He felt safe and happy.

After a couple more songs Emma said, "I'd best be gettin' back to the shop. Mind you go straight home now, Erich."

Erich slid off the bench and headed on his way. But he didn't go straight home. Once outside the door he went around the corner to the forge behind the post office. Dan O'Rourke, the blacksmith, and his son, John Patrick, who everyone called Sonny, were working on a large farm horse. As evening approached a chill was creeping into the air. Erich went eagerly into the forge, basking in the heat inside. He watched as the blacksmith pounded a piece of hot, glowing metal into a horseshoe on the shiny, scarred iron of the anvil.

"Do ye want to pump the bellows for me?" Mr O'Rourke asked as Erich stood awestruck.

Erich nodded eagerly, reaching for the long handles. He grasped them tightly, drawing them apart and back together as hard as he could. The flames leapt with each puff of air. The heat began to sting his face and he flinched at each thud of the hammer on the anvil but he couldn't take his eyes off the blacksmith.

The horse shifted restlessly in the middle of the forge. Erich stayed by the bellows, keeping his distance from the animal. Despite the dangers posed by the animals and the fire's intense heat, Erich loved coming here. He could watch the blacksmith all day. He loved to see the metal glow as the blacksmith worked on it.

"Ye'd best not tarry too long, Erich. It'll soon be teatime. Off you go," Mr O'Rourke said as he finished the shoe.

Reluctantly Erich said goodbye and slipped out of the door. Leaving the village behind he turned up the road towards home. He passed Miller's shop without stopping. Even if he wished to go in, he had spent his pocket money in the post office.

The rest of the journey was through country lanes and fields. Erich didn't make any faster progress here than through the village. He looked in the hawthorn hedges for birds' nests and in every puddle in the ditches for frogspawn.

Erich was lost in his own world as he strolled along. The other children had already made their way home; the dusty road was quiet and deserted. Potholes littered it. He gathered twigs and branches and tried to fill in the depressions, levelling them off as he did so. His work would be swept away by the next cart or feet that passed by but he didn't mind.

He worked to a background of bees buzzing and a skylark's incessant trilling. A ladybird landed on his arm and he stopped to gaze at it for a moment before making a wish. He closed his eyes tightly and wished *Mutti* would find him. She could stay here with me, he thought. She would like it here. There were cows in the fields like she said there used to be in Germany. And there was always lots to eat. She would be so pleased with their new home. Opening his eyes, he knew his wish must come true. He hummed to himself as he walked on.

Further along the road a snail's progress across it caught his attention. He lay on the road to watch its slow march. He thought it might take all night to get across. Maybe someone would step on it before it reached the other side. He hoped it would get there safely.

Eventually he lost interest in its slow progress. He got up and headed on, dragging a branch in the dirt behind him, until he came to a small bridge. He leaned over the wall, on tiptoe, to look at the water trickling beneath it. Unable to resist, he slithered down the bank, the branch abandoned, into the bluish-black clay of the bank. Taking off his shoes and socks he dipped his toes into the stream. The water was cold on this spring day. A dragonfly hovered over the surface and Erich watched it transfixed until it darted away. Then he floated a twig in the current, watching it until it disappeared under the bridge. The current also washed the chalky dust from the road off his feet.

Amidst the rustlings at the riverbank he heard a familiar bird cry. "Cuckoo, cuckoo" rose from the hiding creature. In his mind he saw the forest in Germany. He was walking through it with Eva and the other children. Tante Gretchen was singing the cuckoo song and she smiled at him. Erich smiled contentedly, reliving the moment. But then he looked around and saw the river and an empty dirt road above him. Tante Gretchen wasn't here. She was far away where the soldiers spoke sharply to him and bombs fell at night. He tried not to think about it as he climbed out of the river. He put his socks and shoes on wet feet and scrambled up the bank. Images of Germany flooded through his mind as he wandered along the road. I won't think about the soldiers and bombs, he decided. Instead I'll think about *Mutti*. I have the necklace to give her when my wish comes true and she finds me. This thought cheered him and helped to push the terrifying memories from his mind.

When Erich arrived at the track to Derrykeane, he slipped into the field beside it, almost tiptoeing. He would sneak up on Gipsy. But Gipsy was not to be fooled and came bounding across the field. The dog's internal sense of time never failed him and he was watching for Erich. The brown spaniel easily found him. He danced around Erich and leapt up on him ecstatically. Erich hugged him tightly, wrestling with him as the dog licked his face and nuzzled him. This fervent greeting made Germany seem very far away and the last of the disturbing memories slipped from his thoughts.

They raced along the path, through the haggard to the back door. Erich heard his stomach growl and realised that he was hungry. The back door slammed behind him as he entered the kitchen. Hans looked up from the table where he was finishing his homework. Aunt Elsie was setting the plates out for tea. She paused and smiled at him. Daddy Davy came in the door behind Erich. Both adults turned to him.

"Mrs Baird gave me an apple for helping her," he said, still pleased by the praise he'd received from her.

"Aren't you a grand boy," Aunt Elsie said, rather subdued. She looked expectantly at her husband.

"A letter came today," Daddy Davy said, "from Germany."

5

HAYMAKING AND HALLOWEEN
Spring 1948

"*Meine mutter* write!" Erich shouted.

Daddy Davy didn't reply immediately. Aunt Elsie, grasping at her apron, watched them anxiously.

"No, it wasn't your mother, lad. It's from someone at the orphanage where you lived."

"Tante Gretchen!" Erich shouted, happy that his favourite staff member had written to him.

"No, it wasn't."

"Tante Trude?" Erich said less certainly.

"Yes, that's right," he replied.

"What she say? She coming to see me?" Erich asked.

Daddy Davy shook his head. Unnoticed, Hans listened to the conversation. He wasn't excited to hear that Tante Trude had written to them but he was curious to know why. A year younger than Erich, he didn't remember her well.

"She wants to know that both of you are well," Daddy Davy said. "She also has some bad news," he added.

Erich looked at him uneasily. Is it about *Mutti*? What did she say? he worried.

Daddy Davy went to stand beside Erich and put his hand on the boy's shoulder. He hesitated before he spoke, looking from one boy to the other.

"I'm afraid she's found that your mother's dead. She died when the train station where she was working was bombed during the war."

Hans sat looking forlorn. He didn't remember his mother well but he had hoped that he would see her again one day. He wanted to know her. Erich stood stunned. She can't be dead, he thought. She has to come back for me. She will come back; she said she would. She said we would live together one day, Erich thought desperately. His face crumpled and he cried huge sobs, gasping for breath. Aunt Elsie rushed over and threw her arms around him.

"Poor wee mite," she said, rocking him against her. She looked across at Hans sitting opposite, expressionless. Daddy Davy went and put his arm around the boy.

"*Mutti* said I live with her one day," Erich gasped between sobs.

"I know, lad. But you'll stop with us now," Aunt Elsie replied.

"This is your home," Daddy Davy added. Erich's sobs gradually eased. He wiped at his eyes with his sleeve. He couldn't believe he wouldn't see *Mutti* again. He wanted to see her. But at least he had Daddy Davy and Aunt Elsie. He felt safe knowing he would stay with them.

After tea Aunt Elsie watched Erich seated by the fire, head down and shoulders slumped, staring gloomily into the blaze.

"Mind your home is wi' us now," she said. "You're not alone."

Erich nodded, glancing up briefly from the fire. He was glad he lived here. He knew Auntie Elsie and Daddy Davy would take care of him. Staring into the fire his mind wandered to the necklace under his pillow. I won't be able to give it to *Mutti* now, he thought miserably. He had kept it so carefully for her. But now there was no use keeping it if he couldn't give it to her. He looked up at Auntie Elsie's concerned face and knew what to do with it.

Erich went upstairs without a word and returned a minute later with the necklace in his hand.

"For you," he said, thrusting the necklace towards her.

Aunt Elsie looked at him surprised, then reached to take it. It glinted in the firelight.

"It's lovely, Erich. Thank you very much," she said, touched by his generosity. Daddy Davy smiled from his chair on the other side of the fire.

"That's very kind of you, Erich," he said. "Are you sure you don't want to keep it?"

Erich shook his head and threw his arms around Auntie Elsie, unable to tell her how he felt. She squeezed him tightly.

"Well, time's getting on. I'd best make the supper," she said a few minutes later as she rose, dabbing at her eyes. Erich settled back to watch the fire. He couldn't give *Mutti* the necklace but Aunt Elsie had become like a mother to him. He felt pleased to know she would keep it. He missed *Mutti* but he knew he had a family here.

Summer 1948

The weeks quickly passed and the summer holidays arrived. The girls arrived home from boarding school. Now it was two against two in any dispute that arose, though the girls had the advantage of age and size. Even though Erich still resented Hans, he enlisted his support against the girls' bossiness.

Though free from the daily routine of school, the children still had chores to do at home. The girls helped Aunt Elsie in the house. Nell, fastidious and driven, constantly cleaned and swept. Three years younger than Nell, Rose did not have as much responsibility placed on her and had a more relaxed, carefree attitude. She did what was asked of her but did not look for work. The boys helped Daddy Davy with the farm chores.

After breakfast one morning Erich searched the haggard for eggs the hens had laid, dodging attacks from the geese waddling to and fro. When his basket was full he took the eggs to Aunt Elsie. She was feeding table scraps to the piglet fenced in one corner of the kitchen. Erich stooped to pat the piglet, enjoying the soft feel of its skin and the snuffling noises it made as it devoured the scraps.

"Look at all the eggs I get!" he said proudly.

"Isn't that grand! You did a great job. We'll have hard-boiled eggs with the dinner so," Aunt Elsie replied.

She took the basket from him and set it on the table. Pleased with his efforts, Erich went outside. As he crossed the haggard, a stray goose rushed at him and he shooed it away sharply. The goose waddled off cackling petulantly as he entered the byre. Inside Hans was trying to milk a recalcitrant cow. The cow shifted restlessly and knocked over the bucket. A thin trickle of milk seeped into the straw. Erich laughed.

"You'll get the way of it wi' a bit o' practice. You need to be firm wi' her," Daddy Davy, steadily milking another cow in the next stall, called to Hans without lifting his head.

Erich watched Hans's attempt to milk the cow disdainfully, knowing he could do it better.

"I show you how to do it," he said smugly to Hans as he marched into the stall. Hans reluctantly got up and let Erich take his place. Erich's few months' head start showed as he grasped the cow's teat firmly, squeezing rhythmically as Daddy Davy had taught him. The cow tried to shift but he held his grip. After a couple tries to evade him the cow stood still. Erich milked her without any further resistance. When Daddy Davy finished milking the cow in the next stall he came over to them.

"We'll find a more obliging one for you to have another go," he said to Hans, who was hunching dejectedly in the corner.

Hans straightened slightly and followed him as he went to empty his pail into the creamery can.

When all the cows were milked Daddy Davy lifted a pitchfork and began tossing dirty straw onto the wheelbarrow. Erich lifted a shovel and dragged it across the floor, scooping a small pile of straw onto it. He struggled to lift the heavy shovel and swing it up onto the wheelbarrow. Daddy Davy, working quickly, glanced over and smiled at Erich's attempts to wield the heavy shovel. Hans hid a smirk, pleased to see that Erich didn't do everything well.

"Lad, you need a pitchfork for that. Take yon boy in the corner." Daddy Davy pointed to the far corner of the byre. Erich lifted the pitchfork and made another attempt. With the lighter tool he made faster progress.

When the wheelbarrow was piled high Daddy Davy took it out and dumped it in a corner of the nearest field. They repeated the process until all the dirty straw was removed from the byre. Daddy Davy swept the floor vigorously and then Erich and Hans helped him scatter fresh straw on the floor. The bulky straw prickled their arms and chests as they wrapped their arms around it, clinging to their jumpers and their hair. Erich lifted as much straw as he could, trying to carry more than Hans and hoping Daddy Davy would notice his efforts. Straw protruded at odd angles from his curls, a slightly lighter colour than his hair. He brushed at his clothes trying to stop the itching.

As they dusted themselves off afterwards Daddy Davy emerged from the stable leading Paddy, the cantankerous donkey, on a short rope with the water barrel tied across the animal's back.

"I help you!" Erich shouted when he saw him. Hans hung back, wistfully watching them. Erich never tired of the chores; he liked to be with Daddy Davy and to receive praise for his help.

Erich followed Daddy Davy down to the well, being careful to stay clear of Paddy's hooves. Paddy ambled along, head drooping, paying little attention to them. Stopping suddenly he bent his head into some sweet grass beside the path. Daddy Davy pulled his lead trying to raise his head, but Paddy stubbornly kept it down. Erich also grasped the rope and tried to help Daddy Davy pull the beast but Paddy resisted all their attempts until he finished eating. Then he raised his head and ambled on again.

"Yon boyo is a stubborn beast," Daddy Davy said, shaking his head.

After a couple more stops they arrived at the well. Daddy Davy filled the barrel and tied it on Paddy's back.

On the way back Paddy's jerky gait sloshed the water around inside the barrel. The donkey shook his head irritably when some of the cold water leaked from the barrel and splashed over him. He stopped frequently but they coaxed him on, keeping a steady pressure on the lead rope. Eventually the donkey arrived back in the haggard with the water barrel still on his back.

"I think it might be easier to draw water without yon beast. We'd nearly be quicker to carry it on our own backs," Daddy Davy said ruefully.

Standing a bit straighter, Erich grinned at Daddy Davy. He had said "we". He thinks I'm a good helper. And he didn't include Hans, Erich thought, anxious to have a favoured place in Daddy Davy's affections.

Daddy Davy turned Paddy out into the nearest field and the donkey galloped off, kicking his heels in the air. Daddy Davy and Erich watched the animal wearily.

"Dinner's ready!" Aunt Elsie called.

Daddy Davy and the boys trooped into the house. Erich was hungry after the battle with Paddy. The eggs I collected this morning will be good with dinner, Erich thought. Anticipating them he looked at the table but was dismayed to see nothing on it. Where is the dinner? Erich wondered. The other two were also perplexed.

"We're having a picnic," Nell announced in answer to their puzzled expressions.

She led them out of the front door, around the corner of the house, to the tall beech tree. Its branches brushed against the gable wall. Under its wide, leafy arms a table cloth was spread on the ground. Bread, cheese, bacon slices, tomatoes, butter, jam and boiled eggs were placed on it. They sat on the grass around the table cloth filling their plates from the dishes set out.

Erich peeled the shell off an egg and broke it in half, stuffing the top half in his mouth.

"Erich! You'll choke trying to eat such a mouthful!" Nell admonished.

"No, won't," he said, his mouth crammed full of egg.

Hans laughed, watching him; Nell shot him a reproachful glance but he continued to giggle. Rose, copying her older sister, frowned at the boys. Erich swallowed the egg, sputtering as it went down. Then he burped.

"Boys are so rude!" Nell said in exasperation. Erich and Hans giggled, making faces until Daddy Davy gave them a warning look.

"Mind your manners, lads," he said mildly.

After they had eaten they lay back on the grass, content. Daddy Davy leaned against the smooth, grey bark at the base of the beech tree. It made a comfortable back rest, with ample room for two people to lie comfortably against its circumference. Its branches provided an umbrella to shield them from the noonday sun though a few rays escaped their net and darted between the oval, pointy leaves. It was pleasantly warm without the sun beating down on them. Flies buzzed around the food. Aunt Elsie and Nell lazily swatted them away. The buzzing roused the boys and they sat up. Determined to get rid of the pests the boys swatted at the flies more vigorously than the women, competing to see who could hit the most.

"I get that one!" Erich shouted.

"It was mine! But I got this one!" Hans shouted as he darted after another one.

They jumped back and forth across the table cloth.

"Don't be putting your hands in the food!" Nell cried as Hans landed close to the butter.

Her lethargy dispelled by the boys' antics, Nell gathered up the plates and took them into the house. Rose helped her.

"Goodness, I can't be lying here all day," Aunt Elsie said, spurred by the girls' activity. Daddy Davy nodded in agreement. They rose and returned to their chores. When everything was cleared away, the girls returned. The children lazily surveyed the still afternoon, searching for something to occupy them. Nell stared at Hans for a few minutes and her face lit up. He returned her gaze apprehensively, like his brother he had quickly learned what that look meant.

"Why're you staring at me?" he asked.

"I've a grand idea. Let's play weddings. You can be the bride. Rose will be the groom," she said to Hans.

"Yes, that's a good idea!" Rose agreed.

"Why can't I be groom?" Erich asked, annoyed to be overlooked.

"You're too short. Rose is taller. You can be the bridesmaid," she replied. Erich scowled at Hans. He was older, he should have a lead role. Even bride would be better than bridesmaid. It isn't fair, he sulked to himself.

The girls ran upstairs and returned in a few minutes with two of their best dresses and Sunday shoes. They helped the boys pull the white flowery dresses over their heads and pinned an old lace curtain to Hans's head. The boys stepped into the shoes which were several sizes too big for them. Nell picked a few green leafy twigs and wild flowers to form a bouquet. She handed it to Hans, then stood back to observe their handiwork. Daddy Davy came around the corner from the haggard.

"Daddy! Will you get the camera?" she called.

"Goodness! Where did ye get these two fine ladies?" he asked with mock dismay.

The children giggled. Hans took Rose's arm, grinning from ear to ear as she, a head taller than him, hunched beside him self-consciously. They pranced across the lawn pretending they were gliding down the aisle of the church to the accompaniment of its majestic organ. Erich trailed behind them, tugging at Hans's veil, still unhappy to be relegated to a supporting role. Hans jerked his head away, giggling. Aunt Elsie came out to see what the commotion was and laughed when she saw them.

"Oh, we're going to a wedding so. And a grand one it is," she said.

Daddy Davy went inside and returned shortly with the camera. With all the attention they were receiving, Erich forgot his annoyance at Hans. The wedding party posed, grinning widely, as Daddy Davy snapped their picture.

The rain beat down on the window. Though only early evening, the light was quickly fading. Daddy Davy sat in his chair by the fire, engrossed in a book. Rose, her nose streaming with a summer cold, sat huddled beside him. Hans also hunched close to the fire. In its corner the piglet snuffled in search of any scraps it might have missed at feeding time.

Erich sat on the bench at the table watching Nell's slim legs as she ran the iron over her father's Sunday shirt. He leaned forward and pinched her leg. Nell turned quickly, glaring at him before kicking him sharply in the shins. He grasped his shin, moaning.

"Daddy Davy, Nell kicked me!" he whined.

"Nell, stop that! You're old enough to know better!" Daddy Davy said. He went back to his book.

Erich half smirked at her. Nell glared at him but said nothing. She picked up the iron and resumed her work. The iron hissed as she ran it across the white cotton. Erich listened to its hiss as he watched her legs, slim with just a slight roundness. She stepped back and forth, sliding the iron the length of the shirt. Erich leaned forward and pinched her again. This time Nell spun around, aiming a more vicious kick at him.

"Daddy Davy, she did again!" Erich shouted.

"If this doesn't stop I'll have to spank whoever is responsible," Daddy Davy replied, looking from Nell to Erich.

When Daddy Davy returned to his book Erich started to snivel. He screwed up his eyes, with his head lowered, and began to cry, gradually getting louder.

"She did again, Daddy Davy!" he cried, though Nell hadn't moved from the ironing board.

Daddy Davy looked up from his book and his glance swept around the room at each of them. Hans and Rose tried to hide their smirks, gazing determinedly into the fire. Erich sat, still snivelling, and looked accusingly at Nell who glared back at him. Daddy Davy shook his head.

"I don't know who started this but there's only one thing for it. I'll have to punish both of ye," he sighed.

Hans and Rose snickered until Daddy Davy's attention turned to them.

"I didn't do anything!" Rose exclaimed. Hans nodded in agreement.

"Nell, Erich, come here," Daddy Davy said.

Nell shot accusing glances at Erich as she walked over to Daddy Davy. Erich continued to sniff, peering up at Nell; she darted glances behind her to be sure he didn't pinch her when her back was turned. Daddy Davy, ignoring their antagonism, gave them each a sound smack. They returned to their seats, silently eyeing each other.

"Now I don't know which one of you started it but I'm sure I got the culprit. You were bold and you were punished. That's the end of it. It's forgiven now. We'll hear no more about it. I want both of you to come here and give me a kiss," Daddy Davy said.

Nell reluctantly went over and kissed him, throwing a reproachful glance at Erich. He followed her, smiling.

"The Bible teaches us to forgive those who trespass against us," Daddy Davy said mildly, seeing Nell's look.

Erich and Nell looked at each other warily. Then Erich glanced down again, fascinated by her slim, graceful legs.

The hen's wings flapped wildly as it fluttered and struggled in Aunt Elsie's grip. Erich almost walked into her as he came out of the back door.

"This one's a nice fat one for the dinner," she said.

"No! Don't hurt it!" Erich cried.

"It wouldn't do not to have a proper dinner when we have visitors. We'd want something tasty," Aunt Elsie replied.

Erich watched in horror as, grasping its legs, she deftly twisted its neck. The head lolled to one side while the body still twitched in her hands. Erich ran into the house crying.

"What's the matter, lad?" Aunt Rose asked.

"Aunt Elsie killed the chicken!" he cried.

"Did she now? That's so we'll have a nice dinner," she replied.

"I don't want any!" he said, staring at the floor.

"Well, let's go to the river and see if we can find some pearls," she said to distract him.

"Are there really pearls?" he asked, his curiosity aroused.

"If you look really hard, you might find them," she replied. "We'll take the fishing rods and see if we can catch any fish so."

Distracted from his distress over the bird's death, Erich set about looking for his fishing rod. The piglet shifted in its corner, disturbed by Erich running from the kitchen. It was growing well on its plentiful table scraps.

"You get your fishing rod too, Hans," she said to the boy watching them hopefully from the fireside. Hans jumped up and went to look for his fishing rod.

Aunt Rose always spent her summer holidays at her family home and the children loved her company. Though strict, she was also fun and fired their imaginations.

The boys returned in a few minutes with their homemade fishing rods. Daddy Davy had tied some old string to two strong branches and formed the hooks from nails he bent with a hammer.

Aunt Rose led them down the grassy path to the water. The river, like the bridge of a pair of spectacles, connected two small lakes. The smaller lake was directly downhill from the front door of the house, and the larger one, which they called Derrykeane

139

Lake, was a little to the right. They were only a short walk from the house and the front door was easily visible from the river bank.

They walked with the fishing rods across their shoulders, strings and hooks dangling behind them. Gipsy followed them, plunging his nose into the grass on either side of the path and running in circles. At the river's edge they dropped their rods and peered into the water. Aunt Rose looked over their shoulders.

"Do you see any mussels?" she asked.

They shook their heads and leaned closer to the water.

"They hide under the sand. You'll have to get in the water to look for them," she said.

The boys took off their shoes and socks, throwing them on the bank beside their fishing rods. Hans stepped into the water and yipped as he felt its coldness around his ankles. Erich hesitated, fearful yet intrigued. He peered into the river then followed his brother. Lifting his feet in and out of the water as the cold seeped in he cautiously stepped away from the riverbank. Gipsy plunged in splattering them both. Erich shied away, anxious not to fall into the water as the dog jumped around him. Ever since they had crossed the water on the train journey from Germany he did not like to swim or to be immersed in water; he would rather stay at the riverbank.

The boys bent over, sifting the sand with their feet. It rose, small brown granules floating like a cloud above the riverbed, muddying the clear water. Stuck in the sandy bottom of the river near their feet, several mussels lay at an angle. Their brown, ringed shells stuck out of the sand like crashed flying saucers. The boys pulled out a couple and turned them over, looking at the rough, rounded shells.

They tried to pry them open but the mussels resisted. Grunting and straining for several minutes they finally prised the shells open. Inside the light, rubbery animals were exposed but no white jewels were hidden within their blobby bodies. Disappointed, they tossed the mussels back into the water and unearthed a couple more. Again there were no pearly treasures inside them. The boys tired of their hunt.

They picked up their fishing rods and sat beside Aunt Rose on the grassy bank, their hooks dipping into the water. Gipsy emerged onto the bank shaking himself vigorously, then he lay down beside them, his nose resting on his front paws. In a couple of minutes he was snoring.

"Never you mind you didn't have any luck wi' the pearls this time. Sure, you might find them next time," Aunt Rose said.

"Are they very big?" Erich asked. "They must be massive!"

"Ye never know what ye might find. Sometimes they're big," she replied, smiling as she looked at their earnest faces. "But let's see if the fish are biting this morning."

They sat quietly staring at the water for a few minutes. Their strings moved slightly in the river's current, pulling taut and relaxing again. Gipsy continued to doze. Erich watched a bee hovering over a vetch's delicate, pinkish-purple flower. Its buzz had a hypnotic effect. It was very warm on the unshaded river bank and he yawned as he stared at the bee. The boys sank into a sun-induced stupor.

Suddenly there was a tug on Hans's line. He gripped the rod as it almost slipped from his hands.

"I've got something!" he shouted.

"Good lad! Pull it in," Aunt Rose said.

Hans stood up and backed away from the river's edge, pulling his taut line out of the water. The hook was still hidden beneath the surface. He stepped further back. Gipsy raised his head, wakened by the commotion. The hook emerged from the water and a brown speckled fish, approximately ten inches long, fell twisting and flopping on the grass, its dark, staring eye looking towards the sky. Its gills flapped as its body gradually stilled.

The boys ran over to look at it. Hans grinned, jumping up and down and shouting, "I got a fish!" Erich regarded it enviously.

"That's a grand trout, ye have!" Aunt Rose exclaimed.

Erich went back to the river's edge and dipped his hook into the water again. I'll catch a bigger one! he thought determinedly. Aunt Rose unhooked the fish from Hans's rod and lay it in long grass to keep it cool. Hans sat down again, still grinning, and threw his line back in the water. They sat in silence until Aunt Elsie interrupted their concentration.

"Dinner!" they heard faintly as she called them from the front door. Erich frowned. He needed more time to catch a bigger fish than Hans had. Reluctantly he pulled his line from the water. They gathered up their rods, socks and shoes and the trout and headed back to the house. Hans, strutting proudly, held the trout aloft for all to see. Erich walked behind, head down.

"Aunt Elsie cooked a lovely chicken for dinner. And now we have trout for tea. Isn't that grand?" Aunt Rose said as they neared the house.

Everyone will make such a fuss over Hans. If I'd had more time I'd have caught a bigger fish, Erich thought downheartedly.

"It's a lovely evening. Why don't we call on the Walkers? I haven't seen them in a right while," Aunt Rose suggested after tea.

"That's a grand idea. We couldn't want a better evening for it," Aunt Elsie agreed.

Aunt Elsie and Aunt Rose put on their cardigans and combed their hair. Nell tutted as she ran a comb through Erich's unruly hair; Hans's lay down neat and manageable after a couple of brush strokes.

Erich was glad that tea was over and they were getting out of the house. Now he wouldn't have to listen to any more praise for Hans's catch.

Daddy Davy led them down the path to Derrykeane Lake, the bigger of the two lakes occupying the field in front of their house. The Walkers' house was in the field directly across the lake and the fastest way to get there in summer was by boat. Daddy Davy flipped the wooden rowboat upright and slid it into the water. Aunt Rose, Aunt Elsie and Rose stepped barefoot into the edge of the water, holding their skirts and shoes above the water's surface. Erich watched anxiously as they climbed into the boat and Daddy Davy rowed them across. In a few minutes he was back for Nell, Erich and Hans.

It was a warm, sunny evening and the water lapped gently. The boat barely rocked as it moved across the water's surface. Erich avoided looking over the edge as they glided to the other side. He didn't want to see the water surrounding him. Nell and Hans leaned over to watch the water swirling around their trailing hands, shouting when they spotted the movement of a fish beneath the surface. But Erich kept his gaze firmly fixed on the bottom of the boat.

"It's a lovely, calm night for a boat ride," Daddy Davy said to Erich reassuringly.

Erich nodded without looking up. He couldn't wait to get out of the boat and scrambled out eagerly at the other side. He dashed away as Daddy Davy pulled the boat out of the water.

The house was crowded with people. The Halls, who lived on the next farm, had already arrived. Everyone chatted as the women made tea and set out sandwiches, bread and butter. The children, uninterested in the adult conversation, slipped outside to play. Jenny Hall and Nell went off together with Rose and Jenny's younger sister, Joy, tagging after them.

Erich followed Stephen Walker outside. Hans tailed after them.

"Let's go out in the boat," Stephen said. A year older than Erich, he expected to lead their activities.

"You don't..." Hans began before Erich, with a warning glance, elbowed him. Hans's sentence trailed off and he followed behind them, ignoring Erich's scowl.

"Boats are boring. Let's see who can jump furthest in the hay," Erich replied hastily, trying to divert the older boy's attention away from the water.

The boys went into the hayshed and climbed into the rafters. They jumped down onto the hay below over and over.

When they tired of the haystack they went back inside the house, picking bits of straw out of their clothes and brushing themselves vigorously. They helped themselves to sandwiches on the table, then found a corner to sit in. As the evening wore on their heads nodded and they dozed.

It was dark when they left. Daddy Davy held a torch aloft as they walked to the lake. The boys got into the boat and Nell held the torch as Daddy Davy pushed the boat away from the shore. As he rowed out into the water the only light visible was the yellowish glow from the torch. A few sparks flew off it and fluttered through the air to land, hissing, in the water. Erich couldn't see the threatening water surrounding him. The splashes from the oars were his only reminder of it. He felt safe in the darkness as Daddy Davy rowed unerringly to the other shore. His fear temporarily forgotten, Erich looked up at the bright, twinkling stars in the sky in wonder.

Like the week before it, the next day was a glorious summer day. A light breeze brushed the hay in the field, making it wave slightly. Erich wandered barefoot at the edge of the field, through the cut hay, kicking it with his feet. Hayseeds and bits of hay rose up and clung to his clothes. They prickled against his legs. He watched the men working in the middle of the field. Hans and Bobby were playing in the byre but Erich hung about the hay field, wanting to be near Daddy Davy.

The local farmers helped each other with the major farm tasks each year. Today they were at the Elliotts to make hay. Daddy Davy and several of his neighbours swung scythes in wide arcs, cutting the hay. It swished as it fell to the ground. They worked steadily and rhythmically across the field, leaving a soft, yellow bed strewn randomly behind them.

Erich watched the receding line of hay. It was like a thin, yellow forest which, once felled, became a yellow, crackling mat. From within the yellow forest Erich heard a rasping call, "crek,

crek". A corncrake, hiding within the long grass, had been disturbed as its shelter steadily disappeared. Erich stared at the grass for a long time, willing the bird to appear. The calling continued but he couldn't see it. His attention wavered eventually and he shifted his gaze to the tufts of hay lying in front of him. Suddenly a sandy form darted swiftly from the edge of the uncut hay. Erich looked up to see the speckled bird peep out briefly and disappear into the hedge surrounding the field. Brown speckles flashed on the sandy body as it flitted away.

Erich ran over to Daddy Davy, shouting,"I saw it! I saw it!"

"Did you now? And what did you see?" Daddy Davy paused and stood upright in the field. He set the scythe at his side, the tip burrowing into the ground.

"The bird that goes 'crek, crek'," he replied.

"That would be a corncrake then. You're very lucky as you don't often see them. They're very shy," Daddy Davy replied.

"Can I help you cut the hay?" Erich asked. He studied the scythe resting against Daddy Davy's hip.

"I doubt you could lift a scythe. It's a bit heavy for you. There'll be lots to do tomorrow when we're ready to bring the hay in. You can help then," he replied.

Erich wandered back to the edge of the field, keeping an eye on the uncut hay in case the corncrake showed itself again.

The dry, sunny weather allowed the hay, lying in rows in the field, to dry quickly. The next day they began gathering it. The neighbours were back and everyone helped.

The creaking, wooden tumbling paddy made slow progress around the field. It collected hay and, when it was full, a lever was pushed and the hay tumbled into a heap on the ground. Erich, being one of the smallest helpers, jumped on top of the heap to tramp it down. He did this with great gusto and enthusiasm, dancing on it as if it were a large, down feathered bed. He breathed in the sweet smell of the new-cut hay as he jumped. As more and more hay was collected and added to the top the mound grew higher and Erich rose off the ground, still jumping and shouting with delight. When the haycock was complete he slid off, getting bits of hay stuck in his hair and clothes.

"Let's do lots!" he shouted to Daddy Davy after the first one was complete.

Daddy Davy laughed, watching him. "Never fear, lad. You'll get your fill today."

They worked through the morning. The growing heat and dust from the hay made him thirsty but he barely noticed amidst the excitement and activity. The sun climbed in the sky and beat down harder as the morning went on. Sweat ran off Erich and the other workers; he slowed a little but didn't lose his enthusiasm.

Several women made their way from the house to the field, weighed down with buckets. Erich, standing on top of a haycock, spotted them first and alerted everyone else. One by one the workers stopped and waited for them. The women poured cups of tea and buttermilk for them. There were also ham sandwiches, bacon slices, soda bread, brown bread and cakes. Erich tore off hunks of his sandwich, swallowing each bite with a mouthful of tea. The tea lifted the dryness in his mouth and he sighed contentedly. He hadn't known he could be so hungry. Afterwards he eyed the cake eagerly and was quick to reach for a piece when it was passed around.

Lethargy stole over him after he had eaten. The sun beating down lulled him and he dozed. When Daddy Davy stood up a short while later, Erich roused himself and, shaking off bits of hay, got to his feet. The sun made his head feel heavy and he yawned. He could easily go back to sleep again. But one by one everyone stood up and prepared to resume the work.

"I could be on top," Hans said diffidently to Daddy Davy.

"No, I-I-I on top!" Erich shouted, completely awake now.

"Erich is smaller. That's why he climbs on the rucks. We'll find another job for you," Daddy Davy said to Hans.

Erich smirked triumphantly at Hans and followed the tumbling paddy as it sprang to life. For once he didn't mind being shorter than his brother.

The work went quickly with everyone helping. The next day they were ready to bring the haycocks into the barn. Their sturdy pony, Paddy, pulled the flat wagon out to the field and Daddy Davy guided him until the back end of the wagon was lined up with a haycock. The front end of the wagon was tilted upwards until the back end rested on the ground. The haycock was tied and cranked onto the wagon as if lifted by a powerful crane, then the wagon was tilted upright again. Erich watched fascinated as the haycock was raised onto the wagon. He marvelled that it didn't fall apart and that it could be moved so smoothly. He loved to see the wagon tilt and right itself like a giant seesaw.

The wagon continued around the field collecting haycocks, the children running after it, until it was full. Then it started back towards the barn. Erich and the other children scrambled onto it, jostling for the best positions along the back. They swung their feet over the end of the low wagon, dragging them through the stubble. The wagon ride was one of the perks of helping bring in the hay. Erich laughed as the wagon bumped over the uneven ground. They rocked but were not in danger of falling off. The children leaned sideways as the wagon rounded the corner, trying to tip it but the heavy wagon didn't budge.

At the barn everyone helped to unload and stack the hay inside. Erich took his place in the chain passing it into the barn, feeling important when Daddy Davy looked over and smiled at him. When the wagon was unloaded, he raced with the other children to jump on the end for the ride back to the field.

Autumn 1948

"Well done, children. We'll have a wee break. Away outside with ye now," Mrs Baird said.

Books slammed shut and the children rushed outside. The playground stretched across two fields. The children skipped and played hopscotch on the uneven ground in the field in front of the school. They fished, and occasionally tumbled into, the stream that bordered that field. The other field was an over-grown, scraggy, rough one and the boys loved the secrecy it af-forded them. Bobby, Hans, Erich and several other boys headed for this field; it was out of sight of the classroom and a favourite spot for them to play.

"Let's build a fire. I've got matches," Bobby said.

The boys set about collecting twigs, sticks, paper and anything else they thought would burn. When they had a small mound Bobby took the matches from his pocket and struck one against the side of the packet. It hissed to life as he threw it on the pile. A small flame flickered in the paper and settled deeper into the twigs and branches. After a few minutes a small, crackling fire was burning steadily. The flames, like fingers reaching out and beckoning, burst out from the centre of the fire and then retreated again.

Fascinated by the flames, Erich leaned towards them. He liked the popping, snapping sounds the fire made. How exciting! he thought, grinning as the fire flared brightly. Moving closer to watch the flames twist and slither, Erich leaned directly over the blaze. A flame exploded outwards and caught one of the sandy, curling locks, which dangled from his forehead, travel-ling quickly along it. Erich smelled the charring as it burned. He reached up and slapped at his burning hair.

"I-I-It's burning! It's b-b-burning!" he shouted.

"It's grand. Ye've got it out now," Bobby said.

"Will Mrs Baird see it?" Erich asked.

"Naw, she'll never notice it," Bobby replied confidently.

Engrossed in their activity they did not hear Mrs Baird clang the handbell. The other children filed into the school. Suddenly the silence of the playground startled them. Bobby hurriedly kicked dirt at the fire to put it out. They stamped on it, jumping from one foot to the other as the heat travelled through the soles of their shoes. When there was just a thin trail of smoke from its core they ran to the schoolhouse.

As they entered the classroom Mrs Baird looked at them sternly. "Hurry up! You're late!" she said, frowning as she surveyed the dishevelled, panting boys. As the smell of smoke wafted over to her, she noticed Erich's singed hair.

"What've you been doin'?" she asked.

Breathless with excitement and from the run back to the classroom, Erich forgot his worry that Mrs Baird would notice his burnt hair and blurted out, "We'd a fire! It was brilliant!"

The other boys looked around uneasily. They knew better than to admit to such activities. But in his excitement Erich, often impulsive, spoke before he thought about it.

"You should know better! You're not to light fires! That's very bold! I will have to speak to Mr Elliott. And he won't be best pleased wi' your hair either," she replied, still looking at his charred locks. "All of you will stay after school."

Erich's enthusiasm was quelled slightly by the thought of telling Daddy Davy how he had singed his hair. He didn't want Daddy Davy angry with him. He knew he shouldn't have been playing with a fire and he'd be punished. But then he remembered the lovely flames leaping and changing colours. The fire was so exciting, he thought, exhilarated. He pushed the coming reckoning with Daddy Davy to the back of his mind.

The rest of the day passed slowly. Erich refused to think about facing Daddy Davy later. After the other children left the boys sat writing "I must not light fires" until Erich's hand ached. When Mrs Baird finally dismissed them the other boys shunned Erich, annoyed that he had told their teacher about the fire. Hans left with Bobby and they raced each other to Bobby's house. Erich dawdled along the road on his own.

The autumn sun shone with little warmth but Erich didn't mind. He peered into hedges and ditches as he walked along, in no hurry to get home. He picked dark, clumped blackberries from bushes intertwined in the hedges and leaned into ditches to pick purplish bilberries where they grew in soft, peaty ground. The juices stained his hands as he stuffed them into his mouth.

He spotted some sloe berries but knew to avoid their bitter taste. He continued along the road, sometimes detouring into fields, searching for more of the sweet berries.

Later than usual, unable to delay any longer, Erich finally arrived home. As Gipsy bounced around him he heard several voices in the haggard. It was unusual to have visitors at this time of day. Patting the dog, he listened but could not hear what they were saying.

Everyone was huddled in the corner of the haggard as Erich walked through the gap in the wall. Their neighbour, Mr Evans, stood straddling the pig and Aunt Elsie was poised in front of him, holding a metal bucket. The pig squirmed and squealed as he tightened his knees around it. As Erich took in the scene Mr Evans brought the hammer down hard on the pig's head. The pig slumped silently.

"N-n-no!" Erich shouted.

He ran towards them swinging his school bag at Mr Evans and hitting him in the forehead. Mr Evans clasped his head, swearing, as Erich raised the bag to swing again. Before he could swing it Daddy Davy grabbed his arm from behind and held it. Erich looked back in surprise.

"L-L-Let me go! I-I-I d-d-don't let him!" he shouted, furiously.

"Stop that this instant!" Daddy Davy commanded.

He dragged Erich away and held the struggling boy. Erich screamed and cried, still fighting to get loose.

"Erich, stop that! Ye know the pig was fattened for our meat this winter."

"D-D-Don't kill him!" Erich sobbed.

"God gave us animals for food. That's the way He intended it to be," Daddy Davy said.

"No! I d-d-don't let him!" Erich shouted.

"Now stop that and apologise to Mr Evans."

Erich shook his head vigorously, still crying.

"If you won't apologise, I will have to punish you. Go to your room and I will deal with you later."

Erich knew he couldn't argue with Daddy Davy's tone of

voice. Mr Evans deftly cut the pig's throat and Erich heard its
blood pouring into the bucket as he headed into the house. Sobs
shook him as he climbed the stairs.

He sat on his bed listening to the voices outside. Half an hour
later he heard footsteps on the stairs. Daddy Davy came into the
room and stood over him.

"I know you didn't want the pig killed but it had to be done.
That's how we have meat for our dinner. I know you were upset
but you can't hit people," Daddy Davy said.

Erich looked at him mutely. As he spoke Daddy Davy looked
at Erich's head.

"What happened to your hair, Erich?" he asked.

"It got burned," he replied. He had forgotten his charred hair
in his despair at the pig's slaughter.

"How did that happen?"

"We had a fire in the playground."

"Did Mrs Baird allow that?"

"No," Erich said reluctantly, avoiding Daddy Davy's gaze.

"Then ye'll have to be punished for that, too. Stand up and
take your trousers down."

Slowly and miserably Erich complied. Daddy Davy gave him
several hard smacks.

"That'll help you to remember how you must behave. You'll
go and apologise to Mr Evans tonight. Now, come here." Daddy
Davy put his arm around Erich's shoulder and squeezed it.
"You've had your punishment and now we'll put it behind us."

Erich was still upset that the pig had been killed but he felt a
bit better as Daddy Davy hugged him. Daddy Davy wasn't angry
with him now. He knew he had deserved to be punished but it
was over and Daddy Davy still loved him.

Aunt Elsie slapped the ball of dough onto the kitchen table. She
bent over, leaning her weight on it as she rolled it out flat. As
Erich and Hans ran in the back door she stopped for a moment

to get her breath back.

"What kind of pie are you making?" Erich asked, watching her roll out the dough.

"Apple," she replied, still panting slightly.

"Good! Good!" Erich shouted.

The boys dropped their school books and hovered near the table.

"When will it be ready?" Erich asked.

"For tea tonight. Uncle Jim and Aunt Marjorie are coming round," she replied.

Aunt Elsie continued to roll the dough out, then lifted it into the pie tin beside her. She peeled and cut apples, dropping them into the tin. The boys grabbed a few peelings, as they fell to the table, and sucked them into their mouths like spaghetti. When the pie tin was full of apples, Aunt Elsie went to the dresser and reached down a paper bag and a tin full of coins. She opened the bag and pulled out several rings and other trinkets. She dropped them into the pie, then sprinkled a few coins in it too. Erich watched, fascinated, as she put the shiny coins and rings into the pie. She rolled out the other half of the dough and set it on top of the pie.

"Why you put them in pie?" Erich asked.

"It's Halloween. We always do that. When Uncle Jim, Aunt Marjorie and Bobby come round we'll play games too," she replied.

She set the pie into the oven and started to prepare the tea.

After a few minutes Erich asked, "Is pie ready yet?"

"No, not for a wee while," she replied.

Erich thought of the coins Aunt Elsie put into it. He wanted to get a piece with a coin in it. He'd be rich and he wouldn't have to give it back like the half crown he took from Miller's shop. I want the pie now! he thought, excitedly.

The time passed slowly until Aunt Elsie took it out of the oven and set it on the dresser. Erich eyed the pie. He couldn't wait until Aunt Elsie cut it. He kept watch out the window, eager for their visitors to arrive.

It was getting dark when they arrived. Bobby sat down beside Erich and Hans on the bench under the window. Erich pushed against Hans to get more room as the three of them squeezed together.

"Good evening. Is everyone well?" Uncle Jim said with a hint of an English accent.

Uncle Jim and Aunt Marjorie were Aunt Elsie's nephew and niece. The brother and sister were raised in England and neither of them had lost their distinctive accent. Uncle Jim had returned to run the family farm in Ireland just before the Second World War. Aunt Marjorie's husband was killed during the war and she returned with her son, Bobby, to live with her brother after the war ended. Thin and fair-haired, Aunt Marjorie had a strong resemblance to the Elliotts' daughter, Rose.

Uncle Jim went to sit at the fire with Daddy Davy while Aunt Marjorie helped Aunt Elsie set out food for the tea. Aunt Elsie dished bacon and boxty, a traditional potato dish, onto their plates.

"Not a bad price for cattle this year," Uncle Jim said to Daddy Davy.

"Indeed it's not," he replied. The men chatted about the state of farming until Aunt Elsie called them for tea.

The dishes were passed around and conversation lulled as they tucked into the meal. The greasy taste of the bacon and boxty warmed them on the chilly night. Throughout the meal Erich eyed the pie on the dresser.

"Can we have some pie?" Erich asked Aunt Elsie as soon as everyone was finished.

"In a wee while. First ye can have a go at ducking for apples," she replied.

Daddy Davy brought in a bucket filled with water and dropped several apples into it. The boys took turns, hands behind their backs, trying to grasp the apples in their teeth. Erich opened his mouth as wide as he could but the apple kept slipping away from him. Hans almost got one but it slid out of his mouth. Daddy Davy laughed watching them.

"Come on, lads!" he shouted.

Bobby leaned over and plunged his head under the water, surfacing with an apple hanging from his mouth.

"Good lad!" Aunt Elsie called. She reached in the tin on the dresser and, pulling out a farthing, handed it to him.

Then Daddy Davy tied an apple to a string and held it aloft. Erich and Hans took turns trying to take a bite from it. Erich got the biggest bite and was rewarded with a farthing from the tin. He smirked at Hans as he pocketed the coin.

"Sure, you got a bite from it too, Hans. You deserve a reward," Aunt Elsie said, seeing his forlorn expression. His face lit up as she handed him a coin. The boys happily pocketed their prizes, mentally calculating what they could buy at the shop the next day.

When another pot of tea was brewed and ready to pour Aunt Elsie took the pie down from the dresser. She cut generous slices as Aunt Marjorie poured the tea. Erich used his fork like a pick-axe, as if digging for gold, to explore his slice until he uncovered a coin lying flat under a stewed apple. He pulled it out and held it up, triumphantly. Hans pulled a ring from his and smiled wanly. Bobby also found a coin and whooped as he pulled it out. Erich adjusted his mental calculation and smiled. He would definitely get a chocolate bar tomorrow.

When there was only an empty pie tin left everyone left the table and settled down around the fire. The wind whistled outside, rattling at the kitchen window and drawing the boys' eyes towards the sound.

"Do you hear the voices, lads?" Uncle Jim asked.

The boys looked at him, puzzled. He held their gaze, saying nothing.

"What voices?" Erich asked.

"It's Halloween, lads. You never know what walks the earth this night. It's the one night the dead don't rest. If you listen very hard you might hear them," he replied.

The boys sat silently, straining to hear anything above the noise of the wind. Erich wondered if his mother's voice was among the others.

6

HITLER AND MARS BARS
Winter 1948

"ERICH, GET your coat. We've to leave now or you'll miss the bus," Daddy Davy called up the stairs.

"Can I go too?" Hans asked.

"You'll get your turn another time," Daddy Davy replied.

Daddy Davy took Erich in the pony and trap to meet the bus. He flagged it down as it rounded the bend and Erich climbed on, carrying the sandwiches which Aunt Elsie had packed for him. This was the first time Erich had travelled alone and he was excited and apprehensive. From the bus's window the sheep and cows in the fields looked much like the ones at home but the towns and villages caught Erich's attention. Each was slightly different. He rarely went to any place larger than the local village so the shops and people moving about the streets were fascinating. What are they doing? Where are they going? he wondered. But despite his curiosity, after the first few villages his attention began to wander. The bus stopped frequently and Erich began to get impatient at the slow journey. He opened the bag of sandwiches and ate one, staring out of the window as the bus rolled along to Dublin.

When they finally arrived at the city centre bus station Erich was glad to get off the bus. Standing in the large, open building he felt very small. People were hurrying around him, shouting and waving at family and friends. He frowned, watching the hoards of people. Everyone seemed to know where they were going. Daddy Davy told him that Auntie Lizzie would meet him at the bus. But I don't know what she looks like, he thought, suddenly worried. And he couldn't see past the mass of people. Where should I go? How will she find me, he wondered anxiously.

A young woman, with dark, wavy hair walked confidently up to him. He saw a small red cross on her lapel pin as she leaned over and smiled.

"You must be Erich," she said.

Erich nodded.

"I'm Auntie Lizzie," she said.

"Hello," he replied.

"You're a grand lad to get here on the bus by yourself. I'm sure you'll enjoy your visit to Dublin. I think we'll go to the airport first. Would you like to see the airplanes?" she asked.

"Yes! Oh, y-y-yes p-p-please!" Erich shouted.

They left the bus station, skirting around the man hawking newspapers at the front door, and walked up the crowded street. Erich stayed close to Auntie Lizzie. On O'Connell Street she pointed out a huge monument in the middle of the avenue.

"Isn't that a grand big pillar? That's Admiral Nelson's statue. People walk to the top of it and they can see for miles," she said.

"C-C-Can we go up?" Erich asked.

"We won't have time today if we're going to the airport. But maybe tomorrow morning," she replied.

They caught a bus to the airport. Erich held tightly to the handrail as he climbed the curving stairs to the upper deck. In her navy coat and flat shoes Auntie Lizzie followed him nimbly up the stairs. The bus flew along the street, turning corners without slowing. It seemed as if it might topple over. From their seat on the upper deck, near the front window, Erich excitedly watched the city fly past.

"I-I-It's brilliant!" he said. It's better even than riding in the trap, he thought. It's much higher. I can see everything!

"Well, I think you'll be even more amazed by the airplanes," Auntie Lizzie laughed.

When they got to the airport she led him through the terminal building and up the stairs to the observation deck. Erich ran to the rail and hung over it, looking at three airplanes sitting on the tarmac. He studied the brightly-coloured logo on the tail of each, wondering where they were from. Before he could ask Auntie Lizzie, one of the airplanes slowly backed up and turned, pulling away from the metal stairs attached to its front door. The stairs sat on the tarmac as if they were the remnants of a building which had vanished. The plane rolled slowly away from the terminal building and stopped at the first runway. It sat for a few minutes, poised, then its engines roared to life and it trundled down the runway, gaining speed until it lifted off the ground. As it slowly rose into the sky Erich stood, mouth agape, watching it.

"L-l-look!" Erich cried, pointing at the airplane.

"Yes, isn't it exciting?" Auntie Lizzie replied, smiling at his wonderment.

When the airplane had disappeared from sight and nothing else appeared to be ready to move, they went to the cafeteria. Erich chose a bun overflowing with cream and a lemonade. The cream smeared across his face as he took a large bite from the bun.

"Did you like that?" she asked.

"Y-Y Yes! Did you see the airplane g-g-going up and up!" Erich exclaimed.

"I did," Auntie Lizzie smiled.

Erich chattered on about the airplane. When he stopped for a moment, Auntie Lizzie asked, "How do you like where you live?"

"It's great! We've lots of animals. I can ride Paddy the pony. He's very friendly and eats apples from my hand. Paddy the donkey isn't very nice. I always stay away from him and Gipsy is my dog," he replied.

"Do you like Daddy Davy and Aunt Elsie?" she asked.

"Yes, Daddy Davy is the best daddy. Aunt Elsie is almost like *Mutti*," Erich replied, remembering his mother. No one could take her place. He loved Aunt Elsie but she wasn't quite the same as *Mutti*.

"You've lived with the Elliotts almost a year now. I'm glad you're happier than you were in Bray." Auntie Lizzie noted how his face lit up when he talked about his pets and his foster parents. She would be able to report that this foster placement was much more successful than the last one had been. He now had a suitable long term placement.

"Before we leave we can see if there are any airplanes ready to take off," she said. Erich frowned at the thought of leaving the airport. He loved the airplanes. Seeing his expression, Auntie Lizzie smiled. "I think we'll find more exciting things to do before you go home tomorrow," she said.

Erich slurped the last of his lemonade, eager to see the airplanes again. They went upstairs and stood on the observation deck. In the growing dusk they saw a large airplane lit up and rolling towards the runway. Erich followed its lumbering progress until it was in the air and vanished from sight. He shivered in the chilly evening air.

"It's getting a bit nippy now, Erich. Let's go and get our tea," Auntie Lizzie said.

Erich followed Auntie Lizzie back to the bus stop. They didn't have to wait long for a bus. Like a seasoned veteran Erich trooped onto the bus and up the stairs. From his perch in the front seat he watched the brightly lit streets pass by. He'd never seen so many lights anywhere. He stared out the window in amazement. Every street was lit. It was like Christmas.

"This is our stop, Erich," Auntie Lizzie nudged him as she stood up.

Erich followed her, his mind overflowing. Images of everything he'd seen during the afternoon flitted through his head and he barely noticed the walk from the bus to Auntie Lizzie's flat.

For the rest of the evening all he could talk about was the airplanes and the bus trip back to the city.

"Well, tomorrow we've another treat," Auntie Lizzie said. "We'll go up Nelson's Pillar." Erich cheered at this news. "But now it's time for you to get some sleep."

Erich happily climbed into bed and allowed Auntie Lizzie to tuck him in. He would have liked Aunt Elsie to be here to tuck him in but he would see her tomorrow night. He settled contentedly into the bed, thinking about the next day.

In the morning Erich hurriedly ate his breakfast, eager to be off. He skipped down the street beside Auntie Lizzie, dodging passersby and staying close to her. When they reached Nelson's Pillar Erich craned his head back to look up at it.

"It's very tall, isn't it?" Auntie Lizzie said.

"Y-y-yes!" Erich exclaimed. "Let's go to the top! How do we get there?"

"We'll climb the stairs inside it." Erich raced towards the stairs. "Wait for me," Auntie Lizzie called. Erich halted until she caught up with him. She handed him pennies for the entrance fee before he darted off. He ran up a few stairs and then waited for her to catch up to him before he charged off again. Auntie Lizzie was puffing when they reached the top. Erich stood on his tiptoes; he darted glances in one direction then another so quickly that Auntie Lizzie could barely answer all his questions about what he saw below them.

"It's a big city!" Erich exclaimed. "There's so much to see. It would take days and days."

"It would indeed."

"But I don't want to stay here too long. I'd miss Daddy Davy, Auntie Elsie and Gipsy."

"Well, you'll be going home to see them today. You can come to visit Dublin again another time," she reassured him.

"That's good," Erich said relieved. Dublin was exciting but he was eager to get home.

Erich and Hans walked quickly along the road. It was chilly and the frost was lying on the fields. Erich puffed, watching his breath spurt out of his mouth. Bobby, with his hands stuffed down in his pockets, ran up behind them.

"Hi ya," he said.

"Hi ya," they replied.

"It's cold the day. You wouldn't go barefoot this weather," Bobby said.

"I would!" Erich declared.

Bobby laughed. "You're only codding. Ye wouldn't do it," he said.

"Y-y-yes I would!" Erich asserted.

"I dare ye then!" Bobby said.

"I-I-I w-w-ill!" he replied.

Erich's impulsive nature was spurred by the dare; he couldn't refuse it. He quickly unlaced his sturdy leather shoes, took off his socks and tucked them inside the shoes, then hid them in a gap in the hedge. The ground felt cold under his feet but he strode boldly along the uneven surface of the road. His soles were tough from months of rambling barefoot in summer so the rough ground didn't hurt his feet, but the cold seeped in, making them ache. Erich kept walking, ignoring the creeping numbness. Other children they passed stared and pointed when they noticed his bare feet.

By the time he got to school he could not feel his bluish-tinged feet at all. When Mrs Baird rang the hand bell, he stumbled into the classroom and down the aisle to his seat. She stared at his feet as he walked to his desk, limping.

"Where're your shoes, ye silly boy?" she asked. All the children regularly went barefoot in summer to spare the expense of shoes but she knew that every family found the money for shoes or boots in winter.

Shivering, Erich shrugged. "I l-l-lost them."

"D'ye think I'm daft? You don't just lose your shoes on the way to school. Maybe the dog ate them?" she enquired wryly.

"He'd not do that!" Erich exclaimed.

The rest of the class tittered. Erich sat shivering; Hans stared at the scraped wooden floor, avoiding the teacher's gaze. A young girl raised her hand tentatively.

"I heard him tell Lucy they dared him, ma'am," she piped up.

Mrs Baird didn't need to ask who "they" were. She turned her attention to Hans and Bobby.

"Did you dare him to do it?" she asked Bobby, knowing he was the likely instigator. Hans tried to sink into his desk to avoid her stare.

Bobby sat silent for a minute but finally, under her unwavering scrutiny, nodded.

"Do you know where his shoes are?" she asked Bobby. He nodded again.

"Well, you'd best scoot off and get them. And be quick about it," she ordered.

Bobby scurried out of the classroom throwing a glance at Hans who kept his eyes fixed on the floor. Mrs Baird regarded Erich, huddled in his seat, and sighed.

"Sit you up by the stove and warm yersel'. You're foundered and you'll catch your death of cold like that."

Erich pulled a chair over to the stove and sat down, shivering as the heat penetrated his jumper. Mrs Baird poured him a cup of strong, sweet tea from her flask.

"Put these on and put your feet up to the stove," she instructed him, handing him a pair of mittens from her bag. Erich sat with his feet in the red mittens, propped up against the stove. A few of his classmates pointed and tittered.

"Hush now," Mrs Baird said, looking sternly around the classroom.

Despite her exasperation Mrs Baird treated him kindly. She knew Erich could be impulsive and sometimes did things without thinking but he was a good child who had had a tough life so far.

"Sit you there and your feet will be warm in no time," she said.

Erich detected the motherly tone in her voice and warmed to it. He missed *Mutti* and even with Auntie Elsie's love he still craved and latched on to any special attention or concern shown to him. He sat happily unembarrassed, feet up by the stove in the pair of red mittens. He didn't mind what the other children thought. Mrs Baird is worried about me, he realised, comforted by the thought.

"I told you I could walk barefoot all the way!" Erich said to Bobby on the walk home from school. "You had to get my shoes!" Erich laughed.

"Well, you had to sit with mittens on your feet!" Bobby sneered and Hans nodded agreement.

"I don't care!" Erich retorted.

The boys continued to bicker as they passed the track to Derrykeane. They continued along the lane to Uncle Jim's thatched cottage. Inside Uncle Jim sat at the kitchen table engrossed in a newspaper. Always curious about the world around him, after several years back in Ireland he still avidly read a variety of English and Irish newspapers each week.

"Hello, lads!" he said as they entered the room. Bobby and Hans shouted hello, grabbed two apples sitting in a bowl on the dresser and disappeared outside again.

Erich came closer, peering at the Irish Times laid out on the table in front of Uncle Jim. He leaned against the table and bent over the page, peering at it intently, fascinated by the large sheet of paper covered with words. Erich had made good progress learning English since he had arrived in Ireland not understanding a word of it. But he still needed some help with his reading. Uncle Jim enjoyed reading and had the patience to help him make sense of the words on the page.

"What that say?" Erich asked, pointing to a word.

"Palace. That's where the King lives - across the water where I used to live, laddie," he answered, the distinctive English accent becoming slightly stronger.

"Did you live in a palace?" Erich asked.

"No, lad. Nothing as grand as that," Uncle Jim laughed.

Erich skipped from one word to another on the page and Uncle Jim patiently explained the meaning of each one. Erich repeated them to himself to help file them in his memory.

Spring 1949

"Does God have reason for everything?" Erich asked, walking solemnly beside Daddy Davy, Aunt Elsie and Hans.

"Indeed he does," Daddy Davy replied.

"I don't know why he do some things."

"Well, we don't always understand his reasons."

Erich thought about this, amazed that Daddy Davy always knew the answer to everything. He thought of the tadpoles he had seen swimming in the shallow pool beside the road yesterday.

"Why do frogs start like fish? They should just start as frogs," Erich asked.

"That's the way God made them. They grow into what they are meant to be. You change as you grow, don't you? Every creature becomes what it is meant to be," Daddy Davy said.

Erich's usual chattering stopped as he thought about this. Then he nodded, satisfied. He walked on silently, lost in his own thoughts. Sunday morning had a special feel. God must be watching us, Erich thought. A soft rain fell but he barely noticed it.

"Can we sit in the gallery?" Erich asked a few minutes later.

"You can. But you must behave. Sit quietly and no messing," Daddy Davy replied.

As they walked up the short path to the church's heavy oak

door Daddy Davy handed each of the boys tuppence for the collection. Erich put his coin in his pocket; Hans clutched his tightly. A few men loitered at the door, chatting. Strains of a hymn playing on the pipe organ echoed out of the open door. Willy Graham, standing amongst the men, spotted them as they approached and nodded.

"These boyos are very quiet the day. Are ye sure the fairies haven't switched them?" he asked Daddy Davy, winking at the boys. The boys giggled, sneaking a glance at Daddy Davy.

"They know to mind themselves," Daddy Davy replied. "Now, off ye go and heed what I'm after tellin' youse," he added to the boys.

Erich and Hans went inside and climbed the stairs to the gallery. They headed straight to the front row and sat down. Erich loved to look out over the whole church from here. He leaned over the rail to look at the ground floor. Most of the pews were full. Families sat together; children fidgeting beside their parents. There were fewer people in the gallery.

Willy and a couple of other single men in their twenties came down the aisle and slid in next to Erich and Hans. Willy spotted a woman in the middle of a ground floor pew wearing an enormous yellow hat trimmed with gaily-coloured flowers.

Leaning over to Erich he whispered, "I think there's birds nesting in yon hat. Do ye see them?"

Erich's intention to heed Daddy Davy and be well behaved were destroyed. He doubled over giggling. Hans nudged him, asking what Willy had said. Erich repeated it to Hans and he also choked with laughter. Willy put his finger to his lips, nodding towards the pulpit as Reverend Downey climbed the steps into it.

The service began and the boys quietened. The organ's massive pipes lined the back wall. They reverberated through the boys when the first hymn began. Looking down at the ground floor they continued to observe people below them, whispering comments. A thin, hawk-nosed woman and her portly husband, hear-

ing them, twisted around and frowned up at the gallery. Willy
nudged the boys and shook his head. Erich glanced quickly at
the back of Daddy Davy's head below to be sure he hadn't heard
them. Seeing no reaction from Daddy Davy Erich was silent for a
couple minutes then continued to whisper and giggle with Hans,
stopping when anyone looked up at them.

The church warden and his assistant came into the gallery to
collect the offering. Standing at each end of the front pew, they
passed the wooden offering plate along it. Erich reached into his
pocket and pulled out the coin Daddy Davy had given him. Willy
glanced at it, then leaned over and whispered in Erich's ear.

"Ye can take change from the collection plate when you put
that in. Then ye'll have some money for sweets tomorrow," he
said.

"But Daddy Davy will be cross," Erich replied.

"Sure, what's the harm. Why would he be cross?"

Erich smiled, glad that Willy had given him such a great idea.
There was no harm in taking change from the offering plate.
When it reached him, he dropped his tuppence into it and rooted
around for a penny change. He took it out and put it in his pocket
before passing the plate to Hans. Willy suppressed a grin, nudging the man sitting beside him who also grinned. The warden's
grave face remained impassive, only his eyes widened. Hans
dropped his tuppence into the plate and passed it on.

"Why did you put all the money in?" Erich whispered to him.

"Daddy Davy will be cross if I don't," Hans said.

"No, he won't. Willy said it would do no harm," Erich
replied.

They rose to sing the next hymn. Erich sang loudly, enjoying
the organ booming behind them. When the hymn ended he sat
quietly for a few minutes, thinking about the sweets he would
buy in the morning. The sermon began; the church became very
quiet. Rustlings and coughs were suppressed. The young men
sitting with Willy shifted gingerly, leaning forward slightly to
glance furtively at young women sitting in pews below. One of

them winked at Hans and motioned to him to pinch Erich. Hans hesitated, then, encouraged by more winks and grins, he pinched Erich's leg. Erich glared at him, poking him sharply with his elbow. Hans glanced out of the corner of his eye at the young man who encouraged him to try again. Hans pinched Erich harder. Erich turned and pushed Hans. The boys shoved back and forth in the seat, knocking against Willy. He watched amused until he noticed disapproving stares from surrounding pews. Then he grabbed Erich's arm and held him away from Hans, shaking his head. Erich glared angrily at Hans but held still.

When the service ended the boys filed out behind Willy and his friends. Erich, still annoyed with Hans, shoved his brother. Hans shoved him back. A man behind them grasped Hans's shoulder.

"That's enough now, lads," he said.

Hans glared at Erich but continued down the stairs. Outside the church Daddy Davy and Aunt Elsie were waiting for them.

"Did you behave yourselves?" he asked when he saw the boys.

"Ye wouldn't have known they were there," Willy replied before the boys could speak, flashing a smile at them. He ruffled Erich's hair and wandered away.

"I heard some noise from the gallery. I hope it wasn't the two of you," Daddy Davy said. The boys avoided his gaze.

"There's another thing - I've had a word with the church warden just now. Erich, did you take money from the collection plate?" Daddy Davy asked.

"Willy said it would do no harm," Erich replied confidently. "To buy more sweeties tomorrow."

"Did he now? Well, you don't take money from the plate. Just put your offering in. I thought you would know better than that and he certainly should. Give me the money and you can put it in the plate next week."

Daddy Davy looked at Aunt Elsie. "I know he's your nephew but what sort of example does Willy set as a godparent? Maybe he was a poor choice," he said.

"Ye know what a kidder Willy is. I'm sure he didn't mean any harm. And he is right fond of the boys," she replied.

Erich stared at the ground, thinking of the extra sweets he wouldn't be able to buy tomorrow. Hans smirked at him and Erich, catching the look, scowled back.

On his way to school the next day Erich hunched into his coat to keep the lashing rain off, nipping into the post office as a heavy shower started. Water dripped onto the floor as he shook himself. He still had a little of his pocket money left. Though I'd have had more if I'd kept the change from the collection plate, he thought wistfully. He eyed the gobstoppers in a clear jar on the counter, then his gaze strayed to the chocolate bars on the rack beside the till. Gobstoppers were good value as the large, round sweets could be savoured and sucked slowly whereas chocolate would melt quickly and richly in his mouth. It's a difficult choice, he thought. He stared at the Mars bars, then lifted one from the rack. Erich loved chocolate and it was too tempting to resist. After handing over his money to Mrs Henderson he stuffed it into his lunch bag and continued to school, oblivious of the rain as he daydreamed about the smooth, rich chocolate.

Entering the schoolhouse he hung his dripping coat in the cloakroom and went to his seat. Around him his classmates sat with lank, dripping hair and steaming clothes. Boys without coats, only suit jackets, sat in their sodden jackets. Mrs Baird followed the last child into the room and went to the blackboard. Picking up the chalk, she wrote arithmetic equations in several columns across the board, each subsequent column more difficult than the last. She instructed the children to copy down the appropriate equations, for their year, and begin to solve them.

Erich copied the equations in the second column and set to work. Shuffling, fidgeting and coughing ceased as the children concentrated. Mrs Baird strode up and down the aisles checking their work. As Erich studied the equations, he thought about his Mars bar tucked in his lunch bag. He bent to look inside his desk and peeked into the bag. Hearing the rustle, Mrs Baird looked across the room. Erich hastily withdrew his head from his desk and continued working.

A scraping noise drew his attention to the window. The postman leaned his black-framed bicycle against the wall and sprinted to the door. It banged behind him as he entered the class, water dripping off the flap of his postbag.

"Good day, Mrs Baird," he said, brushing the water from the top of it.

"Good day to ye, Mr Mulligan," she replied, looking up from a senior girl's exercise book.

"It's a terrible day, sure," he said.

"Indeed it is," she replied.

"I'll leave these letters wi' the children to bring home so, if ye don't mind," he said.

"That's no bother," she replied.

The postman took several letters from his bag. The children watched him eagerly. Most families didn't receive much mail, so the arrival of a letter was always exciting. Erich watched hopefully. Maybe there would be a letter from Germany. Tante Trude or Tante Gretchen might write to him. He'd like to hear from them. They remembered *Mutti*. Sorting through the letters the postman dropped envelopes on several desks around the room but he walked by Erich's desk without stopping. When he was finished he pulled the flap down over his bag and gave a cheery wave on his way out, pleased that he would only have a few stops to make in the village before he could get out of the rain. Erich watched until he was out of sight, hoping he might find a forgotten letter for him. But the postman didn't turn back.

Erich peered into his desk and his lunch bag again. His eyes sought the Mars bar beside his thick-cut cheese sandwich. Seeing the wrapper made his mouth water. A glance at the clock behind the teacher's desk told him that break time wasn't for half an hour, but he was getting hungry. Erich tried to concentrate on his equations but couldn't resist lifting his desk lid for one more peek. The Mars bar was so tempting; he wanted it. He reached into the bag, pulled it out and surreptitiously unwrapped it inside the desk, glancing around to be sure Mrs Baird was still across the room. He leaned into the desk and quickly bit into it. As he chewed the chocolate and it melted in his mouth he forgot about Mrs Baird. But as he took a second bite of the juicy chocolate her voice shattered his enjoyment.

"Erich, will you put that away! You have every mouth in this class watering!"

Still chewing, Erich glanced uneasily around the classroom. Every pair of eyes was enviously following the progress of his Mars bar. Despite Ireland's neutrality during the Second World War, the economy had suffered and money was not plentiful, especially in farming communities, in the years after the war. Erich and Hans were fortunate to have regular pocket money to buy sweets. But many of Erich's classmates, especially those from large families, considered a Mars bar a rare treat. Reluctantly he folded the wrapper over the bar and put it away.

Erich went back to his sums, frequently glancing at the clock as it ticked slowly towards break time. When Mrs Baird finally dismissed them Erich grabbed his Mars bar and raced into the playground. He ignored taunts from a couple boys as he devoured the chocolate in a few mouthfuls.

After the break Erich returned to his seat with chocolate smeared lips. Mrs Baird shook her head, smiling slightly. Erich could be outspoken and often irrepressible but he never meant any harm. She sometimes had to laugh at his antics.

"Children, open your reading books," she said.

Clattering and banging, the children reached inside their desks for the books.

"Sarah, you may begin," Mrs Baird said to a tall, dark-haired girl in a navy-blue sweater. Sarah read aloud as the rest of the class listened.

She was interrupted by a loud knock at the door. Mrs Baird motioned for Sarah to stop as she went to answer it. Her strong voice mingled briefly with a deep, authoritative one, then she reappeared with the local policeman behind her. He looked around the classroom. The children sat, all faces peering at him, in awe of the uniformed figure. While he was a familiar figure in the village, the children were still intimidated by the tall, uniformed police officer.

"Good morning, children. I'm inspecting the roll today," he announced.

The officer flicked through the pages for several minutes as the class watched him silently. The Gardai regularly inspected the attendance records at the national schools.

In a rural area, with a low crime rate, they had time to take an interest in community activities and institutions.

"Bobby Crawford, Hans Schnell, Erich Schnell, where are ye?" he asked.

The three boys stood up. Hans tensed apprehensively under the police officer's scrutiny.

"Ye had several absences in February. Now why is that?" he asked.

"It was a bad winter, sir," Bobby replied.

"Was it so bad ye could not come to school?" the officer asked.

Disliking the censure in his tone, Erich said impulsively, before Bobby could reply, "I not have to! I get Hitler after you!"

"You do have to come to school and Hitler is dead," the officer replied in a tone that signalled there would be no discussion.

"No, he isn't and I'll tell him!" Erich, unrepentant at his outburst, stubbornly insisted.

Too young to understand the political events occurring when he left Germany, Hitler was a name Erich had heard adults discuss in hushed tones. All he knew was that Hitler was a powerful German so invoking his name seemed a good tactic to combat the policeman's challenge.

The officer looked at Erich's serious face, suddenly amused by the determination and guileless innocence of the earnest eight year old. He obviously doesn't know who Hitler was, Garda Doyle thought. He liked the boy's plucky nature.

"Erich, you will not speak to Garda Doyle like that!" Mrs Baird scolded him.

Suppressing a smile, Garda Doyle said, "Well, I'll forget the matter as long as ye don't miss any more school."

Bobby and Hans nodded meekly as Erich glared at the officer, before reluctantly nodding too. Garda Doyle thanked Mrs Baird and left. Erich, chin jutted out and teeth clenched, watched through the window as he cycled away.

Big men in uniforms always tell you what to do. Just like the soldiers in the forest. One day I will be big enough to stand up to all of them, Erich thought mutinously.

After school the three boys walked home together, meandering from one village shop to the next. Once out of the village they peered into the hedges, looking for birds' nests abandoned by their occupants last summer. The rain had abated, leaving a grey, overcast sky.

"Garda Doyle could've put you in jail," Hans said to Erich.

"I'm not afraid of him. He c-c-couldn't c-c-catch me!" Erich replied defiantly, squinting into the ditch, looking for frogspawn.

"He could if he wanted to," Bobby said.

"He could put you in jail," Hans insisted.

"He couldn't. I'd poke a hole in his tyre," Erich replied.

After this final profession of bravado, Erich lifted a branch lying at the side of the road and dragged it behind him, making squiggles in the mucky road.

When they reached Millers' shop Erich, having spent the last of his pocket money on the Mars bar, waited outside as Bobby and Hans went in. He wandered around the building, kicking at stones on the ground and glancing around idly. Tiring of that, he spotted the byre door open and went inside. One end was piled high with hay and straw. Maybe I'll climb up and jump down on it, he thought, glancing up at the crossbeam. As the light from the open door shone across it something glinted. He went over to look. A wooden handled knife with a gleaming silver blade lay on the crossbeam. He lifted it and looked more closely. The shiny blade, with a small crown and hand stamped on it, was cool to his touch. The smooth beech handle curved neatly into his small hand. He pushed the top edge and the blade folded into the wooden handle. He pulled it out again, fascinated. He hadn't seen a knife like this before. Maybe the crown on it meant it belongs to a king, Erich thought. Uncle Jim said the King lived in England. Why would he leave it here? Erich reached out to set it back on the beam but held it up to look at once more. No one must want it if it's sitting in the byre, Erich told himself. Maybe he could borrow it and bring it back in a few days. No one would miss it. He looked at it once more then slipped it into his coat pocket.

Erich heard the other boys coming out of the shop and went around to meet them. They walked on without speaking, Bobby and Hans sucking noisily on gobstoppers. Erich eyed them enviously. Bobby, chewing the last of his gobstopper, mumbled goodbye as he left them at the track to Derrykeane.

"Don't tell Daddy Davy about Garda Doyle," Erich ordered Hans.

"I wasn't going to tell him," Hans replied irritably.

Gipsy raced towards them, barking wildly. They raced him to the house. Before going inside Erich slipped into the byre. He could hear Daddy Davy moving around in the stable next door. He won't come in here before tea, Erich thought, as he flipped the knife open and closed once more before setting it on the ledge where the wall met the tin roof. He was sure Daddy Davy wouldn't see it there until he had time to think of somewhere to hide it. He would only keep it for a few days then he'd return it. Erich took a last look at it and went into the house.

The boys sat by the fire as Aunt Elsie set out the plates and cutlery for tea. The potatoes boiling in the pot in front of them made Erich's mouth water. His stomach rumbled.

"When's tea ready, Aunt Elsie?" he asked.

"Just a wee while now. We'll have it when himself comes in," she replied.

As she spoke the kitchen door opened. Daddy Davy came in, his gaze fixed on the boys. He had something folded in his palm.

"Whose is this?" he asked, holding up the knife.

Erich stared at the knife, startled that Daddy Davy had found it. He knew Daddy Davy would be annoyed if he discovered Erich had taken it, even though it seemed to be unwanted and he intended to return it.

"Is it yours, Erich?" Daddy Davy asked.

"No, n-n-not mine," he lied.

"Then it's yours, Hans?" he asked.

Hans shook his head, puzzled. Erich stared at the floor, trying to think, as panic engulfed him. He didn't want Daddy Davy to be cross with him.

"It is H-H-Hans's. I saw him t-t-take it from M-M-Millers' shop today," Erich said.

Hans looked at Erich, shocked and reproachful. Erich avoided his gaze, insisting he had seen his brother take it. Daddy Davy regarded them silently, waiting for Hans to confess. The boy sat there mutely, staring at the floor.

"You know it's wrong to steal, Hans. And I'm disappointed you'd lie about it afterwards. I'll have to punish ye. Come here and take your trousers down," Daddy Davy said sternly, pointing to the chair beside the fire.

Daddy Davy unbuckled his belt and waited as Hans walked over to him and pulled his trousers down. Hans bent over and braced himself against the chair as the belt hit his bare flesh, whimpering as the blows fell. Erich hoped Hans wouldn't say anything. Miserably Erich watched, fear and guilt mingled. He didn't want Daddy Davy to discover the truth and be angry with him. But he felt guilty that Hans was being punished for something he had done.

Afterwards Daddy Davy said, "I hope you've learned your lesson. It's wrong to steal. You'll have to take it back to Millers' and apologise."

Hans nodded mutely. When Daddy Davy left the fire and went to the kitchen table, he looked accusingly at Erich, who avoided his gaze. Nothing more was said about the knife that evening. Hans came to the kitchen table, sitting down gingerly to eat his tea.

❦

Summer 1949

Erich pressed his eye to the hole in the wall, staring into the other half of the hut. A tall, red-haired girl sat with her knickers around her ankles. He could see her smooth white legs and slim ankles. He caught a glimpse of her firm thighs as she stood up, holding her skirt aloft with one hand. He stared, wide-eyed, until Bobby pushed him out of the way.

"My turn," he whispered emphatically.

Erich, curiosity making him bold, tried to shove Bobby aside for another look. Hans craned his neck behind them, trying to catch a glimpse through the hole. A dark-haired boy, with a bowl-shaped haircut, came into the toilets.

"Ye'd better get back. Mrs Baird is asking after ye," he said.

Hearing the door open on the other side Erich tried again to push Bobby aside for a last look but Bobby used his greater height and weight to thwart Erich's attempt. Turning from the peephole they hurried from the toilets to rejoin the other children standing around Mrs Baird in the playground.

"Boys under ten stand at that end of the field," she instructed.

Games Day, held in the field beside the school, signalled the end of the school year. It was an exciting day for the children. Unchained from their desks after the long winter months, they were ready to dash about, unleashing their pent up energy. They threw themselves wholeheartedly into the games and races.

Erich, Hans and Bobby joined the other young boys standing in a row at the end of the field. Mrs Baird held up her hand and they bent forward, tensed, waiting.

"Ready, steady, go!" she shouted, swishing her hand downwards.

The boys raced across the field. Bobby gritted his teeth as he held his place in the leading group, while Hans's thin legs propelled him into the middle. Erich ran as fast as his short legs would carry him, arms pumping and panting, but fell to the back of the pack. They reached the other end of the field panting and puffing. Mrs Baird congratulated the blond boy who hurled himself across the finish line first.

The boys went to stand at the edge of the field, watching and cheering, as the older boys and girls had their turns.

Mrs Baird sent one of the older boys to get a thick, woven rope from the shed. She divided the children into two teams and the children took their places along the rope, pulling it taut. Bobby and Hans were on one side, near the middle of the team, and Erich, on the opposing team, was nearest the centre because of his small stature. Mrs Baird grasped the middle of the rope holding it steady.

"Ready, go!" she shouted, letting go of the red ribbon tied in the middle and stepping away from the rope.

Erich dug his bare heels into the ground, using all his strength to pull on the rope. The other team faced him only a few feet away. The rope strained back and forth as the children pulled with all their might. He was dragged back and forth. The bigger children behind him hauled the ribbon steadily towards them but a sharp tug from the other team pulled Erich back towards the mark in the dirt. He tried to back away from it but was dragged across, clinging to the rope. Lying in the dirt Erich saw Hans and Bobby cheering and jumping up and down with the rest of their team. Disappointed, he tried to ignore their glee. He let go of the rope and stood up, puffing and brushing the dirt from his knees.

His feet burned after being pulled through the dirt.

Mrs Baird instructed two of the older boys to set up the high jump rail at the side of the school building. Each child took a turn trying to jump it. The older, taller boys and girls had no trouble clearing the rail. Mrs Baird lowered it for the younger children. They ran determinedly, as fast as they could, jumping at the last second. Some were successful; others were not.

"Erich, your turn," Mrs Baird called.

Erich nodded, then turned and started climbing the scraggy hillock behind the high jump. He stopped halfway up and turned around.

"What's he at?" George asked another boy beside him.

"I haven't a notion," the boy replied.

"Will ye look at that!" George exclaimed.

Erich ran as fast as he could down the hill jumping over the rail at an angle just before he reached the bottom. This gave him a slight advantage and he managed to clear the bar. Despite being smaller than other boys his age, possibly due to the malnourishment he suffered in Germany during the war, he was not easily deterred and was always game to try.

"Well done, Erich!" Mrs Baird called, laughing. The boy never ceased to amaze her. He could be cheeky but he was a bright, resourceful boy. He just needed his impulsiveness curbed. She couldn't help liking him.

Erich grinned proudly, still puffing.

"That's it for today, children. Have a good summer holiday and I'll see you in September," Mrs Baird said in dismissal.

The children gathered their belongings and set off home, Erich, Hans and Bobby walking together. Getting used to bare feet again after the winter, they sometimes winced as they stepped on sharp stones. Erich dragged his toe through the dirt making designs in it. Not to be outdone Bobby drew a castle with his toe.

"Look at my castle," he said.

"I make a bigger one!" Erich exclaimed.

He started to draw beside Bobby's castle. Bobby swept his foot across it scratching out his tower. Erich shoved Bobby away from it and they tussled briefly.

Erich pulled free, shouting, "I can run faster than you!"

He ran off with Bobby in pursuit. Catching up with Erich he stuck his foot out to trip him. Erich stepped around it, laughing. Excited after Games Day, the boys ran off some of their energy on their way home.

They left Bobby, who continued along the lane, at the track to Derrykeane and raced along it followed by Gipsy, barking loudly.

As they ran into the kitchen Erich shouted, "I jumped the high jump!"

"We won the tug of war!" Hans cried.

"Well done, both of you!" Aunt Elsie said.

"No more school!" Erich shouted.

"Yes, you've summer holidays now," Aunt Elsie replied. "Isn't that grand?"

The boys could barely contain their excitement and, grabbing apples from the bowl on the dresser, rushed out to tell Daddy Davy about Games Day.

After tea the boys went out to the haggard. Erich threw a stick for Gipsy to fetch. Hans leaned against the wall, his hand balanced on it to steady himself.

"I hope ye're not causing any trouble!" a voice said behind them. Hans started. He glanced behind nervously but relaxed when he recognised the visitors.

Willy Graham entered the haggard, grinning. Behind him his brother, John, nodded to them. Giving Erich a cuff as he passed, Willy went in the back door. The boys followed them inside. Before a cup of tea could be brewed their neighbour, Jimmy Hall, arrived. Everyone squeezed into the kitchen. The adults talked about the weather and the progress of the crops; the boys listened.

"Are ye courting yet, Erich?" Willy asked, during the first lull in the conversation.

Erich shook his head. Willy looked around the room, gathering his audience in.

"I thought all the girls would be chasing after ye now. Ye must have seen at least one you fancy," he said. Erich blushed but said nothing. He remembered the red-haired girl in the toilet block and his face flamed brighter.

John frowned at Willy. "Don't tease the lad," he said. "He's too young to be taking an interest in girls."

"Well, if ye don't have a girlfriend, have ye taken up smoking?" Willy joked.

"Don't be encouraging him in any bad habits," John said stiffly to Willy.

"I just wondered if he had them already," Willy said with a wink to the boys.

"I think it's time the lads were in their bed before they learn any from you," Daddy Davy said mildly.

The boys groaned, not wanting to leave and miss anything. Daddy Davy motioned towards the stairs and the boys reluctantly said good night to everyone. As they entered their room Erich heard the chicks Aunt Elsie was rearing in the next room, scurrying and chirping, disturbed by the boys' footsteps. They changed into their nightshirts, quickly mumbled their prayers then quietly crept to the middle of the room. Kneeling on the rough floorboards they jostled against each other to get a good look through a small hole they had whittled in the floorboard. Through the hole they could see most of the kitchen. Willy was telling a joke and the boys giggled at the punch line. Daddy Davy looked towards the ceiling, shouting, "You lads should be in bed!"

The boys crept back quietly to sit on the bed, avoiding the floorboards they knew would creak.

Erich shouted, "We are in bed!"

They sat, holding their breath, until the conversation resumed downstairs. Creeping back to their hole, they lay flat on the floor peering through it, listening to the conversation and banter.

"Shouldn't you young lads be out courting on a lovely evening like this?" Daddy Davy asked John and Willy.

"And why would I do that now when I'm waiting for your beautiful daughters to come home for the summer? Meanwhile may I have a dance with your lovely wife?" Willy asked. He rose and extended his hand to Aunt Elsie. Pulling her up he swept her around the room in a silent waltz. Everyone laughed and clapped. Erich leaned closer to the hole, mouth open, breathing into it as he watched them swirl around the room. His breath dislodged a piece of dust hanging from the ceiling below. It landed on Daddy Davy's nose. Twitching his nose he brushed it away. Erich and Hans clasped their hands tightly over their mouths, stifling their laughter. They sat up, away from the hole, afraid that Daddy Davy would look up. But he didn't seem to notice anything amiss and they crept back. Resuming their positions they watched the ceilidh below. Aunt Elsie stood breathless, her face pale, when the waltz ended.

Daddy Davy stood up. Clasping his arm around her waist he said, "Now don't overdo it. Rest yoursel' a while now." Carefully he guided her back to her chair.

"Sorry, Elsie, I forgot about your heart. I didn't mean you to overdo it," Willy said, concerned.

"Don't worry, I'll be fine in a wee minute. I just need to get my breath back," Aunt Elsie said, puffing and pale. Erich wondered what Willy meant about Aunt Elsie's heart. She wasn't sick. He puzzled over it as the conversation continued below him.

As the evening wore on the boys became sleepy, yawning and their heads nodding. Erich lay his head flat on the floorboards, unable to keep his eyes open. The creeping cold woke him and he shivered in his thin nightshirt. He nudged Hans awake. Teeth chattering, they scurried over to the bed and climbed under their blankets. Erich pulled one corner of the blanket tightly around him. It stretched taut as the boys fought each other for a share of it. Wrapped tightly in the blankets and warmed by the weight of them, they sank swiftly into a deep sleep.

Erich set his basket down and climbed the ladder. The hens sometimes flew up and laid eggs on top of the haystack. Erich was determined to find every one. He poked in the hay looking for any eggs hiding in it. The ladder shifted slightly against the loose hay. Spotting a small, brown egg nesting under a light covering of hay he reached for it.

"Hiya. What're you doin'?" Bobby asked, walking into the barn. Hans followed behind him.

"Gettin' the eggs," Erich replied.

Bobby watched the ladder shift slightly as Erich reached into the hay.

"Mind, yon ladder's not steady," he said, laughing as he grabbed the nearest side and rattled it.

"Stop that!" Erich shouted, looking down at him.

"Don't let go now!" Bobby called, mischievously. Grinning, he shook the ladder slightly harder.

Erich gripped the top rung, shouting, "S-S-Stop, I said!"

Without thinking, Hans gleefully grabbed the other side and shook it, caught up in the excitement. Erich clung to the top rung, the eggs forgotten. A sharp jerk loosened Erich's grip and he fell to the ground, hitting his forehead on the sharp edge of a stone lying in the middle of the barn.

"Aaah, Erich!" Hans exclaimed, inhaling deeply, his eyes round.

Erich lifted his head, confused. Blurry-eyed, he looked down at blood splashing onto the dirt floor. Something warm and sticky ran down his face. Bobby and Hans stood wide-eyed, staring at the blood pouring from his head. The blood's mine, Erich realised. He opened his mouth to scream but no sound came out. His breath came in quick, shallow bursts; his face was frozen with fear. Fumbling, he pulled himself up, clasped his hand to his head and ran into the kitchen.

"I'm b-b-bleeding, I-I-I'm bleeding!" he shouted.

7

FAMILIES ARE FOREVER

"COME HERE till I see that," Aunt Elsie said to Erich as he charged into the kitchen. She set the last dinner plate on the worktop for Rose to dry.

Rose stood open-mouthed, gaping at the blood pouring down his face.

Aunt Elsie calmly lifted a cloth and wetting it, wiped his forehead. She drew him, his chin clasped in her hand, over to the window to look at it in the light. Blood flowed from a deep gash. Aunt Elsie wet and wrung out the cloth again, pressing it firmly to his head.

"Now, sit ye down by the fire until himself gets back. Keep the cloth pressed to it," she said as Erich reached up to touch the wound. She pressed his hand against the cloth, then went to make him a cup of strong, sweet tea. His head ached but the bleeding had stopped. He lay back in the chair. Bobby and Hans were nowhere to be seen.

"What happened to ye?" Aunt Elsie asked.

"I fell off the ladder in t' byre, gettin' the eggs," Erich replied. He didn't mention Bobby and Hans. He knew they hadn't meant to hurt him. He remembered the shock on Hans's face. Hans would not be malicious despite their rivalry for the Elliotts' affection.

"Mind yoursel' the next time. It's a long way down from that ladder," she admonished him.

Aunt Elsie took another look at Erich's head. When he moved

his eyebrows the two edges of the wound gaped apart, oozing blood.

"Daddy Davy will bring you to Dr Brown when he gets back from helping Mr Hall," she said.

"I don't need to go to Dr Brown. It's better now," Erich said, hunching down into the chair, fearfully.

"Well, I think we'll let him have a look at it so," she replied, ignoring his protest.

It was late afternoon when Daddy Davy arrived home. Hans trailed behind him and slipped in to sit silently by the fire, glancing anxiously at Erich's forehead.

"Ye're home so," Aunt Elsie said with a tired sigh, as he walked through the door. She was slightly grey but moved purposefully from the oven to the table preparing the tea. She wouldn't give in to her tiredness and let Rose do all the work.

"Aye, yon cow finally calved," he replied.

"I have the tea ready so. Then you may take Erich to Dr Brown," she said.

Daddy Davy looked at Erich.

"What ails ye, lad?" he asked, concern on his face.

Erich pointed to the gash on his forehead, saying, "I fell off the ladder and cut my head. But I don't need Dr Brown."

Daddy Davy came over and inspected Erich's forehead. Hans looked at the floor guiltily, trying not to draw attention to himself.

"So I see. That's a deep one," he said. "You've been a brave boy, waiting here this while. We'd best get Doctor Brown to look at it." Erich sat up a little straighter, pleased that Daddy Davy thought he was brave. He forgot for a moment that he would still need to go to the doctor.

After tea Daddy Davy got out his black-framed bicycle and set Erich, still asserting he did not need to see the doctor, on the seat. Standing in front of the seat, he pedalled vigorously along the bumpy track, jarring Erich's head. The ride became smoother when they reached the main road. It was a calm, clear night but

Erich, his head throbbing, was oblivious to the pleasant evening. The few miles to Cavan Town passed in an aching blur.

The streets of Cavan Town were empty; the shops were closed, only the pubs were open. A man with a bulbous, red nose and grey whiskers shuffled along the street followed by an old sheepdog, its head drooping. He stopped at the first pub he came to and went inside. The dog lay down at the door as if well accustomed to the routine. A couple of young men stood at the doorway of another pub further up the street, talking and smoking.

Daddy Davy dismounted and pushed the bicycle along the street, stopping at a black door. A wooden nameplate embossed with gold letters was attached to it. Doctor Brown's surgery was in a house refurbished for the purpose; he lived above the surgery. Daddy Davy rang the bell and waited. A middle-aged woman wearing a red apron answered the door.

"Hello," she said, patting the bun at the back of her head.

"We've come to see Doctor Brown. It's about the lad," Daddy Davy said.

"He's away out at the minute. I'm not sure how long he'll be. Is it urgent?" the woman asked.

Daddy Davy gestured towards Erich's head.

"He needs that seen to," Daddy Davy replied.

"Well, come in and wait for him so," she replied.

She led them down the wide hallway into a small room with straight-backed, wooden chairs lining three walls. They sat down in the corner. Erich's head hurt and he felt tired after the journey. He leaned against Daddy Davy's shoulder and fell into a doze. The evening crawled on but the doctor did not appear. Erich shifted restlessly on the chair, unable to sleep soundly while sitting upright. Daddy Davy flicked through a newspaper lying on the table in front of them. Eventually Erich slipped into a deep sleep, his head resting on Daddy Davy's knee.

After the pubs had closed and the sounds of the men making their way home had died away, the front door opened. It closed with a bang. Heavy footsteps strode along the hall. Lighter footsteps scurried down from above and a man's and a woman's voices could be heard in the hallway. A minute later a small, flabby man, his crumpled white shirt tail hanging out over his belt, entered the waiting room.

Adjusting his horn rimmed glasses and squinting at them he said, "Good evening, Mr Elliott. Come through please."

Daddy Davy shook Erich gently to wake him and led him down the hall into the next room. The doctor's mahogany desk sat in one corner. The brown paisley curtains were drawn behind it. A glass-fronted, white enamel cabinet stood on the opposite wall.

"Put the boy up there," Doctor Brown said, indicating an austere, black table in the middle of the room.

Daddy Davy lifted Erich onto the high table. The boy looked around the room sleepily as the doctor leaned over him, inspecting his forehead. A sharp smell of alcohol wafted over Erich. He pulled away from it. The doctor gripped Erich's chin as he bent forward and peered at the wound. A stale smell of sweat rose from his armpit. Erich wrinkled his nose, trying to pull away. He was dizzy with tiredness and the throbbing in his head. The unpleasant smells made him feel ill.

"Sit still so the doctor can look at you," Daddy Davy said.

Reluctantly Erich obeyed. The doctor leaned close, staring at the wound. He peered at it intently from several angles, his eyebrows knitted into a line of concentration.

"It'll need stitches," he said at last.

Erich looked at him fearfully. Oblivious to Erich's reaction, the doctor went to the cabinet and took from it thread and a needle. With his back to Erich, obscuring his view, the doctor sterilised the needle and threaded it. He turned around, the needle pinched between his thumb and first two fingers. Erich whined at the sight of it. His head throbbed and the needle blurred in front of his eyes.

"Will you be a brave boy for me?" the doctor asked. "Just a few stitches will do it. They're just like pin pricks." The doctor moved towards him. "You'd better hold him, Mr Elliott," he added.

Daddy Davy gave Erich a reassuring squeeze, then gripped his shoulders tightly. Erich didn't want the stitches but if it had to be done he felt safer with Daddy Davy beside him. He knew Daddy Davy wouldn't let anyone hurt him. Erich's vision blurred as the doctor held the needle up and gripped his chin; he shut his eyes tightly. The needle slid in and out, pulling the edges of the wound together, but it seemed to be happening far away. Dizziness and a hissing noise between his ears overwhelmed him. He slumped in Daddy Davy's grip.

When the doctor was finished Daddy Davy shook him gently and lifted him down from the table; he leaned heavily against Daddy Davy, barely aware that it was over. Gripping Erich's shoulder, Daddy Davy led him down the hallway. The boy shivered as they stepped out into the cool night air. He felt himself lifted onto the bicycle whose dark silhouette he could just see.

"Are you alright there? Hold tight now, lad." Daddy Davy pushed the bicycle along the footpath, then mounted it and pedalled off, Erich grasping his jacket.

Stars shone very brightly in the clear sky above them. Erich looked up, groggily aware of the bright spots of light. A dog barked nearby as they turned onto the pitch black country road. Something rustled in the hedge beside them and an owl hooted nearby. It must be close. It must be watching us, Erich thought hazily. His eyes felt heavy and he just wanted to sleep. His grip slackened on Daddy Davy's waist and he started to slip. He woke with a start.

"Mind you hold tight, lad," Daddy Davy said.

Erich gripped tighter and struggled to hold on. He thought they would never get home. The journey home seemed much longer than the one to the doctor's surgery. His arms and his head ached. Finally they rode into the haggard. Through a fog Erich saw Gipsy at their feet, tail wagging. Daddy Davy carried Erich into the house and straight up the stairs. He was unaware of Aunt Elsie's concerned face peering at him as they passed. Erich relaxed as Daddy Davy undressed him and laid him in the bed beside the sleeping Hans. He was always safe with Daddy Davy. Erich closed his eyes and immediately fell into a deep sleep.

❦

Daddy Davy sliced into the turf bank, cutting one square piece after another. Erich lifted them with both hands, turning them over and heaving them onto the top of the bank, in a relatively straight line, to dry out. In a few days they would have a good supply ready for the fire. In silent concentration they proceeded with their task. The sky was overcast but no rain fell. A bee buzzed near them in the purple gorse. Above there was a loud whooshing of wings. Erich looked up to see Canada geese, in a V formation directly overhead, swooping to land in the lake beside them. Stretching out their black and white heads, honking, and occasionally flapping their wings, they splashed and waddled onto the bank. Erich watched the ungainly birds, fascinated.

"Yon geese find their way back here every year," Daddy Davy said.

"Don't they ever get lost?" Erich asked.

"Indeed they don't. They know where their home is."

"This is their home too. Just like me," Erich said.

"Aye, it is. Are you thirsty?" Daddy Davy asked.

Erich nodded, scratching the wound on his forehead which was almost healed. Gathering a few twigs into a pile Daddy Davy lit them and in a few minutes he had a small fire burning. Filling the metal teapot with water from a depression in the bog, he hung it over the fire. When it boiled, he took it off the fire, added tea leaves and left it to steep.

The strong tea he poured into their cups had a red hue. Erich grimaced at the bitter taste but he was thirsty and drained the cup quickly. They had been working all morning and he was glad of the rest. The task was monotonous but he didn't mind. He had Daddy Davy to himself and didn't have to share his attention with anyone else this morning.

The bog lay beside the larger of the two lakes in front of their house. Even though they were only half a mile from home, Erich felt they were as remote as the jungles of Africa.

"Did you kill lots of soldiers in the war?" Erich asked.

"You don't want to know about that," Daddy Davy answered dismissively, reluctant to talk about the horrors he had seen while serving with the British forces during World War I.

Despite his own experiences in Germany, Erich, like most boys, was fascinated by war and soldiers. He didn't connect the topic with his own frightening experiences.

But Daddy Davy wouldn't be drawn to talk about the war.

"Is Aunt Elsie sick?" Erich asked, changing the topic abruptly.

"Why do you ask?"

"You said she needed to rest."

"She'll be fine. God has her in his care."

"Does God see everything?" Erich asked.

"Indeed He does. That's why you must always do your best to be good. You want Him to be pleased with you."

Daddy Davy wanted to instil his strong Christian beliefs in the boys. They chatted some more until Daddy Davy stood up saying, "I'll have to get some more turf cut before dinner time. I've to meet Helen off the bus after dinner."

Erich stood up and followed him back to the turf bank, happily humming to himself. Today was a good day. He was glad to spend the morning with Daddy Davy and this afternoon he would see Helen. She spent part of every summer with them and he looked forward to her visits. She was one friend who didn't prefer Hans's company to his. He could always count on her loyalty ever since he first arrived at the Elliotts.

"Are ye courtin' then, Erich?" Willy asked, leaning against the wall of the post office.

Erich shook his head as Willy and the other man laughed.

"Ye must be courtin' if she's staying wi' ye. Ye'll have to save your money as women can spend it for ye quick enough," Willy said.

Willy and the other man laughed again; Willy was always teasing them. Helen looked past him, pretending not to hear his comments. Looking for something to do Erich and Helen had walked from Derrykeane to the village. They were pleased to meet Willy as he always had time to chat with them. After a few more minutes of his teasing and banter Erich and Helen left the men.

"Mind ye go straight home. No courtin' on the way!" Willy called after them.

Willy and his companion laughed again as the children walked away. Erich and Helen drifted out of the village, dragging their toes in the dirt, scribbling designs.

"It's shorter through the field," Erich said, stopping at the first gate they came to.

He climbed the gate and Helen followed him, primly smoothing her skirt down as she jumped from the bottom rail into the field. They walked along the edge of the green field, chatting and peering into the hedge, looking for birds' nests. A brown and white dappled cow grazed a few feet away. She raised her head and stared, uncaring, as they passed. Flicking her tail at a fly buzzing on her flank, she lowered her head and continued grazing.

Leaving their search of the hedges, they picked their way towards the middle of the field skirting around flat, round cow pats splattered in the clumpy grass. Cows raised their heads as Erich and Helen passed but, chewing their cuds, they paid little heed to them. The children chattered, equally unperturbed by the cumbersome beasts around them.

In the middle of the field, surrounded by several cows and calves Erich suddenly noticed a large, black bull. As they neared him he raised his head and looked directly at them over the other animals. He snorted, his nose ring rattling as he shifted irritably. Erich slowed, prompting Helen to notice the bull, half-hidden by the cows.

"It's a bull," Erich said.

"I know that, so I do! He's lookin' at us. Do ye think he's angry?" Helen asked, shrinking closer to Erich.

"We b-b-best get out o' here!" Erich said, taking Helen's hand.

The children hurried towards the nearest gate. Their movement caught the bull's attention and he lumbered after them. Panicking, they broke into a run and the bull gave chase, head lowered and snorting. Terror-stricken, they raced across the field without a thought for the cow pats they had been so carefully avoiding. They scrambled over the gate and stood panting on the other side. The bull stopped just short of it; snorting, he tossed his head and returned to the herd.

"I thought the bull would get us, so I did!" Helen said, near tears.

"We're lucky," Erich replied. Helen nodded agreement.

Hearts pounding and still panting, they watched the bull grazing again, oblivious to them. Helen turned primly to Erich.

"I need to do the toilet. Turn around and don't peek!" she commanded him.

Erich turned around as Helen squatted. She watched him anxiously.

"Are your eyes closed? Don't peek!"

"I'm gonna look!" he said, teasing. He half-turned his head towards her.

"No! Don't ye dare! You're a rude boy if ye do!" she replied.

Watching him anxiously, Helen finished and pulled her skirt down.

"Ye can look now," she said.

Erich turned around. They cautiously checked the field they were standing in for any further dangers before they moved but it was empty.

"I was so scared. I thought that bull would get us, so I did," Helen said, her voice still shaky.

"I not let him hurt you," Erich replied, his confidence returning with the bull safely on the other side of the gate.

He reached out and took Helen's hand. They continued across the field, walking the rest of the way home hand in hand.

Erich and Hans raced up the stairs to change out of their best Sunday clothes. In church they had sat tugging at the collars that clung to their necks, feeling hot and restless even with the slight breeze blowing through the open door. On such a hot summer day they could barely wait to shed their restrictive jackets and ties. Helen busied herself helping Aunt Elsie set the table.

Downstairs again, Hans wandered over to the oven and sniffed, catching the smell of roasting chicken. Erich popped his head into the kitchen.

"If you're away out, don't go too far, Erich. Dinner is nearly ready," Aunt Elsie said.

Erich nodded and went out of the front door. He wandered down the path past the lakes to the bog beside them, stopping at the edge of it. Something moving in the bog caught his eye and he squinted to focus on it. A cow, its front legs flailing as it tried to get a grip on solid ground, was stuck in the bog, bellowing pitifully. Its back legs were mired and half its body submerged. Erich's eyes widened and he opened his mouth wide, inhaling sharply. He turned and scrambled back up the path, clattering through the stone hall, into the kitchen.

"D-D-Daddy Davy! A-a-a c-c-cow's stuck in bog!" he shouted.

Erich panted and gripped the door handle, poised to run. Daddy Davy quickly rose from the chair beside the fire and followed him back down the path. After weighing up the situation, he hurried across the field to the Maguires.

Walking in the back door he greeted them, "Good day! Sorry

to disturb you when you're at your dinner. Michael, would you give me a hand? I've a cow bogged down the front field."

Michael rose from the table, dispatching a couple of his children to fetch other neighbours, and followed Daddy Davy back to the bog. By the time the neighbours had gathered Daddy Davy had strong ropes and Paddy the pony standing by. They wrapped the ropes over the cow's back and behind her front legs and Paddy trudged away from the bog, the rope tightening as he went. The cow bellowed and thrashed but slowly started to emerge from the muck, helped by Paddy and the men hauling on the rope. Frightened, she fought, her eyes rolling wildly as she was pulled from the bog. She aimed a wild kick at her rescuers and slipped back into it to curses from the men. They stopped, puffing, then made another attempt, grabbing the rope and hauling again. The pony strained against the rope and suddenly, with a squelch, the cow emerged from the muck. She lay half on her side but quickly scrambled up and, tossing her head, veered away from her rescuers. Erich cheered. Daddy Davy chased her back towards the field she came from.

"Thanks, lads," he said to the assembled men. "Good on you too, Erich, for spotting her." Erich beamed proudly.

"Being a good churchgoer, I didn't think ye would do any work on a Sunday, Davy," one of the men said jokingly.

"Jesus said, 'What man shall there be among ye, that shall have one sheep, and if it fall into a pit on the Sabbath Day, will he not lay hold on it and lift it out?'" Daddy Davy replied with a smile.

"That's an awfully big sheep so," the man replied.

Daddy Davy and the other men laughed as they watched the cow trotting back to the field. Erich stood, listening to the conversation. Daddy Davy always had an answer for any question and, with the naivety of childhood, Erich trusted that Daddy Davy knew almost everything. He walked back to the house for dinner with his head held high. He was so proud that Daddy Davy was his daddy. I have the best family, he thought.

January 1950

Erich mounted the bicycle and, putting one foot on the pedal, pushed himself off. He tried to get his other foot on the opposite one but he wobbled, gripping the handlebars tightly. The bicycle Daddy Davy had given Erich and Hans for Christmas slowed, starting to topple.

"You have to pedal, Erich!" Daddy Davy shouted behind him.

Erich frantically tried to pedal before the bicycle toppled over. Hans watched, grinning. He had learned to ride quite easily and did not see why Erich had not mastered it yet. Because Erich could not ride the bicycle Hans used it most of the time. It was much quicker to cycle rather than walk to school; he and Bobby rode to school together most days now.

After a few more attempts Erich gave up and dropped the bicycle down beside the wall.

"We can try again tomorrow," Daddy Davy said to Erich as Hans retrieved the bicycle and cycled off to see Bobby. Erich nodded, not in any hurry for another attempt.

Late that afternoon Hans raced into the haggard and jumped off the bicycle. Erich came out of the byre at the sound of the tyres bouncing on the stone. Aunt Elsie poked her head out of the back door.

Seeing him she said, "There you are! The tea's ready. What kept you late?"

Hans propped the bicycle against the wall, saying, "Mrs Maguire and I collided. I stopped to pick up her parcels."

"Ye must be more careful. Are you both unharmed? I hope you apologised to her," Aunt Elsie replied.

Hans nodded. "I wouldn't have been late if that damned Mrs Maguire hadn't been in my way," he muttered to Erich.

"What did I hear you say, lad?" Daddy Davy asked, coming

out of the byre.

"Nothing," Hans replied.

"Tell me the truth," he said.

"What did he say?" Aunt Elsie asked, still standing at the back door. With her poor hearing, she had not caught his comment to Erich nor had Hans intended her to.

"He's using language I won't allow," Daddy Davy replied.

Aunt Elsie looked probingly at Hans. "Did ye?" she asked.

After a moment's hesitation Hans nodded. Aunt Elsie disappeared into the kitchen, appearing a few moments later with a small piece of carbolic soap in her hand.

"We can't have that now. My mammy always said there's only one cure for it. Go over to the bucket there and wash your mouth out with soap," she said, pointing to the rainwater bucket sitting in the corner of the haggard.

"Do I have to?" Hans asked, appealing to Daddy Davy.

"You know it was wrong. Do as Aunt Elsie says," he replied.

Reluctantly Hans took the soap and went over to the bucket. Aunt Elsie shuffled after him, watching as he put it in his mouth and swished it around, screwing up his face at the bitter taste. Cupping his hand he sluiced water into his mouth to rinse it out. Bubbles formed at the corners of his mouth as he spat onto the ground.

When he was finished, Aunt Elsie said, "Now we'll have no more of that sort of language around here. Come in and get your tea."

They ate their tea in silence. Erich ate heartily, glancing smugly at Hans, who was struggling to swallow his food. The taste of the soap lingered in his mouth.

When they finished, Aunt Elsie said to Daddy Davy, "It's been a terrible harsh winter so far. A terrible lot of people are ill and worse. Mrs Miller couldn't shake the cold, poor cratur. It's such a shame; she wasn't terrible old."

Daddy Davy nodded in agreement. "Will we go round to the wake tonight?" he asked.

"I'm done in tonight. Let's go in the morning," she replied, sinking into a chair by the fire. Erich watched her greyish face anxiously.

"You aren't too cold, are you, Aunt Elsie?" he asked.

"No, I'm fine by the fire here. Don't be worrying about me," she replied, smiling reassurance.

Erich darted anxious glances at her through the evening as he did his homework. She was always tired lately. He didn't want the cold to get her.

As Erich finished his last sum and closed his arithmetic workbook Aunt Elsie said, "It's late, lads. Go upstairs and get undressed. I'll be up to hear your prayers."

Erich lifted the lantern from the table and they went upstairs. In the cold bedroom the boys threw off their jumpers and trousers and dived into their nightshirts.

Aunt Elsie climbed the stairs a few minutes later, puffing hard as she neared the landing. Dizzy, she held the banister for a moment, before entering their room.

"Are you sick, Aunt Elsie?" Erich asked, noticing her heavy breathing.

"No, lad, just a bit out of puff," she replied.

She leaned against the doorframe listening as, kneeling on the bare floorboards, they recited their prayers. Erich concluded with "God Bless Daddy Davy, Aunt Elsie, Hans, Gipsy, Patch, Paddy and all our animals. And God bless Mrs Miller and keep her warm. Amen."

The boys rose and scrambled under the covers. Aunt Elsie coughed, choking back a laugh, her eyes watering as she pulled the blankets up around their necks.

"Now, go straight to sleep and no messing about," she said, trying to sound stern.

The boys nodded. She lifted the paraffin lantern and left them in darkness.

Entering the kitchen, she closed the hall door and chuckled.

"Erich, in his prayers, said 'God bless Mrs Miller and keep her warm!'" she said to Daddy Davy. He looked up from the fire and laughed out loud.

"Such a meek, God-fearing woman! She's never gone anywhere warm!" he laughed.

"Davy! Mind what ye say!" she said, laughing.

Yearningly Erich watched the older boys, leaning against the wall just out of sight of the post office. They rolled pieces of paper up tightly and lit them. Eyes fixed on the Bruno's Tobacco ad on the wall opposite, the boys inhaled, pretending they were real cigarettes. Between puffs they held the burning papers behind their backs to conceal them from any adults who might pass by. The paper burned quickly and after a few puffs they had to drop the charred butts. Erich wanted to be part of their group but the older boys only shooed him away when he asked to have a puff.

The light was fading and Erich knew it was time to head home. He had lingered in the village as long as he could after school. If he didn't soon head home, Aunt Elsie would be cross. Turning onto the road that led out of the village he held an imaginary cigarette in his hand, waving it about him. He blew out in the cold air, pretending his frozen breath was smoke wafting upwards. He formed rings, watching his misty breath float away from him over the hedges into the surrounding fields.

The warm days of summer were a memory only; the green fields were transformed. Frost spread a delicate, milky wool blanket on fields and hedges. The red berries that the birds had missed, on holly bushes growing up through and intertwined with hawthorn hedges, gave rare dots of vibrant colour to the landscape. They were a reminder of the Christmas season recently past. Water lying on the roads had turned solid, forming miniature skating rinks. Erich whizzed across the first patch of ice he found, balancing precariously as his boots struck bumps on the uneven surface. Then he slid back across the frozen puddle to where he started. He did this several times before continuing along the road. On afternoons when he walked home with his classmates they competed to see who could slide the farthest.

Erich walked slowly. Warm from skating on the puddles, he didn't mind the cold air. Meandering as aimlessly as a smoke-ring, he daydreamed of smoking with the older boys. He would show them he was big enough to smoke. He would be ten this year.

When he arrived at the haggard, Gipsy barked and twirled in circles excitedly around him. Absentmindedly he patted the dog. Entering the kitchen, Gipsy panting behind him, he found it empty. Aunt Elsie's footsteps clipped across the floor above. Hesitating briefly, he reached for a couple of matches from the box sitting on the mantelpiece. He shoved them in his pocket and grabbed an old newspaper lying in the corner. Hurrying out of the door to the back of the haggard, he glanced around to be sure Daddy Davy was not about.

He took a couple of pages from the newspaper and rolled them up tightly into a thin pencil. He felt in his pocket for the matches, searching the folds of the fabric until he felt the rough wood and fished one out. He struck it on the stony ground and, as it flared, touched it to the ragged tip of the paper bundle. A thin line of black smoke curled up as the tiny flame bit into it. The flame brightened as Erich drew on the other end, inhaling the fake cig-arette. He took another puff hurriedly as the flame devoured the paper. On his third puff Erich heard a cough behind him.

"So ye want to smoke, do ye?" Daddy Davy asked, watching him, his pipe dangling from his mouth.

Erich looked up guiltily, not replying. He dropped the burning paper and stamped on it.

"Well, we can sort that out," Daddy Davy said matter-of-factly.

Erich watched him anxiously, wondering why he didn't sound angry. Daddy Davy walked across the haggard and went into the house. Erich followed him meekly. Before he reached the door, Daddy Davy came out again. Aunt Elsie scurried after him, twisting her apron in her hands, puffing at the exertion.

"Davy, you're not serious, are you?" she asked.

"Indeed I am. We'll see what he thinks of smoking after he finishes this pipe."

Daddy Davy held his pipe in his left hand, scooping it out and stuffing the bowl full of fresh Bruno tobacco. He lit it and handed it to Erich. Unsure what to do, Erich looked at him.

"Now ye'll smoke the real thing, lad," he said.

Erich held the pipe, wondering if he were serious.

"Go on. Put it in your mouth and smoke it," Daddy Davy said.

Erich wiped saliva from the wet handle, feeling the teeth marks gashed into it from years of use. He put it in his mouth and sucked on it. As he inhaled the smoke filled his mouth and nostrils. His nostrils burned and his eyes watered. He choked and coughed, pulling the pipe from his mouth. Daddy Davy watched him impassively. When Erich finished coughing, he motioned for him to put the pipe back in his mouth. Erich tried to inhale and sputtered again. The tobacco tasted vile and his mouth was too dry to swallow. The smell and taste mixed together, making him ill. His head felt woozy and his vision blurred. I don't like smoking at all, he thought, wishing it was over. But Daddy Davy stood watching him and made him put the pipe back in his mouth when he took it out. Aunt Elsie hovered at the door, her face creased with concern.

"Oh, Davy, don't ye think he's had enough?" she asked anxiously.

"I don't want him to forget this lesson. He'll have a few more puffs," he replied, watching Erich draw on the pipe.

Erich took the pipe from his mouth and stood swaying, unable to focus. Daddy Davy gripped his shoulder to keep him from falling. His head pounded and he felt sick. Aunt Elsie rushed over and put her arm around his shoulder. He leaned against her, his eyes half-closed. Daddy Davy let go of his shoulder.

"That was very harsh, Davy! He's just a wee lad!" she said

angrily.

"If he won't do as he's bid, he must learn the hard way," Daddy Davy replied. "Best get him to bed, now. A night's rest will mend him rightly." He gently squeezed the boy's shoulder.

With her arm still around him, Aunt Elsie ushered Erich into the house and up the stairs. She put him to bed and sat beside him until he fell into a restless sleep, tossing and turning. His head throbbed and his stomach lurched.

Daddy Davy held the pipe out to him and he ran from his outstretched hand. Then the angry soldier chased him. He hid in the dormitory but the soldier wouldn't stop looking for him. He cried out as the soldier stooped and spotted him under the bed. He scrambled out and ran down the centre aisle. He would have to jump from the balcony. There was no other way out. Then Mutti was leaning over him, smoothing his hair. He knew Mutti would come back. It would be alright now; she would keep him safe. He didn't have to run.

He reached out, grasping her arm. *"Mutti!"* he called.

Aunt Elsie stopped smoothing his hair and closed her hand over his.

Christmas 1950

The familiar colourful paper decorations criss-crossed the kitchen and holly sprigs adorned the pictures on the walls. Daddy Davy sat by the fire, his pipe smoke wafting around the room. Erich liked the smell, despite his experience of smoking earlier in the year. The pungent aroma was more pleasant from a distance.

Erich sat in the chair on the opposite side of the fire. Companionably they watched the fire crackle in the grate, its heat warming the large room.

"Did you have Christmas in your war?" Erich asked.

Daddy Davy gazed pensively into the fire, appearing not to

have heard the question. Erich waited hopefully.

Finally he said, "The First World War was a long time ago. But I still remember it well. On Christmas Day we stopped fighting for one day. That morning we peered over the edge of our trench at the Germans and shouted 'Happy Christmas' to them. They answered and we came out and met in the middle. We sang carols and shared food parcels."

"Didn't they try to shoot you?" Erich asked.

"Not on that one day," he replied.

"How did you know they wouldn't?"

"Because they kept their word, just as we did. Christmas was more important than a war."

"What was it like there?" Erich asked.

"We lived in trenches. They were just holes in the ground. We had to dig them. When it rained they got full of water and mud," he replied. He did not describe the full horror of the freezing, damp conditions in the mud-filled trenches where disease was rampant.

"Did you swim in them?" Erich asked. Daddy Davy merely smiled at the boy's imagination.

"Was God there?" Erich asked.

"God is everywhere."

"Why did He let you fight?"

"God lets us make our own way. He tells us what is right and wrong and we have to do our best to follow it," Daddy Davy replied.

"Did you ever see an angel?" Erich asked.

Daddy Davy was silent for a minute, staring into the fire. He scratched his head and puffed on his pipe. Taking it out of his mouth, he replied, "Yes."

"Did you! With w-w-wings and a w-w-white gown? W-W-Was it here?" Erich asked, wide-eyed.

"No, not here. It was during the war. At Mons we were surrounded by German soldiers and didn't know how we could get out. We were trapped. Suddenly clouds came down covering us.

The Germans couldn't see us. Then we saw bright lights in the sky and angels were all around us. When they left the Germans had gone. The angels saved us."

Erich looked at Daddy Davy, amazed. He could barely contain his excitement.

"I wish I was there!" he said.

"Oh, no, you don't, lad. We've both seen enough of wars."

Erich was pleased Daddy Davy had told him about the war. He never talked to anyone else about it. They sat looking into the fire as the peat burned down to a reddish glow. Erich felt a bit sleepy and closed his eyes for a moment. Daddy Davy thoughtfully puffed on his pipe. Erich shifted, waking from the doze, and looked around the kitchen.

"Where's Aunt Elsie?" he asked.

"She's after doin' all the chores today to be ready for the girls coming home from school the morra. She's very tired, so she's away to bed," Daddy Davy replied.

"She's alright, isn't she?" Erich asked anxiously. Daddy Davy nodded.

Reassured, Erich yawned. Closing his eyes again, his head nodded and fell against his chest. He dozed until Daddy Davy woke him and sent him to bed.

Summer 1951

"I don't want to go. I w-w-want to stay here - with Aunt Elsie. I'll look after her," Erich pleaded.

"It's only for a week. It's a holiday. Ye'll like it in Sligo and Reverend McDermott is very nice. Aunt Elsie will be fine. She just needs some rest," Daddy Davy replied.

Feet dragging, Erich climbed on the bus, followed by Hans. As the bus pulled away he waved, pressing his face against the window until Daddy Davy disappeared from view. Then he slumped into his seat.

The bus sped across the country along narrow, winding roads. Erich looked out at the passing scenery. As the miles sped on he became distracted by the view and allowed himself to enjoy the vehicle's steady movement. The boys revelled in the motion of the bus, especially rounding corners. They bumped against each other, pretending the rocking bus had thrown them, laughing and shoving. Mountains rose to the north as they neared the coast and suddenly they were in the town. The bus crawled through Sligo Town's Saturday morning traffic, surrounded by cars and carts. Erich peered out at the small shops crowded together along the street. When the bus stopped Erich and Hans followed the other passengers off the vehicle.

A black-haired, slightly chubby man with a clerical collar walked over to them.

"Erich? Hans?" he asked, smiling.

Erich nodded and the man extended his hand to shake Erich's hand, then Hans's.

"I'm Reverend McDermott. So you've come for a holiday with us. I'm sure you'll like it. There are other children to play with at the rectory."

"I have my brother," Erich replied, prepared not to like it here.

"So you do. But you'll meet new friends too."

The man led them to his car. A short drive brought them to a rambling, stone rectory set in spacious grounds. Two girls and four boys were playing outside it. Reverend McDermott spoke to them, calling each one by name as they walked up to the front door. He led the boys into the house and upstairs.

"This will be your bed," he said to Erich. "And this will be yours," he said to Hans. He pointed to two beds side by side. Two other beds stood opposite them. Erich wondered who would share the room with them. It must be a couple of the boys I saw outside, he thought.

"Put your clothes away and then come downstairs. I'll intro-duce ye to the other children." Reverend McDermott and his wife, with no children of their own, fostered the six children Erich had seen in the grounds. The sprawling rectory had ample room for a large brood. Erich and Hans put their few possessions in the drawers beside the beds and went downstairs. A plump, dark-haired woman came out of the kitchen.

"Hello, ye must be Erich and Hans," she said. Wiping her hand on her apron, she extended it to them. "You're very welcome here. I'm Auntie Ida. The other children are still outside. Why don't ye go and join them?"

She swung open the heavy oak door. The children were playing hide and seek on the lawn. Spotting the boys, Reverend McDermott called them over and introduced them to the other children. Henry, George, Will, Charlie, Jane and Isobel. The names swam in Erich's mind.

Joining in the game Erich hid his face against the stone wall and counted as the other children scattered. Hans searched for a place to hide in the unfamiliar grounds. When Erich reached twenty he lifted his head, surveying the garden. Seeing the blue ribbons in Isobel's braids, only half hidden by the rose bush she was hiding behind, he pounced on her, tapping her shoulder, then ran on to find the others. He had caught all but two boys when Auntie Ida called them in for tea. With a groan he gave up but, before he went inside, he turned to see Henry slip from behind a shrub in the far corner of the lawn and George drop down from an old apple tree beside the house.

Erich and Hans followed the other children into the scullery to wash their hands. As Erich walked through the dining room doorway Reverend McDermott flicked a switch on the wall. The room was instantly illuminated. Erich had never been inside a house which had electric lighting before. It's wonderful, he thought excitedly. He stared up at the light above the table until he was reminded to close his eyes for grace. Throughout the meal his eyes were drawn to the switch on the wall. He wanted to flip it to see the room go from darkness to light again.

When the plates were cleared away and the dishes washed after the meal, the children went into the sitting room. There were puzzles and games piled in one corner. Henry and George got out their favourites to play. Jane took a book from the bookshelf. She curled her small frame into the corner of the sofa. Pushing her black-framed glasses up her nose she opened the book in the middle and began to read.

"Do ye want to play draughts?" Will asked Hans. He smiled shyly and nodded. The boys set the board on the floor between them.

Erich swept his eyes around the room. No one was paying any attention to him so he crept back into the dining room. He reached up timidly and flicked the switch. The room illuminated immediately. He flipped the switch off, then on again, chuckling delightedly. After several tries he flipped the switch faster until the light flashed like a lighthouse beacon. He leaned against the doorframe, playing with the switch.

"Now, Erich, don't be doing that! You'll break the switch," Reverend McDermott said. Erich jumped; he hadn't heard him approach.

Reverend McDermott led Erich back into the sitting room and gave him a puzzle to work on. Erich glanced longingly over at the dining room doorway. It would be great to see the light flash again, he thought. He opened the box and poured the puzzle pieces onto the floor. As he sifted through them his eyes were frequently drawn to the light switch.

Charlie, standing in front of the bookshelf, noticed Erich's longing gaze. He slid onto the floor opposite Erich and picked up a piece of the puzzle, searching for its place in the whole. "If you're first in for tea, you can switch on the light," he said conspiratorially.

"Really?" Erich asked. He decided he would race to the dining room tomorrow evening. The boys worked together companionably on the puzzle until Auntie Ida instructed the children to get ready for bed.

As he walked up the stairs, Erich wondered who their roommates would be. His question was soon answered as Charlie walked into the room in front of him. Will followed Hans through the door. The boys were in their nightshirts when Auntie Ida came to hear their prayers. Charlie and Will knelt beside their beds. The brothers followed suit. Charlie led them in the familiar bedtime prayers; Erich mumbled the words after him. Before he slipped into bed Erich murmured, "God Bless Daddy Davy, Auntie Elsie, Gipsy and please make Auntie Elsie well this week. She should be well. She's very good to everyone."

As the boys settled in their beds Auntie Ida turned out the light. Erich lay on his back, listening to the other boys' breathing.

"Where are youse from, Erich?" Charlie asked.

"Near Cavan Town. We live on a farm," Erich replied.

"Do you have animals and everything?"

"Y-Y-Yesss! I have Gipsy, he's my dog. And there's Paddy the p-p-pony and Paddy the donkey. And lots of cows. It's the b-b-best place to live!"

"Are you coming to live here now?"

"N-N-No! W-W-We're just here for a holiday. We go home at the end of the week."

"I came here for a holiday. My mother was ill and I was sent here."

"Why didn't you go home again?"

"My mother died and I had nowhere to go."

"We h-h-have Daddy Davy and Auntie Elsie. We'll always l-l-live there," Erich declared. Auntie Elsie will get better soon, Erich thought. He would help her with all her work when he went home. Then she could get lots of rest. She'd soon be as good as new. He repeated a silent prayer asking God to make Aunt Elsie better as he drifted off to sleep.

Erich and Hans quickly settled into the routine of the house. Tuesday morning after the breakfast dishes were washed Erich nudged Charlie.

"Let's go outside."

Reverend McDermott walked into the kitchen as Erich reached

for the door handle. "Wait a minute, lads. I think we might go somewhere a bit further than the garden this morning," he said.

"Where?" the boys asked together.

"To Lough Gill. Have you heard about the silver bell at the bottom of the lake, Erich?" Reverend McDermott asked. Erich shook his head.

"It's from the Abbey in Sligo and was thrown in the lake a very long time ago. Only people who are free from sin can still hear it ringing."

"Oh," Erich said thoughtfully.

Erich's brow creased as he thought about what Reverend McDermott had said. He remembered the time he blamed Hans for taking the knife from Miller's shop and his frequent arguments with his brother. He knew he should treat his brother better and he did try but, it was hard to do sometimes. He had never told Daddy Davy that Hans didn't take the knife either. That would mean he wasn't free from sin. He wouldn't be able to hear the bell ring. He wondered if Reverend McDermott would be disappointed with him when he realised this? Maybe Reverend McDermott wouldn't like him anymore.

"Charlie, will you help me get the bicycles from the shed?" Reverend McDermott asked.

"I can't ride a bicycle," Erich said hesitantly.

"That's a shame, Erich. It's too far to walk to the lough. We'll have to think of something else to do then." The other children groaned.

"I have a few messages to do in town today. Why don't you come with me, Erich?" Auntie Ida asked. Erich nodded eagerly. Reverend McDermott wouldn't find out that he couldn't hear the bell ring and be disappointed with him and he relished spending some time with Auntie Ida. She reminded him a bit of Auntie Elsie. Hans smiled sympathetically at him but he didn't mind missing the outing to Lough Gill. Humming to himself, he waited patiently for Auntie Ida to write the shopping list as the other children bustled around him then went out to claim their bicycles.

When they set off to the town centre Erich walked beside Auntie Ida, proudly carrying her shopping basket. They crossed a bridge leading to the centre then detoured away from it onto a street beside the river.

"I always like to take time to see the river when I'm in town," Auntie Ida said.

"We have a river in front of our house. We fish in it. Does this river have any fish?"

"Why don't you see for yourself."

Erich stopped and peered into the river. Several ducks swam near the shore, bobbing rhythmically under the water. He stared at the water's surface. A dark shape skimmed just beneath it, rippling the water. Erich shouted and pointed at it.

"There's one! I should have brought my fishing rod with me," Erich said.

"Oh, do you have one?"

"Y-Y-Yes! Daddy Davy made it for me. I can catch any fish with it!"

"He must have made a very good one then." Erich nodded agreement, remembering the days he had spent at the river with Aunt Rose and Hans.

Erich straightened up and they walked on. At the next junction they turned and headed towards the centre of town. Erich followed Auntie Ida in and out of a succession of shops, the basket getting heavier after each stop.

"Can you manage the basket, Erich?"

"Y-Y-Yes. I c-c-could carry twice the weight," Erich said, eager to please. He shifted the basket from one arm to the other and stood up straighter.

"Just one more message. The chemist is across the road."

"Do they have medicine for Auntie Elsie?" Erich asked.

"What kind of medicine do you want for her?"

"She gets tired easily. Something to make her feel better."

Auntie Ida smiled sympathetically. "She's gettin' a rest this week. I'm sure she'll be fine. You don't need to worry about her. I think we could make a couple other stops before we go home."

"Where?"

"Wait and see."

Erich followed Auntie Ida as she weaved along the busy street. The shopping basket sometimes clipped other shoppers as Erich passed them and he mumbled an apology. Auntie Ida came to an abrupt halt outside a shop with the name Keohane's written above the window. Erich looked at the books standing on end, face outwards, in the window display. There were all sorts of books. Auntie Ida opened the door and entered. Erich followed close behind her.

Erich could hardly believe it. Inside there were shelves filled with books everywhere. He'd never seen so many books before. The Elliotts had a few old children's books around the house and Uncle Richard had a bookcase in Bray. The lovely fairytale book was kept in that bookcase. But there were so many more books here. Erich didn't know where to begin to look.

"I think you'll like these," Auntie Ida said pointing to a small section in the corner. Erich went over and pulled out titles one by one from the children's shelves. The pictures on the covers fascinated him. Even his favourite comic books were here. He stood reading the latest episodes of Beano and Dennis the Menace until Auntie Ida tapped him on the shoulder.

"You must be gettin' thirsty with all that reading," she said smiling. "Let's go and have a lemonade before we go home." Erich happily put the comic book back on the shelf and followed her out of the shop.

The boys' holiday passed quickly; they barely noticed the week speeding by. Although they enjoyed their holiday, when it was time to leave Erich was eager to get home to Daddy Davy and Aunt Elsie and to see Gipsy and all the animals again. He traded addresses with Charlie and promised to write, gave Auntie Ida a tight hug and waved exuberantly to the other children as he walked with Reverend McDermott and Hans to the car. He was still waving as they drove off to the bus station.

Daddy Davy met them at the bus and the boys both spoke at once telling him about their holiday, tugging at his sleeve to get his attention. Hans was barely back at the house before he raced off to see Bobby. But not before Aunt Elsie gave each of them a tight hug.

"Would you look at youse," she said. "You've grown since I saw you - even without good farm food! You must be weeds, the pair of you."

Daddy Davy went out of the back door without saying anything. Erich followed him into the byre.

"Their l-l-light came on when you pushed a s-s-switch on the wall," Erich exclaimed. "You didn't have to light it with a match. It w-w-was magic!"

"That's electric light. Some folks have that in the towns," Daddy Davy replied.

"I'll t-t-tell Mrs Baird and everyone about Sligo when we go back to s-s-school," Erich said, inhaling sharply.

Daddy Davy said nothing. Leaning on the pitchfork, he shifted his gaze away from Erich.

"I c-c-can help Aunt Elsie s-s-so she can rest more," Erich continued.

"That's very kind of ye, Erich," Daddy Davy said gravely. He glanced at the boy and quickly looked away again. Erich chattered on about his holiday; Daddy Davy listened silently.

During the next few days the boys settled back into the routine of the farm. Erich was happy to be back. He enjoyed his holiday but had missed Daddy Davy, Aunt Elsie and Gipsy. He was even eager to get back to school to tell Mrs Baird and the other children about Sligo.

Erich teased Nell as she worked around the house but she didn't fly off the handle as she normally did. Even when he pinched her she ignored it. She was much quieter than usual and

Rose, normally quiet, hardly said a word as she sat moping by the fire nursing a summer cold. During those first few days Erich sensed something was wrong and wondered about it anxiously.

Several nights later, when the tea was cleared away, Daddy Davy looked at the boys.

"Lads, I have to speak to ye," he said, gravely. Aunt Elsie slid onto a chair by the fire, avoiding the boys' eyes.

They waited, subdued by his tone of voice. He lit his pipe, drew deeply, then cleared his throat. Leaning on the mantelpiece he looked straight at them.

"You know Aunt Elsie has not been the best this while past. She tires quickly; her heart's not able for all the work to look after such a big house and everyone in it. Doctor Brown says she needs to rest. So we must sell Derrykeane and move to a smaller farm."

"Can we keep our animals?" Erich asked.

Daddy Davy straightened up, swallowing hard before he spoke.

"That's the thing, lads. Aunt Elsie isn't able for two lads any more. So we're asking Reverend Downey to help us find a new home for you."

Erich stared at him in disbelief. Hans's eyes widened like a hurt puppy, but he said nothing. Aunt Elsie, her eyes beseeching, looked from one boy to the other.

"No! You s-s-said this is our home! I-I-I want to s-s-stay with you! Why can't I s-s-stay?" Erich shouted, tears welling in his eyes.

"We don't want you to go either but it has to be," Daddy Davy said sadly.

Aunt Elsie rose and went to Erich, her arms outstretched. But Erich dodged her embrace and ran upstairs, flinging himself on the bed, sobbing. Motioning to Aunt Elsie to wait, Daddy Davy followed him and sat on the edge of the bed.

"I d-d-don't w-w-want to leave!" Erich sobbed.

"I know lad, and you wouldn't if we could keep you. But we'll come to visit. We wouldn't just forget you. If there's any problems with your new home you can tell me." Daddy Davy placed his hand on the boy's shoulder; Erich sniffed, wiping his running nose without a word.

The next few days passed in a blur. Hans mutely followed Aunt Elsie around each day, his face drawn and sorrowful. Erich couldn't believe they were leaving and kept asking why they had to leave. There must be some way we can stay, he thought desperately. This is my family. I thought I would stay forever. If they really wanted me they would find a way that I could stay. Why don't they want me? No one seems to want me for very long and *Mutti* isn't coming back to get me now, he thought miserably. What will happen to me and Hans?

8

CLANGING POTS AND APPLE PIE
County Leitrim
Autumn 1951

ERICH PRESSED close to Daddy Davy as he stooped to push open the low iron gate then strode up the short path; Hans tagged behind them dejectedly. Willy poked Hans in the back, winking when he turned to look but the boy barely noticed and responded with a half-hearted smile. Daddy Davy's knock on the plain, solid door was opened by a tall woman, brushing her wavy brown hair back from her solemn face.

"Hello, Mrs Owens," Daddy Davy said.

"Hello, Mr Elliott. You're very welcome," she replied. She opened the door wide to allow them to enter the central hallway.

"This is Erich and Hans," he said as they stepped in.

"I'm Aunt Rachel," she said to the boys, in a tone better suited to a headmistress than an aunt.

Light streamed through the sidelights framing the door. They followed the faded red paisley pattern of the carpet down the hall into the sitting room where a fire crackled in the open grate.

"Such a long journey you've had," Aunt Rachel said to Daddy Davy.

"Sure, it's no length at all."

"Sit yourselves down. You must be famished. I'll go and put the kettle on." Aunt Rachel disappeared from the sitting room.

Daddy Davy lowered himself onto the settee and the boys

perched either side of him on its firm edge. Willy sat opposite them in a worn armchair. The boys glanced around the room which was crowded with dark, solid furniture. The mantelpiece was lined with photos. A man in army uniform peered out of the largest one, his arm around a small blonde girl who gazed up at him, laughing. Erich turned his attention to the other end of the room. Out of the window he saw a long, narrow back garden. It was much smaller than their haggard. Except for a hen run it was unpopulated. Erich thought longingly of Gipsy and Paddy the horse. He even missed Paddy the donkey.

Aunt Rachel reappeared, balancing a tray loaded with tea, bread and apple pie. She set it down on the table under the window. The boys, prompted by Daddy Davy, shuffled over to the table. They munched listlessly on pieces of apple pie, listening glumly to the adults' conversation. Erich struggled with the lump in his throat as he swallowed. He hoped Daddy Davy would stay a while; he didn't want him to leave.

But when his tea cup was empty Daddy Davy stood up, saying, "Well, we'd best head back. Thank you for the tea, Mrs Owens."

"Not at all. It was no trouble," she replied.

The boys clung to his shadow as they followed him to the door. Tears welled in Erich's eyes when Daddy Davy stooped to hug them; Hans stared at him wordlessly. Willy ruffled Hans's hair, but the boy's eyes never lost their forlorn expression.

"I'll come to see you as often as I can. Aunt Elsie will come too. You'll soon settle in," Daddy Davy said, trying to cheer them.

"They'll be fine here," Aunt Rachel said briskly.

"They're good lads. We're sorry we can't keep them any longer," Daddy Davy said to Aunt Rachel. He smiled at the boys again as he straightened up.

Erich and Hans watched until the men got in the car and slowly pulled away. Gripping the boys' shoulders to get their attention Aunt Rachel ushered them in, closing the door firmly behind her.

"You'll need to hurry up with that," Mary said irritably, shaking her red hair out of her eyes. The lodger finished her tea and dashed from the kitchen.

"Don't mind her, Erich. She's just in bad humour," Fanny said, her shoulder length brown hair framing her smile. Good humoured and patient, she was not at all like the other lodger.

Mary's only ever in bad humour, Erich thought. In the few weeks we've been here she's never said a nice word to either of us. Erich brushed savagely across Mary's shoe until the polish disappeared into it, leaving a gleaming surface.

Picking up her shoes, Fanny admired their sheen. Erich had finished them a few minutes earlier and set them aside for the polish to dry. She put them on and prepared to leave for work.

Hans rattled the dishes in the soapy water, unable to see them under the foam. They heard the front door close behind the girls as he set the last one on the draining board and reached for the tea towel.

"The van will be here soon. Hurry or we'll miss it," Erich said to Hans, giving the floor a cursory sweep.

"I'm still hungry," Hans complained. They had rarely been full since they arrived.

Erich eyed an apple pie on the dresser. Aunt Rachel had baked it yesterday for the lodgers' tea. Only two slices had been eaten, leaving a triangular space where they had been. He reached in the drawer for a knife and cut two large slices from one edge. Handing one to Hans, he stuffed the other into his mouth, chewing furiously.

Erich heard Aunt Rachel shuffling from room to room upstairs but he did not have time to worry about what her reaction would be when she found pieces of the pie missing because the school van beeped outside the door. Brushing crumbs from his mouth, Erich rushed down the hall, shouting to Hans to hurry.

The school van left them back at the house late in the afternoon. Aunt Rachel, scowling, was waiting for them when they opened the door.

"Did you take some of the apple pie?" she asked brusquely, without even a hello.

The boys shook their heads. She studied their faces carefully. Hans stared at the floor to avoid her scrutiny but Erich stared back defiantly.

"We didn't," Erich declared, knowing they would be punished if he told the truth. Since they rarely got enough to eat, he didn't feel guilty about taking the pie or his lie. The food shortages in Germany had taught him how to be resourceful when necessary.

"Well, there's a big wedge missing from one side. That pie's for the girls. They pay decent rent money to me. Don't you two touch it," she said to them sternly. "Where's your pocket money?"

"Upstairs," Hans replied reluctantly.

"Well, leave it down here on the dresser," she told them.

"Why?" Erich asked, distrustfully.

"So I can mind it for you," she said.

Erich eyed her suspiciously but knew it was futile to argue; Aunt Rachel never relented. They went upstairs, brought down their Red Cross pocket money and reluctantly set it on the dresser.

When they came down for breakfast the next morning Erich immediately checked the dresser. The money was gone. Scowling, he nudged Hans, indicating the dresser. Hans stared in dismay.

They set out the dishes for breakfast as the lodgers pounded down the stairs and into the kitchen. Fanny smiled, saying, "Good Morning" cheerily; Mary ignored them. Aunt Rachel never joined them for breakfast. The meal proceeded silently. Dipping their bread into their tea, the boys ate hurriedly, then started clearing the table.

As the girls rose from their chairs, Fanny called, "Tara, lads". She headed out of the door; Mary flounced after her.

The boys hurried through their chores. As Hans finished washing the dishes, Erich said, "Bang on the pots and make some noise so Aunt Rachel will think we're still working."

Hans looked at him quizzically but picked up a pot and spoon, banging as if he were a toddler playing in the kitchen cupboard. Erich lifted the apple pie down from the dresser and cut a slice from one side. He handed it to Hans. He cut another slice from the other side, keeping the triangle's shape intact, and stuffed it into his mouth.

"See - it's even. She won't know we've taken any," he said to Hans. Hans laughed as he chewed the last mouthful of his slice.

Erich was pleased with himself. He had found a way to get something more than the pitiful portions Aunt Rachel gave them to eat. He was looking after Hans, just like *Mutti* had told him to do. He hoped she was proud of him if she could see him. Since they had arrived at Aunt Rachel's he didn't bicker with Hans nearly as much as he had before nor did he resent him. Their unhappy situation made them allies.

Erich picked up the broom and quickly swept the kitchen floor. Lifting the pie crumbs, he threw them in the dustbin.

The boys heard the school van beep its horn outside the door as they rushed to finish their chores. The engine had been idling for a few minutes. Suddenly it revved. Erich ran to the door just as it drove away. He waved after it frantically but it didn't slow down.

"Hans! The v-v-van's away! We'll have to t-t-try to catch a lift to school. I h-h-hope someone stops. It's miles to walk," Erich groaned.

They grabbed their coats and school satchels, then hurried out of the door. The cream-coloured house was near the edge of the village, slightly apart from its neighbours on either side. Two bay windows, framing the door in the middle, balanced the wide, squat building. Two chimneys sat companionably close to each other in the middle of the roof.

It was one of the newest houses in the village. Aunt Rachel's husband had built it less than twenty years earlier. It was a fine, handsome house but rather large for Aunt Rachel to run on her own. Her widow's pension wasn't enough to support Aunt Rachel and her daughter who attended boarding school in Dublin so she kept the two lodgers, plus Erich and Hans to supplement her income.

Erich closed the gate and the boys walked down the road, winding through the village. The village's few shops were concentrated near its tiny harbour. A narrow stream burbled into the harbour, flowing through the field behind Aunt Rachel's garden down to the village.

Other children were also walking through the village but they turned into a side street before the harbour to the Catholic National School. The boys continued along the main street. Once they crossed the bridge and left the village Erich flagged down the first passing car. He was relieved to see it; the road was a quiet one with few cars passing. They would have been very late if they had to walk.

When they arrived in Carrick-on-Shannon they thanked the driver and jumped out. Dodging women with shopping baskets, going in all directions, they made their way to the school. Shops crowded together on both sides of the street but they didn't stop to gaze into their windows. They hurried on, passing the wide, low steps of St. Mary's Catholic Church. Its doors stood open and a few women streamed in and out. The boys slipped in the gate in the high stone wall next to the church, and walked up to a stone building set back from the road. Only the ground floor of the two storey building was in use as, like many Protestant schools, enrolment was declining.

The playground was empty. Everyone was inside; classes had begun. They hurried in and tried to take their seats quietly. All eyes turned to watch them.

"You're late, lads," the young teacher said sternly.

"Sorry, Mrs Morgan. We missed the van," Erich said. He thought it was futile to tell her why they had missed it.

"Well, get your books out. You'll need to catch up with the lesson," she said briskly.

The boys sat near the front of the class. Taller children, mostly girls who stayed until the leaving age of fourteen, sat at the back. A girl with a pale face and long, sandy, tousled hair smiled over at Erich from the next row. Joyce was the first friend he had made at the school. Full of life, she was not cowed by the teacher's glance in her direction.

"Hello," she whispered. "Why did you miss the bus?"

"Hello," Erich whispered, smiling. Before he could answer her question, the teacher looked at him, pointing towards the book on his desk. He bent to look at it.

"When did the Nine Years War end?" Mrs Morgan asked Erich.

"1603, Mrs Morgan."

"That's right. What was the name of the treaty which ended the war?" The teacher pointed at an older girl, wearing glasses.

"The Treaty of Mellifont," she replied.

"Who were the Irish chieftains who ruled Leitrim?" she asked, pointing at a curly-haired boy, wearing a blue jumper.

"The O'Rourkes," he replied.

Mrs Morgan recounted the events of the Nine Years War. Erich loved to hear about the battles. He imagined himself as a soldier in a shiny uniform, charging into battle on his horse. No one would stop me, Erich thought, I'd conquer the rebels. And I'd take Aunt Rachel prisoner and punish her for the way she treats us.

As the day passed Erich forgot his annoyance at missing the van. When Mrs Morgan dismissed them Erich waited for Joyce and walked out with her.

"Can you come and play with us?" she asked.

"No, I have to get the van back. Aunt Rachel is annoyed if we're late for our tea. She might throw it out," he replied.

Reluctantly Erich went to the school van. He wished he lived in the town so he could play with Joyce and the other children.

Only a couple of other children from their school lived in their village so they had few playmates. They were discouraged from mixing with the local Catholic children though they did sometimes join their games.

He watched Joyce walk away with two other girls. Her hair bounced and swirled around behind her as she laughed and shouted. Joyce always seemed to be laughing. Erich loved being with her. He so wished he could stay. Joyce was the only good friend he had besides Helen and he didn't know when he would see her again. He wouldn't be spending the summer with her at Derrykeane this year. Nothing is right, he fretted.

When they got home from school that evening Erich marched into the kitchen.

"Where is our p-p-pocket money?" he demanded. Aunt Rachel looked up from peeling potatoes at the sink.

"I took it to pay for the school van," she replied.

"Y-Y-You get money for keeping us. Y-Y-You can't take our p-p-pocket money for the school van," Erich protested.

"Food and the like doesn't come cheap. I can't be paying for the school van too," she replied. Aunt Rachel's only reason to keep the lodgers and the boys was to earn some extra money. She didn't have any affection for them and wouldn't spend any more than necessary to keep them.

Erich knew she shouldn't have taken their money. But he knew it was useless to argue. She would never relent. I'll tell Daddy Davy when he comes to visit, Erich decided. He'll fix it. Erich hoped Daddy Davy would visit soon. He missed Daddy Davy and Aunt Elsie and Gipsy. He wanted to be back with them. It was so different here to the loving home he had at Derrykeane. I don't like it here at all, he thought, miserably.

Erich had waited for this day all week. Daddy Davy was coming to see them. Leaning on the door, he peered out of the sidelight, watching for the car to swerve jauntily to the curb under Willy's hand. Daddy Davy had only ever learned to drive a pony and trap and depended on friends when he wanted to venture out of his own community. Finding the road empty, Erich paced up and down the hall.

"Will you stop that, Erich!" Aunt Rachel scolded.

Erich turned mid-stride to face her, undaunted by her tone of voice. She continued in an anxious tone, "Now mind what you tell Mr Elliott. You're well treated here. There's many wouldn't treat you as well as I do."

Erich nodded but said nothing. At the sound of an engine slowing he flung open the door. The car drew up outside and stopped. Erich was out of the front gate before Daddy Davy could open the door. Hans raced after him. The boys hugged and clung to Daddy Davy as he stepped out of the car. Willy stepped out of the driver's seat, laughing.

"No one ever greets me like that!" he said. "I guess I'll have to get a girlfriend."

"Where's A-A-Aunt Elsie?" Erich asked.

"She was very tired today, so she stayed at home. She'll come to see you next time," Daddy Davy promised.

The boys clung to Daddy Davy's arms, both talking at once, as they walked up the short concrete path to the door. Aunt Rachel stood in the doorway watching them like a hawk eyeing its prey.

"Hello, Mr Elliott. It's good to see you again," she said.

"Hello, Mrs Owens. Not a bad day, is it?" he replied.

"Indeed, it's not," she said. She smiled and stood aside for him to enter.

"How are the boys getting on?" he asked.

"They're grand," she replied. "They're a bit of a handful at times, without a man around, but we're managing fine."

The boys followed him into the sitting room and sat flanking him. Willy stretched out in the armchair. The boys' eyes never strayed from Daddy Davy as the adults talked. After the pleasantries had been exchanged Aunt Rachel went into the kitchen to put the kettle on. As soon as she was gone both boys tried to talk at once. Daddy Davy shushed them, motioning for Erich to speak.

He began hurriedly, in a low voice. "She took our p-p-pocket money to p-p-pay for the school van and we have to do lots of chores in the morning before school. It takes a long time and sometimes we m-m-miss the school van. We make the lodgers' breakfast and do the dishes and polish their shoes and sweep..."

Daddy Davy listened, frowning. He glanced over at Willy who shook his head, tight lipped. Erich stopped mid-sentence as Aunt Rachel opened the sitting room door, balancing a tray in one hand. As the adults sipped their tea, the boys told Daddy Davy about their school.

The afternoon passed quickly. Erich dreaded its end. There was no mistaking the boys' expressions when Daddy Davy stood up, saying he and Willy must leave. Mutely, with long faces, they followed him down the hall.

At the door Daddy Davy turned to Aunt Rachel and said, "I've heard some things I don't like today. The boys should not have so many chores that they are late for school. They are also entitled to their pocket money. If things don't change here, I shall have to speak to the Red Cross."

Aunt Rachel regarded him with an affronted stare but nodded assent. He hugged the boys and Willy winked over his shoulder at them. Aunt Rachel glared as the men walked down the path. As the car started she pulled the boys roughly inside, closing the door sharply.

Erich glanced at the dresser the next morning as they entered the kitchen. Their pocket money was lying on top of it. He raced over and scooped it up, grinning at Hans. Daddy Davy is the only person who could have got our money back, Erich thought. When they got home from school that afternoon Aunt Rachel made no mention of the money and she never asked to mind it for them again.

Erich, Hans and the other children watched eagerly, waiting for the bonfire to be lit. For days the children had been bringing bits of wood and any rubbish they could find to pile on the mound. Working alongside of the village children Erich and Hans quietly contributed to it. Now a mountain of unwanted belongings and scrap wood rose in the middle of the green. Dusk was creeping in and soon it would be lit.

Halloween was a magical night. There wouldn't be boxty or Uncle Jim's stories or bobbing for apples like at Daddy Davy's house. Erich would miss all of that. But they had never had a bonfire in the country; it was a town tradition. It will be even better than the fire we lit at Rathnane School, Erich thought, and this time I won't get into trouble for it. He rocked impatiently on his tiptoes to get a better view. He couldn't wait to see it lit.

A crowd of children, teenagers and a few adults stood around the bonfire. Women watched from the doorways of nearby houses. One of the men struck a match and set it, hissing, in the middle of the pile. Smoke slowly spiralled out of the mound. Small, darting flames followed, gradually growing higher. They crackled and small twigs fell from the top of the pile, disappearing into the burning centre. Soon the flames were leaping high on the bonfire. Erich watched, open-mouthed, mesmerized by the flames.

Dusk brought a chill to the air. Erich moved closer to the fire, enjoying the heat on his face. A light breeze blew against his back. He raised his hands to the heat, pulling them away when they started to sting. The smell of the wood burning reminded him of Aunt Elsie cooking over the fire in the large kitchen at Derrykeane. He wished that she was here to make boxty and to tuck him into bed tonight. He missed her; he wondered if she missed him too.

Children shouted and clapped, watching the fire. Erich stood, immersed in his own thoughts. Two older boys moved to stand beside him but he was oblivious to them, his eyes fixed on the dancing flames. Several more boys moved in behind them. It was getting dark and the fire burned brightly against the night sky.

"D'ye like the fire, Heinz?" a boy named Sean asked Erich. Oblivious to the menace in Sean's voice, Erich nodded, without looking at him.

"But my name's not Heinz," Erich said. The boy looked at his companion, smirking.

"Maybe we should put your brother in it," he said, ignoring Erich's comment and eyeing him like a cat with a toy.

Erich turned to look at them, uneasily. The two boys smirked, watching him. The boys behind them waited to see what would happen.

"That's a good idea now," the other one said, "Let's see if they burn like anyone else. He's a bit scrawny. He'd probably go up right quick." A couple of the boys behind them sniggered.

Erich tried to inch away from the taunting boys, pushing Hans with him, but they closed in on both sides. Behind them the other boys squeezed closer. Hans nervously eyed the semi-circle enclosing them. Erich scanned the crowd for help but no one else seemed to notice anything amiss. He tried to push through the boys behind them but they grabbed Hans. Erich struggled to free him but they held him tightly.

"I think we'll put him on the fire," one of the boys said behind them.

"N-n-noo!" Erich cried, terrified, trying to free their grip on Hans. The boys laughed, holding him tightly. They moved forward slightly, pushing Erich ahead of them. A man Erich recognised from the post office noticed the scuffle and grabbed Sean's shoulder.

"Let go of the lad! What are ye playing at?" he barked.

"We were only messing. Just having a joke," Sean replied.

"Well, the lad doesn't think you're joking. Let go of him."

The boys released Hans and shuffled away, still smirking. Erich was shaking. He had been sure they would shove Hans into the fire and he wouldn't be able to stop them. What would he do without Hans? He couldn't endure living with Aunt Rachel without him. Erich was so relieved they were gone. He didn't know why they were tormenting him. He hadn't done anything to annoy them. He sometimes played with other village children without such animosity. Why does Sean hate me? Erich puzzled.

His excitement about the bonfire was gone. He wanted to get as far away from its suddenly menacing flames as he could. Hans didn't protest when he pushed out of the crowd, dragging the younger boy with him, and headed back to Aunt Rachel's house.

Erich raced down the garden, grabbing at Hans's shoulder. Hans shrugged Erich's hand off, laughing.

"I g-g-got you!" Erich shouted.

"Did not!"

"I d-d-did!"

The boys ran to the bottom of the garden, puffing and shouting, Erich still trying to grab Hans. The noise and movement frightened the hens and guinea fowl and they clucked, scolding like fat, middle-aged women. They puffed their feathers and shifted restlessly in their run; several fluttered into a huddle in the corner. Engrossed in their game the boys were unaware of the birds' displeasure. They stopped beside the run, still scuffling. The birds scurried to the far end of the cage, ruffling their feathers.

Hearing the commotion, Aunt Rachel charged out of the back door, brushing her hands against her skirt. She saw the birds scurrying around in their run and glared at the boys.

"Don't be frightening the hens! They won't lay if ye annoy them. Now come away from there!" she scolded.

Erich and Hans snickered as she went back into the kitchen. She was constantly scolding and they had stopped taking any notice, no matter what the reason for it. They walked back up the garden, stopping at the old apple tree.

"I can climb h-h-higher than you!" Erich declared.

"No, you can't!"

Hans, thinner and taller than Erich, jumped up and grabbed a low hanging branch, hauling himself into the tree. After a couple of attempts Erich also managed to grasp a branch. He hauled himself up, balanced carefully on the limb, then stretched out to reach the next one. The boys picked their way from branch to branch, climbing higher until the branches got too thin and they had to stop. Sitting in the top of the tree, they looked down at the large, open space behind their garden. Erich loved getting up here. He studied the small stream which wound its way through the middle of the marshy ground and meandered to the village harbour. There were no other houses in sight. It was very peaceful. Aunt Rachel couldn't touch him here.

The back door squeaked open and the boys sat very still. Aunt Rachel looked down the garden, then up towards the road.

"Erich! Hans! Erich! Hans!" she called.

It's too early for tea so she must have something she wants us to do, Erich thought. He knew she would be angry if she saw them in the tree. She had told them crossly last week that she wouldn't be responsible if they fell and broke their necks. The boys kept still until she went in and closed the door. They sat for a short while longer but Erich knew they couldn't hide from her forever. So they started to work their way resignedly down. Hanging onto the lowest branch Erich swung himself to the ground. Hans followed him. They walked up the garden and were almost past the kitchen window when Aunt Rachel spotted them.

"There ye are. I'm after calling ye for ages! Where were ye?" she asked through the open window.

The boys looked at her, shrugging.

"I want ye to go a message. Here's the list. Take it to the post office and Mrs Murphy will get everything for you," she said, coming around to the back door.

Aunt Rachel handed Erich the list and a few coins. Erich and

Hans walked around the side of the house and started down the hill. No one was about as they walked through the village. At the post office Mrs Murphy took their list and lifted the items from the shelves, setting them in a row on the wooden counter. She took the coins from Erich and gave him change.

Outside the post office they stopped beside the harbour to watch the stream which passed Aunt Rachel's house ending its journey. It moved quickly, in a tiny trickle, through the middle of the river bed. Erich picked up a stone and dropped it into the water, watching the tiny plop as the stone disappeared under the surface. Hans picked up a bigger stone and dropped it in, laughing and pointing as it made a larger splash. Erich crouched, looking for a bigger stone on the road. Hans nudged him.

"We better get back or Aunt Rachel will be cross," he said.

"Aunt Rachel is a-a-always cross. I'm not s-s-scared of her!"

They looked up the road and both straightened up immediately. Four older boys were walking towards them. They ambled along, seeming not to notice Erich and Hans.

"Let's go," Erich said, changing his mind about loitering any longer at the harbour. He and Hans gathered up their purchases and started walking up the road.

"Where's your bus to take you home tonight, Heinz?" one of the approaching boys asked.

"We're not c-c-coming from school," Erich replied, hoping Sean would walk past them.

"Is our school not good enough for ye?" Sean asked, ignoring Erich's answer.

Erich and Hans made no reply. They knew Sean would not be satisfied with any answer they gave. As the distance narrowed between them Erich and Hans watched the boys warily, hurrying their pace to pass them.

Standing motionless Sean stared as they passed, then shouted, "Sure, we'd not want their sort. The Prods can keep them. Let's clear them out o' here!"

Without waiting Erich and Hans broke into a run, clutching

their purchases to their chests as they strained up the steep road. They ran as hard as they could with the other boys in close pursuit. After a few hundred yards the boys chasing them slowed down and stopped. Erich and Hans ran until they had put a safe distance between themselves and the other boys. Puffing, they turned to check where their pursuers were. Sean and his friends stood at the crossroads watching them.

"Better get the bus from now on! We don't want youse on our streets," Sean taunted. Erich and Hans ignored his comment and continued up the hill.

I don't know why we go to a different school to most of the village children or why Sean plagues us about it, Erich thought. Sean doesn't like us because we're from Germany. But there's something else too. When we play with the other village children Aunt Rachel doesn't seem to like it either. We get on with all the children except for Sean and his gang. But she only wants us to mix with children we go to the Protestant National School with. Why does it matter to everyone? Erich wondered.

The boys entered the hallway, still puffing slightly. As they set their purchases down on the kitchen counter Aunt Rachel called, "Go and feed the hens. And don't be frightening them! No running or shouting or they will stop laying."

The boys walked out of the back door. Erich knew there was no point mentioning their skirmish with Sean. As long as Aunt Rachel couldn't be blamed for any mishap she wasn't interested in their problems. Erich had never met anyone like Sean when he lived with Daddy Davy and Aunt Elsie. But Daddy Davy would know what to do about Sean, Erich thought. I wish I could talk to him about it.

Stones marked out the hopscotch board in the middle of the road. Traffic through the village was light so their game was unlikely to be interrupted. It was Erich's turn. He hopped on one foot, landing between the stones they were using to mark out the first square. He wobbled and took a huge leap into the next square, almost overbalancing. He teetered on one foot until he regained his balance and continued. On his next hop Erich's toe touched the boundary.

"You're out!" the other children shouted.

"Amn't I inside the box?"

"No, you're out!"

Reluctantly Erich stepped off the board and a girl in a blue dress took his place. Erich looked up the road to see Garda Kennedy driving his cattle past Aunt Rachel's house. He grazed them in a field just outside the town. Aunt Rachel was standing in her doorway.

"Good day, Mrs Owens," he greeted her, smiling.

"Hello, Garda Kennedy," she replied.

"Not a bad day."

"Ah, now we've been lucky with the weather, sure."

The police officer slowed as he passed but Aunt Rachel did not continue the conversation. Erich thought he fancied Aunt Rachel. He always chatted with her and was willing to help her with any request. But Aunt Rachel showed no interest in him except when she needed something fixed.

The policeman continued along the road; Aunt Rachel went inside. Erich watched the progress of the hopscotch game, clapping and cheering when the girl in the blue dress stumbled and was replaced by a small boy. One child after another took a turn until it was Erich's turn again. He stepped up to the end of the board and hopped confidently onto the first square. He focused intently, careful to jump into the middle of the next square, waiting until he regained his balance before proceeding. He did not hear Aunt Rachel calling him. He continued to the end of the board and shouted in triumph as he jumped out.

An older girl in pigtails said, "Erich, Mrs Owens is after calling you. You'd best go."

Hans tensed, waiting for his brother's reaction. Erich did not think it was very late. There was no sign of the light fading. It can't be teatime yet, he thought. He decided to ignore her summons; he stood watching the progress of the next child. Hans relaxed, trusting Erich's judgement. A few minutes later Aunt Rachel called again.

"Erich! Hans! Come here at once!"

Erich looked at Hans and shrugged. They watched the progress of a small girl in a brown cardigan until she stumbled in the last square, then they headed up the road.

As they walked in the door, Aunt Rachel shouted, "Where were ye? I called ye twice! Do ye think I have all day to look for the pair of ye? Your tea was ready when I called."

"Where is it?" Erich asked.

"I threw it out. I don't have all day to chase after youse two!"

"You can't d-d-do that!" Erich shouted.

"Oh yes, I can and I did," she replied. "I had another German boy before youse and he wasn't half the trouble ye are! In all the time he was here he never gave me a bit of bother! But ye're never done annoying me! I won't have it!"

Hans looked miserable but said nothing. They were only a few minutes late for their tea. Erich argued and shouted but Aunt Rachel would not budge. She would not give them anything to eat. Erich stormed out and sat on the doorstep.

The sun had disappeared behind a cloud. A breeze blew and it was getting chilly. Erich wrapped his arms around his bare knees to keep warm. A few spots of rain plopped onto his face. The gentle drops soon turned to a steady drizzle. Erich hunched his head away from it. He sat without moving, his stomach rumbling.

Thumping footsteps alerted him to Garda Kennedy's approach, on his way home from turning the cattle out. He spotted Erich sitting on the step.

"Hello, Erich! Bad evening to be sitting out," he said, looking quizzically at the boy.

Erich nodded, hesitating before he spoke. Garda Kennedy liked Aunt Rachel so Erich figured he wouldn't want to hear any criticism of her. But before he could say anything, Aunt Rachel appeared at the door.

"There you are, Erich!" she said, smiling at the police officer. "Come in and get your tea. Would you like a cup of tea, Garda Kennedy?" The policeman smiled and nodded.

Erich rose and went inside, silently. He knew Aunt Rachel wouldn't give him a chance to tell Garda Kennedy why he was sitting outside. She didn't want to lose the officer's good will. While she had no interest in him she depended on him for help with odd jobs. So she brought Erich in and made something to eat for both boys, chatting animatedly with Garda Kennedy as she did so.

December 1951

The children stepped smartly along the street, double file. Erich had made sure Joyce was his partner. It was the end of the term and they were going to sing at St. George's Church's carol service. Their cheeks glowed with the cold and the effort of walking uphill. Erich stuffed his hands into his pockets.

"There's always lots of biscuits and sometimes a chocolate cake too! And there's sweets in a huge bowl!" Joyce told Erich.

"I hope they have chocolate cake this year. It's my favourite!" he replied.

They were not supposed to talk but Erich and Joyce whispered excitedly. Mrs Morgan, walking ahead of the class, ignored the mutterings behind her.

The village church where Erich attended Sunday services was a small, stone building with an equally small, devout congregation. But today they were going to a big church with its pointed steeple and ornate interior. The sound of their voices would echo through the building. Erich loved the sound of voices ringing out in a large space. It was fun; much better than being in class, he thought.

At the door of the church Mrs Morgan stopped them. "Children, when we get inside follow me straight to the choir stalls behind the altar. No talking, please," she said.

She led them down the aisle. Erich glanced from side to side. The church was dark except for the light cast by the chandeliers hanging from the high arched ceiling. Holly sprigs decorated the windowsills. The congregation sat wrapped in heavy coats and scarves, shuffling in the cold building.

A tall, white candle, partially burned, sat on the altar. The children filed past it into the choir stalls. The minister, in flowing black robes, stepped up to the pulpit to welcome the congregation. Erich loved to sing and waited eagerly for the first carol to be announced. The pipe organ, when it began, echoed through the building with much more resonance than the organ in his local church. It filled the room. Mrs Morgan gave the signal and the children stood. Erich sang, proudly, in a strong voice. He stood as straight as he could, aware of the congregation watching them. When the congregation stood to join them, rustling and creaking benches were drowned out by the sound of old and young voices united.

Erich sat swinging his legs restlessly when the minister began his sermon, eager to sing again. The sermon seemed to drag on interminably. He shifted and coughed, nudging Hans who stifled a giggle. He winked at Joyce who was sitting opposite him with the rest of the girls. When the next carol was announced he jumped up eagerly, wanting to hear the echo of voices again. Singing in this big building is magical, Erich thought. He could forget about his troubles while he was in this marvellous place. Daddy Davy said God was everywhere. Maybe He'll see me singing and tell Daddy Davy about it, Erich thought. He smiled, cheered by that prospect.

After the service Erich stood in the church hall balancing a plate in the crook of his arm and a glass of lemonade in his hand.

"Your cake is bigger than mine," Hans said, eyeing his plate.

"Well, I'm older than you," Erich replied.

"But Hans is taller than you. He must be older," Joyce said. Erich shook his head emphatically. Everyone always thought Hans was older. It was annoying sometimes.

"Are most people in Germany short?" Joyce asked.

"I don't know anything about Germany," Erich replied.

"But what was it like when you lived there?"

"I don't remember it very well. I'm not sure," Erich replied, eager to dismiss the topic.

"Don't you miss it? You're so far from your home."

"Germany isn't our home. Our home is at Derrykeane. One day we'll go back to Daddy Davy."

"Will we?" Hans asked.

"Of course we will." Erich stuffed a large piece of cake into his mouth. The children were queuing up to play musical chairs. Still chewing he led Joyce and Hans to join the game. The afternoon sped by as they played games and laughed and talked with their classmates.

When they left the hall Erich walked to the school van waiting outside. But before getting in he darted after Joyce and tugged her hair.

"Get away with you!" she shouted, laughing. "Happy Christmas!"

"Happy Christmas!" Erich replied. He watched her walk away, wishing he didn't have to go back to Aunt Rachel's house. He didn't expect a happy holiday there. He wished he could go with Joyce. He did not know them but he was sure he would have fun with her family. The school van beeped its horn and Erich climbed slowly in. Despite his gloom, he couldn't resist singing some of the hymns which were running through his mind on the journey home. He pushed thoughts of Aunt Rachel aside and began to feel better as he sang.

Erich and Hans tramped into Aunt Rachel's hallway, laughing and singing. Entering the sitting room they stopped, Hans with his hand poised on the door handle.

A blonde girl, slightly older than Erich sat at the fire. She looked up disdainfully. They stared back at her.

"You must be Erich and Hans. Mammy told me about you," she said without expression.

The boys looked at her curiously.

"Who are you?" Erich asked. He hadn't expected anyone besides themselves now that the lodgers had gone home for the holidays.

"Mavis."

Aunt Rachel came in from the kitchen.

"I see you've met Erich and Hans," she said to her daughter. "This is my daughter, Mavis," she said to the boys.

Aunt Rachel had mentioned her daughter, at boarding school in Dublin, but hadn't told them she was coming home for Christmas. The boys walked past and sat opposite her at the fire, watching her warily but saying nothing. She regarded them with a detached stare. Before anyone broke the silence Aunt Rachel came back into the room.

"I'll need some firewood. Erich, go and ask Mr Clarke to cut some," she said.

Erich frowned. It was already late afternoon and the light was fading. Erich hated to walk down Bob Clarke's gloomy lane in the dark. Hans looked at him sympathetically.

"I'll come with you," he said.

"You'll not," Aunt Rachel said. "I've a few chores for you here."

Reluctantly Erich got up, put on his coat and went out. He walked away from the village, to the rise of the hill and entered a narrow lane. Dusk was approaching but he could still see the road clearly. He hurried along, humming melodies from the Christmas carol service. Slightly out of breath he arrived at the Clarkes' house. Mrs Clarke answered his knock.

"Hello, Erich. How are you?" she asked.

"Fine, thank you. Is Mr Clarke about?"

"He's out yonder," she said pointing across the yard.

233

"Thank you."

Erich hurried across to the sawmill. He saw Mr Clarke standing, his back to Erich, sawing a short plank.

"Hello, Mr Clarke," he shouted above the noise of the saw, breathing in the smell of fresh cut wood. He kept well back from the saw; he still didn't like the whine of it. He couldn't clearly remember what it reminded him of but he had vague images in his head of bright lights flashing in the night sky when he had heard a similar sound in Germany.

Mr Clarke stopped sawing and turned to face Erich.

"Hello, lad. How are ye?"

"Grand, Mr Clarke. Aunt Rachel sent me to ask you for some more firewood," Erich said.

"Well, you can help me chop up some of these ends then," he replied.

He handed Erich a small axe and picked up another one lying against the wall. They worked silently side by side. Erich glanced at Mr Clarke. His quiet, sure manner reminded Erich of Daddy Davy. He liked his company. But tonight he didn't want to hang around. Maybe he could get home before dark.

Erich placed a piece of wood on the floor in front of him and swung the axe with both hands. Three strokes broke it apart. Mr Clarke swung his axe with short, swift strokes, splitting each piece of wood with a single stroke. Erich liked the dull thud of the axes. Between them they soon gathered a pile of wood.

"That should do her for a while," Mr Clarke said. "I'll bring it round tomorrow."

Erich nodded, putting down the axe. Darkness had fallen faster than he expected and he was eager to get home.

"Will you have some tea and a biscuit?" Mr Clarke asked.

"No, thanks. I'd best get back. Goodnight, Mr Clarke," Erich said quickly, tempted by the biscuit but wanting to get the walk home in the dark over.

"Tara, lad. Go straight home now."

Erich nodded, walking out of the shed. The soft light inside gave way to a thick blackness outside. He turned onto the road and set a brisk pace, hunching his head against the breeze slipping into his coat. Dark shadows swayed back and forth on the black road in front of him. He looked up fearfully. Trees, moving in the breeze, overhung the lane. Creaking, they reached out to him as if they were alive. They might be hiding someone in the swaying branches, Erich worried. He hunched further down, shivering, trying not to look at them. His steps echoed on the empty road as he hurried. There were no houses and no lights in sight. He hated this eerie road.

"Get away from me! Leave me alone!" Erich shouted at the trees which threatened him.

"What a friend we have in Jesus," he began to sing, in a tremulous voice, his lips quivering and his eyes blurry with tears. No one would know if anything happened to him. No one would miss him and search for him. Well, Hans would notice but who would listen to him? He looked straight ahead, singing loudly as he tore down the road. Something flapped above him but he refused to look. Singing louder, his voice gradually getting stronger, he hurried along. He tensed at a creak to his left. His eyes shifted nervously from side to side but he didn't look. Taking a deep breath he continued singing. Daddy Davy said God is always with you. He hoped so now as there was no one else to help him.

He was glad to see the trees end, a mile later, when he reached the main road. Without the trees to block it, a half moon gave some light. Erich turned onto the road and half ran the short distance to Aunt Rachel's, relieved to see light through the window as he hurried up the path. He burst in the door, puffing as he shrugged his coat off.

"Why are ye making such a commotion, Erich?" Aunt Rachel scolded, hearing him storm into the house.

"I'm n-n-not," he said. "Mr Clarke said he'll b-b-bring the wood tomorrow," he added, panting after his flight home.

"Grand," she replied.

Erich went into the sitting room and flopped down in front of the fire beside Hans. Mavis, sitting in a chair beside the fire, glanced up from her book. She went back to reading without a word. Aunt Rachel settled on the sofa and lifted her knitting.

Erich and Hans whispered and fidgeted, restless in the silence. Mavis ignored them. The evening crawled along until, yawning, Aunt Rachel looked at the clock.

"It's time ye were in bed," she said to the boys. Mavis looked up. "Ye've no need to leave the fire yet," Aunt Rachel added to her.

Mavis stayed by the fire. Erich didn't know whether it was because she was older than them or whether Aunt Rachel was just eager to get the boys out of her sight. Reluctantly Erich and Hans left the heat of the fire and went up to their chilly room.

They undressed quickly in the cold room. Aunt Rachel never even gave them a heated stone to warm the bed. Erich went to their window, overlooking the front of the house. The night sky with the half moon hanging above him was intriguing rather than scary from here. He stared up at it, forgetting the cold. Grabbing the white metal handles on the window frame, he heaved. The window didn't move at first, then jerked upwards, one side rising higher than the other. Erich hauled on the other side until it rose evenly. With the window halfway up, he stuck his head out and looked at the clear stars above. Hans came to join him, peering out through the open space. They shivered as the cold air penetrated their thin night shirts but they ignored it, fascinated by the stars.

"We could see them better outside," Erich said.

"We can't go outside now," Hans replied, "Aunt Rachel would hear us on the stairs."

"We could get out on the ledge," Erich answered.

Erich dragged the single chair in the room over to the window and climbed out, onto the narrow, concrete window ledge. Below him the black slates of the sitting room's bay window protruded. He sat cross legged on the cold concrete gazing up at the stars. Hans squirmed out and sat beside him. They sat, numbness creeping up through them but fascinated with the painting in the sky above. Whispering excitedly, they pointed at the stars.

They didn't hear Mavis's footsteps on the stairs, then along the hallway past their door.

"I hear you talking. You should be in bed," she scolded, entering the room.

Mavis stopped dead when she saw the boys sitting on the windowsill, looking up at the sky.

"You shouldn't be out there! You'll fall!" she exclaimed.

"We've c-c-climbed higher than this. We'll not f-f-fall," Erich replied confidently.

Before Mavis could reply they heard Aunt Rachel on the stairs. They couldn't move fast enough to escape their narrow perch and she appeared in the doorway as Erich and Hans scrambled through the open window.

"Get in here at once!" she shouted. "That's solid concrete below. Have you no sense at all? I'll not have it on my head that youse two managed to break your necks. And I won't have folk blathering about me either if youse kill yourselves!"

Erich slammed the window closed. Dodging around Aunt Rachel, the boys dived into the bed and lay tense beneath the blankets. Erich thought Aunt Rachel would smack them but she ushered Mavis out and closed the door without a word.

Erich wasn't too worried about being caught and scolded. Aunt Rachel is always scolding us for something, he thought. Because her treatment of them was often harsh and unfair he rarely heeded her. He didn't recognise the sound advice sometimes given during her ranting.

Erich gradually warmed up under the heavy blankets. Images of the bright lights in the sky flitted through his head. There are so many different kinds of light. There's Christmas tree lights, electric lights, firelight and lanterns. How do the stars make their light? he wondered. That's a question that Daddy Davy could answer. I'll have to ask him. I hope he visits again soon, he thought as he drifted off to sleep.

Spring 1952

After tea the boys sat by the fire, looking out at the grey, cloudy evening. Hans dug his fingernails into his scalp and then his armpit. Aunt Rachel watched him, frowning. He shifted in the chair, avoiding her stare. He managed to sit still for a moment then his hand crept up to his head again. Aunt Rachel tutted.

"Hans! Will ye stop that scratching! Sit still," she said.

Hans was still for a moment but soon the itching started again and he scratched furiously at his armpit. An annoyed sigh escaped from her as she glared at him.

"If ye can't stop that scratching, go and wash! Anyone would think ye had nits!" she said.

Hans left the room and there was silence for a few minutes. Erich turned the page of the book he was reading and reached up to scratch his head. Aunt Rachel, her knitting held poised, shot a warning glance at him and he stopped. But the itching grew and he raked his hand through his hair. Aunt Rachel snorted, exasperated, watching him.

"You're scratching too. Will ye stop that!"

Erich tried to resist the urge to scratch but couldn't. He rubbed furiously at his head like a dog with fleas. Aunt Rachel glared at him and he stopped. When she looked away his hand crept up to his armpit and he continued to scratch furtively, trying not to attract her attention.

Hans came back into the room, his hair wet and sticking out in every direction.

"Come here," Aunt Rachel said to him.

She took down an old comb, with several teeth missing, from the mantelpiece. Gripping Hans's chin she angled his head downwards, dragging the comb through his hair. She parted it in different directions, looking closely at his scalp. Clucking and moaning, she let go of his head.

"Ye've got nits," she said. " I suppose ye do as well," she said irritably to Erich.

The boys watched her, waiting. She frowned at them, hands on her hips.

"I won't have nits in my house. The lodgers will leave if they hear about this! It's as well they are away out tonight. I can't afford to have youse driving them out!"

The boys said nothing, cowering slightly. Shaking herself, she bustled around the room.

"Get your clothes off and give them to me," she ordered.

The boys took off their clothes while she went to get the tin bathtub. Setting it by the fire, she filled it with hot water, adding a small amount of cold water. She took their clothes and carrying them at arms length, dropped them in the garden. The water was hot and the boys stepped into it cautiously. Taking a stiff scrub brush she washed Hans, then Erich, scrubbing vigorously until their skin reddened. She scrubbed their scalps and underarms until they stung. But a sharp look from Aunt Rachel stopped the boys crying out at the rough treatment.

When they were dried off and dressed again she took each in turn and picked through his hair with the comb, pulling out any nits still clinging to his scalp.

When she had finished and the bathtub was hung up again she said, "Don't they inspect ye for cleanliness at the school? I have a mind to complain to your teacher about this. Not a word of it to the girls, mind! I don't want them to think I keep a dirty house! And don't ye boys be bringing such things home again!"

The boys nodded, huddling by the fire as their hair dried. Aunt Rachel went into the garden. They watched her through the window as she set fire to their clothes. Everything disappeared in a burst of flame.

"It's not our fault we got nits. She blames us for everything," Hans said to Erich. "Thomas who sits beside me is always scratching. He must have millions of them!"

"All she's worried about is the money she gets from her precious lodgers. She doesn't get as much for us," Erich said.

The boys stood watching their clothes burn in the garden. Erich wished again they were back with Aunt Elsie. She never treated them the way Aunt Rachel did. That was their home. Daddy Davy had said it was.

"I want ye to stay inside with Mr and Mrs Elliott. Now, mind what ye say. Don't be telling them any lies. I have my eye on ye both," Aunt Rachel said.

The boys nodded. Erich couldn't wait to see Daddy Davy and Aunt Elsie. It seemed ages since the last time Daddy Davy had visited. Erich paced from the sitting room to the hall door, in his Sunday suit, watching for them. He thought they would never arrive. Hans stood watch at the bedroom window.

Finally the old, black car trundled into view. Hans ran downstairs and Erich flung open the front door before Aunt Rachel could stop them. They raced to the footpath, waving madly as the car came to a stop. Daddy Davy and Aunt Elsie smiled and waved back; Willy, from the driver's seat, gave a mock salute.

Both boys started to talk at once as they got out of the car. Aunt Rachel hovered in the doorway, listening.

"It's lovely to see you again, Mr Elliott. And so nice to meet you, Mrs Elliott. Won't you come in?" she called.

Erich stayed close to Daddy Davy as he led the way to the sitting room. Aunt Elsie followed, her hand resting on Hans's shoulder. The little group were oblivious to Aunt Rachel following behind them.

"It's very mild so early in the season," Aunt Rachel said.

"Indeed it is. Spring is my favourite time of year," Aunt Elsie replied. "My daffodils are blooming well at home." Erich remembered the yellow blanket he had trampled during his first year with them. At least he hadn't done any lasting damage. He would never purposely upset Aunt Elsie; he knew she loved the flowers.

The boys crowded close to Daddy Davy and Aunt Elsie on the settee. Aunt Rachel went to make tea, looking sharply at the boys before she left the room. She left the sitting room door ajar while she was in the kitchen.

As soon as she was gone Erich whispered to Daddy Davy, "She doesn't want us to tell you what it's like here. She's horrible!"

"Well, Willy is outside tinkering at the motor. Go out and tell him what's wrong and I'll speak to him later," Daddy Davy said softly.

Erich slipped out of the door. When Aunt Rachel returned Daddy Davy and Aunt Elsie kept her occupied chatting. She looked around for Erich but did not have an opportunity to ask where he was. He slipped in later without comment.

The afternoon passed quickly and, when it was time for the visitors to leave, the boys followed them morosely down the hall. At the car they hugged Daddy Davy and Aunt Elsie fiercely. Aunt Elsie's eyes welled with tears as she released Erich and slid into the car. He bent to catch a last glimpse of her then looked up at Willy, standing on the pavement. Willy winked and mouthed, "Leave it to me."

GOODBYE GIPSY
County Cavan
Spring 1952

ERICH PEERED out of the window at the branches overhanging the road and the small fields beyond. He didn't know this road but the area looked familiar as they drove down the steep slope.

"Are we nearly there?" he asked Daddy Davy.

"Just a little further down this road," he replied from the front passenger seat.

Erich stared out intently, eager to catch a glimpse of the new house. Daddy Davy and Aunt Elsie had sold Derrykeane and moved to Clonty, a smaller farm, after Erich and Hans went to live with Aunt Rachel. The new farm was closer to the village and roughly three miles from their previous farm at Derrykeane.

"Why can't Hans come to live with us too?" Erich asked.

"There isn't room for both of you here. He'll be grand with Auntie Marjorie and Bobby in Cavan Town. It's not very far away. You'll be able to see him."

There would be more opportunities for Bobby, after he left school, in a large town. So Aunt Marjorie and Bobby had left Uncle Jim's farm and moved to Cavan Town. Much had changed in a few short months.

Erich wondered if his brother would come to visit him. Hans and Bobby had been best friends before Erich and Hans had gone to County Leitrim. Then at Aunt Rachel's, with no one else to turn to, the brothers had come to rely on each other and finally become friends. Erich did not want that to change. But would Hans and Bobby bother with him now they had each other for company? Erich hoped they would.

The car crunched onto a short dirt lane and stopped. As the sound of the engine died away the front door flew open. Aunt Elsie rushed out, waving. Gipsy bounded from the back of the building and lunged himself at the car, barking. Erich stretched his arm out the open window to pat the excited dog.

"H-H-Hi ya, Aunt Elsie!" he shouted, gleefully.

"Welcome home, Erich!" she called.

The car had barely stopped when Erich jumped out and hugged the leaping dog. Willy, sitting in the driver's seat, laughed at the commotion.

"Yon dog hasn't forgotten ye!" he said to Erich.

"G-G-Gipsy would never f-f-forget me!" Erich said, indignantly.

Erich ran over to Aunt Elsie and threw his arms around her. Hugging her fiercely he said, "I'm s-s-so glad to be here! Aunt Rachel was a h-h-horrible woman!"

"Sure, that's past now. Ye're home again." Tears glistened in her eyes as she held the boy.

Grinning, Erich hugged her again, then reached down to ruffle Gipsy's silky coat. The dog's rear end wagged back and forth vigorously. Letting go of Aunt Elsie, Erich raced in circles around the grey pebble-dashed house with Gipsy in pursuit, barking madly. The adults smiled, watching Erich and Gipsy playing together.

Aunt Elsie said, "Come inside, Erich. I've the dinner ready. I made some of your favourite mushroom soup to start with."

Aunt Elsie picked wild mushrooms and added milk to make a cream soup. Erich loved its rich flavour. He ran eagerly through the front door and into the small entranceway. Ahead of him was a flight of battered, wooden stairs.

"In to the left, Erich," Daddy Davy called, following behind him.

Erich stepped into a compact, square room. On the wall opposite, was a low stone hearth. His mouth watered when he smelled the mushroom soup simmering in the pot over the fire. Aunt Elsie ushered everyone inside. Daddy Davy lifted the soup pot off the fire and carried it to the table.

"Sure, I'll get that," she said. But Daddy Davy motioned her to the table and she sat down gratefully. "Ta. That pot seems right heavy lately," she admitted.

Erich, sitting with his back to the window, looked around the room. A pair of comfortable chairs were set near the fire. The old piano, which Nell had used to torment him during his first Christmas at Derrykeane, stood near the door. He was glad they still had it. Despite the girls' bossy ways, Erich had spent many happy hours singing with them when they were home from boarding school. It was comforting to see familiar objects in this new house.

After dinner Daddy Davy and Erich walked into the field in front of the house, with Gipsy trotting happily at their heels. Erich spotted a horse and a donkey grazing placidly.

"You still have Paddy the horse and Paddy the donkey!" he exclaimed.

"Indeed we do. Sure, what would we do without them?"

"Paddy the donkey isn't much use," Erich said.

"He can be a stubborn beast, to be sure," Daddy Davy agreed.

Erich was eager to see the new farm. They thoroughly explored its few, small fields. Fifteen acres were much more manageable than Derrykeane's forty had been.

When they had explored every inch of it they headed back towards the house. Beside the house Daddy Davy stopped and pointed to a plot of soil.

"See yon bit o' land. I'm growing some vegetables there. I'll fence a bit off for you and you can grow your own vegetables. I'll give you seeds to get you started and you can sell the vegetables when they're ready so you'll have a bit of money for yourself."

Erich jumped up and down. "W-W-What will I grow?" he shouted.

"You can grow some potatoes and onions and cabbage. I'll also give you three or four hens and you can collect the eggs and sell them too."

Erich grinned from ear to ear. He would do his own farming. He couldn't wait to get started.

"I-I-I better start digging my d-d-drills for the potatoes," he said.

Daddy Davy smiled, "I think ye can wait until the morning to start."

Summer 1952

"Are you coming to pick mushrooms?" Erich asked Nell hopefully.

"No, I've too much to do here while Mammy's resting. You and Rose may go," she replied.

It seemed almost like old times to have both Nell and Rose home for a visit. Since Nell started working in Dublin she did not get home often. Erich missed having her around and, though he wouldn't admit it, he was even more fascinated with her slim legs than he had been last year. Erich and Rose, with empty metal buckets clanging on their arms, crossed the road and walked the short distance up the lane to Wilsons' farm. Gipsy trotted contentedly behind them. Wilsons' farm was larger than Daddy Davy's and had several greenhouses behind the house.

Wild mushrooms grew abundantly in the Wilsons' fields and the children often picked them for Aunt Elsie to make mushroom soup. This afternoon they worked quickly and their buckets were soon full. The sun beat down as they left the field. They went past the large, whitewashed house and around to the greenhouses behind it to look for Willy. He worked casually for the Wilsons.

As they rounded the corner he was carrying a potted plant down the narrow aisle. Erich waved and held up the full bucket. Willy smiled at them through the steamy glass. He set the plant down and squeezed up the aisle to the door.

"What mischief are you two up to?" he asked.

"We just came to see you," Erich replied.

"A likely story," Willy grinned. "And might ye be wanting some tomatoes then?"

"Oh yes!" Erich exclaimed.

"Yes, please," Rose said, nudging Erich to remind him of his manners.

Willy laughed, motioning for them to come into the greenhouse. It was even warmer inside than outside under the direct sun. He led them down an aisle filled with tomato plants sitting in trays, their stalks tied up to support the weight of the ripe, juicy tomatoes. Willy picked a few and handed them to Erich and Rose. They cradled them carefully, in their arms, not to squeeze and bruise them.

"Ta, Willy," Rose said.

"No problem, beautiful," he replied.

Rose blushed, avoiding his gaze. Willy laughed, watching her.

"Ye're the same colour as those tomatoes," he said as she blushed deeper.

Erich glared at him, suddenly angry and wanting to get Rose away from him. He didn't like Willy looking at her like that. Erich usually enjoyed Willy's company. He was a natural comedian and always made Erich laugh. But he didn't like it when Willy said things like that to Rose or Nell.

"We better get these home. Thanks, Willy," Erich said gruffly, shuffling up the aisle.

Erich and Rose carefully balanced the tomatoes, the buckets hanging from their elbows, as they walked back to the house.

"We'll have mushroom soup for days with all these mushrooms!" Rose exclaimed.

Erich nodded, following Rose into the kitchen. But even the thought of Aunt Elsie's mushroom soup couldn't shake his mood. He thought of Willy looking at Rose and scowled.

They rolled the tomatoes onto the kitchen table and set the buckets beside it. Nell stopped mid-way between the counter and table. Brushing her hair back with one hand, her eyebrows knit together as she quickly sized up the afternoon's harvest and what could be made with it. She nodded approval.

"Well, that's grand! The tea will be ready shortly. But will we have a couple now? " she asked.

Erich, eyeing the sugar tin, nodded as Nell reached it down from the dresser. She cut the tomatoes in half and liberally sprinkled them with sugar. Biting into them, the juice ran down their chins and dripped onto the table. They sucked in, licking their lips to catch the juice before it could escape. Erich sunk his teeth and cheeks into the tomato as far as he could, pulling hunks out of it. He loved the sweet, juicy fruit. Enjoying the taste, he gradually pushed Willy's comments from his mind.

After tea Nell poured hot water into a large basin on the counter. There was no running water in the house so they used it instead of a sink. Nell washed the dishes, thwarting her mother's attempts to help until Aunt Elsie contented herself with wiping the table. She was tired at the end of the day and when she finished she sank onto a kitchen chair, leaving the cloth where she stopped.

Erich wandered outside and sat on the step, watching Daddy Davy light his pipe. He rubbed Gipsy's neck as he watched the smoke patterns curl upwards. Rose squeezed in past them carrying a pail of water from the well.

"Sure, it's a grand night," a voice called from the lane.

Erich looked around and his eyes narrowed when he saw Willy and his brother, John, walking up the lane towards them.

"Indeed it is," Daddy Davy replied. "We'll have good hay if it continues."

The other men nodded in agreement. They chatted about the

weather and farming. Despite his annoyance with Willy, Erich listened avidly, wanting to learn as much as he could. He wanted his own plot and hens to do well.

When the household chores were finished the women joined them outside. Talk turned to the neighbours and news from the community.

"How do you like the big city, Nell? Is the job going well?" John asked.

"The job's grand and I like Dublin. Isn't it fortunate that I can stay with Aunt Rose? But still it's grand to get home whenever I can," Nell replied.

"Before ye know it, Davy, these two lovely ladies will be marrying. Won't ye, ladies?" Willy teased.

Rose blushed but said nothing. Nell giggled, fluttering her hands about her like a nervous butterfly. Willy laughed, seeing the colour in Rose's face. Erich, moving to stand closer to Rose, glared at him. Gipsy huddled in beside the boy.

"And what'll ye be doing, lad?" he asked Erich. "Well, besides smoking, drinking and chasing women. Ye'll be staggering home full on Saturday nights."

"Now, don't be giving him any ideas," John said, shooting a reproving look at Willy.

"Sure, he probably smokes a pipe already, don't ye? I heard ye started when ye were right young," Willy said to Erich, with a wink. Erich ignored the reference to his experimentation with newspaper cigarettes.

Willy had shifted nearer to Rose. He turned his attention back to her.

"So do ye have any suitors yet?" he asked.

"Don't be daft!" she replied, still blushing.

"Well, I might have to ask ye out myself then. Would ye fancy me?" he asked, tilting his head and grinning cockily.

"S-S-Stop that!" Erich shouted, pushing in between Willy and Rose, shoving Willy away from her. Gipsy gave a low growl. Willy just grinned at Erich's sullen expression.

"Well, she's a pretty girl. I can't help myself, Erich. I wonder if she would have me," Willy said, glancing towards Rose.

"Now that's enough of that talk. Rose is too young to be courting young men and she's your cousin," Aunt Elsie said, fixing a stern stare on Willy.

John shot a cautioning look at him but Willy just grinned cheekily. Erich, watching Willy's every move, stayed close to Rose as if he could physically shield her from Willy's banter. Like a determined terrier he wouldn't budge. Preoccupied with his mission to keep Willy away from Rose, he did not notice the adults' amused smiles.

Belfast
Summer 1952

Erich trailed behind Helen through the field. A fluttering motion, a couple feet away, caught his eye and he stopped to watch a small, yellow spotted butterfly, poised on a twig. He cupped his hands and reached towards it.

"Don't catch it! Leave it be!" Helen admonished as she turned to see why he had stopped.

Erich watched the butterfly flit away at her sudden movement. He shrugged then began poking through the tall grass they were standing in.

"Maybe there are grasshoppers here," Erich said. "Or frogs!"

"I don't want to see any old frogs," Helen said shuddering.

Despite having to leave his precious vegetable garden in Daddy Davy's care, Erich was enjoying his holiday at Aunt Sarah's. He was especially glad to be with his friend Helen again. Sometimes he found it lonely at the farm without Hans or Helen for company once Nell's and Rose's visits were over.

They had spent the afternoon exploring in the field behind Helen's street. Although she lived in the city, the Cave Hill rose behind her garden. The children had spent many hours during the week roaming in the surrounding fields. Erich felt very much at ease with the dark Cave Hill towering behind them. Its brooding presence seemed to watch over them.

"Helen! Erich!" they heard from the direction of the house.

"Aunt Sarah's calling us," Erich said.

Forgetting the wildlife in the field, the children headed back to the house without delay. It was near teatime and they were getting hungry.

"There you two are!" Aunt Sarah said as they came through the back door. "We'll have some tea and then we're away to the cinema tonight."

The children cheered. Erich had never been to the cinema. There were none near Clonty. Helen had told him about the films she had seen and he was dying to go. He glanced at the clock on the wall every minute or so as he wolfed down his food. Uncle Jack would be home from work soon; Aunt Sarah said they would go after he ate his tea. Erich willed the time to move forward.

When he arrived, Uncle Jack greeted everyone cheerfully. Aunt Sarah told him about the plans to go to the cinema and he nodded agreeably.

"So you're going to go to the theatre for your first time, Erich," he said.

Erich looked at him puzzled.

"Aunt Sarah said we're going to the cinema," he replied. He did not want to see a play; he wanted to go to the pictures.

"Well, we are. Don't you worry about that," Uncle Jack replied in his drawling tone.

Uncle Jack's American expressions sometimes confused Erich. So he was glad to have the misunderstanding cleared up. They were definitely going to the pictures. He couldn't wait! He tried to sit quietly while Uncle Jack ate his tea but he kept fidgeting and looking at the clock. He jumped up when Uncle Jack pushed his empty plate away but Aunt Sarah motioned for him to sit down again while she washed the dishes.

"Don't you worry, son. We've time, we won't miss the start of it," Uncle Jack said smiling. "I think we'll head off now," he added as Aunt Sarah hung up the tea towel.

Uncle Jack stood up and went to the hallway. Helen walked, with her usual poised air, behind him. Erich raced ahead of her. Aunt Sarah paused, glancing around the kitchen to be sure everything was tidied away, before hurrying after them. It was still light outside as they got in the car. Erich sat up in the back seat as straight as a scarecrow fixed to a pole, staring out of the double panel front window of the Morris Minor. The car jolted on the tramcar tracks, tossing Erich sideways on the seat, as they bumped along the uneven surface of the Antrim Road. A double-decker tram rumbled and screeched behind them. Erich turned to watch and wave at the driver, who smiled at the enthusiastic boy. The tram stopped and its doors opened. A woman carrying a pram stepped down, holding a small child by the hand. They cautiously made their way to the footpath. Erich watched the tram as they drove on. He wondered what it would be like to be sitting on the upper deck, looking down at the cars around it. Tall, staid brick buildings, with narrow, long windows lined either side of the street. Paper signs were stuck on many windows, advertising the wares inside. The end of each block of buildings was covered in dashes of white paint, advertising businesses adjacent to or beneath the signs. Public houses stood with doors open. Men lounged in their doorways, smoking and watching passers-by.

The car pulled in to the side of the road and stopped. When they got out Erich looked around but he did not see the cinema. He wondered if they were in the right place as he followed Uncle Jack down the street. He began to worry. Belfast was such a big place. What if we're lost and can't find the cinema? he thought. He didn't want to miss the start of the film. Then he noticed a large building with pillars supporting the entranceway looming ahead of them. Above the pillars a large sign proclaimed "Capitol Cinema". They were here!

Uncle Jack handed Erich and Helen several coins from his pocket to pay for their tickets. They trailed behind him to the ticket booth and laid the coins on the counter. When the young woman at the booth handed them their tickets Erich clutched his tightly. He did not want to lose it now. Uncle Jack bought a bag of aniseed balls and handed them around before they went into the auditorium.

Erich paused for a moment when he entered the dark auditorium. It was like stepping into a tunnel. All he could see was the tall, dark shadow of Uncle Jack in front of him. Helen reached out and grabbed onto the back of his jumper as he followed the dark form. They slowly made their way up the aisle until Uncle Jack found four seats together.

Once he was in his seat Erich leaned his head back examining the large, high-ceilinged room. He squinted up at the ornately carved ceiling but the details of the pattern were lost in the gloom. Suddenly there was a burst of music and a light grew behind the thick, red curtains at the front of the room. The heavy curtains rolled slowly to the side as the music got louder. Erich forgot the ceiling and stared mesmerised at the screen. A newsreel reported the latest news events. It's strange to see real people on a screen in front of me, Erich thought. How could they be there but not be real? As soon as the newsreel ended cartoon characters raced across the screen. Erich sat entranced. It was as if they had walked off the pages of his comic books. Mickey Mouse swooped Minnie Mouse off her feet with flowers and his charm. Helen clapped; Erich just stared, leaning forward with his mouth hanging open.

When the cartoons ended more real people appeared. The title "Here Comes The Groom" arched across the screen. Erich watched people with accents like Uncle Jack sing and dance. Bing Crosby pursued Jane Wyman, trying to get his ex-fiancee to change her mind and marry him. They left the office, waltzed into the elevator and emerged onto the sidewalk singing, "In the cool, cool, cool of the evening, tell 'em we'll be there...". It was a catchy tune and Erich hummed along. Helen poked him, putting her finger to her lips. He grinned and stuck his tongue out at her. Uncle Jack, leaning his elbow on the armrest, held out the bag of sweets to them. Erich unwrapped his noisily. His humming stopped as he bounced the sticky ball against his cheek with his tongue, sucking it. The music, singing and dancing on the screen were so magical Erich never wanted it to end. He didn't care that it was a love story. When Jane Wyman finally agreed to marry Bing Crosby Helen clapped; Erich made a face at her. When it ended they sat watching the credits roll, unwilling to leave. The newsreel started again and they stood up, following the crowd outside.

"I was so glad when she said she'd marry him. I knew she would in the end," Helen said. "What was your favourite part?"

"The singing was the best," Erich replied without hesitation. He wasn't very interested in the plot.

It was dusk now and the gas streetlights glowed at the far end of the street. Erich stood on the pavement outside the cinema, staring as the crowd streamed past him. A man with a brown peaked cap walked towards them, ladder balanced on his shoulder. He stopped at each pole, leaned the ladder against it and climbed to the top. He lit the lamp then moved on to the next one. Erich leaned his head back and looked up at the square globes at the top of the black, grooved poles. Panes of glass were set in all four sides of each globe, held in place by a thin, black frame. A pointed ornamental top perched above the globe like an angel on a Christmas tree. The lamp's flame flickered red, blue and green. The flame and its changing colours fascinated Erich. These lights reminded him of Christmas tree lights. But they could change colour. Maybe they're even better, Erich thought, gazing up. He walked beside Aunt Sarah, head craned upwards to watch the flickering flames.

"Mind where you're going, Erich. You'll fall," Aunt Sarah said.

Uncle Jack laughed, watching him.

Erich walked on, humming the tune "In the Cool, Cool, Cool of the Evening". The pictures was even better than he had expected. He could not wait to tell Daddy Davy about it.

"How was the theatre, Erich?" Uncle Jack asked.

Erich drew a breath in quickly, pulling himself up taller as he spoke, "It was b-b-brilliant!"

"I think you're having such a good time here you won't want to go home."

Erich looked at the ground, unsure what to say. He loved all the new things he had seen and done since he came to Belfast but he was eager to get home to tell Daddy Davy about all of it. Besides he missed Gipsy and Aunt Elsie.

Seeing Erich's confusion, Uncle Jack said, "Of course, you'll want to get home. You can come and visit us any time you like. You're always welcome."

Erich nodded, relieved. As Uncle Jack unlocked the car door, Erich hummed the film's theme tune.

County Cavan
Summer 1952

"We're away out, Mammy," Helen said to Aunt Sarah as she opened the door.

"Remember what I'm after telling you. Don't be climbing on the extension," she replied, looking at Erich. "Aunt Elsie and Uncle Davy will be home today and I've everything ready for them."

"Erich, see that you behave yourself," Rose added.

Erich nodded. After his visit to Belfast Aunt Sarah and Helen had come back with him to stay at the farm while Daddy Davy and Aunt Elsie went away for a few days. Erich was glad to have Helen's company for a while longer.

The children knew they were not to go too far from the house as Aunt Elsie and Daddy Davy should arrive soon. Aunt Sarah was roasting a chicken for dinner and she said she did not want to have to look for them when it was ready.

Outside it was oppressively grey. There was no wind and everything seemed to be waiting for the rain. The still air emphasized how quiet it was. No one else was around; there was nothing happening. Erich kicked at the ground restlessly. Gipsy stretched out beside them.

"Let's go to the post office shop," Erich said.

"We're not to go away. You know that, Erich!" Helen said with exasperation, "We promised."

They wandered around the perimeter of the house looking for something to do. Gipsy reluctantly got up and followed them. The animals were all out in the fields and they would get their clothes dirty if they went out to them. No other children lived at the adjoining farms and Willy was not working at the Wilsons today as he was collecting Daddy Davy and Aunt Elsie from the station. They had no one to visit.

"Do you want to skip?" Helen asked.

"Noooo," Erich sighed, bored.

"What do you want to do then?"

Erich looked around the garden but didn't see anything that interested him. They wandered aimlessly around the house again and stopped at the back to look at the new, two storey extension that Daddy Davy was building. He was building a separate kitchen on the ground floor and another bedroom upstairs.

"I wonder if Daddy Davy finished the floor upstairs before they went away?" Erich asked.

"I don't know," Helen replied.

"I could get up there and find out."

"Mammy said ye're not to be going up there!" Helen cried.

"I'll just take a quick peek. It won't do any harm."

Erich went around to the side of the house and caught hold of the drainpipe. Gripping it and digging his toes into the grooves between the cement blocks, he pulled himself up. With his feet wedged between the drainpipe and the wall, he leaned over the roof and rolled onto it. He sat up and looked around.

"Come down from there, Erich! Mammy will be furious!" Helen whispered urgently, beneath him.

Ignoring her, Erich stood up and looked across the extension. The floor was not finished yet but there were crossbeams he could walk on. He would just have a quick look around. It wouldn't do any harm.

"I'll be down in a wee minute," he replied.

Helen screwed up her face, exasperated, as Erich started to pick his way across on the crossbeams.

"Be careful where you step!"

"I will," Erich said, glancing backwards. He lost his concentration for a moment as he spoke, and heard a sharp crunch. He felt his foot sinking. He had misjudged the distance and stepped through the plaster between the crossbeams.

"Ohhh! Aaaaggghhh!" he screamed as he fell. He stopped with a jolt, his legs hanging through the plaster.

Hearing the crash, Aunt Sarah and Rose ran into the extension. Erich could hear their muffled shouts below him. Helen stood screaming beside the house, "Mammy! Mammy! Erich fell!" Gipsy barked sharply and paced along the side of the house.

Bits of the ceiling lay, in strips, in the room below; Erich's legs dangled through the hole which was left. He hung suspended, afraid he would fall further. I'd better move quickly before I do fall, he decided. He leaned forward, rested his elbows on the crossbeam and pushed. Rolling onto the beam, he pulled his right leg out of the hole and then dragged the other one out. Carefully he stood up and brushed his knees off. They were scraped and bleeding slightly. Dust covered his shirt and hair. This wasn't supposed to happen, he thought. I'd better get down fast before I get into any more trouble. Helen was right, Aunt Sarah will be furious. Nervously he half-skipped from one crossbeam to the next until he reached the edge of the building. He half-climbed and half-jumped to the ground.

Aunt Sarah and Rose stood waiting for him.

"Are ye alright?" Aunt Sarah asked, lips pursed, glancing at his bleeding knees.

Erich nodded, cowering. Aunt Sarah looked very angry.

"Whatever will Davy say about this? All his hard work! He'll not be pleased," she said, shaking her head. Erich tried to avoid her gaze.

"Erich, I told ye to behave yourself!" Rose admonished, "Daddy will be furious!"

"Well, what he doesn't know for now, won't hurt him," Aunt Sarah said, making a quick decision. "He's got enough on his plate as it is," she added enigmatically. In a suddenly determined manner she said, "Rose, you sweep up the mess downstairs. We'll try to patch it up and, sure, he might not notice this day. We'll give him a chance to settle in afore he gets the news."

Aunt Sarah set everyone to work. Rose and Helen cleared away the debris downstairs while Aunt Sarah got a couple thin planks of wood and some glue. Erich washed his knees and scrambled back onto the roof. Aunt Sarah, standing on a chair, pushed up the pieces of wood and glued them in place while Erich held them. She filled any gaps then looked at the finished product. From a distance it wasn't too noticeable. They cleared away everything and tidied up.

"Sure, that's not a bad job. You'd hardly notice it," Aunt Sarah said, surveying their work. "Now, Erich don't you be telling them that you broke it."

Erich nodded, grinning. What an exciting morning! he thought. After the initial fright, it was exciting falling through the roof. And they had it fixed so it looked nearly as good as new. Erich admired their work, pleased with himself despite having caused the damage.

"Now you two, go outside and play. But don't get up on the extension again! Behave yourselves until Uncle Davy and Aunt Elsie get home," Aunt Sarah warned them.

The children went outside and hung around the front door. Erich hoped Daddy Davy and Aunt Elsie would get home soon.

He couldn't wait to see them.

"Let's see how many butterflies we can find," Helen said. Erich nodded.

The children wandered around the garden, peering at the grass for any sign of movement until the sound of an engine getting closer drew their attention away from their quest. When the car turned into their lane the children and the dog ran to meet Daddy Davy and Aunt Elsie. Willy got out of the car and stood leaning against it, watching the children jumping around it. The shouts and barking brought Aunt Sarah and Rose to the door.

"Did ye have a good holiday?" Aunt Sarah asked.

"Grand. It was such a good rest," Aunt Elsie replied, getting out of the car.

"Indeed, that's just what ye needed," Aunt Sarah said.

Erich listened impatiently as the adults chatted. He thought about the excitement of the morning and giggled, remembering his legs sticking through the ceiling. It was so funny! Daddy Davy looked at him curiously.

"What's so funny?" he asked.

"I fell through the roof!" Erich blurted out. "My legs were hanging down in the room below!"

Aunt Sarah and Rose glared at him, exasperated. They had worked so hard to hide any sign of the accident. They did not want to annoy Daddy Davy or worry Aunt Elsie when they were only back from their holiday, especially when Aunt Elsie's health was so poor.

"Did you now? Well, we'll have to hear more about this," Daddy Davy replied, glancing around at the women.

Erich could barely contain his excitement as he retold the events of the morning, completely forgetting how angry Aunt Sarah had been with him. Aunt Sarah and Rose exchanged defeated glances, avoiding Daddy Davy's eyes. When Erich breathlessly finished reciting the events, Daddy Davy looked at him sternly.

"Didn't I say ye weren't to go up on the roof?" he asked.

"Yes," Erich said with a sharp intake of breath. "But it was only for a m-m-minute…" he rushed to add, as he realised that he might be in trouble for disobeying Daddy Davy.

"Not even for a minute. And Aunt Sarah told you not to go up there too. You could have been badly hurt. I'll have to punish you for your disobedience."

Erich stared at the floor. In his excitement, remembering the events of the morning, he had forgotten that he should not be on the roof. He should have known Daddy Davy would be annoyed with him. His excitement deflated like a burst tyre. Chagrined he wondered what his punishment would be. Helen smiled at him sympathetically.

❦

Autumn 1952

Erich was so happy since he came back to live with Daddy Davy and Aunt Elsie again. He had missed them terribly when he was at Aunt Rachel's. And he was especially glad to be back with Gipsy. All summer, once school finished, Gipsy had rarely left his side and during the school year when Erich was at home he was usually nearby. But when Erich got up this morning he was nowhere to be found.

Erich was not worried as Gipsy occasionally roamed. But he was never gone more than a day or two. He will probably be back tonight or tomorrow morning, Erich thought. Hurriedly he ate his breakfast and headed off to school.

When Erich turned into the lane after school Gipsy did not bound to meet him as usual. Erich looked around the house but there was no sign of him. The place was very quiet since the girls had left at the end of the summer - Helen to Belfast, Nell to Dublin and Rose to Sligo. And Hans had never been to visit him since he came to Clonty. It seemed completely empty without Gipsy as well. Disappointed, Erich went out to weed his vegetable plot alone. Afterwards he collected eggs from the hens, missing Gipsy's panting and padding footsteps behind him. Erich tried not to think about it the rest of the evening.

Erich ran downstairs the next morning to see if Gipsy had returned. He was disappointed to find the dog was not there.

When Daddy Davy came in from the byre, he said, "Gipsy isn't back yet."

"Well, don't be fretting. He'll be back when he's ready. He'll look after himself."

Reassured, Erich got ready for school and set off along the road. He peered into each field as he walked, hoping to catch a glimpse of the dog. But there was no sign of him. At his desk in school he peered out of the window hoping to find Gipsy had followed him but the school yard was empty. On his way home he again scanned the fields for a glimpse of the dog. Dejectedly he did his chores until Aunt Elsie called him in for tea.

After tea Erich got out his favourite book of fairy stories. He loved the heroic tales and could lose himself in their enchanted world. Many evenings he spent dreaming of flying across the water to England on a magical horse. It was so far away and must be an exotic place. But tonight he could not concentrate. He kept wondering where Gipsy was.

Before he went to bed he looked outside the door but Gipsy had not come home. Disappointed he climbed the stairs to the loft. Daddy Davy and Aunt Elsie's double bed filled the middle of the room; his small bed was tucked into the corner, behind a partition. He climbed under the covers, missing the weight of the dog on his feet.

The next morning was Saturday but Erich did not feel his usual excitement to be free from school for the weekend. He trudged downstairs. Before sitting down for his breakfast he opened the door, not wanting to hope.

He stared in amazement at the dirty, dishevelled spaniel curled on the step. Gipsy lifted his head timidly and Erich stooped to pat him. The dog was a mess. His fur was wet, matted and dirty and a gash ran along his side. He hardly had the energy to lift his head.

Erich ran into the house shouting to Aunt Elsie, "Gipsy's back! Gipsy's back!" Aunt Elsie turned to look and was horrified to see the state of the mangy animal lying on the step.

"He looks like he hasn't eaten in days. You'd best give him a bite," she said.

She filled his bowl with scraps and Erich ran back to the door with it. The dog raised his head and took a few mouthfuls, tired and struggling.

Hearing Erich's shouts Daddy Davy appeared from the byre and said, "I told you he'd come home when he was ready. But look at the state of him! We'll have to clean that wound and he'll need a bath."

Aunt Elsie nodded wearily, leaning on the back of a kitchen chair, struggling not to show the nagging pain which began in her chest and ran down her arm.

"Erich and I will bath him in the yard after breakfast," Daddy Davy said, seeing her weary look.

After breakfast Daddy Davy filled an old tin tub from the byre with warm water. Erich called the dog over and coaxed him in. They lathered him with soap, carefully avoiding the wound. When Gipsy got out of the bath he half-heartedly shook himself, shivering. Erich took an old towel and rubbed the dog carefully. Daddy Davy checked the wound and poured some whiskey on it from a bottle on the dresser. The dog flinched but didn't struggle.

When they were finished Erich brought Gipsy inside to lie in front of the fire. The dog drifted into an exhausted sleep and could not be persuaded to move the rest of the day. He only went outside briefly after tea, then crept back to the fire. Erich watched him anxiously from a chair beside the fire, frequently bending to pat the dog and talk to him. Gipsy's eyes followed him but the dog lay still, whining occasionally.

At bedtime the dog struggled up the stairs behind Erich. Erich lifted him onto the bed. He lay, his arm thrown over the dog, listening to the dog's laboured breathing for a long time, before he finally drifted into a restless sleep. He woke several times during the night and listened anxiously to the dog's wheezing.

In the morning the dog watched him listlessly as he dressed. Erich rubbed Gipsy's neck and the dog struggled to lick Erich's hand then his head dropped back onto his paws.

"Come on, Gipsy!" Erich called when he was ready to go downstairs.

The dog lifted his head briefly and then dropped it down again. He did not even try to get up. Erich lifted him clumsily and carried him downstairs to the fire. When Erich put him down he shifted his front legs stiffly to get more comfortable. Erich watched him while he ate breakfast. Gipsy was not interested in food. Daddy Davy and Aunt Elsie looked at each other but said nothing.

"I'll stay home with Gipsy this morning," Erich said boldly.

"No, lad, you'll come to church. Gipsy will be grand on his own," Daddy Davy replied with quiet authority.

When they were ready to go, Erich left reluctantly, eyeing Gipsy collapsed by the fire. In church he could not wait for the service to be over. He sang the hymns without his usual enthusiasm and did not hear the sermon at all. He just wanted to get home again.

Once home he rushed into the house to find Gipsy in the same position he had left him in. Erich sat watching the spaniel all afternoon. He could not tempt him to eat or drink. Gipsy occasionally whined feebly, barely raising his head.

"Can't we do something for him?" Erich asked Daddy Davy in despair.

"We've cleaned the wound. That's about all we can do. Gipsy knows what's best for him. If he won't eat just leave him to rest," Daddy Davy replied.

Erich did not even bother to get his favourite fairy tale book to read after tea. He sat staring into the fire. No one spoke much. The room was very quiet. When bedtime came he carried the dog to his bed and laid him down gently then knelt to say his prayers.

He finished with, "God bless Daddy Davy and Aunt Elsie and please make Gipsy better. Amen."

Erich climbed into bed and hugged the dog tightly, careful to avoid the scabbed wound. Gipsy whimpered, half raising his head to lick Erich's hand.

"You're my best friend, Gipsy," Erich said.

Erich slept fitfully, waking to hear the dog's laboured breathing several times. Finally he drifted into a sound sleep in the early hours of the morning. He lay motionless, his arm stretched protectively across Gipsy. When Erich woke the room was silent. He lay rigid, listening for the dog's breathing but heard nothing. Worried, he sat up and looked at Gipsy. The dog lay completely still, his chest unmoving. Erich stared in disbelief and agony. Tears rolled down his face as he looked at his friend.

When Daddy Davy came into the room to wake Erich, he found the boy slumped over the dog, sobbing uncontrollably. He put his arm around the boy.

"Why couldn't we make him better?" Erich asked brokenly.

"It's not in our hands. Some things can't be mended. I know a lovely spot under a big shady oak tree where I'll dig his grave. It'll be a fittin' place for such a good friend."

Erich heard the clattering and rumbling about a mile outside the village. He walked slowly along the road, dawdling on his way home from school. Without Gipsy there he didn't feel like racing home. Neither of the Elliott girls would be home before Christmas and he did not know when he would see Hans. His playmates were all gone. Ahead a lorry dumped a load of stones onto the ground and workmen raked them flat. Tar bubbled in a machine at the side of the road and they tipped it over the stones.

A large, yellow machine sat waiting its turn. The driver sat high up on the single seat pushing and pulling levers to move the bulky vehicle. When he pulled the lever the huge, rolling pin wheels were set in motion and it rolled forward. Smoothly he flattened the tar and created a level road surface.

Erich stopped and stood watching the amazing machine. The steamroller is brilliant, he thought. I'd love to drive it! He stood, daydreaming, until a workman waved him on. He skirted the edge of the road, trying not to step on the hot tarmac. He did not want it to stick to his boots and ruin them. Daddy Davy had only re-soled them last week and they were supposed to last the winter.

The road crew had been re-surfacing roads in the area all summer. The dusty dirt roads were disappearing, replaced by shiny, black tarmac which melted and burned bare feet in summer.

Most days, on his way home from school, Erich saw the men working. He dreamed of driving the steamroller. He would sit up so high on the seat and be able to see for miles. He would push the lever and, magically, it would roll gently forward. He would be king of the whole world, sitting up above everything. Maybe he would even have a crown. He would drive everywhere and everyone would clear out of his way. Even Aunt Rachel wouldn't dare face him. Nothing could stop him.

These thoughts rolled through his mind as he continued walking. He was lost in his fantasy the rest of the way home. It blocked from his mind the knowledge that Gipsy would not be there to meet him when he walked up the lane. If he allowed himself to think about it, he missed Gipsy terribly.

"Hi Aunt Elsie!" Erich called as he opened the back door. He looked towards the table where Aunt Elsie was always working when he got home from school. But she wasn't there. There was no smell of potatoes boiling from the pot hanging over the fire either. Daddy Davy sat by the fire filling his pipe with tobacco.

"Where's Aunt Elsie?" Erich asked.

"She's upstairs resting for a wee while," he replied.

Aunt Elsie frequently rested during the day since Erich had returned to them. She was pale and often breathless; she did not look very well. Sometimes Erich saw her put her hand to her chest, gasping. It frightened him. Something was wrong with her.

"Is Aunt Elsie poorly?" Erich asked hesitantly.

"She'll be alright, she just needs to rest a bit. I want to talk to you while she's resting."

Erich looked at Daddy Davy. His tone of voice and expression were serious. It was bad news. Erich just knew it. He waited, blinking rapidly and unaware he was holding his breath. He watched Daddy Davy.

"I think you've noticed that Aunt Elsie needs lots of rest lately. Her health isn't good. I hate to say it but, even though we want to, I don't think we'll be able to keep you with us. Aunt Elsie's health isn't able for it. So I must look for a new home for you, Erich."

Before he could continue Erich shouted, "N-N-Nooo! Y-Y-You promised I-I-I could stay here! Y-Y-You d-d-don't love me anymore!"

Erich clenched his hands, shaking his head as tears rolled down his cheeks. Daddy Davy put his hand on the boy's shoulder, looking at him compassionately. Erich shook his hand away.

"I know I did. But some things are in God's hands. We do love you and would keep you if we could."

"I-I-I could h-h-help Aunt Elsie. I c-c-could do the w-w-work for her," Erich said desperately.

"I know you would do anything you could for her but she's just not able for it anymore, lad."

Sniffing loudly, with tears still rolling down his cheeks, Erich stared at Daddy Davy. He did not understand why he had to leave again. He loved Daddy Davy and Aunt Elsie. He was happy here. He didn't want to go anywhere else. He wanted to stay here. He did not want to hear anymore but Daddy Davy was still speaking.

"I'll find a good home for you, so don't fret. I hope to get somewhere nearby so we can still see each other often."

Erich sat down by the fire and stared into it, sobbing. They had told him Hans would come to visit him but he hadn't come. He was busy and happy with Bobby and Aunt Marjorie. It would be just the same with Daddy Davy and Aunt Elsie. I'll never see Daddy Davy, Aunt Elsie, the girls or Hans again, he thought. I'll be alone.

Sniffing loudly, he lifted his face and stared at Daddy Davy with reddened eyes. He could not believe he was moving again. He had thought he would stay here forever this time. If Daddy Davy did not want to keep him then no one would want him. He was sure of it. Erich had never felt so alone. Not even when he found out *Mutti* had died. He did not belong anywhere. And there was no one he could depend on.

10

A Cat For Company

"ERICH, REVEREND Downey's here!" Daddy Davy called up the stairs.

Erich knew he was there. From his window he had seen the large, black car stop outside the house. He sat silently, delaying as long as possible, then dragged his case off the bed with a thud. He trudged down the stairs and into the kitchen, hauling the bag.

"Hello, Erich. Have you got everything?" Reverend Downey asked.

The boy nodded, avoiding his gaze. He had known Reverend Downey ever since he first came to live with the Elliotts almost five years ago. At church or on visits to the school the minister always had a kind word for him. Erich liked him but he was not pleased to see him today. He did not want to go with him. Although he knew he was not moving far away he would not be living with Daddy Davy and Aunt Elsie. Nothing will be the same again, Erich thought. He lowered his head to hide his face, his eyes filled with tears.

Seeing his expression, Daddy Davy said, reassuringly, "Sure, it's no distance to the Manse. We'll still see each other every week. You can come and visit anytime."

Erich nodded but said nothing. He could not put his misery into words. Aunt Elsie hugged him tightly, her jaw clenched and her eyes screwed closed. As they walked through the stone floored hall to the front door Daddy Davy rested his hand on

Erich's shoulder.

Trailing his bag behind him Erich walked to the black, shiny car and climbed in. Reverend Downey's ministerial duties entailed a lot of travelling so he had been one of the first men in the area to get a car. Vehicles were scarce and it was a treat to ride in one but even this prospect did not excite him today. He stared out of the window forlornly as they drove away from the Elliotts' farm.

It was only a short drive, not much more than a mile, to Kilmullagh Church's rectory. The Manse was set prominently on a hill but its entrance was below, hidden in a hollow. Erich had been to the sprawling grounds for Sunday School picnics each summer since he came to live with the Elliotts. Reverend Downey slowed the car as they approached the gate.

"Welcome to the Manse, Erich," he said, glancing over at the boy, who stared straight ahead.

Erich shifted his attention from the road to Reverend Downey's face. His gaze slid over the minister's greying hair and high forehead to his mild, unassuming eyes and thin lips. Erich knew Reverend Downey was a kind man who wanted to help him. He had always taken an interest in Erich and Hans. But he wasn't Daddy Davy. He couldn't take his place. Erich wished desperately that he were back with the Elliotts; he didn't want to live here.

They turned in at the black iron gates and drove up the meandering dirt driveway to the square, grey house claiming the top of the hill. It was imposing, even in its slightly dilapidated state. While Erich had been in the grounds before he had never been inside the house. It looked big and cold. I'd rather be in Daddy Davy's farmhouse, he thought.

Reverend Downey got out of the car and Erich reluctantly followed him to the door. The hallway was wider than any Erich had seen in a long time. It was a bit like the Goldschmidthaus in Germany except there were no children running through it. He looked around, bewildered. There were so many doors into different rooms. How will I ever find my way around here? he thought miserably.

Reverend Downey started up the stairs and Erich followed him, grasping the wide, smooth banister and dragging his bag over each stair. Upstairs there were as many doors as downstairs. The house had sixteen rooms; seven of them were bedrooms. Reverend Downey walked into a room near the stairs and Erich trailed after him.

It was an enormous room, sparsely furnished. Erich put his case on the floor beside the bed. The bag looked tiny in these surroundings. Melancholy descended on him as he looked around; he felt as empty as the room. It were as if he were a solitary prisoner. He felt very small and alone.

"Put your things away, Erich, and then come downstairs," Reverend Downey said, indicating the wardrobe and dresser on the far wall. "We'll have tea shortly."

"Yes, Reverend Downey," he replied.

"Sure, we can't have you calling me that now you're living with us. You could call me Daddy Downey or Uncle Edward. Which would you prefer?"

It seems I have another daddy now, Erich thought. But it doesn't feel like Reverend Downey is my daddy. Not like Daddy Davy is.

"Uncle Edward," he replied without hesitation.

When Erich finished unpacking he went downstairs. His footsteps echoed in the large, empty hallway. He stood looking at the closed doors, wondering which room to enter, until Uncle Edward opened a door and beckoned him in.

A long dining table, capable of seating twelve people, sat in the middle of the room. Mrs Downey came in behind them carrying a teapot. The three of them sat at one end of the long table. Years ago the Downeys and their ten children filled all the seats. But their children were adults now and away from home. Only their youngest daughter, Susan, came home from university to spend her holidays with her parents.

The Downeys were past their child rearing days; they had grandchildren Erich's age. But they had always taken an interest in Erich and Hans since the boys arrived in the community. So they had offered to care for Erich until a permanent home could be found for him.

After Uncle Edward said grace Erich looked perplexedly at the knives and forks beside his plate. There were more than he was used to at Daddy Davy's. Erich picked up the nearest fork and started eating. He was surprised to find he was hungry and he took a large bite, his mouth gaping as he chewed. Mrs Downey watched him and frowned.

"Erich, close your mouth when you chew," she said. "Don't eat so quickly. It won't disappear."

Grudgingly Erich did as he was bid. Daddy Davy and Aunt Elsie had not worried too much about his table manners. Surreptitiously he studied Mrs Downey's longish, thin face and his eyes met her direct, determined gaze. Despite a natural reserve and quiet manner, she would not bend easily. Her thin lips pursed in a prim, contained expression. Only her short, wavy, white hair softened her countenance. After raising ten children she felt that discipline was essential for them.

Why does she have such strict rules? Erich wondered. I didn't have to worry about which fork to use at Daddy Davy's. And she seems to be watching and criticising me all the time. I don't like it. She probably thinks I can't do anything right.

The Downey household was nothing like anything he had experienced previously. The couple were much older than most parents of eleven year old boys and believed in raising children in a much more disciplined, structured way than Erich was used to. He felt as if he had landed on an alien planet.

"See that you mind your manners, Erich. You must set an example for the other children," Mrs Downey said as he picked up his school bag. "Come straight back after school," she added.

"Yes, Mrs Downey," Erich replied, opening the door. Although she had told him to call her Aunt Isobel, he could not say it; she did not feel at all like an aunt to him. He did not see why he should be an example to the other children now that he lived at the rectory. Daddy Davy hadn't expected him to do that. Why should Mrs Downey expect it?

Erich puzzled over this as he wandered down the long, winding driveway. He stopped at the tall gates and looked across the road at Clanefoy School. He would have liked to stay at Rathnane School. Hans and Bobby weren't there now but he liked Mrs Baird. She was always kind to him and encouraged him. But since Clanefoy School was so close it made no sense to walk to Rathnane.

The architecture of Clanefoy's large, one classroom school gave the impression of a railway station stranded in the middle of the countryside far from a railway line. Two rows of windows, one above the other, gave the illusion of a two storey building but the interior revealed one storey with a high ceiling. Dark brickwork arched over the windows, standing out like eye shadow on a pale face.

Miss Lyons, their teacher, lived in the teacher's residence attached to the school. It was a small, two up, two down building. By the time Erich crossed the road that morning she was in the school, lighting the fire and preparing for the day's lessons. Young and pleasant, she was popular with the children.

At precisely nine o'clock Miss Lyons stepped outside, swinging the hand bell vigorously. This was her first term teaching at the school and she was aware of constant scrutiny from the rectory. Mrs Downey had considerable influence over the Church-run school.

Erich filed into the building with the other children. He knew many of them from Church and Sunday school. He smiled at a couple of the girls and was rewarded with answering smiles. He was taking more notice of girls lately and was pleased they were friendly to him. He tried to hang around them as much as he could. It was not difficult to do so as, being smaller than many of the boys his age, the girls thought he was cute and fussed over him.

As Erich took his seat a fair-haired boy with a slight squint pounded into the room. Miss Lyons closed the door behind him. Erich knew the boy's father was a farm labourer at the rectory. He smiled at John and got a cheeky grin in reply.

"Class, copy the problems from the board and solve them," Miss Lyons said as she wrote several columns of arithmetic problems.

Erich copied them down hurriedly, scribbling across the page in his haste. He gripped his pencil tightly, staring intently as he worked. There were muffled whispers and coughs around the room but Erich was absorbed in his task and he did not hear them. He finished quickly, tossing his pencil onto his desktop, and sat, fidgeting impatiently, waiting for the teacher to check the answers.

Miss Lyons pushed her chair back from her desk and walked to the blackboard. Pointing to the first problem, she asked, "Who can tell me the answer?"

Erich's hand shot up and he held it stiffly in the air, shoulder extended until it nearly popped out of his socket, as she looked around the room. Ignoring his fervour, Miss Lyons pointed to a tall girl in a mousy-brown cardigan at the back of the class, who was avoiding her gaze.

"Jennifer, what's the correct answer?"

"I don't know, Miss Lyons."

Miss Lyons surveyed the classroom again. Most pairs of eyes avoided hers; John stared lazily out of the window. Erich strained to raise his hand as high as he could but Miss Lyons looked past him. He stared at her intently, keeping his hand high in the air.

"Do you know the answer, Erich?" she asked eventually.

"Eighty four," Erich replied.

"Well done," she replied.

Erich beamed, sitting up straight in his seat and basking in the teacher's praise. His hand shot up to solve each of the subsequent problems on the blackboard but Miss Lyons chose some of the more reluctant children. Disappointed each time, Erich lowered his hand. He fidgeted, eager to go on to something else.

After the arithmetic lesson Miss Lyons set them the task of writing a composition about the harvest season. Erich bent his head over his desk and scribbled furiously. He wrote about helping Daddy Davy build haystacks and bring the hay to the barn. He remembered the hot sun and Daddy Davy encouraging him. He always let me climb on top of the haystacks. That was the best part, Erich thought, smiling at the memory.

He was oblivious to Miss Lyons walking around the classroom, reading their work. Erich worked urgently, setting his thoughts on paper as quickly as he could. When he was finished he set the page in front of him and squirmed in his seat, impatient for the others to finish. When most of the children had finished writing Miss Lyons asked for volunteers to read their compositions. Erich's hand shot in the air. Full of happy memories, he wanted to tell everyone about his harvests with Daddy Davy. Miss Lyons looked around the room and chose a boy and girl near the back of the room, who had been very quiet during the arithmetic lesson, to read their compositions.

The morning passed quickly. At dinner time Miss Lyons sent the children outside. Erich ate his lunch leaning against the school wall, watching several girls skipping in the middle of the playground. A couple of boys, near Erich's age but taller, walked over to him.

"Trying to be the teacher's pet," Walter, the dark-haired one, said.

"That's why you wanted to answer all the arithmetic questions," Tommy said.

"I-I-I'm not the teacher's pet," Erich replied, his eyes blinking rapidly.

"You are, surely!" Walter replied.

"I-I-I'm not!" Erich stuttered, his voice rising.

"And you talk funny," Tommy added.

The boys nodded, laughing at Erich's agitation. Erich screwed up his fists, his face contorted and his voice rose to a shout.

"I-I-I don't!"

Other children turned to look. Miss Lyons came to the door, peering out. As soon as she appeared the boys slunk away. Why do they have to taunt me? Erich thought. And why does someone always notice my accent? I never fit in with everyone else. If I never had to speak maybe no one would notice, he railed inwardly.

His thoughts were interrupted by the bell signalling the end of the dinner hour. Erich filed in with the other children, avoiding Walter and Tommy. John fell in beside him.

"Are you living at the rectory now?" John asked. Erich nodded.

"I'll see you around there on Saturday then. I help me Da in the garden. When I'm done I'll show you the old fort."

"Where's the fort?"

"Take your seats quietly, children," Miss Lyons instructed.

John smiled and mouthed "Saturday" as the boys went to their seats. A spelling quiz began the afternoon. Erich quickly became absorbed in the lesson and forgot about Walter and Tommy.

When Miss Lyons dismissed them at the end of the afternoon, Erich filed out with John and several other classmates, talking and laughing. He did not notice Miss Lyons call Walter and Tommy aside and set them to washing the blackboard.

"Who can run to that big tree first?" John asked, pointing to an oak tree at the first bend in the road.

The children raced along the road, arms outstretched to be first to touch the tree. Erich fell against it, laughing, behind John.

Mrs Downey said I must come straight home after school but this is fun, Erich thought. I don't want to go back yet. There's no one to play with at the manse. He pushed her instructions from his mind and tagged along with the other children.

"Let's see who can count the most crows," Ruth, a small girl with braids, said.

The children peered up into the sky looking for the black creatures. Engrossed in this activity, Erich continued walking with the other children.

"Four!"

"I see six!"

"Seven!"

The shouts became less frequent as one by one children dropped out of the group. When they reached John's house he stopped, calling to the other children, "I'm away! See you tomorrow!"

Erich had not paid any heed to the time or the distance he had walked. He saw the track that led to Daddy Davy's house just ahead. I'll visit them, he decided.

"Bye bye!" he called. There was a chorus of farewells as the other children walked on. Erich turned and headed down the track. At the break in the wall he hurried across the haggard and into the kitchen.

"Erich!" Aunt Elsie cried with delight. He ran over and hugged her.

"Hi Aunt Elsie!"

"What a surprise! Isn't it grand to see you so soon! I'll make us a drop o' tea."

Erich nodded happily and sat down at the table while Aunt Elsie boiled the kettle. I'm hungry, he thought. It must be teatime soon but I won't worry about going back to the manse yet. I'd rather to stay here. While she worked Erich told Aunt Elsie about his new school.

"I don't like Walter and Tommy but John will show me the old fort on Saturday," Erich said.

"Won't that be good," Aunt Elsie replied, stopping to watch his lips as he spoke.

"But I'd rather come round here. I could help Daddy Davy with the chores."

"Don't you fret about the chores. Just come to see us when

you're able."

The back door opened and Daddy Davy walked in. He smiled when he saw the boy. Before he could speak Erich bombarded him with questions about the animals and the farm.

When the boy paused for breath Aunt Elsie said, "Will you stay for a bite to eat?" Erich nodded happily.

"Did you tell Mrs Downey you were stopping here?" Daddy Davy asked. Erich didn't reply immediately.

"She isn't bothered where I am," he said finally.

"That's not true, Erich," Daddy Davy replied. "She'll be worried if you haven't been home since school finished."

"That's not my home. This is!"

"You're always welcome here. You know we'd like nothing better than to have you with us. But with Aunt Elsie's health we're not able for it or you'd still be living here." Erich hunched his shoulders and stared at the floor.

"I think we'd best postpone having you stay for tea until another day when Mrs Downey knows you're coming here, lad."

"Tea at the manse is awful. There's so many forks and knives and rules."

"Well, you won't be there forever. It's just for a wee while. We'll see you at church on Sunday."

Erich nodded slowly then he half-smiled, brightening. Sunday wasn't too far away. He gave each of them a tight hug before he set off back to the manse. He knew Mrs Downey would be angry that he was late for tea. But he decided not to worry about that yet.

His return journey was very quiet. He glanced into the hedges as he walked, looking for birds sheltering in their branches. A few yards in front of him a honey-brown bird darted out from underneath the shrubbery. Its bluish head bobbed as it ran along the ground. The pheasant frantically ran several feet then disappeared under the hedge again. Erich stood watching it until the bird disappeared, then continued his journey. Nothing else broke the monotony of the walk.

As he approached the school and the rectory he slowed his pace. The school yard was empty. All the children had left the school grounds ages ago. Miss Lyons would be inside her house, probably eating her tea. Uncle Edward was bent over the rectory gates, inspecting a hinge. He did not see Erich approaching.

"Hello, Uncle Edward," Erich said, self-consciously. The man didn't seem like his uncle.

"Hello, Erich. School finished for the day?" he asked, still concentrating on the hinge.

Erich nodded. Uncle Edward was engrossed in his task and had not noticed the time. He did not realise that school had ended more than an hour ago. Erich watched him inspect the hinge. Uncle Edward peered at it, nodding to himself.

"I'll have to get the screwdriver to fix that," he muttered.

Erich stood with him for a few minutes, then wandered up the long drive to the house. His empty stomach told him it was time for tea.

"Where have you been, Erich? You're late!" Mrs Downey said as he walked into the hall.

"I was at school," Erich replied.

"Not until this hour! You didn't come straight home," she said. "You disobeyed me. I think you'd learn a lesson if you didn't get your tea tonight!"

"I'm h-h-hungry! I w-w-want my tea!" Erich shouted plaintively. "I did come straight home!" he lied. That's not a big lie, Erich thought. I only spent a while with my friends and went to see Daddy Davy and Aunt Elsie.

It was so silent and lonely when he returned to the house each afternoon. He wanted some company. He wished Hans were here living with him or that Helen could come to visit. John, the farm labourer's son, would come on Saturday but Erich knew Mrs Downey would not approve of the boys playing together. She had told him that a child living at the manse should not associate with one living in a labourer's cottage. So the only company he could expect was Uncle Edward, lost in thought, or Mrs Downey, stern and demanding.

"Mind how you speak to me, young man. I will not tolerate impertinence! You'll definitely not get any tea tonight," Mrs Downey said, her lips pursed.

"I was w-w-with Uncle Edward at t-t-the gate after school!" Erich whined. He decided not to mention that he had walked down the road to the Elliotts first.

Thinking about how hungry he was, Erich became more agitated and shouted louder, working himself into a frenzy. Mrs Downey remained firm and refused to give him anything to eat. The argument had not been resolved by the time Uncle Edward walked in the door. Erich ran to him.

"She w-w-won't give me any tea! I-I-I hate her! I was with y-y-you at the gate after school!" Erich cried, so agitated that he could hardly speak.

Uncle Edward looked from one to the other, trying to grasp the gist of the argument in mid-stream. He heard Erich's statement that he had been at the gate and nodded in agreement.

"Indeed, he was at the gate with me," he said.

"Well, in future he must come straight to the house to get his tea," she replied curtly, then disappeared into the kitchen.

Erich breathed a sigh of relief. He would get his tea now. He hated all the rules here; they were so rigid. Aunt Elsie didn't worry about the things that Mrs Downey did. Why can't I just go back to Daddy Davy's? Erich thought miserably.

A few minutes later he was sitting at the table with Uncle Edward and Mrs Downey, eating silently. He felt dwarfed at the end of the long table. He could not imagine a time when the rest of the seats had been occupied by the Downey children. Uncle Edward had told him that they had played table tennis on the large table between meals. That time, long past, seemed to belong to another family, not the people sitting with him.

Erich wandered around the sitting room after tea as if he were in a china shop. Even without any visitors Mrs Downey expected him to behave impeccably. He could look at but not disturb the photographs and ornaments on the mantelpiece and tables. He did not feel at ease. This sitting room was nothing like Daddy Davy's warm, comfortable kitchen where friends and neighbours gathered in the evenings. He felt as if he were in an elegant prison. It was too large and fancy; the space needed children to fill it. But they had already come and gone, grown and left the house. One boy on his best behaviour could not lift the oppressive silence. Erich gazed around the room despondently.

The bright eyes glinting on the mantelpiece always seemed to watch him. Erich walked over and looked up at the slinky black cat sitting there. Her diamond-like eyes danced in the light, seeming to see him. Erich found her expression warm and welcoming. She liked him. He knew she did. She was so tiny, only a couple of inches tall, but so composed and serene, sitting on her haunches with her tail pulled in around her like a stole. Erich was drawn to her the first time he saw her. He felt that he had found a friend in this empty house. He often stood gazing at her, wondering what she was thinking. When he was very lonely he talked to her and felt that she listened and understood. He trusted his tiny glass friend.

Tonight he looked at her and said, conspiratorially, "I h-h-hate her! She always has r-r-rules! I've no one to play with. I h-h-hate living here. It's miserable! Why c-c-can't I go with my friends after school? Better still, why can't I go back to Daddy Davy?"

The cat looked at him sympathetically and Erich felt better, knowing he could confide in her. When Mrs Downey came into the sitting room a few minutes later, Erich joined her by the fire. As soon as they had finished tea Uncle Edward had gone out on church business. He ministered to three churches and he frequently had meetings to attend in the evenings.

Erich opened the children's book of Bible stories which he had been reading to the page where he had left David and Goliath the previous evening. Mrs Downey also sat reading. The clock on the wall ticked, punctuating the odd words of conversation they exchanged. Occasionally her head nodded forward until her chin touched her chest and she jerked it upright again. Her face was tired and strained. Except for the farm labourer's wife, Mrs Doyle, who came to do the cleaning once a week, Mrs Downey ran the large house herself. It was a strenuous task for a person nearing retirement age. The strain of the day showed in her face as she sat by the fire. Jerking her head upright once more, she looked up at the clock on the wall.

"It's time you were away to bed, Erich. Don't forget to say your prayers."

Erich nodded and stood up.

"Goodnight Mrs Downey."

"Goodnight, Erich."

Erich left the warmth of the fire and walked out into the dim hall. The shadows seemed longer and the dark corners more threatening than during the daytime as he climbed the long staircase. He tried not to look around him until he was safely through his bedroom door. He undressed quickly and knelt on the small rag mat by the bed to say his prayers, ending with "God bless Daddy Davy, Aunt Elsie, Nell, Rose, Hans, Helen and Uncle Edward." He paused before he stood up and thought for a second. Then, sighing, he reluctantly added, "God bless Mrs Downey," before getting into bed.

Once under the covers he pulled the blankets up to his chin and closed his eyes to shut out the yawning darkness. He wished his tiny glass friend were with him. Her glinting eyes would light the darkness and make it a less scary place. He felt very uneasy and lonely in the empty space.

I love Daddy Davy and Aunt Elsie but I can't stay with them, Erich thought. And *Mutti* is gone. I'll never have a family of my own. I hate it at the manse but I've nowhere else to go. If I can't stay with Daddy Davy where do I belong? Life will never get any better, he thought miserably. He scrunched up his face, crying silently. He buried his face in the pillow. The silent sobs wracked Erich's body until he finally fell into a troubled sleep.

As he slept he dreamt he was alone and lost in a forest but no

one missed him. He wandered deeper into the forest then he was
looking at a huge pile of bodies, some in tattered grey uniforms,
lying broken and bleeding. He groaned and tossed in his sleep.

Erich followed Uncle Edward around the orchard as he inspected
the raspberry bushes which were full of bright red, juicy fruit.
The minister farmed in his spare time. He had needed the extra
money to support and educate his large family as they grew up.
Now he continued to farm as a hobby.

His farm labourer, William Doyle, took care of the day-to-day
running of the farm but Uncle Edward worked on it whenever
he could find the time. It was a place he could lose himself in
thought without interruption. From his first week at the manse
Erich liked to spend Saturdays in the orchard and vegetable
patch. It was away from Mrs Downey and almost like being back
with Daddy Davy.

Uncle Edward, with a bucket in his hand, moved over to the apple trees. He pulled gleaming red apples from the lower branches
of the nearest tree. The tree was weighed down and needed to
be relieved of its burden before the fruit fell to the ground and
spoiled. The apples would make delicious pies and preserves.
Erich's mouth watered, thinking about it.

Pears and plums also hung in plentiful supply, waiting to be
picked. Uncle Edward gave Erich an apple from his bucket and
he munched on it as he watched the minister. When the bucket
was full Uncle Edward set it down.

"Would you take the bucket to the kitchen for me, Erich?" he
said before he headed to the beehive. Erich sauntered up to the
kitchen, set the bucket inside the kitchen door and scurried away
before Mrs Downey noticed him. I don't want to see her, Erich
thought. She'll just find something to criticise.

He hurried back to the orchard where he found Mr Doyle rooting in the vegetable garden. The Downeys, with the labourer's
help, grew all their own vegetables. He shook a bunch of freshly

pulled carrots to free the bits of earth clinging to them. His son, John, stood next to him holding a sack filled with the vegetables he had dug up. When Erich spotted the other boy he smiled. John was the only person near his own age he had seen at the rectory since he arrived.

John set the sack down, left his father working in the vegetable garden and walked over to Erich.

"Hi, John. Will you show me the fort today?" Erich asked, pushing to the back of his mind Mrs Downey's instructions not to play with the labourer's son.

"Da, do you need me for a wee while?" John asked.

"I'm grand. Off you go, lad," he replied.

Erich and John left the rectory grounds and walked along the road until they came to a marshy field. They squelched across it to the remains of an ancient fort. The ground was raised into a small mound with a flat top. Around it the sunken earth marked where the ditch which protected it used to be. The faint outline was all they needed to mark out the boundaries of their kingdom.

"Approach if you dare! I will defend my fort to death!" John cried, climbing onto the top of the mound.

With a wild cry Erich ran at the fort and they met in mock battle, arms raised to swing their imaginary swords. Their hands criss-crossed the air in sweeping blows but neither fell wounded. Erich finally forced John off the mound.

"I win! You've left the fort!" he cried.

Reluctantly John conceded defeat. Erich shouted triumphantly. They re-enacted their battle scene several times with variations until they grew tired of it.

"Let's head back. Mammy baked a fresh loaf this morning," John said.

The boys tramped back across the sodden field onto the road. On the way back to the rectory they stopped at John's home.

"Hello, lads. Are you after coming from the manse?" Mrs Doyle asked as they came through the door. The boys shook their heads and told her about their adventures at the old fort. She gave the children tea and thick slices of bread. Erich sat happily drinking tea and chatting with the Doyles. He felt more comfortable with them than at the manse; their house was more like the home he was used to.

As tea time approached Mrs Doyle said, "You'd best get back, Erich. Mrs Downey will be vexed if you're late for tea." Erich reluctantly headed back to the manse.

"Where have you been, Erich?" Mrs Downey asked as he came through the door.

"I was playing at the fort," he replied.

"I saw you talking to Mr Doyle's son. Was he with you?" she asked.

"Y-Y-Yes."

"Haven't I told you that I don't want you to play with him? Why don't you play with some of the other children?"

"They don't live near us! W-W-Why can't I play with him? I like him!"

"Because it's not fitting. He isn't suitable."

"I can't go to play with my friends after school and I can't play with John here. You just d-d-don't want me to have any friends! I h-h-hate you! You're s-s-so horrible to me!" Erich shouted at her.

"That's enough of that. We won't have such outbursts. If you can't behave, you'll go to your room," she said with finality.

Erich glared at her, silent and powerless. Why does she have so many silly rules? he thought, frustrated by her unbending attitude. I don't want to lose the only friend who ever comes to the manse. I like John. Why can't I play with him? Turning, he stomped up the stairs, ignoring Mrs Downey's admonishment to lift his feet.

"Erich, it's time you were away," Mrs Downey said.

"I'll take you to church after Sunday School," Charles said to his mother. The army chaplain was home for a few days leave.

Uncle Edward was already at the church preparing for his first service. He had two more at other churches after the service at Kilmullagh.

Erich shrugged on his jacket, stopping for Mrs Downey to inspect his hands and face before he went out of the door.

"How are you managing with Erich?" Charles asked his mother thoughtfully, watching the boy through the window as he walked down the driveway.

"We're doing grand. I raised ten of you remember," she chided him.

Charles smiled. "I know you did but Erich seems rather difficult. He seems a bit of a handful. You don't have anyone to help you and you should be resting more," he replied.

"Don't be worrying about me. God doesn't give us more than we can bear," she replied, with a determined smile.

Erich walked down the driveway, scuffing his boots in the dirt. He hated walking to church on his own. At Daddy Davy's the whole family went to church together. But at the manse everyone went at different times; he missed the company. At least I'll see Daddy Davy and Aunt Elsie this morning, Erich thought. I'll tell Daddy Davy about my harvest composition. The thought made him walk a bit faster.

After Sunday School, as Erich left his class, he saw Mrs Downey and Charles walking up the path. Erich found Charles rather intimidating in his uniform and tried to avoid him. Many of the parishioners stopped Charles to speak to him as he led his mother into the church. They had not seen him for a long time and knew he was only home for a few days. Erich took the opportunity to try to disappear into the crowd.

Erich was happy to see Daddy Davy and Aunt Elsie were sitting in their usual pew. But before he could slip in beside them, Charles spotted him and motioned him over. He did not want to sit with the Downeys but reluctantly he obeyed the summons. As he passed the Elliotts' pew he trailed his hand over the end, hesitating and waiting for an invitation to join them. Aunt Elsie and Daddy Davy smiled a welcome but before they could say anything Charles turned around and beckoned again. Erich continued down the aisle.

Erich sat quietly beside Mrs Downey in the front pew. He knew he must behave. There would be no arguing and wrestling as in previous years with Hans. The Downeys would not tolerate it.

Uncle Edward stepped up to the pulpit. Standing tall and serious, he spoke authoritatively in a quiet voice. Erich listened to the sermon as if hearing a stranger. The man behind the pulpit was a different figure from the unassuming man who pottered in the grounds of the rectory the rest of the week. Despite sitting with the Downeys, Erich forgot his unhappiness for a while in the peaceful atmosphere of the church. The prospect of seeing Daddy Davy and Aunt Elsie afterwards also cheered him. As the service progressed he sang each hymn with more gusto than the last one anticipating the end of the service.

After the benediction Erich slid out of the pew before Charles could stop him, and trotted up the aisle, grinning widely as he stopped at the Elliotts' pew. Aunt Elsie hugged him.

"How are you gettin' on, Erich?" Daddy Davy asked, reaching over to ruffle his hair. Barely pausing for breath, Erich told him about the harvest composition that he had written.

"That's grand. I'd love to read it. What else have you been at?"

Erich launched into an account of all the week's happenings, not mentioning that Mrs Downey had been annoyed with him on the day he had visited them because he was late for tea.

"Good morning, Mr Elliott, Mrs Elliott. It's a grand day," Mrs Downey said as she came up the aisle to them.

"Indeed it is. How's Erich getting on with you?" Aunt Elsie asked.

"He needs a firm hand but it's nothing we can't manage," she replied. Aunt Elsie frowned but made no comment.

"Well, we'd best be getting on. Come along, Erich," Mrs Downey said. She shook hands with the Elliotts and continued up the aisle. After another quick hug from Aunt Elsie, Erich reluctantly followed her, glancing back every few feet. Aunt Elsie watched him, her eyes troubled.

Now that he had seen Daddy Davy and Aunt Elsie the best part of the day was gone. Erich dreaded going back to the rectory. Sunday was a long day. It was his least favourite day of the week. He had to be on his best behaviour in that huge, silent house. He could not go anywhere and there was no one to play with. Mr Doyle didn't work on Sundays so there was no chance John would be there. Though it didn't really matter if he were, Erich thought. Mrs Downey won't let me play with him anyways.

Christmas 1952

The dog's barking alerted them. Uncle Edward opened the door in time to see Maggie bounding down the driveway, barking madly. The pointer, though she was a hunting dog, mainly kept watch in the rectory grounds. She raced over the gravel and, barking excitedly, bounced up on the person approaching, welcoming rather than aggressive.

"Down, Maggie!" Susan said, laughing, "Hello, Daddy!" she called to the figure in the doorway.

"Hello, Susan! We didn't expect you until tomorrow."

"My exams are finished so I thought I'd come up early."

The Downey's youngest daughter had arrived home from university in Dublin for Christmas. Before she was even in the door her infectious laugh reverberated around them, breathing life into the place. Hearing her voice, Erich ran to the door.

"Hello, Susan!" he shouted. He was delighted to see her. Ever since he had first arrived in Cavan she had always been friendly to him. He was glad she was home.

When Susan had settled her things into her old room she came down to the sitting room. Elated by her arrival, Erich could barely sit still as he listened to her telling her parents about her studies and life in Dublin.

"And how are you both?" Susan asked her parents.

"We're grand, dear," Mrs Downey replied.

"But the doctor wants your mother to rest more. Her weak chest is giving her a bit of bother," Uncle Edward said.

"Well, I can help her while I'm at home," Susan said. "And there's a couple of chores Erich can help me with," she said, looking at him. Erich nodded eagerly.

"Tomorrow we'll chop some more wood for the fire," she said, speaking to Erich as an equal rather than a child; very few people ever did that. He beamed at her.

The next morning Erich and Susan, in their oldest jumpers, went out to the woodpile. They set to work breaking the large blocks of wood into small pieces. Susan, pausing for a moment, laughed when Erich's attempt to swing the axe went amiss and he split off only a small sliver from a log. Erich joined in her laughter, feeling accepted rather than ridiculed. Susan swung the axe expertly, splitting the logs evenly. She quickly amassed a pile of sticks; Erich's pile grew more slowly.

It was clear and frosty; they could see their breath as they worked but they were warm from their exertions. When they finished they carried the wood to the house and stacked it against the wall. Erich piled up sticks in his arms until he could barely see past them, then followed Susan almost blindly to the house, laughing and chatting with her as they walked. It took several trips to stack all the wood.

"Mind how you stack them," Mrs Downey called from the kitchen door as Erich carelessly dropped a load against the wall. He bent to tidy them, tossing them roughly into a neater pile.

"She never thinks I do anything right," Erich complained to Susan as they walked back for another load.

"Mam's particular but she's not as stern as she sounds. She just wants to raise you properly," Susan replied.

"She's not like Daddy Davy and Aunt Elsie. What's wrong with the way they raised me?"

"You liked living there, didn't you?" Susan asked, sympathetically. Erich nodded.

"I want to go back but they don't want me."

"It's not that they don't want you, Erich. They just can't manage to care for you. They'd have you there if they were able."

"I wish you were always here so I wouldn't be alone. You never scold me."

Susan smiled and ruffled his hair. "Don't take it to heart. Mam's not as bad as her bark. I can't stay all the time. I have to go to university. But I'm here for a couple weeks."

Erich brightened at the thought of Susan's company. It was amazing how one person could change the atmosphere so much. Christmas would be much less bleak than the autumn had been. Erich enthusiastically lifted another load of wood and trotted up to the house.

January 1953

Erich opened the front door. He had not walked far with the other children after school but he tensed, expecting to be greeted by Mrs Downey's scolding. The hall was silent; the house seemed lifeless again now that Susan was back in Dublin. Not seeing anyone downstairs, he went upstairs and dropped his books on his bed. Heavy footsteps clicking below drew him downstairs again.

"There you are, Erich. It's teatime," Uncle Edward said as he crossed the hall.

He ushered Erich into the dining room. There were two plates set at the table. Uncle Edward sat down at the nearest one and Erich sat opposite him.

288

"Where's Mrs Downey?" Erich asked, cautiously. He was not upset not to see her but was curious about her absence.

"Mrs Downey's chest is bad. She's gone to rest," Uncle Edward replied.

Erich was not surprised by this news. She had been coughing since Christmas. The meal passed with companionable chitchat. Erich felt relaxed at the table for a change. He did not worry about using the correct fork or keeping his elbows off the table.

Afterwards Erich sat at the fire with Uncle Edward. He felt carefree, untroubled by scrutiny. He enjoyed the sense of freedom he had all evening and went to bed content. I wish it was always like this, he thought. Life here might be bearable.

When Erich came in from school the next day he heard men's voices in the dining room. I expect a parishioner has come to see Uncle Edward, Erich thought. The minister often had callers. Knowing he had to be quiet, Erich started up the stairs to his room. Before he reached the landing, the dining room door opened.

"There you are, Erich. Come in a wee minute," Uncle Edward said.

Erich came back down the stairs and into the dining room. Standing by the fireplace was a tall, slim man, younger than Uncle Edward. His sallow face was the colour of aged paper. Dark, curly hair sat incongruously atop it. He scrutinised Erich, as if sizing him up.

"Henry, this is Erich," Uncle Edward said. "Mr Moss is my niece Dorothy's husband," he said to Erich. "They live in County Kildare."

"Hello, Erich," the man said, smiling but never losing the solemn look in his eyes. Erich thought he must be a strict headmaster; he had that appearance.

"I asked Mr Moss to help me find a new home for you. He's the church warden in his parish and knows quite a few people."

The statement jarred Erich. He looked at Uncle Edward with dismay. He knew he would not stay at the rectory forever but he thought he would stay in the parish. Daddy Davy and Aunt Elsie were here. He had spent almost half his life here. He did not want to go somewhere else. Uncle Edward can't mean it, Erich thought, panic rising. He stared at Uncle Edward as he continued.

"Sure you know Mrs Downey hasn't been too well. Her chest is weak and it's been at her lately. It's too much work for her to care for you much longer. Unfortunately I haven't been able to find a home for you in this parish but Mr Moss has found one in his."

"S-s-she doesn't w-w-want me here! That's w-w-why I have to l-l-leave!" Erich shouted.

"Indeed not, Erich. Since we're older than the Elliotts maybe we shouldn't have offered to bring you here. Maybe it wasn't for the best. But, sure, I thought I would have you sorted in no time. But now, with Mrs Downey's illness, we need to find a suitable home for you sooner than we thought. So Mr Moss agreed to help us. He will take you back to Kildare with him to meet a couple in his parish who are looking for a boy about your age."

Shocked and unhappy, Erich fled to his room. He lay on his bed, thinking about this news. He couldn't believe he was going so far away. Who are the people I'm going to? What are they like? Living with Aunt Rachel in Leitrim had been terrible. And Hans won't be there this time. Daddy Davy can't help me either. Kildare is further than Leitrim. He won't be able to come to visit. I'll be on my own, Erich thought miserably.

Mrs Downey must want me to leave, Erich thought. I always argue with her and she doesn't like it. That's why she's spent so much time in her bed lately. She isn't really ill. She's decided to stay there until I leave. Erich nodded to himself. That was the reason, he decided. It can't be anything else. She's forcing me to leave. I know she is, he thought bitterly.

Erich frowned, thinking about it. Why can't Uncle Edward find a home for me around here? Only strangers will have me. What's wrong with me? Does it matter that I sound different to the other children? Am I really so different from everyone else? Doesn't anyone who knows me want me? Tears ran down his face as he thought about it. He couldn't ask all the questions in his head; he had no one to ask. He already felt very alone.

❦

County Kildare
Winter 1953

"Do you have children?" Erich asked.

"Yes, three of them," Mr Moss answered.

"That's good. I'll be able to play with them. Not like at U-U-Uncle E-E-Edward's. I didn't have anyone there," Erich said. Maybe this won't be a terrible place, Erich thought cautiously.

Mr Moss made no reply. He did not think such boldness should be encouraged in a child.

Erich had discovered on the drive to County Kildare that Mr Moss was not a chatty man. He spoke no more than necessary. Like Mrs Downey, he expected Erich to be on his best behaviour. Erich wondered what his children were like. He was sad to be going so far from Daddy Davy and everything familiar but he would welcome having other children in the house again even if it were only for a few days. He was glad to get away from the cold, silent manse and Mrs Downey's strict regime.

They stopped outside a rambling country house opposite a grey stone church like many Church of Ireland buildings dotted around the countryside. This must be it, Erich thought. Mr Moss got out of the car. Erich jumped out and followed him to the door. As they entered the house three children, all younger than Erich, ran to meet them.

"Who's he, Daddy?" the oldest boy asked.

The children came to an abrupt stop in front of them and waited for their father to answer. He waited until they were quiet, then spoke.

"This is Erich. He's staying with us for a few days."

A woman appeared behind them, smiling.

"Hello, Erich. You're very welcome. I don't know if you remember me, from our visits to my uncle, Reverend Downey. My goodness, you've grown since I last saw you!" Mrs Moss said. Erich didn't remember her but she seemed nice so he smiled at her.

"Henry, will you take Erich into the sitting room with you," she said to the oldest boy.

"Do you have any c-c-comic books?" Erich asked. Henry shook his head as he led Erich to the sitting room.

"I have a new puzzle. I started it this afternoon. Do you want to help me do it?"

There were pieces of the puzzle lying everywhere in one corner of the sitting room. Erich studied the loose pieces then nodded. He sat down and was soon absorbed in finding the right place for each piece. Henry hovered beside him, watching his progress.

Erich was completely absorbed in the puzzle when Mrs Moss called, "Tea's ready!" The Moss children went to the dining room promptly when she called but Erich lingered over the puzzle, unwilling to leave it.

"Erich! Mrs Moss told you tea's ready." Mr Moss leaned into the room and looked pointedly at Erich. Slowly the boy stood up and dragged himself into the dining room. The Moss children were already seated at the table. They sat up straight, silently waiting for their father to say grace. Erich slumped into his seat. Glancing up, he caught sight of the light switch beside the door. He eyed it keenly; he loved the mystery of light switches, flicking them to watch the light come and go.

"Electric l-l-light's great! They h-h-had it at the rectory in County Sligo," Erich exclaimed.

"Light's great!" Sam, the Moss's youngest son, echoed.

"Quiet now, children, for the blessing," Mr Moss said, ignoring Erich's comment.

Excited at having the other children's company, after Mr Moss said grace Erich prattled on and on. He voiced his thoughts on many matters, trying to impress the younger children. Sometimes Sam echoed him. Henry eagerly jumped in with his own comments. Tea time was much noisier than usual for the Moss family.

After he finished eating, Mr Moss, his elbows resting on the table fingertips touching, regarded Erich. He found Erich less biddable than his own children. The boy needed to be ruled with a firm hand.

Erich put down his fork and jumped up exclaiming, "I'm going to finish the puzzle!"

Henry followed him crying, "Me too!"

"Erich, Henry, you haven't asked to be excused from the table yet," Mr Moss said sharply.

"Sorry, Daddy. May I be excused?" Henry asked sheepishly.

Erich looked mutinously at Mr Moss, resenting the censure. He had only left Mrs Downey's stern regime. I don't want to be in another home like that, he thought. Henry watched him. After a tense silence he asked, "May I be excused?"

"You may," Mr Moss replied.

Erich darted into the sitting room and, after a quick glance at his father, Henry dashed after him. When Mr Moss excused the younger children, they followed the boys. Mr Moss sighed, watching his wife clearing the dishes from the table.

"Dear Lord, give me patience! We need to ensure he is kept in check while he is with us," Mr Moss said.

"He's not a bad child. He's just spirited," his wife replied.

"He is altogether too excitable. He has no discipline. It isn't good for the child and we don't want our children learning his habits either," he said, exasperated. Mrs Moss nodded agreement.

"I will speak to Mr and Mrs Wray tomorrow to finalise the arrangements. If everything goes well, the Wrays will adopt Erich and they will have an heir to inherit their farm. It will be a great opportunity for the boy," Mr Moss said.

11

QUICKER THAN HIS TEMPER

"HOW BIG is the farm?" Erich asked Mr Moss.

"Seventeen acres," he replied.

"That's not very big. Daddy Davy had forty acres at Derrykeane," Erich said, choosing to forget that Clonty was only fifteen acres.

"Do they h-h-have children?" Erich asked a few minutes later.

"No, they don't. So they are pleased that you are coming to live with them," Mr Moss replied, glancing away from the windscreen to the boy beside him.

The last mile, down a single track lane, seemed as if it would never end. Tall hedges on both sides obscured Erich's view. He felt as if he had disappeared into a dense forest. Finally they emerged into a clearing. Two gates faced them.

Across a field to the right Erich saw several children of various ages playing in front of a two storey farmhouse. The house was painted a delicate yellow.

"You said they d-d-don't have any children," Erich said, his forehead furrowing.

"That's correct. They are the Mulligans' children."

"Oh, I'll be able to call round to them then," Erich declared without hesitation. He was delighted to find he would have playmates so near him.

"I shouldn't think so, Erich. You will meet new friends at your school."

The invisible barrier that divided the communities rose between Erich and his immediate neighbours, separating them before they even met. Wistfully he watched the children playing as he got out of the car and opened the left hand gate. They drove across the field to a low, whitewashed cottage. Two unpainted stone buildings stood behind the house. Tin roofs capped all three buildings.

A skinny, small man in his mid-forties, his threadbare jacket hanging loosely over his baggy jumper, came out of the nearest shed. Pushing his battered hat back on his forehead and scratching beneath it, he fixed them with a fierce stare. A black greyhound mongrel sat a few feet away, timidly watching.

"Hello, Robert," Mr Moss said. "I've brought Erich." Robert Wray nodded at Mr Moss.

"Hello, lad," he said, gruffly, his expression never changing. Erich was immediately alert. He did not like this man.

"Erich, this is Uncle Bob. You'll be living with him and Aunt Annie," Mr Moss said.

A woman appeared in the doorway of the house, hovering, unsure whether to come out. Although in her early forties, she looked older, strained and careworn. Her eyes watched her husband, anxiously, for a sign of what was required of her.

Seeing her, Mr Moss said, "Hello, Mrs Wray. I've brought Erich to you."

"Hello, Mr Moss. Hello, Erich. I'll put the kettle on," she said in a halting voice, and darted inside again.

"There's a couple of papers I'll need you to sign," Mr Moss said to Robert Wray.

"He's smaller than I expected," Uncle Bob replied, eyeing Erich.

"I expect he'll grow. Sure, you can see how you get on. The arrangement isn't irrevocable."

Uncle Bob nodded towards the house and they followed him inside.

A rooster crowed from somewhere in the haggard as Erich stepped out of the door. There was only a slight glow on the horizon at this hour. He could just discern the solid form of the pump handle, blacker than anything around it, as he passed. He walked to the outhouse, shoulders hunched against the cold. When he was finished, Erich hurriedly fastened his trousers. It was too cold to expose his bare skin to the air any longer than necessary.

Erich half jogged back to the house, stopping at the water pump. Shivering, he pumped the handle and splashed freezing water on his face. He was loathe to let the cold water touch him and jumped involuntarily as it stung his skin. He quickly rubbed his face and hands. Uncle Bob watched him through the window.

"I wouldn't call that washing!" Uncle Bob shouted, slamming open the back door. He strode to the pump and clamped his hand on Erich's shoulder. Pressing the boy's head and neck under the spout, he pumped the handle vigorously. He scrubbed Erich's neck until it burned. The cold water stung his raw skin. When he was finished Erich pulled away, shaking the water from his head and neck like a dog emerging from a river. He shivered as the cold air brushed his wet skin.

"Away and get the turnips for the cows," Uncle Bob said.

Erich's stomach rumbled. He was hungry but he had his chores to do before he could have breakfast. He trudged out to the field, his hands shoved into his pockets, the sack stuffed under his arm. His nose ran and, without taking his hands out of his pockets, he wiped it on his sleeve. His legs were red and stinging below his knee length trousers as the breeze whipped them.

The turnips, piled in a heap in the corner of the field, were preserved from last summer's harvest. Erich, fingers splayed wide, randomly grasped the hard, uneven balls and stuffed them into the sack as quickly as he could. When the sack was full he dragged it back to where the mangle stood in the haggard.

Stretching up Erich dumped the contents of the sack into the mangle's funnel. He fought to turn the handle until, groaning, it grudgingly gave in to him and its teeth-like rollers crunched and shredded the turnips. The pieces fell into a bucket on the ground.

Numb with cold, at first he did not notice the drizzle as it started to blow across him. His clothes were soon covered in a film of water which seeped through them, adding to the cold. His hands were red and deadened on the handle. When the funnel had emptied its chopped contents into the bucket he carted it into the byre. Lifting the bucket, he let the pieces tumble into the trough.

"T'byre needs mucked out," Uncle Bob called, from the far end of the building. He milked slowly and rhythmically, dry and comfortable in the shed.

Barely able to feel his fingers after the cold outside, Erich lifted the pitchfork and began tossing dirty straw into the wheelbarrow. He was warmer inside, sheltered from the blowing rain. Draughts slipped through cracks in the stone walls but it was not the full force of the wind. When the wheelbarrow was piled high with straw Erich threw the pitchfork on top and grasped the handles. He pushed it through the doorway, aware of Uncle Bob's critical eyes on him. He never heard warm praise from Uncle Bob like he had from Daddy Davy.

I wish I was back at Daddy Davy's. We'd work together and soon be finished. He'd be pleased with my work but I'll never satisfy Uncle Bob. I hate him, Erich fumed.

The boy knew that nothing he did would please this man but he didn't care as he felt no desire to do so. He wasn't Daddy Davy. Irregardless, Erich knew he had to complete the work. His life would be miserable otherwise.

Balancing carefully, he steered the wheelbarrow to the field and dumped its contents. He repeated the process until the floor of the shed was bare then trundled the empty wheelbarrow, bouncing on the uneven ground, to the shed opposite where he forked clean straw into it. He hurried, as fast as he could go without overturning the wheelbarrow, between the two sheds, trying to dodge the rain. It took several trips to cover the floor of the byre with fresh straw. By the time he was finished Uncle Bob had finished the milking and gone inside the house.

Erich's first sight as he walked in the back door was Uncle Bob sitting at the table, eating a bowl of porridge and slurping loudly from his cup of tea. He seethed knowing Uncle Bob had been sitting there while he finished the chores. Daddy Davy would never have done that, Erich thought angrily. Tired and cold, he flopped onto a chair at the table. He grasped the hot cup of tea Aunt Annie set in front of him with both hands. He felt a little better as he swallowed the warm liquid. Feeling somewhat revived he hunched over to hurriedly eat his breakfast. No conversation passed between them at the table as Aunt Annie fluttered about the kitchen, ready to take flight at the slightest rebuke from her husband.

It was quite light outside now. The school van would be here soon. Erich finished his tea then went to pick up his school satchel.

"Bye!" he called, as he hurried out of the door. Uncle Bob grunted; Aunt Annie watched him from the window.

"Bye," she said softly to his retreating figure.

Erich hurried along the track worn in the grass and climbed the gate at the other side of the field. Walking up the long lane the relentless drizzle accosted him. He slung his satchel over his shoulder and stuffed his hands in his pockets. Rain drops ran off his curls, bouncing over his forehead and dripping onto his face. He shook his head to clear the water away, like a spaniel shaking himself after a swim, then burrowed his chin into the collar of his jumper, flipping up the lapels of his jacket.

The high hedges on either side of the lane obscured his view but Erich never even glanced up. He just kept plodding forward, eager to reach the van and get out of the rain. He splattered mud over himself with each step. As he hurried it splashed higher until his face was dotted with brown specks. Erich met no one on his walk up the lane. Hidden between the high hedges he could have been the only player in a huge maze.

A mile later he emerged from his green tunnel. Standing on the main road, he strained to spot the van coming. He did not have long to wait. The battered old van soon pulled off the road, stopping on the shoulder a few feet past him. Erich picked up his satchel and sprinted to it. With a last shake of his shoulders to free himself of the penetrating rain, he climbed into the van and flopped into an empty seat to a chorus of hellos. His neighbours and the first friends he had made since he arrived, the Cooke girls and their brother, Tom, were already in the van. Eleanor, who was nearest his own age, smiled and they started to chat. The windows were clouded over with steam rising from the children's wet jackets and coats. The driver, Mr Grainger, had to wipe the front window to see past the fog created by the wet clothing. He glanced quickly down the road then pulled out.

The children were so familiar with the scenery along their route to Athy that no one bothered to try to peer through the heavy fog shrouding the windows at the fields beyond which were also half covered in fog. Pre-occupied with their conversations, they did not notice anything beyond the van and the journey passed quickly.

With a dwindling Protestant population in the county, the school accepted children within a several mile radius of Athy in order to keep the enrolment large enough to stay open. Several parents had collectively bought the van so their children could attend the school.

The school was located at the edge of Athy, just outside the town and slightly separate from it. The grey-black, two storey stone building, just past its centenary, sat in its own grounds. Its regal appearance gave the impression of a private boarding school rather than a local national school. Double and triple chimneys sat at intervals atop the tall, pointed roof. Above each second floor window the stonework protruded to a roof-like point. Pale quoins and window borders contrasted with the darker stone of the building.

The van dropped them off in front of the school. Over the narrow, painted door an ornately carved stone proclaimed Athy Model School. This was the first school Erich had attended since he lived in Bray which had more than one teacher and classroom.

When they left the van the boys and girls separated into their respective playgrounds on opposite sides of the school. Erich wished they didn't have separate playgrounds. He liked the Cooke girls' company. Tom went to join some of the younger boys. Left on his own, Erich stood near the door, hunched to avoid the worst of the rain.

When the teacher rang the bell a few minutes later, Erich walked down the hall into his classroom. Leaning on his cane, Mr Keown watched the children file past. Water dripped from their jackets and coats. Though most children's hair hung limp, the moisture tightened Erich's curls.

"Put your chairs by the fire," Mr Keown instructed them, his cane tapping in time with his footsteps as he walked across the classroom. Eagerly they pulled their chairs over to the warmth of the fire. Shivers and steam rose from them as its heat seeped in. Mr Keown poured cups of tea from a flask on his desk, passing them to the huddled children.

Mr Keown taught the senior years. Barely nine stone, he was small and thin but he commanded the respect of his pupils and never had difficulty maintaining discipline. He was also dedicated to teaching and Erich's keen, diligent attitude pleased him; he took pains to encourage his new student.

When all the children were seated, Mr Keown said, "*Dun an doras, le do thoil,* Eleanor."

Eleanor Cooke closed the classroom door and hurried back to the fire.

"*Go raibh maith agat, Eleanor,*" Mr Keown thanked her.

"*Conas a ta tu?*" he asked, turning his attention to Mervyn sitting next to Eleanor.

"*Taim go maith*, Mr Keown," Mervyn replied.

"*Cad e seo?*" Mr Keown asked, pointing through the small panes in the sash window to the road outside. He turned to Erich, waiting for an answer.

"*Ta se an sraid*," Erich replied. Erich tried to remember the word for road in German. He didn't know why he thought of it. He didn't remember many German words anymore.

"*Ta se*," Mr Keown agreed. "*Go maith*, Erich."

The Irish lesson continued in the question and answer format until Mr Keown was satisfied the children understood the vocabulary. Afterwards he returned their English essays. Erich studied the first page of his. Several stars sat proudly above the title. He grinned and sat up straighter in his seat. Eleanor, noticing the stars, nudged him. When he turned to her she smiled, pointing to the essay. Erich beamed with pleasure, glad Eleanor had noticed.

"Return to your desks, please," Mr Keown instructed, noticing the children's clothes and hair had stopped creating pools beneath their chairs.

As they settled into their desks, Mr Keown handed a short, fair-haired boy, seated at the front of the class, a stack of paper to distribute. The teacher set a blue vase, filled with snowdrops, near the front edge of his desk, clearing books and papers out of the way. When each child had a sheet of paper he said, "Take your pencils and draw the flowers and vase, class."

The children bent their heads in concentration. The room fell silent as they worked. Erich studied the vase intently then started to draw. Mr Keown watched the boy from behind his desk, but Erich, intent on the task, was unaware of the scrutiny. Mr Keown liked his attitude; he obviously put an effort into his work. The teacher stood up and ambled down the aisle leaning on his cane, head bent looking at the children's work. Some drawings were very basic and amateurish while others showed potential.

He stopped beside Erich's desk. The boy drew meticulously, replicating the vase in front of him. Mr Keown was impressed by the talent shown in his work. Erich should spend more time developing his drawing, the teacher thought. But it was unlikely he would get much time or encouragement for his drawing from his foster family. Practical farming matters were all they were interested in. It's a shame the boy's talent will be wasted, Mr Keown thought, walking on along the row.

"Time to finish, class. I'll collect your drawings to mark," Mr Keown said.

Papers and bodies shuffled as the children passed their drawings to the front of each row.

A sharp rap at the door preceded the entrance of a stooped, black-haired man in flowing black robes. His large nose protruded from his wizened face like a signpost as, peering sharply at the children, he crossed the room. All he needs to complete his witchlike appearance is a pointed hat, Erich thought.

Erich scowled when he saw him; he had quickly decided that he did not like Reverend McKenna, the local minister. He was nothing like Reverend Downey.

"Good morning, Reverend McKenna," Mr Keown greeted him, standing and gathering his papers from the desk. With the children's drawings tucked under his arm, Mr Keown limped out of the room.

Reverend McKenna regarded the children without smiling. He would brook no rowdiness or disorderliness. The children sat still and attentive under his watchful gaze. He settled into the teacher's chair and began his lesson.

Erich tried to concentrate so as not to incur the minister's displeasure, wishing the religion lesson was over. It was almost lunch time and he was hungry. Stealthily he looked at the clock on the wall, willing it to move forward - or backward to the drawing lesson. He had enjoyed that. It was a brief escape. He loved any activity he could lose himself in and forget everything that made him unhappy.

The children raced from the school van to the large, stone water trough on the grassy square in front of the Cookes' house. The property was shielded from the road by large trees and a high hedge. The eldest Cooke girls disappeared into the house. The younger children, Erich and another classmate, Rebecca, who lived at an adjoining farm to him, went into the hay shed.

Erich came as often as possible to the Cooke farm after school. Sometimes, like today, one or two other friends came too. On good days they played rounders on the grassy square; on wet, miserable days they played cards in the kitchen. But no matter what the weather, they eventually found their way to the hay shed to bounce in the soft straw. It was a game they never tired of. They chased each other, climbing until they were high above the ground, then jumped into the pile.

"I'll be king of the castle!" Erich shouted, starting to climb.

"No, you won't! I'll climb it afore you!" Rebecca shouted. Tall and lively, she loved a challenge and started to clamber up, quickly catching up with Erich. She passed him, laughing. Erich darted his hand under her dress and grabbed the waist of her knickers. There were gasps and laughs from the children below.

"No, you won't!" he shouted holding on. He would like to peek into her knickers but he also wanted to get to the top first. His conflicting desires kept him rooted to the spot, undecided what to do.

Rebecca laughed, pulling away from him. Her waistband stretched out digging into her stomach but she kept straining forward. Suddenly it snapped. She pitched forward, her knickers dropping to her ankles, as Erich tumbled backwards. Laughing uproariously, she pulled them up and held them at her waist. The girls below giggled.

Erich had found to his advantage that he was popular with the girls in his new school too. Since he was smaller than the other boys his age the girls treated him like a favourite pet. No one could be angry with him no matter how bold he was.

"Wait till your mammy sees that!" Eleanor exclaimed.

"Sure, she can sew the elastic back together," Rebecca said, still giggling. "I'd best go home and tell her the good news." Unconcerned, she climbed down and headed home. Erich also climbed down, forgetting he meant to be king of the castle. He didn't have the same enthusiasm for the game without Rebecca.

The Cooke girls and Erich went outside to play a game of rounders. When it was his turn, Erich hit the ball easily. He ran quickly, sliding as he ran. Mrs Cooke came to the door of the large farmhouse and watched them, arms folded against the chilly air.

"Tom, girls, come in and get your tea! You too, Erich!" she called. The Cooke children often had visitors and Mrs Cooke fed everyone who sat down to the table. With five children of her own, another one or two made little difference.

The farmhouse was a sprawling, two storey building. Its dark stone was covered with plaster and whitewashed. A chimney sat at either end of the black slated roof, like two lonely diners at a long, banquet table. Tall, narrow windows allowed thin beams of light into the sitting room and kitchen. But the light was fading in the late afternoon.

Erich followed the Cooke children through the olive green door into the large kitchen. His stomach rumbled as the aroma of bacon and potatoes wafted from the plates the older girls carried from the range to the battered wooden table. The children ate noisily and heartily. Mrs Cooke tried to keep some semblance of order and manners as everyone chewed and talked at once.

Erich joined in the conversation, teasing Tom, the youngest Cooke child, as if he were his own brother. Looking at Tom he thought of Hans. I wish I knew how he's gettin' on. I'd love to see him, Erich thought.

This household was such a contrast to his silent, grim existence at the Wrays. Mrs Cooke didn't look fearfully at her husband as Aunt Annie did, nor was she cowed and afraid to move.

It felt relaxed and safe here. Erich loved being with this noisy, happy family. He wished he had been sent to live here. It would be almost as good as going back to Daddy Davy.

After the meal Eleanor lifted a worn deck of cards from the dresser. She shuffled and dealt them into piles around the table. Erich reached for the nearest pile. Lifting it, he searched his hand for matching pairs, triplets or runs. He had a pair and a four card run; he smiled to himself. Blinking rapidly and frowning slightly with concentration, Erich watched as each child in turn laid cards on the table. As they worked their way around the table he realised his hand was not as promising as he had first thought. Eleanor won the round with a run which included a king, queen and jack. They played several rounds, quiet with concentration. Erich sighed as Eleanor lay down three kings. He had only three sixes. Eleanor had won another hand.

"Pity you didn't have better luck, Erich," Mrs Cooke said, shaking her head, as Erich dropped his cards on the table. "Goodness, look at the time, now. You'd best be gettin' on," she added.

Erich nodded and stood up. With a chorus of goodbyes trailing after him, he walked out into the darkness. His eyes took a few minutes to adjust to it as he walked along the road. No vehicles passed him during the half mile walk to his lane. He turned into the lane, disappearing between the hedges. It was blacker here than the road had been but the hedges either side of him were visible in the light cast by the half moon. Their solid, dark bulk steered him down the lane. He walked along happily, thinking of the fun he had had at the Cookes' house. And, best of all, Rebecca had been there. He had liked her from the first time he met her. He was always eager to be anywhere that she was. And he had almost seen into her knickers. It was a brilliant afternoon, he thought.

The shadows on either side did not disturb him; he walked boldly. This journey did not frighten him as his trips to get firewood for Aunt Rachel had done. He was not afraid of the dark now. At twelve his natural impulsiveness was developing into an assertive, plucky attitude. His experiences during the past few years had strengthened his resolve rather than cowed him.

Erich climbed the gate and trotted across the field to the Wray's cottage. Entering the back door he saw Uncle Bob in his usual spot at the kitchen table, the newspaper spread out in front of him. He looked up when the door slammed.

"What kept ye till this hour?" he asked.

"I was playing at the Cookes and they a-a-asked me to stay for tea," Erich replied.

"Well, there was work waiting to be done here while ye were off larking about. I had to do it all myself."

"It's not my f-f-farm," Erich muttered.

"What did ye say?" Uncle Bob shouted.

"Why s-s-should I have to do s-s-such a lot o' work? I-I-It's your farm!" Erich shouted back.

"Don't ye dare speak to me like that! Ye should be grateful I keep ye! Not many would!" Uncle Bob rose from the table, his hand raised. Erich backed away as he advanced. He sprinted, quicker than Uncle Bob's flaring temper, out of the door and around the side of the cottage. He knew better than to face Uncle Bob when he was in this mood. Before the ill-tempered farmer was out of the door Erich was sitting up in an apple tree's branches, silently watching him tramp back and forth through the yard, in and out of the sheds, looking for the boy.

"Get ye in here now, Erich!" Uncle Bob shouted. "I've a letter here from the Elliotts for ye. I may set it in the fire if ye don't come in."

Erich was tempted by the knowledge that a letter from Daddy Davy waited for him. He loved hearing from Daddy Davy. But he knew better than to face Uncle Bob until he calmed down. Muttering and stamping, Uncle Bob searched both sheds. Erich wrapped his arms around himself and leaned against the tree trunk, waiting until the search was completed. When Uncle Bob's efforts proved futile he went back inside the house, slamming the door. Erich crept down from the tree and tiptoed to the nearest shed. Shivering, he hoped Uncle Bob would go to bed early. His temper would not burn itself out before morning and it would be best to avoid him. But it was cold outside. An hour passed as Erich sat silently watching the window, willing Uncle Bob to go to bed.

Finally he saw the flickering flame from the paraffin lamp dancing briefly in each of the windows along the back of the house. The light's waltz ended at Uncle Bob's room; a few minutes later it went out. Uncle Bob must have gone to bed. Aunt Annie often went to bed when her chores were completed, unwilling to sit with Uncle Bob and possibly provoke his anger. Erich waited a few minutes then he quietly slipped in the unlocked door. He spotted a flat, dark object on the kitchen table. Lifting it he could see it was a letter. It must be the one Uncle Bob said Daddy Davy had sent. Uncle Bob didn't burn it, Erich thought, relieved. He grabbed it and hurried to his room. He got under the blankets fully clothed and rolled into a ball, tucking the letter under his pillow. He could not read it in the dark and had no lamp. His hands and feet were numb. He was glad to be under the thin blankets; it was warmer than outside. He listened tensely for any sound from the other end of the house until, exhausted, he dropped off to sleep.

Erich woke early and eagerly ripped the envelope open. He recognised Daddy Davy's heavy, even writing and quickly read the letter. He could see Daddy Davy sitting at the kitchen table to tell him about Aunt Elsie and the girls' visits home. Reading the news he could almost imagine himself there. There was no mention of Hans. Erich wondered how his brother was getting on. Did Daddy Davy ever see him? Daddy Davy said it was quiet with all of them away. He asked Erich to write and tell them about his new home.

Erich lay back on the bed. What can I tell them? he thought despondently. Nothing that wouldn't upset them. He knew they couldn't do anything about his misfortune this time. They wouldn't come to rescue him like they did from Aunt Rachel's.

He mulled over the situation in his mind. They're probably really glad I'm gone. If they had wanted me, they wouldn't have sent me away, he thought bitterly. What is the point of replying? I'll never see them again. I don't even have a stamp to post it anyway. Erich tucked the letter under the mattress, unwilling to discard it though he had no intention of replying.

Spring 1953

The gentle, grey horse followed Erich without any prompting from the lead rope as the boy walked in front of the plough. The horse had more years experience than Erich did. They walked back and forth across the field as the plough, like a boot with its pointed toe dragging behind them, cut a straight line in the earth.

Uncle Bob gripped the handles of the plough and steered it in a straight line, turning the corners in a neat semicircle. He fixed his eyes on the ground in front of him to keep the line straight, adjusting with one hand or the other if the plough wandered. Erich enjoyed working with him like this. Concentrating on the work at hand, Uncle Bob did not have time to shout or threaten; he became bearable for a while. It was almost like helping Daddy Davy. Erich could imagine himself back at Derrykeane again.

They had been ploughing all day. Erich's legs ached but the steady plodding across the field soothed him. He walked half in a daze. Trying to shake the hypnotic effect of the task, Erich looked around for some excitement or challenge. He glanced over his shoulder at Uncle Bob steering the plough. It did not look difficult. He could do that.

"Can I have a g-g-go, ploughing?" Erich shouted to Uncle Bob.

"Not until ye're a bit older," Uncle Bob replied.

"I could d-d-do it," Erich asserted. "Let me t-t-try it."

"Well, we'll see next year. Ye need to be a bit stronger to hold the plough steady," Uncle Bob said. He was thin but wiry and his arms were much stronger than his frame would suggest. Erich would not be able to control the plough as he did.

Erich continued walking in front of the horse, bored now that he was fully alert. He would love to be able to play with his friends but the chores would keep him busy all day. But tomorrow was Sunday. No work other than that which was absolutely necessary was done on Sunday. So Erich would have some time to himself after church. He smiled, thinking about the church service. He would see Rebecca. Even though he was at school with her all week, he would not miss a chance to see her. Her boisterous personality drew him and she always had time to talk to him. Thinking about Sunday cheered him and kept him awake as he walked up and down the field.

The next morning was overcast. Erich left before the Wrays to walk the couple of miles to the village. The church and a few houses comprised the whole village.

When he entered the church hall Erich spotted Rebecca sitting beside her older brother, Peter. Disappointed, he sat a few rows behind them. He would not get a chance to speak to Rebecca with her brother there. Peter would be sure of that.

After Sunday school Erich stood around with several boys who were also in his class at school, scuffing his shoes on the gravel, beside the church door, watching the parishioners arrive. Erich stared up at the pointed spire above him. Its turret-like tower reminded him of a castle. He imagined a damsel in distress trapped in the tower, leaning over and calling him. It would be Rebecca, of course. He would race to her rescue and she would be overawed by his bravery. He darted a glance at Rebecca chatting with several other girls nearby. Peter stood a few feet from them, his watchful eye on her.

The entire church building was grey, a deeper grey than the sky surrounding it this morning. It was an identical twin to many other country churches Erich had seen since he arrived in Ireland. Set in the middle of its own graveyard, it had a sombre presence. The latticed, plain glass windows were reminiscent of a window in a prison cell. The only splash of colour was the stained glass window at the rear of the building which allowed warm, glowing colours, like a kaleidoscope, to dance inside on bright days.

The sanctuary was quite small, able to seat one hundred parishioners. When most of the congregation had arrived Erich went to sit at the front with two other boys. Together they comprised the male section of the choir. Elderly women and young girls made up the rest of the choir.

When the hymns began Erich sang with gusto, surreptitiously searching the congregation to catch a glimpse of Rebecca. The other boys, dragged by their mothers to the choir, eyed him quizzically. But Erich did not notice. He loved to sing and sang each hymn with relish, putting some life into the tired choir. Glancing down the aisle he caught Rebecca's eye. She smiled at him. He sang even more heartily.

After the service Uncle Bob stood chatting with Mr Cooke outside the door. Mrs Cooke and Aunt Annie, the task of making Sunday dinner for their families awaiting them, walked out of the gate together and headed home.

"It's been grand weather this week," Mr Cooke said.

"So it has. I finished most of the ploughing yesterday," Uncle Bob replied. He didn't mention my help, Erich thought, listening to them.

"Please God, we'll get a good day for Punchestown this year," Mr Cooke said.

"Indeed, it'll be no good if the ground's sodden. They won't run worth tuppence," Uncle Bob replied.

Erich wandered away, uninterested in the conversation. Uncle Bob won't take me to Punchestown races. He never takes me anywhere. Daddy Davy always took me when he went anywhere. If I were at Daddy Davy's, Hans and I would be going to Ballylea Fair this summer, he thought wistfully. Daddy Davy would give us both pocket money and we'd spend ages looking around the stalls before we decided what to buy. Will Hans and Charlie come up from Cavan Town for the fair? he wondered.

Mr Moss stood in the doorway talking to two elderly sisters. His eyes scanned the grounds, vigilantly monitoring children playing. Seeing him Erich veered away from the door. At the rear of the church, under the St Brigid's cross and away from their parents' gaze, a group of children were loitering. The imposing stone cross stood over a large, old plot. The younger children chased each other around it, jumping over the low iron railing surrounding the grave, until the church warden rebuked them. Erich went to join a couple of boys standing beside the cross. Together they watched girls from their Sunday school class, trying to appear uninterested, teasing them as they passed. Several girls called hello to Erich. He smiled, pleased they noticed him. Rebecca waved as she walked to the gate with her parents. Her brother, turning to see who she was waving at, scowled when he saw Erich. Hiding his disappointment, Erich waved back, watching her leave. He wouldn't have a chance to even say hello to her.

"Erich!" Uncle Bob called.

Erich peered around the corner of the church and caught a glimpse of Uncle Bob looking for him. After a quick glance in the direction of the St Brigid's cross Uncle Bob strode towards the gate.

"Tara, see you tomorrow," Erich shouted to the other boys and hurried after him. He half ran as they strode without speaking along the road and down the lane to the farm.

Smelling the boiling potatoes as he entered the back door, Erich was glad the dinner was nearly ready. He was hungry. He went to wash quickly and sat down at the table. Between glances at her husband Aunt Annie darted a small smile to Erich as she set his plate in front of him. The meal was silent; Uncle Bob and Aunt Annie rarely conversed with each other. Erich ate ravenously and then sat waiting for the activity on the farm each week which he enjoyed best.

Uncle Bob relaxed at the table for a few minutes after the meal, then he stood up and lifted his hat from the peg by the door. He went out of the back door without a word. Erich stood up and followed him. Every Sunday afternoon Uncle Bob walked the perimeter of the farm, checking hedges for gaps to be repaired and looking for any other work that needed doing. He checked each field to see if it had been well enough grazed to warrant moving the cows to another field. He also looked for rabbit holes that could injure valuable animals. When he was finished he proudly surveyed his small domain.

"I'll mend yon gap tomorrow. The heifers are grand in the front field for a few days yet," he said, nodding to himself after he finished the inspection.

At times like these Erich enjoyed listening to him and learning about farming. He wanted to be a farmer when he left school. Just about everyone, except the minister and his teacher, farmed. What else would I do? Erich wondered. He liked working with the animals and he wanted to be like Daddy Davy. I can leave here and go back to help Daddy Davy. We can farm together. I'll even see Hans again. It'll be great! Erich thought. This daydream always cheered him.

Relaxed in his domain, Uncle Bob was sometimes eloquent in his discourse about farming. Erich eagerly absorbed any information he could get. At these times Uncle Bob was pleasant and interesting company, devoid of outbursts of temper. Erich tried to enjoy these brief moments on Sundays. He never knew what mood Uncle Bob would be in the rest of the week.

Summer 1953

Erich's forehead wrinkled in concentration, head bent towards the floor, as he listened to the radio. He was near the front of the group but the cracklings and buzzing made it difficult to hear. The children sat huddled around the radio, subdued in the strange surroundings of their teacher's house. They were only next door to the school but it seemed miles away. Coronation Day was a mild June day but no one noticed the weather with the excitement of being out of class. The presenter said that Princess Elizabeth, a slim, dark-haired woman with elegant robes flowing around her, walked confidently down the aisle of Westminster Abbey. Erich imagined the Chapel stretching out in front of her, tall pillars rising like ancient oak trees on either side.

Erich listened enraptured. England was far away like the lands in the fairy stories he sometimes read and Princess Elizabeth's Coronation sounded just like one of those. It did not seem like a real event at all. Mr Keown said the Abbey was far grander, larger and more ornate than any church Erich had seen. He listened in awe to the descriptions of the horses and splendid carriages slowly trooping through the streets of London. He could hardly believe that it was happening as they listened. Sometimes fairy stories could be true. I'd love to see such a wonderful place, Erich thought. Maybe one day I'll go to England and see all the grand places that Uncle Jim talked about. Thinking of Uncle Jim reminded him of Charlie. And of Hans. Maybe Hans will come to England with me, he thought.

Erich sat up in the tree, lying back against the trunk, head bent to peer between the leaves. The path below was bordered by trees as if providing a guard of honour. Erich thought Rebecca deserved a guard of honour. There wasn't a prettier girl at school. Her shoulder length dark hair framed lively eyes dancing in her composed face. Her family farm was up the hill from the Wrays and the tree-lined path connected the two farms. Rebecca came to visit whenever she could get away. Erich hoped she might come today. So when he had finished his morning chores he rushed up the tree to sit and watch for her.

Erich heard rustling along the path and leaned forward to get a better view. He caught a flash of dark hair and a cotton floral pattern. He scampered down the trunk and eagerly went to meet her.

"Hi, Rebecca!"

"Hi, Erich! How're you?"

"Alright."

"What humour is he in the day?" She nodded towards the Wrays' farm and screwed up her face.

"As b-b-bad as ever. He was giving out this morning, while I w-w-was milking, because he saw me drinking some milk. I h-h-hate him! It's a-a-awful there!"

Rebecca smiled sympathetically, listening to Erich as they walked along the path. There was no one else he could talk to about Uncle Bob. He didn't even tell the Cooke girls what it was like at the Wrays. Boisterous and the centre of attention in a group, Rebecca was serious and perceptive on her own. Erich did not know anyone who was better company and eagerly anticipated any time he could spend with her. And he relied on her as his confidante. It made living at the Wrays bearable.

When they reached the house Aunt Annie was filling a bucket at the water pump. With Uncle Bob out working in the field, Aunt Annie was almost relaxed and stood to chat with them. She leaned on the water pump, making no effort to get back to her chores.

"Would you like a cup of tea?" she asked Rebecca. "There's some fresh bread too." Out of Uncle Bob's shadow she was kind and caring. She lavished as much affection on Erich as she dared without provoking her husband's temper.

Before Rebecca could answer footsteps approached briskly from the tree-covered path. A tall, sandy-haired boy, a couple years older than Erich, his jacket tight over his thick shoulders and arms, emerged from the path. He frowned when he saw Rebecca chatting happily with Erich and Aunt Annie.

"Ye don't have time to be gossiping with yon boy, Rebecca. Mammy is asking for ye," her brother Peter said, eyeing Erich suspiciously. Twelve year old girls were not encouraged to have male friends, especially foreign ones and strangers to the area. Although the Cookes and Rebecca had welcomed Erich some people were suspicious of him.

"Maybe I'll s-s-see you t-t-tomorrow, Rebecca," Erich said.

"She'll not have time to be calling on you," Peter said to Erich with finality. Rebecca did not protest but gave Erich a cheeky grin over her shoulder as she left with Peter.

Erich felt a weight tightening his chest despite Rebecca's obvious disregard for her brother's orders. Visitors were rare at the farm, especially other children. Everyone was afraid to come near the taciturn but volatile farmer and his odd, cowering wife. Rebecca was the bright spot in his grey world. He should have expected interference. Something always happened when he made a friend.

Why am I always the odd one out? he wondered. After seven years in Ireland he did not feel different from his classmates. But some people obviously thought he was. He knew he sounded a bit different, his accent a mixture of German and Irish, but was it even very noticeable? And why did it matter? Why was he not suitable?

Dispirited, Erich watched Rebecca disappear into the leafy path. Maybe it's better not to get too close to anyone, he thought. Every time I do I get hurt. If I don't get too close then it can't hurt. That might be the best idea, he concluded.

"Do you want a cup of tea and a wee bit of bread, Erich?" Aunt Annie asked, smiling sympathetically at him. He shook his head. He knew Aunt Annie was fond of him and wanted to cheer him up but bread and tea wouldn't help.

"I'd best get on now," Aunt Annie said when he refused the offer. "Don't fret. No doubt she'll be round the first chance she gets." She smiled fleetingly then picked up the bucket she had set beside the pump and went into the house.

The afternoon was very warm. Erich took a drink from the water pump and wandered off to the nearest field. It was empty. He walked across it to the next one. He stopped and looked around. The house was hidden from sight. Uncle Bob was not here. He must be in the far field, Erich thought. Several cows ambled through the field, noses in the grass. A couple others lay under the hedge, in the shade, chewing their cuds and tossing their heads to keep the flies away. The grass was long. You could tell the cows were recently put in this field, Erich thought idly. He stood watching the placid, slow beasts, depression holding him in place like a heavy weight. He felt so alone.

The heat was overpowering. The sun beat down making him wearier than he already was. He watched the cows, half-sleeping, under the hedge. Slowly he walked over to them but they took no notice of him. Their incessant chewing and placid bulks were comforting. Erich sat down beside one of the cows and she swung her head towards him, mildly curious, but made no attempt to move. Erich lay his head back on her round belly which bounced like a waterbed under her soft, silky hide. He closed his eyes, hearing her rhythmic chewing and the occasional flick of her ear. She snorted gently but didn't move. Animals are always nicer than people, Erich thought. They never think I'm strange or different; they never laugh at me. He drifted into a heavy, heat induced sleep, feeling safe and not as alone as he had a few minutes earlier.

12

MONEY FOR STAMPS
December 1953

E RICH OPENED the low, wooden gate, walked up the path to the neat stone house and knocked on Miss Woods' door. Set back behind a tall hedge her H-shaped house gave the impression of a miniature manor house. Two identical ends, with bay windows, were joined by a short corridor. The symmetry gave it an elegant air. With the church spire visible above its pointed roof, it could easily be mistaken for the manse. But the manse, set on the other side of the church, was not nearly so grand.

Miss Woods answered his knock without delay. "I thought I would see you today," she said brightly, as she ushered him inside.

The elderly spinster lived alone and welcomed the boy's company. She had been kind to him since he arrived, providing a sanctuary in her home. Sunday afternoon was a good time to call.

The atmosphere in the house was so different to where Erich lived. Light streamed through the large, bay windows into the airy, tastefully decorated sitting room in contrast to the small, dirty windows at the Wrays' cottage that let little light into its gloomy, cramped interior. Miss Woods pushed open the sitting room door and waved him in. Following their well established routine, he slid onto a chair near the window. Miss Woods disappeared down the hall.

She returned a few minutes later carrying a tray laden with tea and biscuits. As she poured the tea she asked, "How are you getting on with your lessons?"

With his mouth full, Erich replied, "I passed my arithmetic test but it w-w-was very hard." After another bite of a biscuit, he said, "I got four stars on my English c-c-composition this week."

"That's grand! You're doing very well!" Miss Woods replied.

As they continued to chat Erich took a biscuit from the plate each time Miss Woods passed it to him. Periodically he glanced over at the bookshelf against the wall. He loved to peruse her books. They were different from the comics and children's stories he usually read. Sometimes she let him borrow one. Seeing his gaze, Miss Woods said, "Would you like to look at the books, Erich?"

"Yes, please!" He did not need a second invitation and was already standing in front of the bookshelf. He lifted a well worn book about Irish history and thumbed through the pages gingerly and slowly, reluctant to replace it on the shelf. He loved to read about the soldiers, chieftains and battles. Miss Woods smiled, watching him.

"Would you like to borrow that one? You may keep it until after the Christmas holidays," she said.

"May I?" Erich asked excitedly.

Miss Woods nodded. Erich happily walked back to his chair with the book clutched under his arm. There was so much more in Miss Woods' books than in the comics he bought whenever he could afford them or the children's books they had at school. He could not wait to read it when he got home.

Balancing the book on his knee, Erich strained to see the words on the page. The plain glasses the doctor had given him did not help to penetrate the deep shadows the oil lamp cast but he persevered.

Erich studied the page, engrossed in the voyage of the Spanish Armada. He had been reading about it all week. He loved the world that books opened up to him. It would be so exciting to travel across the water in a ship, ready to fight anyone who opposed me, he thought. He also loved cowboy tales. It would be great to ride a spirited horse instead of their placid animal. Then I could gallop across miles of open country with no one to stop me. I'd leave everything behind. When I'm older I'll go somewhere like that, Erich decided. There was such an amazing world beyond his foul-tempered guardian's struggling farm. There must be so many exciting adventures out there. I just have to go out and find them. One day I'll go to the places I've read about, he promised himself. Hans will come too.

Since he had arrived in Ireland, he had mostly lived in isolated rural areas. He did not know much about what lay beyond his own farm. Until recently he had always wanted to be a farmer just like Daddy Davy. But he wasn't so sure now. What if he couldn't go back to Clonty? He didn't want to stay on this farm with Uncle Bob. It wouldn't be the same. Besides, there were so many other things he would like to do. Erich pondered his options.

"Bedtime, lad," Uncle Bob said gruffly from the other side of the fireplace.

"Goodnight," Erich said as he stood up and walked down the narrow, dark hall clutching the book to him, careful not to bend the pages.

Tomorrow will be fun, he thought as he got into bed. It was the end of the term and classes finished at dinnertime. They were singing at St Michael's Carol Service and then there was a party in the church hall. Erich smiled as he closed his eyes, anticipating lemonade and sweets. The Children's Christmas Party was a tradition in most parishes and Erich never tired of it year after year, no matter where he was.

The next afternoon the whole school went into the town, walking double file along the footpath, tightly packed together. They crossed the river and continued along the wide main street, spreading further apart as they walked. Athy had the air of an old market town. People bustled up and down the street between shops, stepping around the chain of children.

St Michael's Church was much bigger than the village one. Erich eagerly marched up the aisle to take a seat in the choir stalls. The children combined with St Michael's choir formed the largest choir he had ever sung in. Erich always loved hearing voices echo in cavernous church buildings.

The church was full. Erich scanned the crowded pews, feeling as if he were on stage. He shivered as the organ boomed out the first carol. Standing with his class and the rest of the choir, he opened his mouth wide, singing clearly and heartily. He wished he could do this every day. It was such a great feeling.

When the hymns ended, he listened to the sermon patiently, on his best behaviour. The younger children wriggled in their seats, eager to go to the church hall to eat cake and biscuits. Reverend McKenna's black robes didn't look as witchlike in the holly and ribbon-decked church as they did when he came to their school, Erich decided, watching the minister. But he still didn't like him. This minister wasn't genial and friendly like Uncle Edward.

When the service ended the children giggled and jostled each other, queuing up to enter the hall. They would have run through the door like a herd of cattle if their teachers were not keeping a watchful eye. Erich and the other older children tried to appear nonchalant but there were gasps and oohs when they saw the Christmas tree in the corner with a large stack of parcels under it.

Mr Keown, leaning on his cane, stood at the door beside Miss Phair, the first and second year teacher, watching the children hurrying back and forth in the hall. He smiled indulgently. Erich stopped beside him.

"What do you think Father Christmas left you under the tree?" he asked Erich, surveying the tree and parcels. He liked the boy and tried to be kind to him, knowing the unhappy situation where he lived.

"I don't know, Sir. I doubt anyone will g-g-give me any presents," Erich replied honestly.

"Well, I wouldn't be surprised if Father Christmas has something for you," Mr Keown said, encouragingly. "But first you had better get over to the table before all the cakes and lemonade are gone," Mr Keown added. Erich went to join the queue.

"Erich's such a bright boy but he has little future on the Wrays' farm. It'll give him a living but such a hard life. Sure, it's a terrible shame. The boy's capable of more." Mr Keown sighed.

Miss Phair nodded agreement, glancing at Erich in the queue. He stood behind Rebecca and tapped her shoulder, ducking down as she turned. Laughing, she batted his head.

"They seem so young yet their school years are almost over. They won't be children much longer," Mr Keown said, watching their childish antics. With fourteen the leaving age, they would be finished school next year.

❧

Spring 1954

"You take it now," Uncle Bob said to Erich as he rounded the turn at the end of the furrow. Several neat rows were cut into the field. The rest of it lay undisturbed, tufts of tall grass sticking out in the muddy field, bent under the weight of the moisture on them. It always seemed to be raining at this time of year and the ground was wet and muddy. Erich did not mind the mess. He rushed from the horse's head back to the plough and gripped the handles as Uncle Bob had shown him. The horse lurched forward in the mud on Erich's command and he almost lost his grip. The plough jerked to the left and Uncle Bob grabbed the handles to steady it.

Letting go he said, "Keep it straight now."

Erich wrestled with the heavy plough and, with great effort, steered it in a straight line for a few feet. Hitting a stone partly buried in the earth, the plough lurched to the left and started a new track. Erich pulled hard to the right. He managed to shift it into the original track and continued down the field. When it threatened to waver again, near the end of the row, Uncle Bob grabbed the handles and steered it back on course. At the end of the row Erich turned to survey his work. A slightly wobbly line, like a child's scribbling on a wall, stretched behind him.

"That's not too bad, boy. Ye'll learn," Uncle Bob said approvingly, looking back.

Erich nodded. Uncle Bob led the horse around the turn and Erich walked steadily into the next row. Halfway along the row the plough lurched against buried stones and Erich struggled to keep it in a straight line.

Uncle Bob shouted, "No! Keep it straight, boy!"

Concentrating, Erich didn't reply. He focussed his attention on the ground in front of him. They continued in silence except for the odd curse or order from Uncle Bob when the plough wavered. Uncle Bob's patience was tenuous and if the plough strayed too far from the row he became agitated, yelling furiously. But Erich enjoyed ploughing and was not upset by Uncle Bob. His attention was focussed on the row ahead of him.

By the end of the day Erich was muddy and tired but he barely noticed. He loved the concentration of walking behind the horse and the satisfaction of surveying his finished work. For once he didn't mind even when Uncle Bob yelled at him. Daddy Davy would be so proud of me, he thought, unconcerned with Uncle Bob's opinions. Maybe when I leave school I will go back to Daddy Davy and help him run the farm. I can be a cowboy or go to sea later, he decided. He had no idea how many times he had changed his mind about his future career. There were so many possibilities and sometimes one choice seemed better than the others. But then another quickly took its place.

Erich followed Albert, the casual labourer who worked for Uncle

Bob each spring and summer, along the row, sacks over their heads to keep the worst of the rain off. They worked without coats. It had rained all morning and a steady breeze blew. Albert shoved the spade into the ground and poked a hole. Erich followed behind dropping a seed potato into it from the sack he carried. Albert swished the spade across the hole to fill it in. They trudged along, methodically planting the seed potatoes. Each row seemed to stretch on forever in the rain.

When they stopped for dinner there was no sign of the rain stopping and they hunched against the hedge bordering the field, trying to shelter under it. The grey sky seemed to muffle sound and isolate them from the rest of the world. It was peaceful standing there with the water dripping off them.

Aunt Annie brought them sandwiches and tea. They ate silently, taking large bites, swallowing them quickly and gulping the hot tea. Erich shivered as the tea warmed his insides.

"We'll get this field done today," Albert said.

"Good! Uncle Bob says he'll give me some pocket money for helping with the farm work," Erich said. "I'm working really hard to earn lots. Then I could buy some new comic books." I'll also save for my bus fare to Daddy Davy's, he thought to himself.

"Don't count your chickens before they're hatched," Albert advised. "Mind he keeps his word."

Erich nodded. I'll be sure to get my money, he thought. I'm not busting myself for nought. I'll be sure to get all that's owing to me.

After tea that evening Erich said to Uncle Bob, "I haven't had any pocket money from the Red Cross since I came here. Are you keeping it?"

"Sure, you don't get any money from them now. That finished when you came to stop here for good. They mind foster children."

Ignoring Uncle Bob's comment about his permanent residence on the farm, Erich pursued their financial agreement. "When will you p-p-pay me for the farm work?"

"Sure, I won't have the money until after the harvest," he replied. "I'm only giving you a bit because ye've got stuck in well. Most lads help their Das and get nought. Ye're lucky to be getting it."

Satisfied, Erich nodded. His plans for the money were already well formed. He sat by the fire and dreamed about the latest comics and a trip to Daddy Davy's. He would not dwell on Uncle Bob's comment that he was stopping here now. Although he knew he was meant to stay, it still sounded ominously final.

Autumn 1954

"Will you get married when you leave school?" Erich asked Rebecca, leaning against a bale of hay in the Cookes' shed. The children had finally tired of jumping in the hay and were lounging against the bales.

"Sure, I'm not courtin'," she replied laughing.

"You might be then," Erich replied, wondering whether he stood a chance with her.

"I'll help Mammy about the farm. I could teach for a few years then get married. You'll work the farm with Mr Wray?"

"That's what I'm supposed to do. But I h-h-hate it there. Where I lived before was much better."

Erich imagined what it would be like to work the farm with Daddy Davy. *I'd love that! I don't want to think of years and years stretching ahead on the Wray's farm. I have to get away from there somehow even if it isn't to Daddy Davy's,* he thought.

"I could go to sea. I could go after Christmas," Erich said, enthusiastic about any way to get away from Uncle Bob.

"Wouldn't you be scared to go to sea?" Rebecca asked.

"I've read about it. It's brilliant! There's always exciting adventures. It's not like here."

"I'll miss you if you go away."

"But I'll come back often to visit." Erich was glad to hear that she would miss him.

Engrossed in the conversation, he did not notice the time passing until the shed grew grey and gloomy in the spreading dusk. The odd afternoon at the Cooke farm was the only time he could spend with Rebecca, free from her brother's disapproving presence, and he tried to spin out the time as long as possible. But he knew it was getting late and Uncle Bob would be looking for him. Reluctantly he got ready to leave.

Mrs Cooke came to the door to call the children for tea. Seeing Erich and Rebecca she asked, "Will you stay for tea?"

"Ta, Mrs Cooke," Rebecca replied.

"I'd better get back," Erich replied, thinking of Uncle Bob's anger if he didn't get his chores done. Besides, he wanted the pocket money he'd been promised for his work. Erich waved to Mrs Cooke; he tugged Rebecca's hair as he passed her then sped up the short lane to the main road.

He walked along the shoulder of the road, singing to himself. "On Top Of Old Smoky" had been a hit a couple years ago and he liked it. He hummed it, thinking of the future. He would have to find a way to save enough money to get away. The money he earned for the farm work wouldn't be enough. He was certain he didn't want to work for Uncle Bob when he left school even if the farm would be his eventually. It would be unbearable. He would have to find a way to get away.

Erich walked mechanically, oblivious to his surroundings. He turned off the main road into the long lane and tramped along, unable to see it in the dark, but unerringly following its path.

Uncle Bob came out of the byre as Erich entered the haggard. His hat was pulled well down on his forehead, his eyebrows hidden under the brim. Erich could only see his eyes beneath it.

"Where have ye been 'til this hour?" Uncle Bob roared.

"I was at the C-C-Cookes'," Erich replied.

"Ye should have come straight back from school. There's work enough to do."

"I-I-I'm not your l-l-labourer. Why should I d-d-do all your work?" Erich shouted, tensing and blinking rapidly.

"I've taken you into my house! Ye should be grateful and not mind a bit o' work."

"None of the other lads do as much as I do!"

"Don't be cheeky! I want ye here when there's chores to be done!"

"Why don't you d-d-do a bit more yourself? A-A-And you haven't given me the money you promised yet!" Erich shouted, angrily puffing his chest out.

"How dare ye, boy! Ye'll not speak to me like that!" Uncle Bob shouted.

He lifted the pitchfork, lying against the wall, and lunged at Erich. Reacting quickly, Erich dodged him. Still shouting, Uncle Bob followed.

Hearing the commotion, Aunt Annie came out of the back door and stood watching them, wringing her hands together. She gasped as Uncle Bob lunged again with the pitchfork, stabbing it at the boy.

"Don't, Bob! You'll kill the lad!" she cried, fear for Erich making her bold enough to speak out.

The pitchfork missed Erich by a couple inches and stuck into the ground. Uncle Bob cursed as he leaned back to pry it out then sprinted after Erich. Aunt Annie's high-pitched wail drowned out Uncle Bob's curses as he pursued the boy across the haggard. Erich darted a glance over his shoulder and tripped on a stone protruding from the rough ground. He sprawled, like someone making an angel in the snow, arms and legs flying in all directions. Uncle Bob stabbed the pitchfork into the ground as Erich twisted to look behind him, missing the boy by less than an inch. Erich jumped up, ignoring the searing pain in his knees, and ran into the nearest field. Heart pounding and puffing he crouched to listen for Uncle Bob's footsteps, glad of the almost complete darkness. He heard curses and Uncle Bob's boots stamping around the haggard; they stopped short of the field. Aunt Annie whimpered, pleading with Uncle Bob not to hurt the boy.

Erich stayed hidden until he heard the back door slam. There was silence; the Wrays must have gone in. He shivered in the cool air, his skinned knees throbbing. He could not sit out here all night but he could not go into the house either. He weighed up the options until, suddenly, he knew where to go. Quietly he crept back to the haggard and into the shed opposite the byre. Hay was piled up inside it, in a high stack. Uncle Bob's greyhound mongrel, always adept at avoiding his master's temper, had dug into the side of the stack and fashioned a burrow for himself. Erich peered inside and saw the curled form of the dog. Whispering, he called the dog and coaxed him out. The dog slunk out, whimpering and wagging the back half of his body in his joy at the attention. Erich patted him briefly then crawled into the burrow. He sat down, scratched knees drawn to his chin and leaned against the solid form of the hay. It was warm and safe.

During the evening Uncle Bob came outside several times. Erich heard him rooting around the haggard, looking for the boy. He stayed very quiet but Uncle Bob didn't come near the haystack.

"What are ye doin' running about at this time o' the night?" Uncle Bob asked late in the evening.

Erich knew he must be talking to the dog, who would normally be curled up out of sight, by now. The boy tensed but stayed quiet. He heard footsteps approaching and held his breath. Uncle Bob peered in the end of the burrow, silently.

"Come you out and get in yon house," he said calmly. After hesitating for a moment, Erich crawled out and darted to the opposite side of the shed.

"Get in the house and away to your bed. I'll not touch ye," he said.

To Erich's surprise Uncle Bob's temper had dissipated and he made no move toward the boy. Erich walked quickly across the haggard and into the house. Aunt Annie stood in the kitchen, her hat on her head, some of the pins almost falling out of it. It looked as if she had been preparing to go somewhere but had not done so. In her anxiety, she had not pinned it on properly but she did not seem to notice.

"Thank God you're alright, so," she said. "I was in half a mind to fetch Mr Cooke to reason with himself." She clasped his shoulder and let go quickly, afraid Uncle Bob would appear.

Erich went to his room. He lay under the covers, listening for a long time to be sure Uncle Bob was not coming down the hall, before he fell into a fretful sleep. He never knew when Uncle Bob's mood would change.

"It isn't working out, Mr Moss. Sure, the boy isn't much help and he's right cheeky," Uncle Bob said.

"That's a shame as I had great hopes that he would be a help to you on the farm and inherit it one day. It would've been grand for both of you. But I've seen the boy can be a handful. He's excitable and needs to be kept under strict control."

"Sure, I know it, Mr Moss. We've done our best. He couldn't find a better, kinder home but I don't know what ails the lad. He won't mind me."

"I will make some enquiries," Mr Moss replied. "The Red Cross may be able to suggest something."

"Thank you, Mr Moss," Uncle Bob replied.

Erich urged the horse forward, towards the byre. A motor rumbled down the lane and stopped across the field at the gate. The normally quiet, obedient horse whinnied and shied away from the byre door. Erich tried again. The horse stamped, tossing his head, unwilling to move. A car door slammed.

Erich and the horse turned at the sound of footsteps entering the haggard. A tall, thin man approached; Erich could see his outline in the darkness. The horse sidled towards the door, away from the stranger.

"Hello, you must be Erich," the man said.

"Yes," Erich replied with a sharp intake of breath. From the corner of his eye he watched the man warily. They never had visitors. What does he want? Erich wondered.

The man smiled and extended his hand. Erich looked at him but did not shake it.

"I'm Mr Griffith, from Dr Barnardo's Homes. I've come to speak to you." Erich nodded, shrugging his shoulder slightly.

"I've to get the horse into the byre," he said, brusquely.

"I'll wait for you," Mr Griffith replied.

Erich spent several minutes coaxing the horse through the door and into its stall. Mr Griffith watched him thoughtfully.

"That's a difficult job," he said when Erich was finished.

"I always do it," Erich replied.

Mr Griffith regarded the diminutive boy and wondered why the child had to do such a task. The animal was so much bigger and stronger than the boy. Mr Moss had reported that the child did not do his chores satisfactorily. He wondered what was expected of the him.

Erich led the man inside the house without any further comment. Mr Griffith introduced himself to the Wrays.

"I thought the Red Cross would send someone," Uncle Bob said.

"They care for the children who were sent here for short term foster care. But, since there are no plans for Erich to return to Germany, we will assume his case."

"You'll stay for tea with us, Mr Griffith?" Aunt Annie asked anxiously, glancing at her husband for his permission.

"Thank you. That would be very kind indeed. It's a long journey down here from Belfast," he replied.

During the meal Mr Griffith chatted to the Wrays, who avoided his gaze, uncomfortable with a stranger, even one they had requested, in their house. They were quiet, unsure what to say. Mr Griffith chatted easily, trying to relax them. Erich answered any questions directed at him but otherwise remained silent. As soon as the meal was over Uncle Bob went to the sitting room, leaving Erich and Mr Griffith at the kitchen table. Aunt Annie busied herself washing the dishes. She tried to avoid catching Mr Griffith's eye, afraid she might have to speak to him.

"You've been living with the Wrays for two years now, Erich. Do you like it here?"

"It's a-a-alright," Erich replied noncommittally, aware that Aunt Annie was listening to their conversation. He wondered what the man wanted.

"Do you have many friends?"

"S-s-some."

"Do they come here to visit you?"

"No. Not h-h-here. N-n-never into the house."

"That must be rather lonely at times."

"Y-Y-Yes," Erich replied, breathing in sharply and blinking rapidly. Mr Griffith noticed the tension as Erich answered each question.

"It's rather far from everything here. Would you like to live where there was more company?"

"W-W-Where?" Erich asked, suspiciously. He knew, from previous experience, that he might move anytime with no say in the matter. What was this man trying to do? While he wasn't happy here, somewhere else might be worse.

"I've come to talk to you about the possibility of coming to live in a Barnardo's Home. You don't have any relatives nearby, do you?" Mr Griffith asked, knowing the answer.

"I d-d-don't have anyone, except my b-b-brother, Hans."

"That must be very difficult."

"Yes." Again there was a sharp intake of breath and Erich shrugged slightly. Mr Griffith felt keenly how alone and vulnerable the boy was. He had moved so often and had no one constant in his life. Reports stated that one set of foster parents had shown considerable interest in him. They seemed keen to keep in contact with the boy. It was a shame they were unable to care for him.

"I believe your former foster family, the Elliotts, write to you?"

"Y-y-yessss," Erich replied hesitantly. Was the Home near Daddy Davy? he wondered. Will I be able to see him again? Or maybe they could take me back to live with Daddy Davy.

"Do you write to them often?"

Erich didn't know what to say. He didn't want to admit that he hadn't written. He was angry with Daddy Davy for not finding a way to keep him. But he would go back in an instant if he were given the chance. Maybe he wouldn't be allowed if he told the truth.

"When I h-h-have s-s-stamps," he whispered, hoping Aunt Annie wouldn't tell the truth. But she kept her back to them.

"Do you remember Germany at all?"

"A little bit. N-N-Not very much."

"Do you still remember how to speak German?"

"N-N-No. I never s-s-spoke it since I came to Ireland," Erich asserted, dismissing the topic.

Most of the refugee children who had parents living were returned to Germany after their three year foster placements ended. Erich had lived in Ireland much longer than most of the children and he had no one to return to in Germany. Mr Griffith noted to himself that he must recommend that this option could not be considered for the boy.

"Have you thought about what you would like to do when you leave school?"

"I k-k-know how to farm. Or I c-c-could be a midshipman! Can I do that if I g-g-go to the Home?" Erich asked. Maybe I could join the navy and come home to visit Daddy Davy, he thought with growing enthusiasm. Or maybe I could be a sailor and a farmer. The possibilities quickly grew in his mind.

"Well, first you would go to the Home and continue in school for another year."

"But I finish school this year."

"In England you have to go to school until you are fifteen.

Then we'd do some assessments and decide what is the best career for you. We'll do our best to find a suitable placement in the field you choose."

"I wouldn't go to Cavan?" Dismayed Erich stared at him. He thought they were talking about going back to Cavan but that didn't seem to be the idea at all. As the information tumbled through Erich's mind, disappointment seeped in. He wasn't going back to Daddy Davy.

"I'm afraid not, our Homes are in Northern Ireland and England. You would probably go to England as you must be born in Northern Ireland to work there when you leave school."

He thought about what the man was saying. England. He'd read about it in books and heard the Coronation on the radio. And Uncle Jim had told him so many stories. He'd imagined what it must be like. And there would be other children. He wouldn't be on his own all the time. And best of all he'd get away from Uncle Bob. No more yelling and heavy chores. If he couldn't go back to Daddy Davy it would be better than staying here.

"A-A-Are we g-g-going tonight?" Erich asked hopefully.

"No, not tonight. It will take a few weeks to get everything organised so it will probably be in January." Mr Griffith smiled at Erich's change in attitude.

"My b-b-brother isn't h-h-happy in Cavan," Erich suddenly declared.

"You haven't seen your brother for a couple of years, have you?" Mr Griffith asked gently.

"N-N-Nooo," Erich admitted reluctantly.

"You don't write to him either, do you?"

Erich shook his head, hunching forward. From the little Daddy Davy wrote in his letters, he knew that Hans was happy with Bobby and Aunt Marjorie. But he missed him. He didn't want to go to England without him.

"How do you know he isn't happy?"

"He i-i-isn't," Erich insisted stubbornly, shrugging one shoulder in a reflexive movement. If I can't go to Daddy Davy's then

Hans must come with me, he decided.

"I will try to find out about your brother for you," Mr Griffith said kindly. He did not pursue the topic any further; he would need to get some details first.

"I will make the arrangements and let you know when you are going to England," Mr Griffith said as he stood up to leave. Erich walked Mr Griffith across the haggard and waved enthusiastically as he crossed the field to where his Ford Prefect was parked at the end of the lane.

Uncle Bob and Aunt Annie never mentioned Mr Griffith's visit. Uncle Bob was his usual, taciturn self though Aunt Annie cast despondent, sidelong glances at Erich as she went about her work. But Erich barely noticed. He was leaving Uncle Bob. With only his pocket money if he ever got it, it would have taken him a very long time to save enough to get away. But now circumstances had turned in his favour. He was going to England and would never have to see Uncle Bob again! He could hardly believe it! He wished Rebecca could come too. But he would come back to see her. Once he had a good job no one could say he wasn't good enough for her.

"You sign here, Robert, and date it," Mr Moss said, pointing to the space for his name and address. Robert Wray nodded and lifted the pen. He briefly scanned the agreement.

"Point 6 does not apply to you. It would only apply to a relative. You would not be required to receive him back for any reason since the adoption isn't proceeding," Mr Moss stated, looking at the document. Again Robert Wray nodded. He wrote his name and address in large, shaky letters. Beneath it Mr Moss and Mr Lambe squeezed their signatures onto the page, as witnesses.

"When will he leave?" Robert Wray asked.

"I think it will be after Christmas. I will do my best to get Mr Griffith to arrange it as quickly as possible."

"That'll do. Ta."

January 1955

The rasping cough filled the room as Erich opened the door. He carried a cup of tea and bread, smeared with jam, into the Wrays' bedroom. Aunt Annie sat propped up in the bed, pale and drawn. Her shoulders shook as she coughed. She had been ill since before Christmas.

Erich had not returned to school after the Christmas holidays. At fourteen he had finished his education. So he made the meals and cared for her, as well as doing his farm chores. Uncle Bob took little notice of her illness. Erich had not had time to see Rebecca or his other friends since the last school term ended. But he was rather relieved as he did not want to say goodbye to everyone. He had done it too often; he just wanted to leave quietly. I'll write to Rebecca to explain, Erich thought.

Last night he had packed reluctantly. They were coming for him today. Sadly he watched Aunt Annie pick at her breakfast. He did not know how she would manage after he left. Erich fretted about this as he watched her eat. Aunt Annie spoke seldom and rarely showed affection to him but he liked her. And he knew she liked him. She wasn't Aunt Elsie but he'd grown fond of her. He wasn't sure about leaving now. Desperation to get away from Uncle Bob warred with compassion for Aunt Annie. He didn't want to leave her alone with her fierce tempered husband, especially while she was ill.

He heard Uncle Bob open the kitchen door and he walked down the hall to him.

"You s-s-still haven't paid me for the farm work. You o-o-owe me fifteen shillings," Erich said in a fierce whisper.

"I'll not pay you that!" Uncle Bob said.

"You o-o-owe it to me! A labourer would get more," Erich said, his voice rising.

"Nonsense!"

"You s-s-should have paid me after the harvest. I did the w-w-work. You said you w-w-would give me my money after you went to market," Erich insisted. Uncle Bob looked at him and scowled.

"I'll give ye five shillings. Sure, an' that's thievin'," Uncle Bob replied.

He went to the cupboard, took a tin from the shelf and counted out the coins. He tossed them onto the kitchen table without another word. Erich scooped them up as Uncle Bob stomped out of the door.

Erich returned to the Wrays' bedroom. Aunt Annie had slipped into a doze, her loose hair fanned across the pillow. He rarely saw her hair loose. She always pinned it up under the small, round hat she wore. The long, straight hat pins lay on the dresser. It was the first time he'd seen her face relaxed, devoid of her customary anxious, darting glance. Sleeping she was a different person. Erich lifted her cup and plate, careful not to wake her, and carried them to the kitchen.

Returning to the bedroom, he stood watching her sleep. He heard a motor stop out at the gate but he did not move. Uncle Bob shouted from the haggard; Erich ignored him. How can I leave her like this? Erich thought. She needs someone to look after her.

When Erich did not answer, Uncle Bob pounded down the hall, the kitchen door slamming behind him.

"Did ye not hear me calling ye? They're here. Get your gear," Uncle Bob said sharply.

Aunt Annie's eyes opened with the commotion. Erich ignored Uncle Bob and waited for her to speak.

"Best you were away then," she said with a wan smile. "Good luck, lad."

Erich walked to the door and turned to look at her again, lying frail and weak in the bed. Tears welled in his eyes. He didn't know how to put his feelings into words. Seeing his compassion and concern, she smiled determinedly.

"I'm nearly mended, lad," she said. "I'll be grand."

He nodded. Reluctantly he walked down the hall and picked up his few possessions.

"Tara then," Uncle Bob said brusquely as he passed. Erich nodded but did not reply as he went into the haggard, crossed the field to the van and climbed in. He turned and stared at the ramshackle house for the few seconds it was visible then slumped in his seat as it disappeared behind the hedge.

"So you're away to Belfast, lad?" the driver said.

Erich nodded but made no comment. He could not think of his new adventure with the image of Aunt Annie in his mind, alone in the house with her brutal husband.

"We haven't seen Erich this long time - it was afor Christmas," Olive said to Lizzie at the kitchen table in the Cookes' farmhouse.

"Sure, he's busy working on the farm. He won't have much time now he's left school," Lizzie replied.

"I went a message there today and he was nowhere in sight," Eleanor said. "Mrs Wray's poorly and not able to get out o' the bed. Mammy sent her some dinner. Mr Wray was in the byre."

"Do you know where he is, Mammy?" Lizzie asked.

"Erich has gone away," Mrs Cooke said.

"He never told us. Aren't the Wrays adopting him? Where's he away to, Mammy?" she asked.

"No, they'll not adopt him." Before the girls could question her she continued, "You children should mind your own business and don't go poking your noses into other people's." Mrs Cooke refused to be drawn any further on the topic. She lifted several plates and went into the kitchen. The children looked at each other, shocked.

"He never told Rebecca he was away and they're thick as thieves," Eleanor said. "She'd have said if he had."

Tom whispered, "I think Mr Wray killed him and buried him

in the haggard!"

Belfast
January 1955

Erich stood with Mr Griffith at the Belfast dock waiting to board
the boat to Liverpool. Though he still regretted having to leave
Aunt Annie, he was glad to be away from Uncle Bob. The Wrays'
farm seemed very far away already. I can scarcely believe I'm
going to England, he thought excitedly. I'll see the Queen and
her huge palace. I'll join the navy, fight pirates and travel all over
the world. It'll be just like in the books.

"I've made some enquiries, Erich, about your brother. He
seems very happy with Mrs Crawford in Cavan Town. But we
will keep in touch with him to be sure he is alright," Mr Griffith
said.

Erich nodded. He knew that already and he understood. He
desperately wished his brother would join him but wasn't surprised that Hans wanted to stay where he was. I'd go back to
Daddy Davy if they'd have me, Erich thought. I know why Hans
wants to stay.

He would be starting his new life in England on his own. But
it doesn't really matter. I'm getting used to being on my own. I
can look after myself, Erich thought.

"You can write to Hans. He'd like to hear from you. The
Elliotts would also like to hear from you," Mr Griffith said.
Erich didn't reply.

"They didn't send you to Kildare because they didn't want
you. They hated having to let you go and they haven't forgotten
you," he reminded him gently.

Erich thought about this. When he left Clonty he was heart-
broken and he was angry at Daddy Davy for sending him away.
But he knew there wasn't any choice. If he admitted it to himself, he always knew they cared about him and had wanted him

to stay. Why else would Daddy Davy have continued writing to him even when he never replied? He couldn't stay angry or blame them for sending him away. I'll write to them and Hans when I get to England, he decided. It's as well I finally got the money for the farm chores. I'll need lots of stamps if I'm to write to Rebecca too.

One day, when I'm a sailor, I'll come back to see them, Erich thought, bolstered by the knowledge that Daddy Davy and Aunt Elsie would wholeheartedly welcome him.

"I w-w-will write to t-t-them," Erich replied emphatically as he and Mr Griffith boarded the boat. He was starting a new adventure but he didn't have to leave all of his past behind.

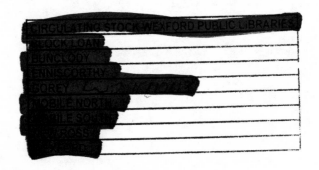

Printed in the United States
141412LV00003B/113/P